BOX 21

BOX 21

Anders Roslund and
Börge Hellström

SARAH CRICHTON BOOKS

Farrar, Straus and Giroux

New York

Sarah Crichton Books
Farrar, Straus and Giroux
18 West 18th Street, New York 10011

Distributed in Canada by D&M Publishers, Inc.
Printed in the United States of America
Originally published in 2004 by Piratförlaget, Sweden
English translation originally published in 2008 by Sphere,
Great Britain, as *The Vault*
Published in the United States by Sarah Crichton Books /
Farrar, Straus and Giroux
First American edition, 2009

Library of Congress Cataloging-in-Publication Data
Roslund, Anders, 1961–
    [Box 21. English]
    Box 21 / Roslund / Hellström. — 1st ed.
       p.   cm.
    Translated from the Swedish.
    ISBN-13: 978-0-374-28295-0 (hardcover : alk. paper)
    ISBN-10: 0-374-28295-1 (hardcover : alk. paper)
        1. Prostitutes—Sweden—Fiction.   2. Revenge—Fiction.   3. Human
    trafficking victims—Fiction.   4. Human trafficking—Sweden—Fiction.
    5. Criminals—Sweden—Fiction.   6. Police—Sweden—Fiction.
    7. Stockholm (Sweden)—Fiction.   I. Hellström, Börge, 1957–   II. Title.

PT9877.28.R67B6913 2009
839.73'8—dc22

2009004449

www.fsgbooks.com

1   3   5   7   9   10   8   6   4   2

EXTRACT FROM AN ACCIDENT &
EMERGENCY PRIMARY ASSESSMENT
SÖDER HOSPITAL, STOCKHOLM

. . . Unconscious female, unknown identity, brought in by ambulance 09:05. Neighbour called emergency services to flat at 3 Völund Street.

Circulation	Pale, cool peripheries. Pulse 110, regular. Weak/thready, BP 95/60
Disability	Unconscious (AVPU scale). No response to voice or painful stimuli.
Exposure	Multiple lacerations to the back, approximately 10–30 cm in length, recent origin. Small abrasions and bruises to face. Large swelling, lateral aspect of left proximal humerus.
Abdomen	Tense/rigid.
Impression	Female, approx. 20 yrs, injuries consistent with multiple external violence (inflicted with whip?). Shocked, signs of decompensation. 1. Likely intra-abdominal bleed, splenic source 2. Fracture left humerus.
Plan	Transfer to ITU for continued care . . .

ELEVEN YEARS EARLIER

She clung to her mother's hand.

During the last year she had done this a lot, held on tight to her mother's soft hand and felt it squeeze hers back.

She didn't really want to go to the big city.

Her name was Lydia Grajauskas and she already had a sore tummy when they boarded the bus outside the ugly bus terminal in Klaipeda. The further away from home they went, the worse she felt.

Lydia had never been to Vilnius before – she had only imagined it and looked at pictures and listened to people's stories – but now she didn't want to go there at all, because it wasn't her kind of place; she had nothing to do there.

It was more than a year since she had seen him.

She was about to turn nine and she had thought a hand grenade was a kind of cool present.

Dad hadn't noticed that she was watching him. He had his back turned to her and Vladi, and he was excited about being with the other men; they all drank and shouted and hated the Russians. She was lying top to tail with Vladi in the sofa, a huge brown thing with a worn corduroy cover that smelt horrible; they used to lie there sometimes when school was closed and Dad was working. They listened.

7

There was something special about the men's loud voices and guns and boxes of ammunition that fascinated them, that made them hide on the sofa to listen and watch more often than was perhaps good for them. Dad's cheeks had been so red, which they weren't normally, only sometimes at home, when he had been drinking straight from the bottle and sneaked up behind Mum and pressed himself against her bum. Of course, they had no idea that Lydia noticed what they were up to and she didn't let on. He'd always drink just a bit more and Mum would have a taste too, her mouth to the bottle and then they'd go into the small bedroom, chase everyone out and close the door.

Lydia liked to see her dad's flushed cheeks. At home or with the other men, polishing the weapons in front of them all. He seemed more alive then; he didn't look as old as normal, after all he was twenty-nine.

She peeped cautiously through the window.

Her stomach hurt even more when the bus started and then hurtled along roads full of potholes, and every time one of the front wheels bumped over an especially rough bit, her seat shook and something sharp jabbed her insides, somewhere under her ribcage.

So this was what the big world really looked like. The unexplored world, the whole stretch of land between Klaipeda and Vilnius. She had never been allowed to go before; it was expensive, and the important thing was that Mum went, as she had done every second Sunday for almost a year, with food and the money she had somehow managed to get from somewhere. It was hard to tell how Dad really was, what he would say. He probably missed Mum more than her.

On the day with the hand grenade, he hadn't even seen her.

Leaning forward out of the sofa, she had rooted around in the boxes of plastic explosives and grenades, shushing Vladi with her finger against her lips; he had to be quiet because the men didn't want to be disturbed. She had known by then how all these things worked, the explosives, the grenades and the small handguns. She always watched when they practised, and if she had to, she could handle the weapons at least as well as some of the men.

She kept staring through the dirty window of the bus.

It was raining hard, so the windows should have been clean, but instead of washing away the dust, the raindrops whipped up a spray of brown mud that made it more and more difficult to see anything. The road was better now: no potholes, no jolting and no more jabs under her ribs.

She was actually holding the grenade when the police broke the door down and burst into the big room.

Dad and the other men shouted to each other but they were too slow off the mark, and just a few minutes later they'd been pushed up against the walls, handcuffed and beaten. She couldn't remember how many police had come into the room, maybe ten or even twenty. All she remembered was that they kept screaming *zatknis* again and again and that they carried the same kind of gun that Dad sold, and that they won before they even started.

Their shouts had mixed with the sound of gunshots and breaking bottles.

All the noise had hurt her ears and then, suddenly, when Dad and his friends had been pinned to the floor, a strange silence fell.

Perhaps that silence had stayed in her memory more clearly than anything else; it had been a silence that had seemed to take over everything.

Mum's hand. She grabbed it and pulled it closer, making it rest on the seat next to her, and she held on until the skin went white and she couldn't squeeze it any harder. She had clung to her Mum's hand just as hard when they sat outside the courtroom in Klaipeda, during the trial against her dad and his friends. She and Mum had sat there holding hands, and Mum cried for a long time when the court official in a grey suit came and told them that all of the accused had been sentenced to twenty-one years in prison.

It was a year since Lydia had seen him. He mightn't recognise her now.

She prodded the cloth bag Mum had brought with her. It was bursting with food. Mum had told her about the porridge that they had to eat, almost always a nasty, mealy mess. Mum rattled on about vitamins, that you'd get ill if you didn't get enough and how everyone in that place needed them and that's why people who came to visit tried to bring good food.

The bus was driving quite fast now. The road was wider and there was more traffic than before, and the houses beyond the muddy window were larger as well and seemed to grow bigger the closer to Vilnius they got. The first houses she had seen along the bumpy road had looked old and poor. Now it was mostly blocks of flats, all grey walls and tin roofs, but sort of modern-looking. Then came some more expensive houses and then all the petrol stations, all in the same place. She smiled and pointed, she had never seen so many garages together before.

The rain had almost stopped, which was a good thing. She didn't want her hair to get wet, not today.

The bus stop was near the Lukuskele prison, only a few hundred metres away. It was a great big place, taking up almost a whole city block, with a high wall going all the way round it. It had originally been a Russian church, but it had been converted and new buildings had been added. Now more than a thousand prisoners lived there.

Other mothers and children were already queuing outside a massive iron door set into the middle of the concrete wall. One family was let in at a time to face the uniformed and armed guards who were waiting in the room behind the door. Everyone had to answer questions. Show their identity papers. Show what they had with them. One of the guards smiled at her, but she didn't dare to smile back.

'When we're in there, if anyone coughs, leave the room.'

Mum turned to her while she said this and she looked stern, as she always did when she was serious. Lydia wanted to ask why, but held back, as it was clear that her mum didn't want to say any more.

They were led out of the main building and on to a path running alongside a high fence with barbed wire on top. Behind it white dogs were barking and throwing themselves against the wire mesh. She saw two faces watching them from a barred window and they waved and called out to her.

'Hey, sweetie! Up here, darling!'

She marched on, looking straight ahead. It wasn't far to the next building.

Mum was carrying the bag in her arms and Lydia reached out for her hand. It wasn't there. Another jab in her tummy, like on the bus when it bumped over the edges of potholes. They went up a staircase with harsh green walls; the colour almost hurt her eyes, so she kept looking at Mum's back instead, putting her hand on it as they walked upstairs.

They stopped on the third-floor landing, followed the guard who pointed down a long, dark corridor that smelt stale and of bleach at the same time. Every door they passed had a bin with TBC written on it. She looked in one that wasn't properly closed and saw tissues with blood clots.

This place was called the hospital wing, and the room they entered had eight beds in a row along one wall. The men's heads had been shaved, and they all looked pale and tired. Some were lying down. Some were wrapped in a sheet and had been propped up in a chair and a few were standing talking by a window. Dad was sitting on the bed at the far end.

Lydia stole a look at him and thought that he looked smaller than before.

He hadn't spotted her. Not yet.

She had to wait for quite a long time.

Mum went to him first. And they spoke to each other, argued about something, not that she could hear what they said. Lydia kept watching him, and after a while she realised that she didn't feel ashamed, not any more. She thought about the last year, about her schoolmates' taunts that didn't hurt any more, not when she stood here, so close to him. That sick feeling inside her and the pain in her tummy had gone away too.

Later, when she hugged him, he coughed, but she didn't leave the room like she had promised her mum. She just held him tighter and wouldn't let go.

She hated him; he should be coming home with them.

NOW
PART ONE

MONDAY 3 JUNE

The flat was silent.

She hadn't thought of him for a long time, or indeed of anything that belonged to that time back then. And now she was sitting there thinking about it. She thought about that last hug in the Lukuskele prison ward when she was ten years old and he had looked so small and coughed so his whole body rattled and Mum had given him a tissue, which filled with blood clots before he scrunched it up and put it in one of the big bins in the corridor.

It was the last time, but she hadn't realised it then. Perhaps she still hadn't taken it in.

Lydia took a deep breath.

She shook off the feeling of sadness, smiled at the large mirror in the hall. It was still early in the morning.

A knock on the door. She still had the hairbrush in her hand. How long had she been standing there? She glanced in the mirror again, her head a little to the side. Another smile, she wanted to look good. She was wearing the black dress; the dark material contrasted with her pale skin. She looked at her body. It was still a young woman's. She hadn't changed much since she came here, not on the outside.

She waited.

Another knock, harder this time. She should answer it. She put the hairbrush on the shelf by the mirror and took a few steps towards the door.

Her name was Lydia Grajauskas and she used to sing her name; she sang it now to the tune of a children's song she remembered from school in Klaipeda. The chorus had three repeated lines and she sang *Lydia Grajauskas* for each line. She had always done this when she felt nervous.

Lydia Grajauskas
Lydia Grajauskas
Lydia Grajauskas

She stopped singing when she reached the door. He was there on the other side. If she put her ear to the door, she could quickly pick up the sound of his breathing. She knew its rhythm so well. It was him. They had met often, was it eight or maybe nine times? His smell was special. She could sense it already, the smell of him, like one of her dad's workmates from that filthy room with the big sofa where she had hidden when she was a girl. Almost like them, a mixture of tobacco and aftershave and sweat that seeped through the closely woven material of his jacket.

He knocked for the third time.

She let the door swing open. There he was. Dark suit, light blue shirt, gold tiepin. His fair hair was short and he was suntanned. It had been raining steadily since the middle of May, but he still had a late-summer glow, as he always did. She smiled at him, the same smile as at the mirror a moment earlier; she knew he liked her to smile.

They didn't touch each other.

Not yet.

He came in from the stairs, into the flat. She looked quickly at the hallstand and nodded at one of the coat hangers, as if to say let me take your jacket and hang it up for you. He shook his head. She guessed he was about ten years older than herself, maybe thirty-something, but it was only a guess.

She felt like singing again.

Lydia Grajauskas. Lydia Grajauskas. Lydia Grajauskas.

He raised his hand, as he always did, touched her black dress lightly, slowly sliding his fingers along the shoulder straps, across her breasts, always on top of the material.

She kept very still.

His hand traced a wide circle over one breast, then towards the other. She hardly breathed. Her chest had to be still, she must smile, must stay still and smile.

She kept smiling when he spat.

They were standing close together then; it was more like he let it go rather than spat. He didn't usually spit in her face, instead the spittle landed in front of her feet in their high-heeled black shoes.

He thought that she was too slow.

He pointed.

One straight finger, pointing down.

Lydia knelt, still smiling – she knew he liked that. Sometimes he smiled as well. Her knees clicked a little as she pressed her legs together and went down on all fours, her face looking ahead. She asked him to forgive her. That was what he wanted. He had learnt how to say it in Russian and insisted on her getting it right, making sure she used the right words. She lowered herself in stages by bending her arms until she was almost folded double and her nose touched the floor. It was cold against her tongue as she licked the gob into her mouth, swallowed it.

Then she got up, like he wanted her to, closed her eyes and, as usual, tried to guess which cheek.

Right, probably the right one this time.

Left.

He hit her with the flat of his hand, which covered her whole cheek. It didn't hurt that much. His arm came right round and the slap left a pink mark, but mostly it just burned. It stung only if you wanted it to sting.

He pointed again.

Lydia knew what she had to do, so the pointing wasn't necessary, but he did it anyway, just waved his finger in her direction, wanted her to walk into the bedroom, to stand in front of the red bedspread. She went in front of him. Her movements had to be slow, and as she walked she had to absently stroke her bottom and breathe heavily. That was what he wanted. She could feel his eyes on her back, burning, his eyes already abusing her body.

She stopped by the bed.

She undid the dress, three buttons at the back, rolled it down over her hips and let it fall to the floor.

Her bra and panties were black lace, just as he wanted and he had brought them personally, making her promise to use them only for him. Only him.

The moment he lay down on top of her, she no longer had a body.

That was what she did. It was what she always did.

She thought of home, about the past and all the things she missed and had missed every single day since she came here.

She was not there, she had absented herself. Here she was just a face with no body. She had no neck, no breasts, no crotch, no legs.

So when he was rough, when he forced himself into her from behind, when her anus was bleeding, it wasn't happening to her. She was elsewhere, having left only her head there, singing *Lydia Grajauskas* to a tune she had learnt long ago.

It was raining as he drove into the empty car park.

It was the kind of summer when people held their breath when they woke up and crept over to the bedroom window, hoping that today, today the sun would be beating against the slats of the venetian blinds. It was the kind of summer when instead the rain played freely outside. Every morning weary eyes would give up hope as they scanned the greyness, while the mind registered the tapping on the window pane.

Ewert Grens sighed. He parked the car, turned the engine off, but stayed in the driver's seat until it was impossible to see out and the raindrops were a steady flow that obscured everything. He couldn't be bothered to move. He didn't want to. Unease crawled all over him; reluctance tugged at whatever there was to catch. Another week had passed and he had almost forgotten about her.

He was breathing heavily.

He would never truly forget.

He lived with her still, every day, practically every hour, twenty-five years on. Nothing helped, no fucking hope.

The rain eased off, allowing him a glimpse of the large red-brick villa from the seventies. The garden was lovely, almost too carefully tended. He liked the apple trees best, six of them, which had just shed their white flowers.

He hated that house.

He relaxed his grip on the wheel, opened the car door and climbed out. Large puddles had formed on the uneven tarmac and he zigzagged between them, but the wet still soaked through the soles of his shoes before he was halfway there. As he walked, he tried to shake off the feeling that life ended a little with every step he took towards the entrance.

The whole place smelt of old people. He came here every Monday morning, but had never got used to the smell. The people who lived here in their wheelchairs or behind their Zimmer frames were not all old. He had no idea what caused the smell.

'She's sitting in her room.'

'Thanks.'

'She knows you're coming.'

She didn't have the faintest idea that he was coming.

He nodded at the young care assistant, who had come to recognise him and was just trying to be friendly, but would never know how much it hurt.

He walked past the Smiler, a man of about his own age who usually sat in the lobby, waving cheerily as people came and went; then there was Margareta, who screamed if you didn't pay attention to her and stop to ask how she was. Every Monday morning, there they were, part of a photograph that didn't need to be taken. He wondered whether, if they were not lined up and waiting one morning, he would miss them, or whether he would be relieved at not having to deal with the predictability of it all.

He paused. A quiet moment outside her room.

Some nights he would wake, shaken and covered in sweat, because he had clearly heard her say *Welcome* when he came, she had taken his hand in hers, happy to hold on to someone who loved her. He thought about it, about his recurring dream and it gave him the courage to open the door, as he always did, and enter her space, a small room with a window overlooking the car park.

'Hello, Anni.'

She was sitting in the middle of the room, the wheelchair facing the door. She looked at him, her eyes showing nothing remotely like recognition or even a response. He went to her, put his hand against her cold cheek, talked to her.

'Hi, Anni. It's me. Ewert.'

She laughed. Inappropriate and too loud as always, a child's laughter.

'Do you know who I am today?'

Another laugh, a sudden loud noise. He pulled over the chair that was standing by the desk she never used, and sat down next to her. He took her hand, held it.

They had made her look nice.

Her fair hair was combed, held back with a slide on each side. A blue dress that he hadn't seen for a while, that smelt newly washed.

It always struck him how bafflingly unchanged she really was, how the twenty-five years, wheelchair-bound years in the land of the unaware, had left so few traces. He had gained twenty kilos, lost a lot of hair, knew how furrowed his face had become. She was unmarked, as if you were allowed a more carefree spirit that kept you young to make up for not being able to participate in real life.

She tried to say something as she looked at him, making her usual gurgling baby noises, which always made him feel that she was trying to reach him. He squeezed her hand and swallowed whatever it was that was hurting his throat.

'He's being released tomorrow,' he told her.

She mumbled and drooled and he pulled out his hankie to wipe away the saliva dribbling down her chin.

'Anni, do you understand? From tomorrow, he'll be out. He'll be free, littering the streets again.'

Her room looked just the same as when she had moved

in. He had picked out which pieces of furniture she should have from home and positioned them; he was the only one who knew why it was important for her to sleep with her head to the window.

Already on the first night she had looked at peace.

He had carried her in, put her in the bed and tucked the covers round her slender body. Her sleep had been deep and he had left her in the morning when she woke up. Leaving the car there he had walked all the way to police headquarters in Kungsholmen. It was afternoon by the time he had arrived.

'I'll get him this time.'

Her eyes rested on him, as if she were listening. He knew this was an illusion, but because it looked right, he sometimes pretended they were having a talk the way they used to.

Her eyes, were they expectant or just empty?

If only I had managed to stop.

If only that bastard hadn't pulled you out. And if only your head hadn't been softer than the wheel.

Ewert Grens bent over her, his forehead touching hers. He kissed her cheek.

'I miss you.'

The man in the dark suit with the gold tiepin, who usually spat on the floor in front of her feet, had just left. It hadn't helped this time to think of Klaipeda and have no body, only a head. She had felt him inside her; it happened sometimes that she couldn't shut out the pain when someone thrust themselves into her and ordered her to move at thc same time.

Lydia wondered if it was his smell.

The smell she recognised reminded her of the men who sat with her dad in that dirty room full of weapons. She wondered if it was a good thing that she recognised it, if that meant that she was still somehow connected to what had been back then and which she longed for so much, or if it was just breaking down even more, that everything she could have had, and that was now so far away, was being forced deeper into her.

He didn't speak afterwards. He had looked at her, pointed, one last time – that was all. He didn't even turn round when he left.

Lydia laughed.

If there had been anything between her legs, she would have been aggrieved that his bodily fluids had filled it and she would have felt him inside her even more. But she hadn't. She was just a face.

She laughed as she lathered one part of her body after another with the white bar of soap until her skin was red; she rubbed hard, pressing the soap against her neck, shoulders, over her breasts, her vagina, her thighs, feet.

The suffocating shame.

She washed it away. His hands, his breath, his smell. The water was almost painfully hot, but the shame was like some horrible membrane that would not come off.

She sat down on the floor of the shower cubicle and began to sing the chorus of the children's song from Klaipeda.

Lydia Grajauskas.
Lydia Grajauskas.
Lydia Grajauskas.

She loved that song. It had been theirs, hers and Vladi's. They had sung it together loudly every morning as they walked to school through the blocks of flats in the housing estate, a syllable for each step. They sang their names loudly, over and over again.

'Stop singing!'

Dimitri shouted at her from the hall, his mouth close to the bathroom door. She carried on. He banged the wall, shouted again for her to get out of there fucking pronto. She stayed where she was, sitting on the wet floor, but stopped singing, her voice barely carrying through the door.

'Who is coming next?'

'You owe me money, you bloody whore!'

'I want to know who's coming.'

'Clean up your cunt! New customer.'

Lydia heard real anger in his voice now. She got up, dried her wet body and stood in front of the mirror that hung above the sink, put on her red lipstick, put on the nearly cream underwear in a velvet-like material that Dimitri had handed to her that morning, sent to her in advance by the customer.

Four Rohypnol and one Valium. She swallowed, smiled

26

at her reflection and washed the tablets down with half a glass of vodka.

She opened the bathroom door and stepped into the hall. The next customer, the second of the day – a new one, someone she'd never seen before – was already waiting on the landing. Dimitri was glaring at her from the kitchen, watching as she passed him, the last few steps before opening the front door.

Before opening it she made him knock once more.

Hilding Oldéus gave the wound on his nose a good hard scratch.

The sore on his nostril wouldn't heal. It was the heroin: whenever he shot up, it itched and scratched. He'd had a sore there for years now. It was like it was burning; he had to rub, rub, his finger digging deeper, pulling at the skin.

He looked around.

A crap room at the welfare office. He hated it, but he always came back, as soon as he got out there he was, ready to smile for a handout. It had taken him one week this time. He'd been brown-nosing the screws at Aspsås prison. Said 'Cheerio' to Jochum. He'd been kissing the big boy's arse these last few months; he needed someone to hide behind, and Jochum was built like a brick shithouse. None of the lads even thought of messing with him as long as he hung out with Lang. And Jochum had said 'see you' back. He only had one bleeding week left. (Hilding suddenly realised he'd be out tomorrow. A week had passed: fuck, it was tomorrow.) They'd probably never meet up again outside. Jochum had protected him for a while, but he didn't do drugs and people who didn't just sort of disappeared, went somewhere else.

Not many people waiting here.

A couple of gyppo birds and a fucking Finn and two bloody pensioners. What the fuck did they want?

Hilding scratched the sore on his nose again. They were just taking up time, a crowd of losers getting in his way.

It was one of those days, a day when he was all sensitive. He didn't want to feel anything, mustn't, and then one of the days from hell hit him, when he knew, felt, felt, felt. He needed a hit badly, had to get rid of this crappy feeling. Had to get some fucking kit. But all these bloody awful people were sitting there, in this crappy room, holding him back. It was his turn now, fuck's sake, it was his turn.

'Yes. Who's next?'

That fat old cow opened her office door again.

He hurried over to her, his jerky movements propelling his thin body forward. Everyone could see that here was another young person, not even thirty yet, whose childish face somehow blended in with his punctured junkie skin. He was heading somewhere, but it certainly wasn't life.

Hilding scratched his nose again and realised that he was sweating. It was June, but raining non-fucking-stop, so he was wearing a long raincoat. It didn't let any air in or out. He should take it off, but couldn't be arsed to. He sat down on the visitor's chair in front of the bare desk and empty bookshelves. A nervous glance round the office. No one else there, no other fucker. There were normally two of them.

Klara Stenung settled on her side of the desk. Klara was twenty-eight, the same age as the heroin addict facing her. She had come across him before, knew who he was and where he was going. She knew the type; she'd worked as a social worker's assistant in the suburbs for two years, and then at the Katarina-Sofia office here in the city for three years. Thin, stressed out, noisy, just out of prison. They came and went, disappeared for ten months at a time inside, but always reappeared.

She stood up and reached across the desk. He looked at

her hand. He looked at it, considered spitting in it, but then took it in a flaccid shake.

'I need some cash.'

Her eyes met his; she didn't say anything, just waited for more. He was on her books, filed away. She knew everything about him. Oldéus was just like the rest. No father, not much of a mother, a couple of older sisters who had done what they could. He was very bright, very confused, very lost. Alcohol at thirteen, cannabis at fifteen. By now, he was on the fast track. Smoked heroin, then started to inject. First prison sentence at seventeen. Now, at twenty-eight, he had been inside ten times in eleven years, mostly for burglary and a couple of times for dealing in stolen goods. He was a petty criminal, the kind who had waved a bread knife at the assistant in the late-night corner store and then hung around outside the shop for the first dealer to come along, bought some kit and mainlined in the nearest doorway and couldn't understand it when someone in the shop pointed him out to the police when they turned up. He still didn't get it when the police bundled him into the back seat of a patrol car and sped off towards the station.

'You know the answer. No money.'

He twitched nervously in his chair, rocking backwards and forwards, nearly losing his balance.

'But I'm just out. For fuck's sake!'

She looked at him. He shouted, he scratched his nose and then the sore started to bleed.

'I'm sorry. You're not registered. As unemployed, or as a job-seeker.'

He got up.

'You fat cunt! I'm fucking skint. Fuck's sake. I'm hungry!'

'I understand that you need money for food. But you aren't registered so I can't give you any money.'

The blood dripped from his nose on to the floor. It was flowing fast and the yellow lino was soon covered in red. He hurled abuse, of course, threatened her as well, but never any more, it never got worse than that. He was bleeding, but didn't fight; he didn't have it in him and she knew it. It didn't even occur to her to call for support.

He slammed his fist on the top of the bookshelf.

'I don't give a fuck about your fucking rules!'

'Whatever you say. You still won't get any money. All I can do for you is give you two days' worth of food vouchers.'

A lorry rumbled past outside the window, the sound pushing its way up between the solid buildings that lined the narrow street. Hilding didn't hear it. In fact, he heard absolutely nothing. The stupid old slag in front of him had been banging on about food vouchers. And since when could you get fucking kit with food vouchers? He stared across the desk at the fat woman, glaring at her big droopy tits and fucking pathetic necklace of big round wooden beads. He burst out laughing, then shouted and knocked over the chair, kicked it into the wall.

'I don't give a toss about your fucking tickets! I'll have to find the fucking cash myself then! Fucking cunt!'

He almost ran through the door, through the crappy waiting room, past the Finn and the two gypsy slags and the old buggers. They all looked up at him, didn't speak, sat in silence, hunched up. He shouted at them, *fucking losers*, and something else that it was impossible to make out in passing, his shrieking voice breaking up and mixing with the blood dripping from his nose, which marked a trail down the stairs, out through the main door and all the way along Östgöta Street, towards Skanstull.

Not much of a summer.

Windy, rarely above seventy degrees except the odd morning with fleeting sunshine, otherwise the rain fell steadily on the rooftops and barbecue covers.

Ewert Grens had held her hand for as long as she let him, but after a while she became restless, the way she did when she had laughed enough and her babbling was done and the saliva no longer dribbled down her chin. So he had hugged her, kissed her forehead and said he'd be back in a week, always in a week's time.

If only you had managed to hold on just a bit longer.

Then he got into the car and drove back across Lidingö Bridge on his way to see Bengt Nordwall, who now lived in Eriksberg, some twenty-odd kilometres south of the city. Ewert was driving far too fast and suddenly saw himself, as he often did, behind the wheel of another kind of car. The police van he had been in charge of twenty-five years ago.

He had spotted Lang on the pavement, just ahead of the van; he knew that he was wanted, so he did what they had done so many times before, drove up alongside the running man while Bengt pulled the door back and Anni, who was sitting nearest the door, grabbed hold of Lang and shouted that he was under arrest, as she was supposed to do.

She was sitting in that seat, nearest the door.

That was why Jochum Lang had been able to drag her out.

Ewert blinked and swung off the road for a moment, away from the queue of stressed morning commuters. He switched off the engine and sat very still until the pictures faded from his mind. In recent years, the same thing happened every time he visited her, the memory pounding inside his head, making it hard to breathe. He stayed where he was for a while, ignoring the idiots with their horns, just waited until he was ready.

A quarter of an hour later he pulled up outside his friend's home.

They met in the narrow suburban street, stood together and got wet while staring up at the sky.

Neither of them smiled very often; it could be their age, or maybe they had always been the kind who rarely smile. But the impenetrable greyness and the wind and the pouring rain were too much; you had to smile because there was nothing else you could do.

'What do you think about all this, then?'

'Think? That I can't be bothered to let it get to me any more.'

They both shrugged and sat down on the rain-sodden cushions on the garden sofa.

Their friendship had begun thirty-two years earlier. They had been young back then, and the years had passed quickly; they had less than half of their lives left.

Ewert looked at his old friend. The only one he had really, the only person he talked to outside work, the only one he could bear to be with.

Bengt was still in good shape, slim, lots of hair. They were roughly the same age, but Bengt looked much younger. Maybe that was the effect of having young children. They forced you to stay young, as it were.

Ewert had no children and he had no hair and his body

had grown heavy. He had a limp, while Bengt walked with a light step. They were both policemen and shared past and present in the Stockholm city force. Both had been given a finite gift of time, but Ewert had used up his faster.

Bengt let out an exasperated sigh.

'It's so bloody wet. I can't even get the kids out of the house any more.'

Ewert was never sure why the family asked him over for breakfast, whether it was because they thought it would be nice or whether it was out of duty. Maybe they felt sorry for him, so lonely, so naked outside the four walls of the police headquarters. Whenever they asked, he went and never regretted it, but still he could not help wondering.

'She seemed well today. Sent her regards. At least, I'm sure she would have.'

'And what about you, Ewert? Are you all right?'

'Why do you ask?'

'I don't know. It's maybe just that you look . . . heavier these days. No, more burdened. Especially when you talk about Anni.'

Ewert heard him say this, but didn't reply. He looked around and observed with disinterest the suburban life that he could not understand. The small villa was actually quite nice. Very normal. Brick walls, a bit of lawn, a bunch of neatly trimmed shrubs. Sun-bleached plastic toys scattered here and there. If it hadn't been raining, the two children would've been running about in the garden, playing whatever kids of that age played. Bengt had had children rather late in life, when he was nearly fifty. Lena, who was twenty years his junior, had given him another chance. Ewert had no idea what a pretty, clever young woman like Lena saw in a middle-aged policeman, but he was pleased for Bengt, of course, even if he didn't understand.

Their clothes were soaking and started to hang heavily. They didn't notice any more and forgot about the weather.

Ewert leaned forward.

34

'Look, Bengt.'

'What is it?'

'Jochum Lang gets out today.'

Bengt shook his head. 'Ewert, you're going to have to let go of that one day.'

'Easy for you to say. You weren't driving.'

'And I wasn't in love with her, you mean. Never mind, you must let go. Leave the past behind you, Ewert. It was twenty-five years ago.'

He had turned to look back.

He had seen her reach out and grab the fleeing body.

He sighed, rubbed his wet scalp, felt the old anger rise inside him.

Jochum reacted to the hand holding him back and half turned, still running. He grabbed her and pulled hard, and Bengt, who was sitting next to her, had not been able to hang on to her.

He sighed and rubbed his head again.

In that moment, as she fell and the rear wheel bumped over her head, he had realised the rest of their life together was no more.

Lang had laughed as he ran away. And he laughed when he was later sentenced to a few lousy months for grievous bodily harm.

Ewert hated him.

Bengt undid the top button of his shirt and tried to make eye contact with his old friend.

'Ewert?'

'Yes?'

'Lost you for a moment, there.'

Ewert stared at the sodden lawn, at the tulips drooping in the neat border.

He felt tired.

'I'll nail that bastard.'

Bengt put his arm round his shoulder. Ewert pulled back. He wasn't used to it.

'Ewert, let it go.'

It wasn't long since he had held her hand; she had laughed like a child. Her hand had been cool, limp. Absent. And he remembered what it had once been like, warm and firm and very much present.

'From today he'll be walking the streets. Don't you understand? Lang is walking, laughing.'

'But Ewert, whose fault was it? Was it Lang's? Or mine? I couldn't hold on to her. Maybe it's me you should hate. Maybe it's me you should nail.'

The wind was back, catching the rain and whipping it into their faces. The terrace door opened behind them. A woman came out holding an umbrella and smiling, her long hair tied back.

'What are you two doing there? You're crazy!'

They turned round and Bengt smiled back.

'Once you're wet, it doesn't matter any more.'

'Well, I want you indoors. Breakfast time.'

'What, now?'

'Now, Bengt. The kids are hungry.'

They got up. Their clothes stuck to their skin.

Ewert looked up at the sky again and it was just as grey as before.

It was still only morning; she could hear the birds outside singing to each other, as they always did. Lydia sat on the edge of the bed and listened. It was so nice; they sang just like the birds around the ugly concrete blocks of flats in Klaipeda. She didn't know why, but she had woken several times last night, always after the same dream about her and her mum's trip to Vilnius and the Lukuskele prison, so many years ago.

In the dream her father was standing in the dark corridor of the tuberculosis ward, waving goodbye to her as she walked away, past the room called the HIV ward with its fifteen beds occupied by slowly decaying inmates. Then, from a distance, she turned to look back at him and saw him collapse. She stood still for a moment. When he didn't get up from the flagged floor she ran to him as fast as she could, dragged and pulled at him until he was upright again, coughing and emptying himself of the blood and yellow stuff he had to get rid of. The whole scene was actually a rerun of something that had really happened, but it was her mum who had been crying and screaming until some of the ward orderlies turned up to take Dad away. The dream recurred every time she fell asleep last night and she had never dreamt it before.

Lydia sighed deeply and shifted position a little. She had to sit further out on the edge of the bed to part her thighs just as widely and slowly as the man in front of her demanded.

He was sitting about a metre away. A middle-aged man, in his forties, the age her father would have been now.

He was her third customer today.

He had come to see her punctually every Monday morning for nearly a year. He always knocked on the door just as the church bells started pealing outside her locked window.

He didn't spit. He didn't want to force himself inside her. She didn't have to do anything with his sexual organ. She didn't even know what he smelt like.

He was one of those who hugged her when she opened the door, but then didn't touch her again. All he wanted was to sit with his cock in one hand and wave at her with the other to get undressed and do other things.

He wanted her to thrust her crotch backwards and forwards while he squeezed his cock harder and harder. He wanted her to bark like a dog he once had. In the meantime, he kept squeezing his dick, which would go more and more pink until he fell back into the armchair and let his stuff flow over the black leatherette.

By twenty past nine he was done. When the bells rang out for half past he would be gone. Lydia stayed where she was, sitting on the edge of the bed and listening to the birdsong. She could hear it again.

The blood was dripping from the raw sore on his nostril, down on to the Östgöta Street pavement. Hilding was almost running. He was in pretty poor shape despite having been inside. He had never been one of those guys who worked off their hatred, or built up respect, in the prison gym, but now he was jogging along, raging at the fucking bitch at the Katarina-Sofia social and panicking, desperate for heroin, and was therefore out of breath when he arrived at the Skanstull metro station on the ring road.

Sod their fucking handouts. He would just have to get the money himself.

'Hey, you!'

Hilding prodded one of the kids standing just in front of him on the platform. She was twelve or thirteen, that sort of age. She didn't respond and he poked at her again. She turned away deliberately to look in the direction of the train they were waiting for.

'Hey, I'm talking to you.'

He'd seen her mobile phone. He reached out for it, took a step forwards, grabbed it from her hand and dialled the number, despite her protests, then waited for the line to connect.

Hilding cleared his throat.

'It's me, sis. Hilding.'

She said nothing, so he continued.

'Listen, sis. You got to lend me some.'

She sighed, then replied. 'You won't get any money from me.'

'Sis, I need food. Clothes. That sort of stuff. That's all.'

'Try Social Services.'

He glared angrily at the phone, drew a deep breath and shouted into what he figured was the speaking end.

'Fuck's sake! I'll have to sort it out myself then. Whatever, it's your fault!'

She answered in the same tone of voice as before. 'No, it's your choice, Hilding. And your problem, not mine.'

She hung up. Hilding shouted abuse into the electronic void. He threw the bloodstained phone on to the platform. The fucking kid was still standing there crying when the train pulled in and he got on.

He stood in front of the doors and kept scratching at the red, dripping wound on his nose. His pale, emaciated face was spotted with blood and crusty with drying sweat. Some kind of smell hung around him.

At the Central Station he took the up-escalator. It was hardly raining at all when he emerged from the underground. Maybe it hadn't rained all morning. He looked around; he was still sweating inside his buttoned raincoat, his back soaking. He crossed Klaraberg Street and the pavement on the other side, then slipped in between the houses near the Ferlin statue and through the gate to St Klara Cemetery.

Empty, just as empty as he had hoped.

On the grass, a bit away, some guy who was off his head, but nobody else.

He walked past the large Bellman statue, to the bench behind it, under a tree he thought might be an elm.

He took the weight off his legs, humming to himself. Felt

with his hand inside the right coat pocket. There it was. Bag full of washing powder. He sifted it between his fingers.

He put his other hand in the left pocket and pulled out the pack of twenty-five small plastic stamp envelopes, eight by six centimetres, each containing a little amphetamine, which was barely enough to cover the bottom. Hilding topped up all the bags with washing powder.

He needed cash and would have it soon.

It was evening. Her working day was at an end. No more customers.

Lydia walked slowly through the flat, which was pleasantly dark, lit only by a few table lamps. It was quite big, with four rooms. Probably the largest she'd been in since she came here.

She stopped in the hall.

She had no idea why she kept looking for something hidden in the wallpaper pattern, somewhere behind the fine stippling of lines filling the barren surfaces between floor and ceiling. She often stood there, forgetting everything else; she realised that the wallpaper reminded her of something she had seen on another wall, in another room, long ago.

Lydia remembered that wall and that room very well.

The security police had stormed in and her dad and the other men in the room were pushed up against the wall, and voices were shouting things like *Zatknis, zatknis!* Then a strange silence.

She had known that her dad had been in prison once before. He had put up a Lithuanian flag on the wall at home and was sentenced to five years in Kaunas prison for it. At the time she was too little to understand. She had shaken her head. It was just a flag. She still couldn't understand. Of course they hadn't given him back his army job afterwards. Once, she remembered it well, when the vodka was finished and his cheeks were flushed and they were all in the room with the stippled wallpaper, surrounded by weapons that were about to be sold, he had noisily demanded explanations, shouted out: 'What choice did I have? When my children were screaming with hunger and the state wouldn't help, what the hell was I supposed to do?'

Lydia stayed in the hall. She liked evenings, the silence and deepening darkness that slowly wrapped around you and brought peace. She let her eyes follow the little lines upwards and had to crane her neck; the ceiling was high, as it was an old flat. She remembered times when she had worked alone in much smaller flats, but usually there were two of them, giving the men who knocked on the door a choice of girls to paw.

Every day she had to have twelve customers. Sometimes there were more, but never fewer, because then Dimitri would beat her up or rape her from behind, again and again, to make up for the missing gigs. Always up the arse.

She had her own ritual. Every evening.

She showered. The too-hot water washed away their hands. She took her tablets, four Rohypnol and one Valium, washed down with a little vodka. She put on large, baggy clothes that hung on her body, so she had no curves, no one could see, no one could touch her. Even so, sometimes the aching pain down there couldn't be silenced.

Tonight she felt jabs of pain and knew why. There had been a couple of new customers and they were always a bit too harsh. She rarely complained; she understood now how important it was that they came back.

Lydia got bored with the lines on the wall and turned to look at the front door. It was ages since she had been outside. How long was it? She couldn't say for sure, but she thought maybe four months. She had thought about it, breaking the kitchen window; you couldn't open it, or any of the others. She had thought about smashing the glass and jumping. The flat was on the fifth floor, though. Looking down scared her too much; she couldn't imagine what it would feel like to fall through the air towards the ground. She went to the door, touched it, sensing the cold, hard surface of the steel, closed her eyes and stood with her hand over the red light, breathing deeply and cursing herself for not understanding the electronic lock. She had tried to see what Dimitri did, but he knew she was spying and always made a point of standing in the way.

She left the hall, walked through the unfurnished room that was inexplicably known as the sitting room, past her own room with the large bed she despised but had to sleep in.

She walked to the end of the corridor, to Alena's room. The door was closed, but Lydia knew that Alena was finished for the day and had showered and that she was alone.

She knocked.

'Yes?'

'It's me.'

'I'm trying to sleep.'

'I know, but . . . can I come in?'

Silence, just for a few seconds. Lydia waited and then Alena made up her mind.

'Of course you can. Come in.'

Alena was lying naked on the unmade bed. Her skin was darker than Lydia's and her hair was still wet. If she left it like that it would be hard to brush tomorrow. At the end of the day Alena would often lie like this, staring at the ceiling and thinking about Janoz, that she had never told him she was going, that the years had passed, that she could still feel his arms and longed to be held again; it would only be for a few months, then she would come back to him, to Janoz, then they'd get married, later.

Lydia stood still. She looked at Alena's nakedness and

44

thought about her own body, the one she had to hide in baggy clothing afterwards – she knew that was what she was doing, hiding. She looked and she compared and she wondered how Alena could bear to lie in the same bed without clothes on, and she realised she was looking at her opposite, someone who somehow let things linger, who didn't hide it, who almost clung to it.

Alena pointed at the bed, the side that was empty.

'Sit down.'

The room was just like hers – same bed, same set of shelves and nothing else. She sat down on the rumpled sheets. Where someone else had just been. For a while Lydia stayed inside the red wallpaper, watching its swirling little velvety flowers. Then she reached out for Alena's hand, squeezed it and spoke in a near whisper.

'How are you?'

'You know . . . as usual.'

'Just the same?'

'Yes.'

They had met on the boat, so they had known each other for more than three years. Back then, they had laughed together. They were on their way. The frothing white water in their wake. Neither of them had ever been at sea before.

Lydia pulled her friend's hand closer, still holding it tight, caressing it, interlocking her own fingers with her friend's.

'I know. I know.'

Alena lay very still. Her eyes were closed.

Her body wasn't bruised, not like Lydia's, at least not in the same way.

Lydia lay down beside her, and in the shared silence their minds wandered, Alena's thoughts drifting back to Janoz, and Lydia's back to Lukuskele prison, to the shaven-headed men who coughed their lives away in the shabby prison hospital.

Then suddenly Alena sat up, pushed a pillow between the

small of her back and the wall and pointed at the evening paper on the floor.

'Look at that, Lydia.'

She let go of Alena's hand, bent down and picked it up. She didn't ask how Alena had got hold of a newspaper. She realised it was from one of the men who had been there today, one of the ones who took things with them, wanted something extra and got it. Lydia didn't have many customers who gave her things. She wanted money. Cash was all Dimitri cared for, and she liked cheating him of it. Anyone who wanted extras had to pay, a hundred kronor each time.

'Open it, look at page seven.'

The customers were charged five hundred kronor and she knew what five hundred times twelve per day came to. Dimitri took nearly everything; they were only allowed to keep two hundred and fifty. All the rest was taken from them for food and their room and to repay their debt. In the beginning she had said she wanted more money, but then Dimitri had sodomised her over and over, until she promised never to ask again. It was then that she had decided to keep an extra hundred when she could. Do it her own way, more for the sake of cheating Dimitri-Bastard-Pimp than for the money itself.

Some men wanted to beat her.

She let them. They paid an extra hundred and she took the blows. Most of them didn't hit her that hard; it was their way to get in the mood before sex. She took six hundred, gave Dimitri his five and kept her mouth shut. This had been going on for quite a while. She had saved quite a bit and Dimitri-Bastard-Pimp was none the wiser.

Lydia didn't speak Swedish and she certainly couldn't read it. Whatever it said in the paper was lost on her, the bold headline as much as the small print. But she saw the picture. Alena held the paper up so she could see and her eyes stopped at the picture. Suddenly she screamed, burst into tears, ran from the room, then came back and stood there staring at the paper, hating it.

'The swine!'

She threw herself on the bed, close to Alena's nakedness, crying now more than screaming.

'The stinking, rotten swine!'

Alena waited. There was no point in talking; she had to let Lydia cry, as she herself had cried not long before.

She held her friend tight.

'I'll read it for you.' Alena knew Swedish quite well. Lydia couldn't understand how she could bear to learn the language.

She and Alena had been in this country for just as long as each other and met just as many men, but that wasn't the point. Lydia had decided to shut it out, never to listen, never to learn the language in which she was raped.

'Do you want me to read?'

Lydia did not want her to. Didn't. Didn't.

'Yes.'

She huddled closer to Alena's naked skin, borrowing her warmth. She was always so warm. Lydia felt frozen most of the time.

The picture was dull. It showed a middle-aged man leaning against a wall. He was tall and slim, with blond, smooth hair and a moustache. He looked pleased with himself, like someone who has just been praised. Pointing to him, Alena read out the headline, first in Swedish and then in Russian. Lydia lay still, listening, not daring to move. The article was badly written, in a rush, a drama that had been resolved early that morning, just before the paper went to print. The man leaning against the wall was a policeman who had managed to get a small-time crook, who had in a panic taken five people hostage and held them locked up in a bank vault, to enter negotiations. In the end, the hostage-taker had been talked round by the policeman and all his captives were freed.

It wasn't a very exciting story. Routine police work, see page seven. Tomorrow, another page, another policeman.

But he was smiling. The policeman in the picture was smiling, and Lydia cried with hate.

The Plain was packed with them, speed freaks who couldn't get enough. Needed more.

Hilding made for the stairs to Drottning Street, where he usually hung out, and stood a few steps up. Easier to spot him there. He didn't give a toss about the pigs with their telephoto lenses. Fuck them.

She was waiting by the metro entrance. Tiny chick, smallest brownie customer he knew. No more than one metre fifty tall. She wasn't old, not even twenty and ugly with it. Big tangled hair, a greasy sweater. She must've been using for three or four days and now she was going off her head. Randy as hell too; all she wanted was to shoot up and fuck and shoot up and fuck. He knew her name was Mirja and she spoke with a foreign accent that made it hard to understand what she was on about and it was fucking impossible when she was really freaked out; it was like her mouth couldn't cope any more.

'You got it?'

His grin was mean. 'Got what?'

'You know. Some.'

'What? Fucking what?'

'A gram?'

Christ, what a slag. Speed and shagging. Hilding straightened his back, checked out the Plain. The cops were taking no notice.

'Crystal or ordinary sulphate?'

'Ordinary. Three hundred.'

She started rooting inside one of her shoes, near the laces, pulled out a wad of crumpled notes and handed him three.

'Like, just ordinary.'

Mirja had been on a bender for almost a week. She hadn't eaten, just had to have more, more, more, needed to get away from what seemed like high-voltage circuitry inside her head, thoughts that hummed and pulled her brain this way and that, making it hurt, like high-voltage shocks.

She walked away from Hilding as fast as she could, away from the Drottning Street steps, past the statue in front of the church and into the cemetery.

She heard the people she passed talking about her. Such loud voices, and it was scary, the way they knew everything, all her secrets. They talked and talked, but soon they'd stop and go away, at least for a few minutes.

Mirja was in a hurry now, sat down on the seat nearest the gate, slipped her bag from her shoulder, took out a Coke bottle half filled with water, held it in one hand and a syringe in the other. She drew the water up into the syringe and then squirted it into the plastic bag.

She was crazy for it; she had waited for so long. She didn't notice that the contents in the bag foamed a little.

Smiling, she drew up the solution, put the needle in place and held it still for a moment.

She had done this so many times before – the tie round the arm, find a vein, pull back blood into the syringe, shoot up.

The pain was instant.

She stood up quickly, cried out but her voice didn't

carry. She tried to pull back what she had already injected. The vein had swollen up already, an almost centimetre-high ridge running from wrist to elbow.

Then the pain passed and her skin went black, as the washing powder had corroded the blood vessel.

TUESDAY 4 JUNE

Jochum Lang was not asleep. The last night was always the worst.

It was the smell. When the key turned in the lock for the last time, it always hit him: the small cells all smelt the same. It didn't matter which prison it was, even in the police cells, the walls and the bed and the cupboard and the table and the white ceiling smelt the same.

He sat on the edge of the bed and lit a fag. Even the air pressure in the cells felt the same. That sounded plain fucking stupid and he couldn't tell anyone, but it was the truth that every cell in every prison and every jail had the same air pressure and it wasn't like in any other room.

He felt like belling the security desk – he always belled on the last night inside – so he went over to the metal plate with the intercom and pressed the red Call button long and hard.

Fucking screw took his time.

The red lamp went on and the central security desk replied.

'What's up, Lang?'

Jochum bent forwards to speak close up into the pathetic microphone.

'I want a shower. Get this fucking smell off.'

'Forget it. You're still locked up in here. Like the rest.'

Jochum hated the lot of them. He had done his time, but these little shits had to show who was on top to the bitter end.

He went back to the bed, sat down and looked around the cell. He would give them ten minutes and then try again. They usually gave in after the third or fourth try, came along to open up and stood aside just enough for him to push past. With only one night left, he obviously wouldn't want to do anything out of order, but once outside they might meet him anywhere in town, and sometimes it was wise not to have too much shared history with inmates.

He got up, walked about. A couple of paces to the window, a few more back to the metal door.

He packed as slowly as he could, cramming two years and four months into a plastic carrier bag. Two books, four packets of fags, soap and toothbrush. Radio and the pile of letters. An unopened packet of tobacco. He put the bag on the table.

He belled again. The fucker still took his time. Irritated, he put his mouth close to the microphone and growled. His breath misted the metal surround.

'I want my clothes.'

'Seven o'clock, mate.'

'I'll wake the whole fucking wing.'

'Whatever.'

Jochum banged on the door. Someone banged in response on a door on the other side of the corridor. Then another. Quite a noise. The screw was faster this time.

'Lang, you're creating a disturbance.'

'That's right. Like I said.'

The duty officer sighed.

'So you did. Look, I'll have you escorted to the sacks and the desk to check your stuff out. Then back you go. You won't get out until seven.'

The corridor was empty.

No one was up and about. The others, with years to wait behind their locked doors, had fallen quiet again. Who had any use for the dawn? He walked through the unit, along a corridor with eight cells on each side, passed the kitchen, passed the room with a billiard table and a TV corner. The screw was right in front of him, a little runt with a thin back. He could easily do him over, ten minutes after he'd finished his time – he'd done it before.

The screw unlocked the main unit door and led the way through the long underground corridors where Jochum had walked so many times before. The store was located next to the central security desk, behind the wall with CCTV monitors. Being there meant getting out. Just wandering among the hundreds of hessian sacks that smelt of the cellar, then finding the right one – opening it, trying on the clothes. Too small, they were always too small. This time he had put on seven kilos, bigger than ever. He had worked out regularly and bloody hard. He looked around. No mirrors. Rows of cardboard boxes with name tags, the belongings of the lifers who had no digs outside and kept what they owned boxed up in a storeroom at Aspsås prison.

He had taken the Karl Lagerfeld bottle back with him. The screw hadn't noticed or else didn't give a fuck either way. Jochum hadn't smelt like a free man since they stripped him on Day One. No alcoholic fluids allowed in the unit. He undressed and, standing naked in the middle of his cell, emptied the aftershave over his shaved head, its contents flowing over his shoulders and torso and dripping down over his feet and on to the floor, the powerful scent stripping off his prison coating.

Ten to seven. The screw was punctual.

The cell door opened wide. Jochum grabbed his carrier bag, spat on the floor and walked out.

All he had to do now was change into the tight clothes

he had just tried on, collect the release money, a pitiful three hundred kronor, and the one-way train ticket, tell the screw to go to hell as the gate slowly swung open, and walk out, bag in hand, giving the finger to the guard at the security camera. And turn sharp right, to the nearest stretch of wall, open his flies and piss against the concrete greyness.

The wind was blowing outside.

At the far end of the ground floor of the police headquarters, the dawn chorus was competing with Siw Malmkvist. As ever. Ewert Grens had served in the force for thirty-three years and had an office of his own for thirty. His cassette player, a present for his thirtieth birthday, had been around for almost as long. It was one of those large, lumpy things which combine a mono speaker and a tape deck. Every time he moved office he would carry it himself, cradled in his arms. Ewert only played Siw Malmkvist. A home-made rack held his collection of all her recordings, Siw's entire repertoire, in different orders on different tapes.

This morning it was 'Tunna skivor' (1960), the Swedish version of 'Everybody's Somebody's Fool'. He was always the first one in and turned the sound up as high as he liked. The odd bod might complain about the noise, but as long as he acted the sour old bugger they let him be, on the whole, left him to it. He kept life at bay behind his closed door, buried in his investigations while Siw belted out Sixties pop.

His mind was still caught up in yesterday. It had been good to see Anni in her crisply ironed dress, her hair neatly combed. She had looked at him more often than usual, almost made contact. As if, for a few moments, he was more than just a stranger sitting beside her and holding her hand.

And later that morning, Bengt's nice home, so full of life. Breakfast with messy kids and kind looks. As always, he had been full of gratitude. As always, he had nodded and smiled, while Bengt and Lena and the kids treated him like a member of the family, just as they always did. Yet he had felt lonelier than ever and that bloody awful feeling was still hanging around him now.

He turned up the volume and started pacing up and down on the worn linoleum. He had to think about something else. Anything but that. No doubting today, not any more. He had made a decision, chosen this place, this job. If the working life of a policeman meant missing out on some of the good things in life, so be it. That was how things had panned out. One day followed the other, making it thirty-three years in the end. No woman and no children and no real friends, just his long, devoted service, due to end in less than ten years from now. When it ended, he would cease to be.

Ewert looked around the room. The room was his only for as long as he put in the hours. When he retired this would become someone else's office. On he paced. Limping, his large, heavy body turning at the bookshelf and then at the window. He was not good-looking, he knew that, but he had been powerful, intense and brooding. Now he was just angry most of the time. He pulled his fingers through what had once been hair and now was grey, cropped tufts.

That song.

The tears I cried for you could fill an ocean,
But you don't care how many tears I cry.

And so, for a while, he forgot. It was morning now and his mind turned to the piles of documents on his desk, reports to be read and investigations to be completed. He had to deal with them, come what may.

A knock on the door. He ignored it. Too early.

Whoever it was opened the door.

'Ewert?'

It was Sven.

Ewert didn't say anything, he simply pointed at his visitor's chair. Sven Sundkvist came in and sat down. He was one generation younger than his colleague, a slightly built, straight-backed man with pale, short hair. Apart from Bengt Nordwall, Sven was the only one in the police house whom Ewert didn't detest. The lad had a good head on his shoulders.

Sven said nothing, because he had realised long ago that Siw's songs were Ewert's past, another, happier time that Sven knew nothing about. He sensed how powerful these memories were, though.

No one spoke. Only the music.

A buzzing noise as the tape came to an end and then the snap when the elderly machine's Play button popped up.

Two and a half minutes.

Ewert stood still, cleared his throat and spoke for the first time that day.

'Yes?'

'Good morning.'

'What?'

'Good morning.'

'Morning.'

Ewert walked over to his desk, his chair. He sat down, looked at Sven.

'And what do you want? Apart from saying good morning?'

'You know, don't you, that Lang gets out as of today?'

Ewert made an irritated gesture.

'Yep. I know.'

'That's all. I was actually on my way to an interrogation. The heroin addict who flogged washing powder.'

A second passed, maybe two. Ewert suddenly hit his desk with both hands. Sheets of paper showered on to the floor.

'Twenty-five years.'

He hit the desk again. Now that the documents had scattered, his hands slapped against wood.

'Twenty-five years, Sven.'

She was lying under the car.

He stopped, he jumped out, ran over to her motionless body, over to the blood that was gushing from somewhere in her head.

The piles of papers were all over the floor. Sven could see that Ewert was clearly caught up in thoughts he had no intention of sharing with anyone. He bent down and randomly picked up a few of the scattered documents and read out loud.

'"Trainee teacher, found naked in Rålambshov Park,"' he read aloud. '"One leg broken below knee. Both thumbs broken. *Criminal Act Not Confirmed*."'

He started on the next sheet of paper, his finger following the lines.

'"Insurance office worker, found in Eriksdal Wood. Knifed in the chest, four times. Nine potential witnesses. No one noticed anything. *Criminal Act Not Confirmed*."'

Ewert felt the anger, the rage. It started in his stomach and made his whole body ache. It had to be released. He waved at Sven, to make him move out of the way. Sven moved over. He knew.

Ewert took aim and kicked the waste-paper basket across the room. Its contents rained down everywhere. Silently and almost automatically, Sven started to make a pile of the empty tobacco tins and coffee-stained paper cups.

When he had finished he went on reading aloud.

'"Suspected grievous bodily harm. *Criminal Act Not Confirmed*. Suspected manslaughter. *Criminal Act Not Confirmed*. Suspected murder. *Criminal Act Not Confirmed*."'

Sven had interrogated Jochum Lang more times than he could remember. He had used every technique recommended in the college textbooks and quite a few others besides.

Once, a few years ago, he had almost managed, he had just about won his trust through showing him that he could cope with anything, no matter how shitty, if he wanted to open up. If Jochum talked, Sven would listen. Regardless. Jochum had taken this on board, but backed away just when he seemed ready and carried on as before, asking for fags, staring out the window. Later he clammed up totally, admitting nothing, not even to taking a dump now and then.

Sven turned to face his boss.

'Ewert, these papers that you flung all over the floor – I could go on for ever.'

'Enough.'

'"Intimidation of court witnesses, aggravated abduction . . ." He's under suspicion on twenty different counts.'

'I said, enough.'

'Found guilty on only three occasions. Short sentences. The first time . . . Let's see. Yes, for "causing serious injury".'

'Shut the fuck up!'

Sven jumped, didn't recognise the face of the man who was shouting at him. Ewert was often loud and aggressive in Sven's presence, but his anger was normally directed at someone else. This time was different.

Ewert turned away, marched over to the cassette player. The ancient apparatus started up again, playing the same tape.

Yes, everybody's somebody's fool.

I told myself it's best that I forget you.

Ewert listened and Siw's voice cooled his rage. I can't take much more, he thought. It could all end here and now. At this moment in time. Jochum Lang was one of those villains who had kept him at it for thirty-three years, nose to the grindstone and never a thought of stopping, of drawing breath, until the sentence had been pronounced. If he couldn't nail scum like him by now, he might as well give up. Drop it, go home and dare to live. During the last year, thoughts of this kind had bothered him; he dismissed them, but they came back, more distinct, more often.

Sven sat down in front of him, touched his chin, pulled his fingers through his blond fringe.

'Look, Grens . . .'

Ewert raised his finger.

'Shush.'

Another minute.

And there are no exceptions to the rule.

Yes, everybody's somebody's fool.

Sven waited. Siw stopped singing. Ewert looked up.

Suddenly Ewert spoke.

'What is it, then?'

'Look, it's just a thought. Aspsås prison. And Hilding Oldéus. You know who I mean, that emaciated junkie. The one I'm about to question.'

Ewert nodded. He knew exactly who Hilding Oldéus was.

'We know Oldéus was inside at the same time as Lang,' Sven went on. 'And we know they got friendly, as friendly as anyone can get with a lunatic hard man like Lang. Hilding crawled to him, produced some home-brew early on; it had been hidden in a fire extinguisher. They were nearly put in the slammer at one point when a guard caught them at it, pissed out of their heads.'

'Right. Hilding laid on the brew and Jochum gave him protection in return.'

'Exactly.'

'And what was your idea?'

'After questioning Oldéus about the washing powder, then we'll talk about Lang. Let him help us get him.'

The music had stopped. No more Siw. Ewert looked around the room, though there wasn't much to see. It was small and, apart from the cassette player and the tape rack, totally impersonal. Everything was regulation issue. Pale wood furniture, bits and pieces identical to the furnishings in the Inland Revenue offices on Göt Street and the National Insurance building in Gustavsberg. Impersonal or not, he spent more time in the room than anywhere else, from dawn to dusk, and later too. Quite often he didn't go home at night, preferring to sleep on the sofa by the window. It was small in relation to his big body, but it didn't matter. Oddly enough, he slept well here, much better than in his proper bed. Here he escaped the sleepless nights, the endless hours battling with the dark that plagued him in his own flat, where he could never find peace. Sometimes he didn't go home for weeks on end, without understanding what kept him away.

'Oldéus and Lang, eh? I don't think so. They exist in parallel worlds. Oldéus is hooked on heroin. It's all he wants. Lang is a criminal, not a junkie, even if he has pissed classified substances at Aspsås once or twice. And that's that. They have nothing in common, not outside.'

Sven shifted about in the visitor's chair, then leaned back and sighed. Suddenly he seemed tired.

Ewert looked intently at his friend.

He recognised what it was: resignation, hopelessness.

He thought about Oldéus. He had no time for people like that, small-time junkies who picked holes in their noses. Life was too short and there were too many idiots.

'OK. What the fuck. One nutter more or less. We can always ask him about Lang. Can't do any harm.'

A shiny brand-new car crept towards the large gate in the grey wall. The kind of car that would smell of leather upholstery and pristine wooden dashboard if you opened one of the front doors.

Jochum Lang spotted it as soon as he had passed through central security and started to cross the yard. He hadn't talked to them and hadn't asked for a car, but he understood all the same: they would be waiting outside, that was part of the deal.

He nodded a greeting and the man at the wheel nodded in response.

The engine ticked over while Jochum gave the finger to the security camera and pissed against the concrete wall. No hurry, the car was waiting and nothing disturbed his ritual. All the time in the world to finish having a piss, show the finger again and drop his trousers down, as the gate slowly swung shut behind him. Somehow, he wasn't really free until he'd done it, pissed on the wall, shown the guards his arse. He knew it was childish and pointless, but with his freedom came the urge to prove that none of those bastards could humiliate him any more and that, after two years and four months, he was the one who'd do the humiliating.

He walked over to the car, opened the passenger door and got in. They stared at each other in silence, without knowing why.

Slobodan looked older. At thirty-five his long hair was already going grey at the temples, he'd grown a thin moustache that was also tinged with grey, and there were new wrinkles at the corners of his eyes.

Jochum tapped lightly on the windscreen.

'New car. Traded up, I see.'

Slobodan looked pleased.

'Sure thing. What do you think?'

'Too flash.'

'It's not mine. It's Mio's.'

'Last time you were driving one you'd just nicked. Started it up with a screwdriver. Suited you better.'

The car moved off smoothly, just light pressure on the gas.

Jochum Lang took the train ticket from his trouser pocket, tore it up and threw it out the window, shouting abuse loudly in a broad Uppsala dialect, roaring about what he thought of the prison service's parting gifts, not fit to wipe the shit off your arse, and let the pieces blow away in the strong wind. Slobodan was talking on his mobile, which had been ringing for a while. He accelerated, leaving the gate and the high, grey wall behind them. Then, after a minute or two, the rain started up, the windscreen wipers going slowly at first, then faster.

'I'm not picking you up because I wanted to. Mio asked me to do it.'

'Ordered you.'

'Whatever. He wants to see you as soon as.'

Jochum was a big man, broad-shouldered, who took up a lot of car space. Shaved head, a scar from his left ear to the corner of his mouth. Some poor sod had tried to defend himself with a razor. Jochum talked with his hands, waving them about when he was upset.

'Look, last time I did something for him, I ended up here.'

They left the narrow prison drive and moved out on to a wider road that was quite busy already, people on the way to work.

'You took the rap, sure. But we looked after you, and your family. Right?'

Slobodan Dragovic turned to Jochum smiling, showing off poor-quality dental work, as he answered his phone, which was ringing again. Jochum stared silently straight ahead, absently following the wipers as they spread the water over the windscreen. Right enough. A total screw-up when he'd done a cash collection and that fucking witness who should've known better, who talked and pointed until the court passed a sentence. He followed the paths of the rain-drops, thinking that he knew all the hazards, but shit happens, that's true enough. Mio was always close at hand, watching him with borrowed eyes and ears every morning when he woke up and looked around his cell, looking out for him, looking out, that's what they did.

The gleaming new car gathered speed on its way through the landscape as it changed from rural to urban, and then through the northern suburbs, on towards central Stockholm.

Suspects were questioned in a room below the custody cells.

Wasn't much of a room, really.

Filthy walls, which had been white once, a heavily barred window at the far end, a worn pine table in the middle of the floor and four plain wooden chairs, straight out of some school canteen.

Sven Sundkvist, interview leader (IL): Please remain seated.
Hilding Oldéus (HO): Why the fuck are you picking up innocent people?
IL: Mixing amphetamines with washing powder, you call that innocent?
HO: Don't know what you're on about.
IL: Crap drugs. Cut. So far we've got three users with corroded veins. They gave us your name.
HO: What the fuck are you talking about?
IL: And you were in possession.
HO: Wasn't mine.
IL: We took the bags of white powder from you at the time of your arrest. All six were sent to the labs.
HO: Weren't fucking mine.

IL: Twenty per cent amphetamine, twenty-two per cent Panadol Extra and fifty-eight per cent washing powder. Oldéus, sit down.

Ewert Grens opened the door and went in. He had to pass through eight locked doors to get here, but hadn't even noticed. His mind was on the reports, and he could still hear Sven's voice reading aloud, 'causing serious injury', over and over in his head. And he saw the police van that hadn't stopped in time, him holding her in his arms until the paramedics put her on a stretcher and carried her off, away from him.

He was fighting Sven's voice, trying to rid himself of the words, and looked up briefly into the harsh overhead light. Then he concentrated on the man sitting opposite Sven, noted his thin face and how a finger was scratching nervously at a wound on one nostril, the drops of blood trickling down towards his mouth and chin.

IL: DSI Ewert Grens enters at oh nine twenty-two.

HO: [inaudible]

IL: What was that, Oldéus?

HO: Wasn't fucking mine.

IL: Stop messing about. We know you sold cut speed on the Plain.

HO: Know fucking everything, don't you?

IL: We arrested you there. With the bags full of washing powder.

HO: Wasn't fucking mine. Some guy handed it to me when I got there. What a cunt, passing on crap like that. I'll sort him when I get out of here.

Ewert Grens (EG): You're going nowhere.

HO: What? Fucking pig.

IL: Plenty of people who'd like to get hold of you, Oldéus. And if just one customer who bought that shit off you reports it, we'll charge you with attempted murder.

That's you inside for between six months and eight years.

Hilding got up, walked jerkily about in the tight space, suddenly stopped and struck out with one arm, lowered it and walked on a few more steps, stopped again and started speaking incoherently. He rambled on, his head first shaking, then tossing from side to side. His thin body, that was screaming for heroin, that ate and spewed, was disintegrating as they watched.

Ewert looked at Sven. They had seen all this before, of course, and knew he might sit down again and tell them all they wanted to know. Or he might lie down on the floor in the foetal position and shake himself unconscious.

EG: Six months at least. Up to eight years. But you're in luck. We're in a good mood today. What if the impounded bags got lost?

HO: What the fuck d'you mean, lost?

EG: Well, there are things we'd like to hear more about. Tell us about a friend of yours called Lang. Jochum Lang. You know him.

HO: Never heard of him.

Hilding's face was twitching violently. He grimaced, his eyes rolled back, his head turned this way and that. He scratched the wound. He was terrified. Jochum's name clawed at his mind and he wanted to shake it off, dump it, he didn't want it.

Not here. He was about to protest when someone knocked on the door. A woman detective put her head in. Ewert couldn't remember her name, but she was a summer locum, Skåne dialect.

'Sorry to interrupt. It's for you, Superintendent. I think it's important.'

Ewert waved her inside.

71

'Don't worry. This is all going to hell anyway. This little smack head seems to be in a rush to get out and die.'

Sven nodded when she glanced at him. She walked towards the table to stand behind Hilding. He got up, pointed at her, thrust his crotch at her lamely a few times.

'Got yourself new pussy, Grens? Pig's pussy, eh!'

She swung around, slapped him hard with the flat of her hand.

He lost his balance, stumbled forward holding both hands against his cheek, which flared bright red.

'Fucking pig!'

She stared at him.

'Inspector Hermansson to you. Get out. Now.'

Hilding, one hand covering his flushed cheek, kept swearing while Sven took a firm grip on his arm and escorted him out of the room.

Surprised, Ewert glanced at Sven, then turned to his young female colleague.

'You're Inspector Hermansson?'

'That's right.'

She was young, maybe twenty-five, no doubt in her eyes. She showed nothing. Neither surprise nor anger, unfazed by being called 'pig's pussy', unexcited by having dealt a violent blow to Hilding's face.

'Something important, you said?'

'The central switchboard called. You're needed at an address in the Atlas district. Völund Street. Number three.'

Ewert took note and searched his memory; he'd been there before, not long ago.

'It's somewhere along the main railway line, isn't it? St Erik's Square area?'

'That's right. I checked it on the map.'

'What's up?'

She had a sheet of paper in her hand, torn from a police notebook, and she looked at it quickly, didn't want to make a mistake. Not in front of Ewert.

'Our local colleagues have forced entry, following a report of serious physical abuse in a flat on the fifth floor.'

'And?'

'It's . . . quite urgent.'

'Anything else?'

'There's a problem.'

It was one of the older properties in a good area and had been carefully restored. Each street door was flanked by well-kept lawns with small trees dotted about, despite the lack of room, and narrow borders glowed with red and yellow flowers.

Ewert Grens got out of the car and scanned the long façade with its rows of windows. Turn-of-the-century building, the sort where you could hear your neighbours, their heavy steps in the kitchen, when they turned up the volume for the news, when they went out to put something in the rubbish chute. He looked at the windows with their expensive curtains. Flat after flat where people lived and died, only a breath away from their neighbours. But they never met, never knew anything about the person next door.

Sven Sundkvist, who had parked the car, joined him.

'Völund Street. Looks expensive. Who can afford to live here?' he muttered.

Eight windows on the fifth floor. Violence had broken out behind one of them. Ewert compared them. They all looked the same, the same damn curtains, the same damn plants – different colours, different patterns, but still the same.

He snorted in the general direction of the decorous façade.

'I don't like physical abuse cases anywhere, but it's worse in this sort of place. Which is as a rule where they happen.'

He looked around. An ambulance and two police cars with their chilly blue lights rotating. Maybe ten or so curious neighbours standing about near the parked cars, not crowding in on the place, decent enough to show a little proper respect, something that didn't always happen. The street door was held open by a rope tied to a bicycle rack. Ewert and Sven walked along the flagged path and into the lobby. Large wrought-iron numerals set into the wall near the doorway said '1901'. So it was built at the turn of the century. Satisfied, Ewert nodded to himself and started to study the list of tenants' names. Four of them on the fifth floor: Palm, Nygren, Johansson, Löfgren.

Couldn't be more Swedish. Only to be expected, given the kind of place it was.

'Do you spot anybody familiar, Sven?'

'No.'

'They don't exactly put it on show.'

'You?'

'No idea.'

Pretty poor lift, narrow with a folding grid gate, room for three, no more than 225 kilos. A uniformed policeman stood guard, an older man whom Ewert hadn't seen around for a long time.

I always forget how many idiots there are in the force, he thought. Like this one. If you don't clap eyes on them day in and day out, these sad bastards fade from your mind.

He smiled grimly while he observed the man.

Legs well apart, the stance of a cop on the telly, a cop with an important mission, keeping an eye on things as the music builds up, with lots of long notes from the string section. He might even click his heels if you asked him a question, and he'd almost certainly spell words aloud when working on a report. In short, the sort who should be allowed to guard lifts, but not much else. That sort.

The constable didn't return Ewert's smile, because he sensed the contempt. He deliberately addressed Sven when he started on his account.

'We were called about an hour ago, sir. An extremely drunk pimp. And a badly beaten prostitute.'

'That so?'

'Yes. Some neighbours phoned the police, but by then he'd already beaten her black and blue. She's unconscious. She needs to go to hospital. And there's one more in there. Another prostitute, by the look of her.'

'Beaten up too?'

'Don't think so. He didn't get round to her, I suppose.'

Ewert listened in silence while Sven talked to the idiot guarding the lift, but eventually he couldn't take it any more.

'Alerted an hour ago! Exactly what are you waiting for?'

'We aren't allowed in. Apparently it's Lithuanian . . . er, territory.'

'What? When someone is being physically abused, you go straight in!'

Five bloody flights. Ewert had a problem breathing, every step cost him. He should have used the lift, but his temper had flared up and he had run past that flaming imbecile on guard duty. He heard voices discussing the case above him, getting louder as he climbed. Two ambulance men and a paramedic seemed to be conducting a case conference on the fourth-floor landing. They exchanged brief nods as he passed them. Only one more flight.

He was gasping for breath and out of the corner of his eye he saw that Sven was catching up with light steps. Ewert couldn't give up now and forced his legs to move. They didn't want to. He could hardly feel them.

There were four doors on the top-floor landing. One of them had a gaping hole in the panel and was guarded by three uniformed men. He didn't recognise any of them, but further back he saw the familiar face of Bengt Nordwall, in civvies like himself and Sven. Barely twenty-four hours had passed since Ewert and Bengt had met on that rain-sodden morning outside the happy family home where Ewert had been given breakfast and caring attention. It was rare for their paths to cross at work, and Ewert stared at his friend, feeling almost let down.

They shook hands briefly, as was their habit.

'What are you doing here?' Ewert asked.

'Russian. The guy in there doesn't speak anything else.'

Bengt Nordwall was one of a handful in the force who could speak Russian. He went on to explain a little more.

'A pimp was beating the shit out of one of his whores and she kept screaming to high heaven. When the police arrived they broke the door down and came face to face with that lowlife you can see over there.'

Bengt pointed at a man just inside the doorway, apparently standing watch over the badly damaged door. He was in his forties, short and fat and flabby. His shiny grey suit looked expensive, but didn't suit him and didn't fit him either.

'Then he waves his diplomatic passport at the lads and claims that the flat is Lithuanian territory and that the Swedish police have no right of entry. He won't hand over the woman and refuses to admit our medic. Or any other doctor, except one from the Lithuanian embassy. The victim seems to be well beyond saying anything, but the other woman in there has shouted abuse at the pimp, calling him "Dimitri-Bastard-Pimp" in Russian. He doesn't like it one bit, but for as long as we're around, he doesn't dare do anything except shout back at her.'

Sven had stopped a few steps down, by the rubbish chute between floors four and five. He was just finishing a call on his mobile and waved at Ewert to catch his attention. He closed his phone, came up the remaining steps, looking at Ewert as he spoke.

'I've just been talking to the housing association that's responsible for this place. The flat belongs to a Hans

Johansson, which fits with the board downstairs. It's not a regular sublet.'

Ewert Grens turned to look at the man in the shiny suit, who claimed that his diplomatic status gave him the right to beat up women, and at the same time held out a hand towards the three uniformed men behind Bengt.

'One of you lot, hand over a truncheon. Right, Mr Dimitri-Bastard-Pimp, try waving your diplomatic credentials this time.'

As he approached the door, the smartly suited man demonstrated that he intended to block the way by taking a few steps back and holding both his arms out to the side. Ewert walked on until he was close enough to ram the tip of the truncheon into a vulnerable gap in the unbuttoned jacket, which made the body standing in his way double up. The Lithuanian representative hissed something in Russian and collapsed, clutching his belly with both hands. Ewert called out to the doctor and the ambulance men on the floor below, then waved at the officers to follow him and marched on, through a long hall and an empty sitting room.

At first he couldn't quite take in what he saw in the next room.

The bedspread was red and a woman was lying on it naked, with her back towards the door, but there seemed to be no difference between her body and the top of the bed, the red colours blending.

He had not seen anyone so badly beaten for a very long time.

The light is always the same in the Söder Hospital casualty department.

Early morning and late, lunchtime and afternoon, evening and night, the light stays on and on.

A young doctor, tall and thin, let his tired eyes follow the string of lamps in the corridor ceiling as he accompanied a patient trolley. He was trying to focus and listen properly to what the nurse was saying. This must be the last patient on his shift, then he could go out into the other light, the kind that changed with time.

'Unconscious female, almost certainly subjected to a beating. Head injuries, a broken arm and probably internal haemorrhaging. Laboured breathing. I'll call the trauma team and ITU.'

The young doctor stared at her. He had had enough, didn't want to hear any more about how people went about exterminating each other.

'She needs an airway.'

He nodded, but stayed by the woman on the trolley for a moment, just a few more seconds, on his own. It had been a long day, and for some reason he had seen more young people than usual, his own age or younger. He had mended their damaged bodies as best he could, knowing that none of them would carry on living as they had until now. They would always carry today inside them, wouldn't be able to let go, regardless of what showed externally.

He studied her face. Somehow she didn't look Swedish. From somewhere not very far away, though. She was blonde and probably pretty. She reminded him of someone, but he didn't know whom. The ambulance staff had jotted down some details and he pulled the notes out of the plastic pocket. He learned that her name was Lydia Grajauskas, or at least that was what another woman had stated, the one who was in the flat where the abuse had taken place.

He looked at her.

All these women.

What had the expression on her face been while he beat her?

What had she said?

Green- and white-clad staff came hurrying along and sought some kind of confirmation from the doctor with the dark, exhausted eyes, indicating that they were ready to start. The patient was wheeled into the trauma room, expertly lifted on to a theatre trolley and wired up for monitoring her pulse, ECG and blood pressure. They opened her mouth to introduce a tube into her stomach and sucked away its contents. She became less human, less of a body, more statistics and graphs, it was easier then, easier to deal with.

Had she actually said anything?

Or screamed? What do you scream when someone is beating you?

He, of the tired eyes, couldn't bring himself to leave her.

He wanted to see . . . What? He didn't know what he wanted to see.

One of his colleagues had now taken over and was standing about a metre away carefully moving the woman they knew was called Lydia Grajauskas, turning her light body on its side to inspect the blood-soaked, shredded skin.

The sight upset him.

'Hey, somebody! I need a hand.'

The tired young doctor stepped forward and saw what the doctor beside him had seen.

He counted.

When he reached thirty he stopped.

The stripes were red and swollen.

He sensed the tears coming and forced himself to hold them back. It happened from time to time. The obligation to stay professional took a physical effort. Must see her as statistics, as a set of graphs. *I don't know her, I don't know her*; it didn't do the trick, not this time. Today there had been too much of this pointlessness he couldn't understand.

This torn, red mess.

He said it out loud, maybe to hear what it sounded like, maybe to inform everyone, he couldn't be sure which.

'She's been flogged!'

He repeated it more slowly, in a quieter voice.

'She has been flogged. Multiple injuries. From the back

80

of her neck all the way down to her behind. Her skin is . . . has been lacerated.'

The flat was lovely, he had to admit it. High ceilings, sanded floorboards and a tall tiled stove in every room. A home like this ought to be peaceful. Ewert Grens had settled down on one of the four folding plastic chairs in the kitchen. With Sven and two technicians in tow, he had investigated all the rooms now.

Who was the woman called Lydia Grajauskas? Who was her friend, who said her name was Alena Sljusareva? And who was the would-be Lithuanian diplomat, who said the flat was foreign territory and was known as Dimitri-Bastard-Pimp for short?

After the beaten Grajauskas woman had been carried off on a stretcher and before the technicians turned up on the scene, the other one, Sljusareva, had disappeared. Both women were prostitutes and came from one of the Baltic states, or possibly Russia. He had come across the sort before. The story was always the same. Some guy with the gift of the gab would arrive in the village and target girls with promises of work and good money in a Scandinavian welfare state. Young and poor, the girls would bite on the bait. The moment they accepted the false passports, they were transformed from hopeful teenagers into supposedly horny female slaves. Their passports cost money, of course, and the debt was too big for them to pay off outright. It had to be recovered from their earnings. A few of them would try to refuse, but would promptly be taught a lesson and would learn with time what a beating could mean. The girls were raped, over and over again, until they bled. With a gun pressed to their heads, they would be told to do it again and again – spread your fucking legs and do it, you've got to pay for your passport and the sea crossing. If you won't fuck them, I'll take you up the arse again! He, the persuader, who had beaten them and raped them at gunpoint, would sell them

81

on afterwards, three thousand euros for every teenage girl shipped from east to west, who had learnt to groan with desire whenever someone penetrated her.

Ewert sighed and looked up when Sven came into the kitchen. He was ready to report on the contents of a cupboard they had missed the first time round.

'Not a damn thing there either. No personal belongings at all.'

Several pairs of shoes, a couple of dresses and quite a few sets of bra and panties. And bottles of perfume and plastic toilet bags containing assorted make-up, a box of condoms, dildos and handcuffs. That was all. They had found nothing in the flat that couldn't have been predicted if you started with the assumption that their life stories were all about sexual penetration.

Impatient, Ewert flapped his arms about.

'These children without faces.'

These girls did not really exist. They had no identity, no work permit, no life of their own. They breathed, cautiously, inside a fifth-floor flat with electronic door locks in a big city which was very different from the one they had left.

'Ewert, do we know how many of them we've got here in Stockholm?'

'As many as the market demands.'

Ewert sighed again and bent forward to finger the wallpaper. The pimp had beaten her in here and her blood had congealed on the flowered pattern. In fact blood had splashed all over the place; even the ceiling was dotted with red spots. He was angry and tired and felt like shouting, but found himself whispering instead.

'She's here illegally. She'll need to be guarded.'

'She's being operated on now.'

'I mean afterwards, in the ward.'

'It will take another couple of hours, the hospital tells me. Before she's done.'

'Sven, please get a guard for her. I don't want her to disappear.'

Outside the house with the imposing façade the street was silent and empty.

Ewert examined the windows in the house opposite. Nothing new there; they looked as blank and as orderly, with the same sort of curtains and flowerpots.

He felt deeply ill at ease.

The beaten woman, the pimp in the shiny suit and Bengt and the rest of his colleagues, waiting for nearly an hour while she lay unconscious and bleeding.

He felt chilly and tried to shake it off, together with the bad feeling, but did not know how to get rid of something like that.

It was half past ten in the morning. Jochum Lang served himself from the breakfast buffet in Ulriksdal Inn. Typical Yugo tactic: treat someone to something expensive and then start talking business. They had driven through the northern suburbs, heading straight for the talk that was due to start any time soon. One more piece of omelette. A cup of coffee to follow. Might as well make use of the mint-flavoured toothpicks too.

Lang let his eyes sweep over the breakfast room, all white tablecloths and heavy silver-plated cutlery and conference delegates eating their fill. Women with red cheeks were lighting cigarettes, men sitting as close to them as they could, after pouring themselves yet another cup of coffee. He laughed at the encounters and expectations; he didn't do things like that, never had done, had never understood the point of such a predictable game.

'So what's on your mind?'

They hadn't exchanged more than a word or two on the way, since Slobodan had met him at the gate of Aspsås prison in the shiny car and Jochum let himself be driven away, had sat in the leather passenger seat and thrown away the shreds of the standard one-way train ticket.

Now the two of them were waiting and watching each other across the beautifully laid breakfast table in the expensive restaurant ten minutes from the centre of Stockholm.

'Some business of Mio's.'

Jochum, with his large shaved head, sunbed tan, scarred cheek, remained stubbornly silent, just sat there taking up space.

Slobodan leaned forward.

'He'd like you to have a word with a guy who is selling our goods cut with washing powder.'

Jochum waited. He said nothing. Not until Slobodan's mobile phone, lying in the middle of the table, rang and he reached out for it. Then Jochum grabbed his wrist.

'You're talking to me. Do the rest of your fucking business some other time.'

A flash of defiance in his eyes.

Slobodan withdrew his hand, just as the ringing stopped.

'Like I said, this guy sells bad shit. And one of the buyers was Mio's niece.'

Jochum picked up the salt cellar from the starched tablecloth waste between them, rolled it over the table, watched it go over the edge of the table and roll across the floor towards the window.

'Mirja?'

Slobodan nodded.

'Mio never bothered about her before. A smack head whore.'

Muzak flowed from wall-mounted speakers, lift music. The women with red cheeks laughed and lit fresh cigarettes, the men undid the top buttons on their shirts, tried to hide their ring fingers as best they could.

'I think you know the bloke.'

'What's your point?'

'Look, it was cut with washing powder. And it was ours. Don't you get it?'

Jochum didn't comment and leaned back in his chair. Slobodan had gone red in the face.

'That little creep is ruining our street cred. The story that punters were mainlining fucking Persil will do the rounds in no time.'

Jochum was starting to get fed up with the whole place: the conference women's smoke, the smell of cooked break-fasts, the too-polite waitresses. He wanted to get out, out into the daylight, to another day. This posh scene might be everything that some people longed for in Aspsås, but it wasn't his idea of the good life. On the contrary. The more years he spent inside, the more he resisted any kind of fancy pretence.

'Get on with it. Tell me what I'm supposed to do, for fuck's sake.'

Slobodan responded to his impatience.

'No fucker's going to sell washing powder in our name. So, a few broken fingers. An arm, nothing more. That'll do.'

Their eyes met. Jochum nodded.

The muzak piano played worn-out pop. He got up, made for the car.

The morning had almost passed, but Stockholm's Central Station was still yawning, still not quite awake. Some people were in transit, some were snatching a little sleep. Always room for those who struggled with loneliness. It had been raining since midnight, and the homeless had sought shelter in the massive doorways, tried to lie down on the benches in the hall that was as large as a football pitch. They had to keep moving to avoid the security guards, hiding in amongst the hurrying crowd of travellers carrying bags and suit-cases and paper cups of café latte steaming under plastic lids.

Hilding Oldéus had just woken up.

A couple of hours' kip in the middle of the day. He looked around.

His body ached from the hard bench. Some sodding guard had been prodding him non-stop.

No food, not since the morning, when one of the cops had given him a couple of custard creams at the joke hearing. Not that it made him grass on Jochum.

He wasn't hungry now. Not randy either.

He was, like . . . nothing.

It made him laugh out loud. Two old bags stared at him

and he gave them the finger. He was nothing. Had to get more kit. Then he could carry on being nothing and shut them all out and have no feelings.

He got up. He smelt of piss, his hair was greasy and matted and the wound on his nose was coated in dried blood. He was thin and filthy and twenty-eight years old, closer to the other side than ever before.

Hilding walked slowly towards the escalator that wasn't working. When it rocked too much he clung to the black rubber railing. The left-luggage lockers were down a concrete corridor. The door was opposite the johns, where some cow demanded five kronor every time you needed to take a leak. Not fucking likely. Stood to reason you pissed in the metro tunnel instead.

Olsson was tucked away at the back as usual, somewhere between boxes 120 and 150. He was asleep. One foot was bare, no sock, no shoe. The fucker could afford shoes, no problem, but who cares about fucking shoes.

He was snoring. Hilding pulled at his arm and shook him a little.

'I want some cash.'

Olsson was still half asleep and stared vacantly at him.

'You hear? I need cash. Now. You were going to settle last week.'

'Tomorrow.'

Olsson wasn't his real name. Hilding had no idea what it was, but he knew it wasn't Olsson. They had been stuck in the same drug rehab place once, down in Skåne.

'Olsson, you heard. One fucking thousand, right now! Or did you take all the shit yourself?'

Olsson sat up, yawned, stretched.

'Hilding, lay off. I haven't got any!'

Hilding scratched the wound. The bastard didn't have any money. Just like that cow at the Social Services. Like his sister. He'd phoned her and begged for money again, like he had a few days ago from the metro platform. Same again: she'd stuck to the same old tune, like *It's your choice, it's your problem, don't try to involve me.*

He started on the wound again, the crust came off and it bled quite a lot.

'Got to get some cash, you fucking cunt. Get it?'

'I haven't got none. Tell you what I've got. Information, well worth a thousand.'

'What fucking info?'

'Jochum Lang is looking for you.'

Hilding couldn't leave the wound alone. He sighed and tried to make out that he didn't swallow.

'So what? I don't give a shit.'

'What does he want you for?'

'I don't know. Meet up? We did some time together in Aspsås.'

Olsson's cheek twitched upwards, over and over, making his eye open and close. He was caught in his junkie tic.

'Worth a thousand, wasn't it?'

'I want my cash.'

'Haven't got it.' Olsson patted his anorak pocket. 'But I have got some smack. Powder.'

He pulled the plastic bag from its hiding place and held it up for Hilding to see.

'One gram, what about it? Take it and we're even.'

Hilding stopped scratching.

'A gram?'

'Fucking strong too.'

Hilding reached out, waved his hands around, slapped Olsson.

'Let's see.'

'Pure heroin. Real strong.'

'I'll take a quarter now. I'll just shoot up a quarter. OK?'

The train to Malmö and Copenhagen was late, the loud-speakers in the ceiling filled the hall, fifteen minutes more to go, sit down on your seats, keep waiting. From some-where else, café noises, the smell of brewing coffee and greasy pastries sneaked about and clung to everything. They didn't notice, didn't notice the great space around them filling up with commuters hurrying to their platforms – young people with rover tickets and huge, flag-covered rucksacks, families travelling at inconvenient times on the special saver tickets that the businessmen despised. All that passed them by. Jerkily they walked to the photo booth near the main entrance. Olsson stood guard; he was to stop anyone wanting to get in and make sure that Hilding didn't OD and flake out. Hilding sat on the low folding seat and drew the curtains. He was shaking and his legs showed, so Olsson moved over a little.

The spoon was in the inside pocket of the raincoat.

He filled the spoon with white heroin powder, added a few drops of citric acid on top, cooked the mixture over the flame of his cigarette lighter, then mixed it in the water and drew the solution up into his syringe.

He had lost a lot of weight. It used to be enough to take the belt into the third or fourth hole, but now he got to the seventh. He pulled it tight, and enough was left to go one more time round his arm. The leather cut deep into the flesh.

He bent forward and grabbed the end of the belt between his teeth to keep the ligature tense, looked for a vein at the elbow. Nothing there. He prodded with the tip of the needle, pushed it against stringy, tough cartilaginous bits, past them and into the big hollow that had formed inside his arm where innumerable injections had eaten away the substance of his body.

He searched about, tried, tried again, and then suddenly felt the wall of a vessel give way under the needle.

He pulled back and smiled. Usually it wasn't this easy. Last time he had had to find a track in his neck before he could shoot up.

The thin stream of blood was held suspended in the transparent fluid inside the plastic wall of the syringe for a moment, then dispersed into a spreading plume, like the petals of a red flower opening. It was so pretty.

Hilding collapsed, unconscious, within a second or two.

He fell forward from the seat, became easily visible below the curtain. He had stopped breathing.

WEDNESDAY 5 JUNE

Lydia had just woken up.

She tried to turn over in bed. Resting on her right side meant that her back hurt a little less. She waited, alone in the large room. She had been unconscious for twelve hours, at least that was what a nurse, who spoke Russian, had told her.

Her left arm was broken. She couldn't remember everything, had no idea how he had done it. She must have lost consciousness before he did it. It was in plaster and the cast was to stay on for a couple of weeks.

She remembered him kicking her in the stomach, over and over, and screaming, *Whore, whores like you fuck when you're told*. And when he had done with kicking her, he buggered her, first pushing his organ up her anus, then his fingers.

She knew that Alena had tried to stop him, shouted at him and thumped his back, but he had pushed her into her room, made her take her clothes off and locked her in. It would be her turn next.

Lydia remembered what had happened right up to the time he started to use the whip on her. She remembered everything before that.

He struck her on the back above her backside. *I won't do your arse, your back is OK, nothing to fuck there, it's useless.*

She had counted to eleven, that was as many as she could remember. The nurse had said her back showed many more marks than that.

'Good morning.'

The nurse was called Irena, a dark-haired woman from Poland – you could tell from her accent. She had lived in Sweden for nearly twenty years and was married to a Swede. They had three children. Irena said she was happy in Sweden, that it was a good place.

'Good morning.'

'Slept well?'

'Now and then.'

Irena cleaned Lydia's wounds as she had the day before. She started with the face, then the back. The bruises on her legs would go away by themselves.

She twitched when the nurse's hands touched her back.

'Does it hurt?'

'Yes.'

'I'll be as gentle as I can.'

A guard had been stationed outside her room. His green uniform reminded her of the security staff on the big Scandinavian railway stations which she and Alena had been hurried through every time Dimitri had panicked and forced them to move to another city. He would order them to pack quickly and then off they'd go, five times in three years, though the flats had been all alike. Always on the top floor, with red bedspreads and electronic locks.

Lydia felt how her back ached, how the sterile fluid stung her open wound. She couldn't think why, but her thoughts wandered back to a graveyard in a village somewhere along a country road between Klaipeda and Kaunas. Her father's mother and father were buried there, and that's where her dad was put into the ground too. She realised that she no longer missed the man with the shaved head who had seemed so small when she saw him in Lukuskele prison. He didn't exist any more; he had finally disappeared while she wept for him, standing next to her mum in that cemetery. Since then he hadn't existed for her.

Lydia became restless, anxious, had to stop herself from crying out. The cuts on her back were burning. She fixed her eyes on the green-uniformed guard, if she concentrated on him it didn't hurt as much.

She didn't know why he was standing there. Maybe they thought Dimitri-Bastard-Pimp would come back. Or maybe that she would run away.

Irena talked while she washed Lydia's back, asked questions about the notebook on her bedside table and the hospital food – did she like it? They both knew that they were meaningless questions, that the answers didn't matter, but chatting would help Lydia to think of something else and relax a little, forget the pain from her torn skin. Lydia told Irena that the notebook was just for writing her thoughts in, about the future and things like that, and that the food didn't taste of much, but it was hard to chew, because her cheeks ached.

'My dear . . .'

Irena was looking at her and shaking her head.

'My dear, I have no idea what you have been through.'

Lydia didn't answer. She knew. She knew what she had been through. She knew what her body, the thing she tried not to feel, looked like now. Also, she knew what she had written in that notebook on the bedside table.

She knew that it would never happen to her again.

'There you are, dear. That's it for now. I'll come back in the afternoon, but it's going to hurt less and less every time. You're very brave, dear.'

Irena caressed Lydia's shoulder quickly and smiled at her. As she left the room, a doctor entered with four other white-coated people in tow – three men and a woman. The doctor spoke to the guard and then to Irena, who came back to Lydia's bedside and pointed at the doctor and the others.

'Lydia, this is the doctor who has looked after you. He examined you when you arrived here. The other four are medical students. Söder Hospital is one of the hospitals where students train to help ill people. The doctor wants them to see your injuries. To learn about them. Is that all right?'

Lydia only registered their faces. She didn't know them. She was tired, didn't want people to stare at her, she hurt so.

'Let them look.'

The doctor waited as Irena translated and nodded a thank you to Lydia. He asked Irena to stay and translate. It was important that Lydia could understand. He told the students about what happened when someone was admitted to Casualty, about Lydia's journey from the ambulance, through the hospital to the department of surgery. Then he produced a laser pointer and let the red dot wander over her naked back, demonstrating her injuries.

'Marked redness and swelling. See . . . The beating was carried out with quite a lot of strength. See . . . We believe an ox-hide whip was used, some three to four metres long. See . . .'

Irena turned to Lydia again and tried to hold her gaze while she translated. Lydia nodded in agreement. The four students said nothing. They had never seen a lashed back of a human being before. The doctor waited for their comments and then continued.

'Ox-hide whips are used for cattle droving. This patient had thirty-five lashes.'

He talked on for a bit longer, but Lydia could not bear to listen any more. They left a little later – she hardly noticed.

She looked at her notebook.

She knew.

She knew what had been done to her.

She knew it would never happen again.

One floor down.

There were three patients in Ward 2 of Söder Hospital's medical department.

None of them knew anything at all about the woman upstairs with the flayed back.

She knew nothing about them.

The floor in Lydia Grajauskas's ward was their ceiling. That was all.

Lisa Öhrström stood in the middle of Ward 2 and looked at her three patients. She stood there for a while. She was thirty-five years old and she was tired. After a couple of years of work, she was as tired as her contemporaries on the medical staff. They often talked about it. Lisa worked almost all the time, but never felt she did enough, and carried this sense of inadequacy home with her, falling asleep with it at her side. The feeling of never spending enough time with patients, let alone talking properly to them once she had dealt with the diagnosis and general health survey and appropriate treatment. She could hear how she speeded up before hurrying off to the next bed, the next ward, the next clinic, always making important decisions on the hoof, never being able to stop and dwell on them.

Now she made herself look at the patients, one at a time.

The elderly man was awake and propped up against the pillows. He hurt somewhere inside, and was clutching his abdomen while he used the other hand to search on his bedside table for the bell-push. It should be somewhere near the food he hadn't touched.

The man in the next bed was much younger, more a boy actually, eighteen or nineteen years old, who for the last five years had been in and out of just about every department in the hospital. His body had been strong before he was suddenly taken ill, and ever since he had been hanging on for dear life, crying and swearing, refusing to die. His breathing was very slow and he had lost most of his body mass long ago, together with his hair and youthful looks, but he still lay in his bed, angrily staring at the wall until he was certain that he would wake up to see yet another morning.

The third man was a new admission.

Lisa sighed. He was the one who made her feel exhausted, the reason why she was standing still while a patient's bell was ringing irritably in the corridor.

He had been admitted last night and put in a bed at the far end, opposite the older man. Strange and somehow unfair too, though she knew she shouldn't follow this thought to its conclusion, that he was the only one of these three patients who would leave this hospital with a beating heart.

And he was the only one of them who acted as if he was intending to end his life. She knew that she could not make him understand how completely he drained her energy and robbed her of time. It didn't matter that he had just been more dead than alive. He didn't understand, or perhaps he did and he would do the same thing over and over and over again. And every time, she or one of her colleagues would end up standing in the middle of the ward feeling apathetic and furious. Again.

She hated him for it.

She went over to his bedside. That was part of her job.

'Are you awake now?'

'Fuck. What happened?'

'You overdosed. It was a struggle to bring you round this time.'

He tugged with one hand at the bandage round his head and scratched the sore on his nostril with the other, probing and prodding it in the way she had tried to stop because it distressed her, back in the days when she still cared about him. She read through his journal.

His history was familiar – she knew it by heart – but she ran her finger down the list of dates, anyway.

Hilding Oldéus (28). Twelve acute admissions following an overdose of heroin.

He had needed hospitalisation twelve times. To begin with, she had feared for his life, been terrified, wept the first five or six times. Nowadays she was indifferent.

She had to share her strength, make sure that everyone got the same care.

But she couldn't help it.

She couldn't bring herself to care much for his future any more.

'You were lucky. The guy who made the emergency call, one of your mates apparently, gave you mouth to mouth and heart massage on the spot. Inside a photo booth at Central Station. Or so I'm told.'

'That was Olsson.'

'Your body wouldn't have coped on its own. Not this time.'

He scratched the sore. She was on the verge of trying to stop him, as she usually did, but reminded herself that his hand would be back there straight away. Never mind, let him. Let him tear his whole face to bits.

'I don't want to see you here again.'

'Hey, sis. Don't hassle me.'

'Never.'

Hilding tried to sit up straight, but collapsed back on his pillows. He was dizzy, put his hand to his forehead.

'You see what gives, don't you? I mean, you don't lend me any dosh and that's it. I take what gives, like pure powder. Get it?'

'Sorry?'

'Can't fucking trust nobody.'

Lisa sighed.

'Look, it wasn't me who dissolved the heroin in citric acid. It wasn't me who loaded the syringe. It wasn't me who injected it. You did all that, Hilding.'

'So? What's all that in aid of?'

'I don't know. I truly don't know what anything is in aid of.'

She couldn't take any more. Not today. He was alive, that was enough. She thought of how his addiction had slowly become hers. How she had somehow felt the effect of every injection, joined every treatment centre, stopped breathing when he OD'd. She had attended therapy sessions for relatives, participated in self-help courses, taken on board that she was a co-dependent, and then, finally, grasped that her feelings had never been of any consequence. For long stretches of time she simply ceased to exist for Hilding. It had been his addiction, but it had ruled her and the rest of the family too.

She had scarcely stepped out into the corridor when he called her back. She had decided not to go back, to continue on her rounds, so he carried on screaming, louder and louder. She couldn't take it and ran back, tearful out of sheer anger.

'What do you want?'

'Sis, for fuck's sake.'

'Tell me what you want then!'

'Am I just supposed to lie here? Like, I've OD'd.'

Lisa sensed the eyes of the others on her. The older man and the very young man who refused to die were watching her and hoping she would support and encourage them, but she couldn't, didn't have the strength, not now.

'Sis, I need something to help me come down.'

'Forget it. We won't give *you* any drugs here. Ask the doctor who's dealing with you, if you must. He will say the same.'

'Stesolid?'

She swallowed, the tears running down her cheeks. As usual he had reduced her to this. 'We've stood by you for years, Hilding. Mum and Ylva and I. We've had to live with your paranoia. So stop whining.'

Hilding didn't hear a word she said. He didn't like it when her voice sounded like that.

'Or Rohypnol.'

'We were pleased every time they locked you up. Every time. Aspsås, wherever. Do you understand that? Because at least we knew where you were.'

'Valium, eh, sis?'

'Next time, just do it properly. Take a fatal overdose so you're put away for good and all.'

Lisa was bending forward, clutching her stomach. The tears were coming faster and she turned away. He mustn't see her cry. She said nothing more, walked away from his bed to see the older man, the one who had pressed his bell. He was sitting up straight with one hand pressed to his chest. He needed pain relief, his malignant tumour demanded it. Lisa said good morning and took his hand, but addressed Hilding over her shoulder.

'By the way.'

Her brother didn't answer.

'There's a visitor for you. I promised to let him know when you were awake.'

She had to get out, and disappeared down the bluish-green corridor.

Baffled, Hilding stared at her back. How could anyone know he was here? He hardly knew himself.

*   *   *

Jochum Lang got out of the car when it pulled up outside the hospital entrance. It was good to escape the smell of leather upholstery. In just a couple of hours he had learnt to detest it as much as that of the cell where he had been locked up for the past two years and four months. Both smells meant being under someone else's power and control. He had been around for long enough to know that it didn't actually matter who you had to take orders from, a screw in prison or Mio outside it.

He walked past the patients who hung out near the hospital doors, longing for home, along the corridor with a constant traffic of people on their way somewhere else, and stepped into one of the big shiny lifts where a recorded voice informed you sweetly which floor you were on.

He's only got himself to blame. It's his own fault.

Jochum had his own mantra. He used the same ritual every time, knew it would work.

He's only got himself to blame.

He knew where to find him. General Medicine. Floor 6. Ward 2.

He moved quickly now. It was a job and he wanted to be done with it.

The room was much too quiet. The others were practically asleep, just two of them, an old boy in the bed opposite and a lad who looked more dead than alive. Hilding didn't like silence, never had. He looked around nervously, stared at the door, waited.

He saw his visitor the moment the door opened. His clothes were soaked. It must be raining outside.

'Jochum?'

His heart was pounding. He clawed at the sore on his nose and tried to ignore the fear that tore at his insides.

'What the fuck are you doing here?'

Jochum Lang looked exactly the same as before. Just as fucking big and bald. Hilding felt all sorts of things. He didn't want to feel them, but couldn't help himself. No way. All he wanted was some Stesolid. Or Rohypnol.

'Sit up.'

Jochum was impatient, his voice low but clear.

'Sit up.'

Jochum grabbed the wheelchair by the older man's bed, released the brake and pushed it across to Hilding, waiting until he was sitting on the edge of the bed.

He pointed from the bed to the wheelchair.

'I want you to sit in this.'

'What do you want?'

'Can't say here. Got to get you to the lifts.'

'What do you want?'

'Fucking sit here!'

Jochum pointed at the wheelchair again, his hand close to Hilding's face. *He's only got himself to blame.* Hilding's eyes had closed. His thin body was weak; only a few hours earlier he had collapsed in a photo booth. *It's his own fault.* He was obeying now, slowly, stopping to scratch at the sore, the blood running down his chin.

'I didn't. Didn't say a word.'

Jochum stood behind him, then started to wheel him out, past the man and the boy, both asleep by now.

'I mean. Listen, Jochum, for fuck's sake. I didn't talk. Do you hear me? The pigs asked, sure, had me in for an interview and wanted to know about you, but I didn't say a thing.'

The corridor was empty. Blue-green floor, white walls. And cold.

'I believe you. You wouldn't have the guts.'

They met two nurses, who nodded a kind of greeting to the patient in the wheelchair. Hilding wept like he hadn't done since he was a child, since before the heroin.

'But you've been dealing in cut speed. And flogged it to the wrong punters.'

They had left the wards now and entered the lift area.

The corridor was wider here and the colours had changed; it had a grey floor and yellow walls. Hilding's body trembled violently. He had no idea fear could hurt like this.

'The wrong punters?'

'Mirja.'

'Mirja? That slag?'

'She's Mio's niece. And you're so fucking stupid that you sold her half-half Yugo whizz and washing powder.'

Hilding tried to stop crying. The tears seemed weird, nothing to do with him.

'I don't get it.'

They stopped in front of the lifts. Four lifts, two on their way up.

'I don't get it.'

'You will. You and me. We're going to have a little chat.'

'Jochum! Fuck's sake!'

The lift doors. He could reach them, grab hold of them and maybe hang on.

He couldn't tell.

Couldn't tell why the fucking tears kept coming.

Alena Sljusareva ran along the quay at Värta Harbour.

She stared down into the dark water. It was raining, had been raining all morning; what could have been a sunlit blue sea was black. The waves crashed against the cement walls of the quay. It was more like autumn than summer.

She was crying and had been for nearly twenty-four hours, from fear at first, then from rage and now from a frail sense of longing mixed with hopelessness.

During the past twenty-four hours she had relived the three years since she and Lydia had boarded the Lithuanian ferry. Two men had escorted them, their hands politely opening doors and their mouths smiling and telling the two young women how lovely they looked. One of the men had been a Swede, who spoke good Russian and had false passports ready and waiting, the key to their new life. Their cabin was really big, larger than the Klaipeda bedroom she had shared with three others. Alena had been laughing and happy then. She and her new friend were leaving the past behind.

She had been a virgin.

The ship had barely left the harbour.

She could still feel the sensation of the blood running down the inside of her thighs.

Three years. Stockholm, Gothenburg, Oslo, Copenhagen, then back to Stockholm. Never fewer than twelve men. Every day. She tried to recall just a few of them, see their faces in her mind's eye, any of them, the ones who liked hitting or humping you or simply looking at you.

She couldn't remember a single one.

All faceless.

Like Lydia felt about her body, but the other way round. Lydia said her body wasn't there, something that Alena had never understood. She was aware of her body all the time, knew it was being violated, counted the number of times; she'd lie there naked and calculate the total of twelve times a day for three years.

She had a body, no matter how hard they tried to take it away from her.

For her, they didn't have faces, that was how she coped.

She had tried to warn Lydia, calm her down. Nothing worked. It was as if she changed the moment she had seen the newspaper article. Her reaction had been so strong, her eyes glowing with hatred. Alena had seen Lydia humiliated, resentful, but never like this, so full of hate. She regretted having shown Lydia the newspaper, should have hidden it instead, or thrown it away, as she had thought at first.

Lydia had stood up to Dimitri, straight-backed in front of him and said that from now on she intended to hold on to the money, it was her they screwed and she deserved to keep what they paid. He'd struck her in the face at first, it was his usual reaction and Lydia must have expected it. She hadn't backed off, just told him that she didn't want any customers for a bit, no one lying on top of her, she was too tired and didn't want to do it any more.

Lydia had never protested before. Not aloud to Dimitri, that is. She had dreaded the blows, the pain and the gun he sometimes pointed at their heads. Alena sat down on the edge of the quay with her legs dangling. Three years. She missed Janoz so much it tore at her. Why had she gone away, why hadn't she told him that she was going?

She had been a child.

Now she had grown into someone different.

It had happened suddenly, in that ship's cabin. The Swedish man had held her down and spat in her face, twice, while he forced himself into her. The change had continued afterwards, a little more for every time someone stole from inside her.

She had stood in the doorway of her room, watching. When he got the whip out and held it in front of Lydia's face, she had rushed in and jumped on him. Dimitri had never beaten them with the whip, only threatened to. When she tried to grab it, he kicked her in the stomach, shoved her into her room and locked the door, shouting that she'd get hers later.

She stared down into the water, waiting. She should go back. Home to Klaipeda. Home to Janoz, if he was still there. But not yet. Not until Lydia had been in touch.

She had counted the sounds, every lash, one by one. The police had arrived at stroke thirty-six. She had heard every single impact through the shut door, heard Dimitri lifting the whip to strike Lydia's bare skin once more.

Her feet. If she stretched her legs, they would touch the water. She could jump in. Or she could get up and board the ship. Go home.

But not yet.

They had seen each other being raped. She had to wait.

They had searched the flat and someone had unlocked her door. Dimitri had been lying on the floor, clutching his stomach. She had been alone for a few seconds, minutes maybe, then suddenly she saw the policeman they knew, and panicked, ran the few steps to the front door, which had a big hole in it, but turned back to kick the knocked-down Dimitri-Bastard-Pimp hard in the balls with the pointed tip of her shoe. Then she had carried on running, out on to the landing, down the empty stone stairs, all five floors.

She reacted to the ring tone at once. She knew who it was.

'Yes?'

'Alena? It's me.'

Hearing Lydia's voice made her feel good. She was in pain, Alena could hear that. It was difficult for her to speak, but her voice, it was so good to hear her voice again.

'Where are you?'

'At the harbour.'

'You're going home.'

'I was waiting for you to phone. I knew you would. Then . . . Then I could go home.'

The mobile phone had been a present from one of the faces she couldn't remember. Alena had wanted gifts from customers who asked for extras, Lydia had preferred money. The things she got might be clothes, a couple of necklaces and sometimes a pair of earrings. Dimitri didn't have a clue and didn't know about the mobile phone either, of course. It was quite new; in return the forgotten face had been allowed to do extras with both of them together. Lydia had wanted the mobile; she thought it would be good to have at least one between them, just in case.

'What are you going to do?'

'When?'

'When you get back home.'

'I don't know.'

'Do you miss it a lot?'

Alena caught her breath. She had a vision of what it had been like, kind of grim and messy. Klaipeda hadn't been very nice.

'Yes, I do. I want to see them all again. See what they look like. Maybe to find out what we would've looked like.'

She told Lydia about her escape, how she had fled down into Völund Street without turning back to look, not once, just running from the place she hated. Now, after twenty-four endless hours of wandering around in the city, she wanted to sleep, simply sleep for a while. Lydia didn't say much. A bit about the hospital where they had been taken a couple of times, a bit about the bed, the food, the nurse from Poland who spoke Russian.

Not a word about the gashes on her back.

'Alena?'

'Yes, what?'

'I need you to help me.'

Alena looked down again. For the moment the water was calm and she could see a blurred image of herself, the dangling legs and the arm and the hand holding the phone to her ear.

'I'll help you. Ask anything.'

Lydia's breathing came slowly. She seemed to be searching for words.

'Do you remember the cellar with the storerooms?'

Alena remembered well: the hard floor, the impenetrable dark at night, the damp air. Once, when Dimitri had some visitors to stay, he locked Alena and Lydia up in the cellar for two days. He needed their beds, he said, but never told them anything about the guests.

'Yes, I do.'

'I want you to go there.'

The calm surface rippled in the wake of a passing motor-boat, the wavelets dispersing her image.

'But they're after me; I might be on the wanted list. I've got to be careful.'

'I want you to go back.'

'Why?'

Silence. Lydia didn't reply.

'Lydia, tell me. Why?'

'Why? Because it's not going to happen again. What happened to me will never happen again. That's why.'

Alena got up. She paced up and down along the quayside, between the iron posts, which were taller than a man.

'What do you want me to do there?'

'There's a bucket with a towel in it. In the storeroom. Underneath the towel you'll find a gun. And Semtex.'

'Semtex?'

'Plastic explosive. And a detonator. In plastic carrier bags.'

'How do you know?'

'I saw it there.'

'How do you know it's Semtex?'

'I just know.'

Alena Sljusareva had been trying to take all this in, listening but not quite hearing what Lydia said. She said shush into the phone. Lydia kept talking, so Alena shushed her again, more loudly, hissing until the line was her own.

'Lydia, I'm going to hang up now. Phone me back in two minutes. Two minutes, that's enough.'

There was an afternoon sailing in a few hours. She could take it. She had the money. She had everything she needed in her shoulder bag. She wanted to go home, to see the place she called home; she wanted to close her eyes, forget about the last three years, be seventeen again and happy and lovely, be someone who had never left Klaipeda, not even to see Vilnius.

None of it was true or ever would be. That was then. Now she was someone different.

The phone rang.

'I'll help you.'

'Thank you, Alena. I love you.'

Alena felt nervous, carried on marching between the iron posts, up and down with the phone pressed to her ear.

'Number forty-six, you'll see the figures quite high up the door. There is a small padlock, nothing special. The bucket is just inside the door, to the right when you go in. The gun and some ammunition is in one of the bags, the Semtex is next to it. Take the lot and then go to the Central Station, to our box.'

112

'I was there yesterday.'

'Was everything all right?'

Alena took her time.

Their box was a small, square metal lock-up, set into the stone of a waiting-room wall. Their lives were stored in box 21.

'Everything was fine.'

'Get the video.'

That video. Alena had almost forgotten about it and the faceless man who liked being filmed. Once, he had asked her to make love with Lydia. Alena had refused, but Lydia had caressed her cheek when he was watching and said they could touch each other, that he could film them, if they could make their own film afterwards.

'Now?'

'Yes, it's the right time. We'll use it.'

'Are you sure?'

'Dead certain.'

Lydia cleared her throat before starting to explain.

'I've been lying here just thinking about everything. My arm hurts and my back feels like it's on fire. It's hard to sleep. I've written down my thoughts. Worked it all out, read it, scribbled bits out and rewritten. Alena, I am absolutely sure. Someone has to know. This must never happen again.'

Alena looked at the large blue ferry waiting a few hundred metres away. She wouldn't get back to the harbour in time. Not today. But tomorrow was another day and the departure time was the same. All she had to do was vanish for one more night. It could be done.

'Then what?'

'Then come here, to Söder Hospital. There's a guard keeping an eye on me, so we can't talk. I'll be sitting in the patients' dayroom and watching TV. There are other patients around most of the time, people I don't know, so I won't be alone. There's a toilet next to the dayroom. If I sit on the sofa, I'll see you when you go past. Go into the toilet and put everything you've brought into the bin, then stick some used paper towels on top. Keep everything, the gun and the ammo and the explosive and the video, in a plastic bag; the stuff in the bin might be wet. Oh, and some string. I need string too. Can you get hold of some?'

'So I'm to walk past you and pretend you aren't there?'

'Yes.'

Alena Sljusareva turned her back on the water and walked away. When she reached the road the wind had picked up. It was a wide road that cut through the harbour area, passing the warehouses on its way up towards Gärdet.

The city centre was full of people, tourists desperately shopping while the rain fell. Alena was grateful for the crowds. The more people there were in the streets, the easier it was for her to hide.

She took the metro to the Central Station, went to find box 21, opened it and put the video in her bag. Then she stood for a while in front of the open locker, staring into the dark interior where their belongings were stacked on two shelves. Their lives. At least, the only parts they accepted. All that mattered after three years.

She had only been there twice before, on the day they acquired it, and then yesterday.

Almost two years ago, Dimitri-Bastard-Pimp had taken them to the Central Station. He had told them that they were to leave the Stockholm flat for a few weeks and work in Copenhagen instead. The flat there had turned out to be in a building just off the Strøget shopping area and close to the harbour. The customers were mostly drunk Swedes fresh off the Malmö ferry, smelling of lager and duty-free chocolate bars. They often paid for two goes, went off after the first time to drink through the night and returned to slap the girls about or wank in front of them or ride them once more before going back home.

While they had waited for the train to Copenhagen, Alena had said she needed to go to the toilet, simply had to go. Dimitri had been alone with them and warned her not to even think of giving him the slip. If she didn't get back in good time for the train he would kill Lydia. She believed him. She never had the slightest intention of leaving her friend alone with him anyway. Nothing could have made her.

All she wanted was a locker of her own, a kind of home.

One of her regulars was a man with a plumbing business in Strängnäs, who every week would spend hours on the road to come and see her. He had told her about the safe boxes you could hire for two weeks at a time. They were meant as a convenience for visitors to the city, but were mostly used by the homeless.

Instead of going to the toilet, Alena had used her fifteen minutes away from Dimitri to get one of these lockers. It had been frantic, but she had made it and returned happily with a key hidden in each shoe.

Her helpful regular had cut a copy of the key and agreed to take things to the locker and to keep renewing the agreement before it ran out, his part of the bargain if she allowed him to do extras. She always bled a lot afterwards, but it had been worth it.

Standing in front of the open locker, she knew how true that was.

Having a place that was their own, where Dimitri-Bastard-Pimp couldn't get his fingers on their things, no matter how much he threatened, that had been worth every blow.

Alena knew she would never come back and she took all that was hers, the necklaces, earrings, dresses. They each had their own key. She left Lydia's things and her money; when she got out of hospital she would find what was hers waiting for her.

She locked the door and walked away.

The metro again, the green line this time. The train was packed. She got off at St Erik's Square, climbed the stairs to the wet tarmac outside and started walking, keeping a lookout for that Vietnamese restaurant, one of her route markers. After the restaurant it wasn't far to another flight of stairs, though this one was beautiful, with great big angels to anchor the handrails. She followed the steps down to Völund Street.

Alena had reached the last of the steps when she saw the police car with two uniformed cops inside. She bent down, pretending to shake a stone out of a shoe, taking her time and trying to think fast.

She couldn't think.

Her eyes followed two children leading their bicycles. They passed the police car without anyone taking much notice.

Still no thoughts; she seemed unable to think.

This was here and now. It always was here and now.

She put her shoe on, straightened up and walked calmly towards the front door of the building, staring straight ahead, as if untouched by the rain that fell all around her, thinking about what she didn't remember, the men with forgotten faces who came to lie down on top of her.

The men in the car didn't stir, just sat and watched her walk past.

Alena opened the door, stepped inside. Waited.

Nothing.

They must still be sitting there. She counted to sixty. One minute. One minute more and then she would make for the stairs to the cellar.

She had prepared herself for the heavy footfalls and a voice ordering her to turn round, get into the back of the police car.

Nothing. Not a sound.

She shook herself free of the command that was never made and started down the two flights of stone stairs at a measured pace. She had to be quiet, mustn't get out of breath. She thought about the door on the fifth floor, that gaping hole. It had offered a kind of freedom.

She closed her eyes for a second; she could still hear the blows from the fireman's axe on the door panel, a uniformed policeman outside was hammering the wood to splinters. Then a thud when Dimitri let go of Lydia's body, and his footsteps as he ran towards the man who was entering the flat.

Alena had to stop to calm her breathing.

She had waited behind that door for almost a year.

It was beyond all comprehension.

Twenty-four hours of freedom to wander round the city was all it took to make a whole year seem strange and distant. If only she could make up her mind that none of it had happened, then she would never have been in that flat with its two large beds, she would never have stood in the hall staring at the electronic locks.

She carried on down to the landing outside the cellar door. Stopping, she turned to face the broken-down door up there and stuck a finger in the air, for the men who would no longer come and ring the doorbell.

The door in front of her was locked and covered in cold, grey, sheet metal. She wasn't very strong, but could manage to open it with a crowbar. She had done it once in Klaipeda. At the time it had been an awful night, but now she thought of the whole episode as a bit of distant fun and games.

She put her shoulder bag on the floor and unpacked the things from box 21: the dresses, the plastic boxes with necklaces and earrings, the video, the ball of string. She placed them side by side on the floor. The crowbar was buried underneath it all.

The man in the hardware store had laughed. *A crowbar and string, well I never. Planning a bit of break-in, eh? You don't look like a burglar!* She had laughed too, and spoken in English.

I live in an old house. What I need is a strong man with some good tools. She had looked at him the way she looked at her clients, the way she knew they liked to be looked at. The hardware store man had given her the ball of string for free and wished her good luck with her large house and strong man.

It was the smallest crowbar in the shop and quite easy to handle. She jammed the teeth into the lock and pushed, putting her whole weight on it once, twice, three times. Nothing budged.

She didn't dare to try harder in case she made a noise.

But she had no choice.

Once more she inserted the two prongs of the crowbar, jiggled it backwards and forwards against the door frame, tested and then pushed, using all her weight and all her strength.

The lock gave way with a loud crack. The sound travelled up the stairwell. Every tenant who was in could have heard it.

She curled up on the floor, as if it would make her less visible.

She waited. She counted to sixty again.

Her wrist ached. She must have pushed harder than her body could take.

The silence continued.

Then she counted to sixty again.

No doors opened, no one came downstairs to find out what the noise was.

She got up, packed her things.

The cellar door swung open easily. Ahead was a long corridor. Its lime-washed walls seemed to lean in over her. At the far end of the corridor was another door, leading into four passages, with the storage rooms belonging to the flats.

Supporting herself with one hand resting on the metal panel, and clutching the crowbar in her other hand, she steeled herself to break the lock until she suddenly realised that the second door was open. Someone had unlocked it. That someone must be in there and would come back out, lock up and leave.

She stepped inside. The air was stale and smelt of damp carpets.

Her eyes slowly got used to the dark.

There was another smell. Aftershave and sweat. Dimitri smelt like that, and the customers, some of them anyway. She stood very still. It was hard to breathe, the air she inhaled didn't seem enough.

Somebody was in there.

Alena remembered the ferry and her ticket and looking down into the water.

Steps on the rough brick floor. Someone was walking about in there.

She was crying, the tears trickling down her cheeks as she felt her way forward, following the wall into the nearest passage and then along to a pen that stuck out a bit. She closed her eyes and sat down. She would not look until later.

She sat there for so long, she lost all sense of time. The person was wandering about, opening and closing doors, lifting things and putting them down, some must have been heavy. The noises tugged her thoughts this way and that.

Then she heard nothing more. The silence was almost worse.

She was shaking and weeping, hyperventilating, until she dared let herself believe that she had been left alone.

Standing up, her legs felt weak and her head ached. She didn't turn on the light, no need to check the number on the door. She knew exactly where it was.

They had been left in the damp underground darkness for two days and two nights.

Their storeroom was in one of the middle passages. The walls were made of wood, painted brown, with a narrow opening at the top of the door that was too small for her to climb through, more of a ventilation space. A simple small padlock. She weighed it in her hand and took a deep breath.

The crowbar fitted in under the hasp hammered into the board nearest the door. She pushed as she had done before and stared in surprise at the padlock and hasp dangling free.

She stepped inside.

It was not yet midday on Wednesday 5 June. The sky was as dark as on a drowsy night in November and the rain, which had dominated the day since dawn, was still dancing on the tarmac.

Ewert Grens, who had asked for one of the plain cars from the police pool, opened the passenger door and got in. He wanted Sven to drive, as he did more and more often. Ewert found concentrating on the road tiring; the light irritated him and made his eyes run. He was ageing quickly and hated it, though the swift decline of his body didn't matter much; he had lost his woman long ago. No need to look good for anyone else. But his failing strength and energy – that was something else. He used to be able to cope with everything. The engine inside him never stopped, forcing his body to keep up with his restless mind. Fifty-six years old and lonely. What use is the past then?

They were late and Sven drove quickly towards the Arlanda Airport exit. It had been an odd morning. A job that should have been over in a few minutes had turned into a couple of hours spent holed up in Terminal Five. The man, whom they knew as Dimitri-Bastard-Pimp, had been scheduled to board a white and blue Finnair plane to Vilnius, flight time less than an hour. Their idea had been to see him leave and conclude the report on his activities that afternoon.

Ewert stared at the dual carriageway ahead and didn't register the irritation in Sven's voice.

'Got to hurry.'

'What?'

'I have to go faster. Any colleagues out and about?'

'Not as far as I know.'

The Arlanda slip road was practically empty and Sven was driving well above the speed limit. He longed for home and was determined to get there in time.

Dimitri-Bastard-Pimp had been dispatched as effectively as they could have wished.

They first saw him walking towards Departures, accompanied by two heavies. As he queued for security control, Ewert and Sven had been near the check-in counter, just a little bit away, noting his nervous head movements as he rooted through his jacket pockets for the boarding pass. He was still at it when a short, sturdy man in his sixties approached and started to shout at him, gesticulating energetically and at one point slapping Dimitri's cheek. The scene caught everybody's attention. The man, smartly dressed in a suit and a hat, went on shouting at Dimitri, who seemed to shrink and crumble as they watched. Another slap and then the older man pushed him in the back to propel him through the electronic gateway, past the conveyor belt and the X-ray camera, on into the departure hall.

Ewert and Sven didn't intervene. They had wanted to reassure themselves that they'd never have to clap eyes again on the man who beat up young women. That was all. The airport guards could handle anything out of order.

When the man in the suit had stopped shouting and turned away from the departing Dimitri-Bastard-Pimp, he walked briskly towards Ewert and Sven, not hesitating for a moment, as if he had known all along that they were there, keeping an eye.

Surprisingly light of foot, carrying a briefcase in one hand and an umbrella in the other, he had approached them and greeted them politely, doffing his hat and shaking their hands.

Now the car had left the airport area and swung out into the southbound E4 motorway to Stockholm. Visibility was poor, and Sven had to slow down even with the windscreen wipers going at top speed.

Ewert sighed loudly and turned on the car radio.

The suit-and-hat man had introduced himself, though Ewert had forgotten his name instantly, and then stayed where he was, calmly chatting to them while late travellers hurried and elbowed their way past, swearing at them in the passing. He had started talking the moment Dimitri-Bastard-Pimp had vanished out of sight and began by explaining that he was on the Lithuanian diplomatic staff, the head of embassy security in Sweden, and invited them for a drink. Ewert had said thanks, but no thanks. Actually, he could've done with a drop of something alcoholic. It was early but he was tired and thirsty. It wouldn't do, though, not with Sven standing next to him. The security boss insisted. A coffee perhaps, in the upstairs café?

They hesitated for a little too long. Their host had found a table with a view of the runway, brought them all cups of coffee and greasy Danish pastries, then sat down facing them and sipped his drink.

He had been silent at first, but soon started speaking in heavily accented but fluent English, better than either Ewert's or Sven's. He apologised for his behaviour earlier, declaring that he disapproved of raised voices and violence, but sometimes it was necessary, as indeed it had been this time.

Then he launched into a long and complicated thank-you speech, addressing them on behalf of the Lithuanian people.

After a longish pause while he watched them, he explained

how upset he had been when informed of the activities of his embassy colleague, Dimitri Simait, and how embarrassing such revelations were for a country that was trying to recover its reputation after decades of oppression. He was fishing for an agreement to keep the whole thing quiet. They themselves had seen that Dimitri-Bastard-Pimp had left the country and could leave it at that.

Ewert and Sven had thanked him politely for the coffee, got up and, before they left, told him with some asperity that the investigation could not be hushed up, indeed should not be, if they had anything to do with it, that human trafficking seldom was.

The music that rolled out from the car radio was like a wallpaper of sound. Ewert had long since tired of it, it all sounded the same. He produced one of his own tapes.

'Hey, Sven?'

'Yes?'

'You listening to this?'

'Yes.'

'It isn't up to much, is it?'

'I want the traffic info; we're getting closer to the northern access.'

'I'll put this one on.'

Ewert cut the Radio Stockholm talk of vehicle collisions and put in his own home-mixed Siw Malmkvist tape. Her voice. He closed his eyes. He could think now.

When they had suddenly got up from the café table with the runway view, the Lithuanian official had turned pink in the face and asked them to stay and listen to him for just a little longer. Ewert and Sven had exchanged a glance and sat down again. The man's voice had sounded tired. Strands of his thin hair were dangling on his forehead, he was sweating profusely, and his skin shone in the harsh glare of the strip lighting. His hands sought something to hold on to, found one each of their hands and clasped them with his stumpy, sticky fingers.

Several thousand young women, he said. From Eastern Europe. Hundreds of thousands of lives! That was the extent of it, the illegal sex trade with the West. Bought and sold as we speak. More and more. Our girls! Our women!

He squeezed their hands, his voice desperate now.

It's the unemployment, he continued. Persuading the girls is easy. Don't you see? They're young, looking for a job, waiting, hoping for an income. A future. And the men who offer the world on a plate, they're so clever, they promise and threaten until they're ready to sell the goods, kept in rooms with electronic locks, like the two girls you found in the Völund Street flat. That was the address, wasn't it? And when the deal is done, when the cajoling, menacing men have got their bundles of bank notes – then they disappear. You know it's true. No responsibility, no investment, no risk. Cash in hand! Cash in and vanish!

The embassy official had suddenly raised their hands; Ewert had stared angrily at Sven, been about to protest, but decided to stay put while the little man pressed their hands firmly against his cheeks.

Do you understand, he had said, truly understand what I'm telling you?

In my country, in Lithuania, trading in narcotics, say, is a serious crime. Heavy sentences are passed. Long, harsh punishments are meted out. But trading in people, in young women, that's risk-free. In Lithuania, pimps are hardly ever punished. No one is sentenced; no one gets a spell in prison.

I see what is happening to our children. I cry for them, with them. But I can do nothing. Do you understand? Truly?

The car was slowing down on the Nortull access route.

Ewert slowly let go of the image of the despairing man, the official with his hat and his briefcase, pleading with them to understand, and swapped it for the next, the long queues of wet cars. The lights blinked and swallowed ten cars at a time, a quick estimate told him that there were at least a hundred stationary vehicles crowded in ahead of them. They'd have to wait for at least ten minutes.

Sven swore irritably, something he didn't often do. They were late and about to be even later.

Ewert leaned back in the passenger seat, turned up the volume. Her voice:

Today's teardrops are tomorrow's rainbow,
And tomorrow's rainbows I will share with you.

It drowned out Sven's swearing and the idiot hooting of car horns.

Ewert was at peace, resting deep, deep inside himself. Only what had been, long ago, existed for him. Everything had been so simple, like black-and-white photos; he had more of a life then, and lots of time waiting for him. 'För sent skall syndaren vakna', (1964), original English title 'Today's Teardrops'. The empty plastic box in his hand had an insert with his photo of Siw on stage in a People's Palace. He had snapped her and she had smiled into the camera, waved at him and said hello to him afterwards. His eyes wandered among the song titles on the list, tunes he had recorded himself, written down the lyrics.

He was listening to Siw, but couldn't get the despairing little man from the embassy out of his head. When their coffee cups had been drained to the last drop, he and Sven had thanked the diplomat again, freed their hands and had scarcely managed to get out of the café when they heard him calling after them. He had asked them to stop and wait until he caught up with them.

He had walked between them down the stairs and started to tell them what he knew about Lydia Grajauskas and her father. He had come to the airport not only to ensure that Dimitri Simait was dispatched, but also out of respect and grief for the father and daughter; their history seemed to be without end and so sad.

He had fallen into silence until they reached the large entrance hall of the main terminal, then he continued his narrative about a man who had been imprisoned and forced to abandon his family because he refused to deceive the authorities about his pride in flying the Lithuanian flag, a challenge to a society that wouldn't allow it. And then, after serving his sentence, he had been sacked from his army post, only to be imprisoned a couple of years later for treason. He had been deemed a risk to state security because he and three erstwhile colleagues, still in defence jobs, had stolen and smuggled weapons and sold them to a foreign power.

At this point the Lithuanian suddenly interrupted his story to bemoan the tragic fate of the girl. Then he shook hands with them and walked off, disappearing among the queues of suitcases lined up at the check-in counters. Ewert and Sven followed him with their eyes for a long time, both of them with the feeling that he had done what he set out to do and had expressed in words a series of events which for some reason had clearly moved him, and so had tried to unload some of it on the two Swedish policemen.

Ewert stopped looking at the cassette player for a moment and glanced along the queue of stationary cars. Still as long as before. In the driver's seat, Sven was twitching restlessly, revving the engine now and then.

'Ewert, we'll be late.'

'Not now. I'm listening. To Siw.'

'I promised. I promised this time.'

Today was Sven's forty-first birthday. When he left in the morning, Anita and Jonas had still been asleep, they had all agreed to celebrate later on. He had taken the afternoon off, promised to be back home by lunchtime. His birthday. On his birthday, at least, he wanted to make sure that he was allowed to take his Anita in his arms, the woman he had loved since they met in senior school, and to be next to Jonas and hold his hand hard enough to make him protest.

For almost fifteen years they had waited for a child, for Jonas.

They had agreed early on to try to create a life that was

a combination of them both, but failed and failed. Anita had been pregnant three times. The first time she had a still birth after seven months: an induced labour in a hospital bed, complete with pushing and contractions and pain. Afterwards, with their dead baby girl next to her, she had wept in his arms. The next two pregnancies ended in late miscarriages, tiny hearts that suddenly stopped beating.

Their shared longing was something he could feel any time. For years it had tainted everything they did together, robbing them of pleasure and almost suffocating their love for each other. Until one day, almost eight years ago to the day, when they had travelled to a small town some twenty kilometres west of Phnom Penh. The representative from the adoption bureau had met them at the airport and taken them on a journey through an unknown landscape.

And then there he was, waiting for them, lying in a simple little bed in the local orphanage. He had arms and legs and hair, and was already called Jonas.

'I should be sitting on the bus back home.'

'You'll make it.'

'Or be waiting at the bus stop at Slussen. At the very least.'

'You'll get there soon.'

He had promised. This time too.

He remembered it well, his fortieth. It had been a very hot day and his birthday cake had gone sour in the back seat of a police car. A five-year-old girl had been raped and tortured and dumped in a wood near Strängnäs. He had promised, had been on his way home to the table, all set for his little party, and it had been hard to explain to Jonas on the phone why someone would hurt a child with a knife and why it meant that he had to wait for his dad to come home.

He wanted to be with them so much.

'I'll turn on the blue light. Fuck the rules. I want to get home.'

Sven glanced at Ewert, who shrugged. He stuck the plastic dome on the roof of the car and waited for the siren to kick in. Then he pulled out of the queue, crossed the double white lines and zigzagged between cars that were trying to get out of his way into some space that hadn't existed before. In a minute or two they were clear of the hold-up and the three sets of lights.

Sven accelerated towards the centre of town. That was when the emergency call came through.

They missed it the first time. What with the siren and Siw's singing, it was drowned out.

A doctor had found Hilding Oldéus's dead body on a staircase, near the ward where he was being treated for a heroin overdose.

Oldéus had been badly beaten. Difficult to identify. The doctor, a woman, had said that he had had a visitor; she had taken him in herself. Her voice had sounded very weak, but her description of the visitor was clear. He had been tall, heavily built, shaved head, sunbed tan, a scar running from the corner of his mouth to his temple. That was why the emergency call had been for Grens and Sundkvist.

Ewert stared straight ahead. There was something like a smile on his face.

'Twenty-four hours. Sven, twenty-four hours was all it took.'

Sven looked at him.

He was thinking about Anita and Jonas, who were waiting, but he said nothing. He just changed lanes to get to Väster Bridge and on to Söder Hospital.

She was sitting at the back of the bus. It was almost empty now, with an older woman a couple of rows in front of her and a woman with a pushchair in one of the centre seats. That was it. Alena Sljusareva would have preferred to hide among lots more passengers, but most people had got off two stops before, at Eriksdal Sports Complex – the athletic type, off to some event.

The bus turned off the ring road and drove on, past the Söder Hospital Casualty reception. She had been there a year or so before, with Dimitri trailing her. Someone who had wanted extras had lost his cool and done things they hadn't agreed on. Up a small slope, a half-turn to the bus stop right in front of the main hospital stairs: the end of the journey.

She looked around. If someone was watching out for her, that person was keeping a low profile.

She tipped her umbrella forward to cover her face. It was bucketing down.

In the entrance hall she cautiously scanned the walls, hung with artwork made of metal, glanced at the hard benches full of people with paper cups of coffee and then quickly looked down the four corridors.

No one took any notice of her at all. They were all pre-occupied with getting better.

She went to the kiosk, bought a box of chocolates, a magazine and a bouquet of flowers already wrapped in transparent plastic. She was obviously going to see someone who wasn't well; she was one of the people who popped in to visit during their lunch break. One of the many.

The lift to the surgical wards was the one furthest away. The long corridor wormed its way into the interminably large building; she met recent admissions, off to some test or other, and slowly fading long-stay patients, and lost souls who didn't know what was going on and never would. Every now and then new corridors opened up, going this way or that, all identical to the one she was in. Too many corridors, she didn't like them.

The lift was waiting for her with its door open. She had to go right to the top, all seven floors. Alone in the tight space she watched someone in the mirror, a twenty-year-old wearing an oversized raincoat, someone who wanted to go home, nowhere else, just home.

The door opened. She hid behind her shield, kept a firm grip on the box of chocolates and the bouquet of flowers. A doctor passed her in a hurry and vanished through a door halfway along the corridor. Two patients walked towards her, in the usual plain hospital clothes with plastic bands around their wrists. She glanced at them quickly and wondered how long they had been there, if and when they would ever leave.

The TV room was on her left. She heard the sound of the news as she approached, a burst of music that was trying to sound important. She spotted the guard, who stood near the door, his arms crossed on his chest. Green uniform, truncheon at his side and a holster for the handcuffs. He was looking at the patients on the sofa: two boys, wearing their own clothes, and next to them a woman. Her face was badly damaged and one of her arms was in plaster. Her eyes were fixed unseeingly on the news presenter. Alena wanted to meet those eyes – just a moment would be enough – but the woman on the sofa sat motionless, isolated from the world around her.

A few more paces carried Alena past the guard and the people on the TV sofa. The corridor ended here. The door facing her had a toilet sign and a disabled symbol. She stepped inside and locked herself in.

She was shaking, her legs felt weak and out of control, and she leaned forward, letting go of what she was holding to support herself against the wall.

Again, she saw someone reflected in the mirror, someone who wanted to go home. Just wanted to go home.

Alena put her shoulder bag on the lid of the toilet seat. She had wrapped the plastic bag tight round its contents, trying to make the package as small as possible. Pulling it out, she weighed it in her hand before putting it into the waste-bin. She saw the tap, swore at herself as she turned it on and flushed the toilet. Noises which had to be there, in order not to be noticed. The paper towel dispenser was nearly empty, but she got out a wad, scrunched the towels up one by one and hid the plastic bag underneath them.

Lydia hurt everywhere.

Her body punished her every time she moved. A little earlier she had asked the Polish nurse for a couple of morphine tablets.

She sat on the TV sofa next to the two boys, whom she had seen before and smiled at several times but never talked to. She didn't actually want to know them, there was no point. She wasn't interested in the news broadcast and didn't understand a word anyone said. The guard didn't take his eyes from her.

From the corner of her eye she had noticed the woman walking past, holding a box of chocolates and a bouquet.

Ever since, her breathing had been laboured.

She waited for the sound of the toilet door opening again

and for the woman's footsteps to pass and fade away. She wanted to close her eyes, to lie belly down on the sofa and sleep through it all, only waking up when it was all over.

It didn't take long. Or maybe it did. She wasn't sure.

The woman opened the toilet door. Lydia heard it perfectly clearly. Shutting out the noisy TV programme was no problem. She only registered the sounds from the corridor. The woman's steps came closer; she picked up the moving shape without turning her head, barely an awareness of the passing body, a glimpse of a person walking swiftly back in the direction she had come from.

Lydia stole a glance at the man in the green uniform.

He had noted the passing visitor but no more. He didn't get up to follow her, and her presence passed out of his head the instant she left the ward.

Lydia let the boys know she wanted to get up from the sofa and passed them. Then she looked at the guard, nodded to him, pointed at her bladder and then in the direction of the toilet. He nodded. It was fine for her to go to the toilet. He would stay here.

She locked the door, sat down on the lid and took several deep breaths.

It must never happen again.

She got up. Dimitri-Bastard-Pimp had kicked her hip and she limped a little. She turned on the tap and let the water run. She flushed the toilet twice. She went over to the bin and with her good arm, removed the top layer of paper towels.

Lydia recognised the plastic bag, an ordinary supermarket carrier. Inside was everything she had asked for. The handgun, the ammunition, the Semtex, the video, the ball of string. She didn't know how Alena had managed to do what she wanted, but she had. She had gone to box 21 at the Central Station, evaded the policemen who presumably guarded number 3 Völund Street, and got through the two locked doors to the cellar.

She had done her bit.

Now it was all up to Lydia.

Almost all the patients wore white, baggy items of regulation hospital clothing. Lydia's long white coat had been much too large to start with, but she had asked for an even bigger one. It flapped round her body, which didn't exist. In one coat pocket she had a roll of white hospital tape. First she secured the gun with it, after winding tape twice round her waist, and then the Semtex. Gun to the right, plastic explosive to the left. The video and string she left in the bag, which she pushed down inside her panties, adjusting them to make sure it was secure.

One last look in the mirror.

Her battered face. Cautiously, she fingered the many large bruises round her eyes. Her neck was a thick roll of white bandage around a supporting collar. Her left arm hung there, stiff with plaster.

It would never happen again.

Lydia opened the toilet door and limped out. Just a few steps along the corridor. The guard saw her, but she shook her head at the TV sofa and pointed towards her room. She wanted to get back to bed. He understood, nodded. She moved slowly, making signs to show that she wanted him to follow her to her room. He didn't get it. She tried again, pointing at him, then at herself and then the room: he was to come with her, she needed his help. He raised his hand, understood, no need to explain any more. He mumbled 'OK' and she thanked him by curtseying as well as she could manage.

She waited for him to get safely inside her room, until she could hear him breathing behind her.

Then everything happened fast.

Still with her back to him, she pulled at the tape that held the gun on the right-hand side of her ribcage. Then she swung round. She showed him the gun, and released the safety catch in one quick movement.

134

'On knee!'

Her English was clumsy, and heavily accented. She pointed with the muzzle of the gun to the floor.

'On knee! On knee!'

He stood still in front of her. Hesitated. What he saw was a young woman who had been admitted to Casualty yesterday, still unconscious. She limped, had a plaster cast on one arm and a bruised face. The sagging coat made her frail, like a nervous bird.

Now she was threatening him at gunpoint.

Lydia saw him hesitate, raised her arm and waited.

She had been only nine years old.

Death had been on her mind then. She had never thought of it before, at least not like that. She only had nine measly years behind her, when a man in uniform, not that different from the man in front of her now, had held his gun to her head and screamed *Zatknis, zatknis!* with his spit spraying into her face. Dad had been shaking and crying and shouting that he'd do anything they wanted, just take the gun away from his daughter's head.

Now she was pointing a gun at another person. She pressed it to the man's head, the way others had done to her. Lydia knew exactly how it felt, knew the hellish fear that tore at your insides. Just a little extra pressure from the finger on the trigger and, from one moment to the next, your life would be over. She knew he'd had time by now to think of everything ending: no more smells, tastes, sights and sounds, no more sensations of being touched, no more being with others in any way. Everything will carry on as before, only I won't be there. I'll have ceased to be.

She thought of Dimitri and his gun, which he had pressed against her head more times than she could count, and of his smile, which was just like the smile on the face of that military policeman when she was nine, and like the smiles of all the men who had later gone down on her, invaded her, forced their way in.

Lydia hated them all.

She stared at the guard and knew how he felt, understood what having a gun against your head was like, and kept it there, holding her arm raised high and glaring at him in silence.

He sank to his knees.

Then he clasped his hands behind the back of his neck.

Again Lydia used the gun to point; he was to turn his back to her.

'Around. Around!'

He didn't hesitate this time, turned round on his knees until he was facing the door. She grabbed the gun by its muzzle, aimed with the handle at the back of his head and hit out as hard as she could.

He fell over forwards, unconscious before he hit the floor.

She pulled out the bag, carried it just like any ordinary shopping bag and hurried out of the room, down the corridor towards the lifts. It took a minute or so before one came. People passed her, but didn't see her, absorbed as they were by their own journeys.

She stepped inside and pressed the lowermost button. Standing there, she didn't think of anything in particular. She knew what she had to do.

All the way down. And when the lift stopped, she stepped out and walked along the bright white corridor towards the mortuary.

Jochum Lang was sitting on one of the seats by the entrance to Söder Hospital when Alena Sljusareva walked past him. He didn't see her, because he didn't know her. And she didn't see him, because she didn't know him either.

Jochum felt uneasy and was trying to shake it off. It was a long time since he had beaten up someone he knew.

It's his own fault. He's only got himself to blame.

He just needed a few minutes alone, that was all, just a sit-down, to think things through and try to get a grip on why he felt so tense.

Hilding had clung on to the lift doors. All the time he was weeping and pleading and calling Jochum by his first name.

Sure, Hilding was a fucking addict, at it all the time. And he would keep at it until his emaciated body couldn't take any more. He had his kit and he would do anything, grass on anyone, to get another hit. On the other hand, he had no enemies, there was no real hate, and no purpose in life whatsoever, except messing up his blood with Class A substances in order to shut off all the feelings he didn't want to have.

Jochum sighed.

This time had been unlike any other, somehow. Before, it had made no difference whether he knew who they were or not, or if they had wept and pleaded for their lives.

None of it mattered a shit, not really.

It's his own fault.

The hospital entrance hall was a strange place. Jochum looked around. People were moving about all the time, some sentenced to stay, others relieved to get out. No one laughed here, it wasn't that kind of place. He didn't like hospitals at all. They made him feel naked and vulnerable, powerless, unable to control other people's lives.

He got up. The doors opened automatically for him. It was still raining; small lakes had formed on the tarmac, floods of water trying to find somewhere to go.

Slobodan was waiting in the car, a few metres away from the bus stop. He was parked in the taxi zone, two wheels up on the kerb. He didn't turn round when Jochum opened the car door, he had seen him coming out.

'Took your bloody time.'

Slobodan looked ahead, turned the key and revved the engine. Jochum grabbed his wrist.

'Hold it.'

Slobodan stopped the engine and turned to Jochum for the first time.

'What?'

'Five fingers. A kneecap. As per the tariff.'

'That's what you pay for messing with our goods.'

Slobodan was acting the boss. He was picking up bad habits, like his loud sighs and the way he waved his hands about to show how little he cared.

'And?'

Jochum had been doing the rounds with Slobodan since way back, before the little shit even got his driving licence. His bossiness was hard to take and Jochum considered telling him so.

Not now. He'd make himself clear some other time.

'The guy struggled, hung on to things. I couldn't push him

into the lift. Suddenly he got hold of one of the wheels on the chair and off he went. Down the stairs and into the wall.'

Slobodan shrugged, started the engine again, revving it, turned the windscreen wipers on. Jochum's rage was gnawing at his insides and he grabbed Slobodan's arm, forced his hand off the wheel, pulled out the car key and pocketed it. He grasped the other man's face with his hand, pressing his fingers into the cheeks, turning his head so that they were face to face, forcing Slobodan to pay attention.

'Someone saw me.'

Sven drove into Söder Hospital via the Casualty entrance, the way he often came on professional business. They were known here. Plenty of parking space too.

They didn't say anything. They hadn't spoken since the alert, when Sven changed direction and headed for Väster Bridge, away from his birthday celebrations that he had promised to be home in time for. Ewert understood how important it was to Sven, even though he didn't understand why; he had rejected all that from his life. Or maybe it was actually the other way round. He found it hard to think of anything suitable to say, something comforting, and though he tested out several phrases in his head, they all sounded awkward and pointless. What did he know about missing a woman and a child?

Everything.

He knew everything about it.

They got out and hurried up the ramp into Casualty. Side by side they marched towards the lifts. General Medicine, sixth floor.

When they emerged, a woman was waiting for them, a doctor called Lisa Öhrström. She was quite young, quite tall and quite good-looking. Ewert's eyes rested on her too intently and he held her hand for a fraction too long. She noticed and looked quickly at him. He felt embarrassed.

'I let the visitor in,' she said. 'But I didn't see them leave the ward together.'

She pointed at the stairs, just next to the lift. A body was lying face down on the first landing. The blood had flowed out into a large reddish pool around it.

He was still now, blood congealing around his mouth, his hand didn't scratch his nose, his eyes didn't flicker, his arms didn't flap. This bodily peace was new. It was as if his damned twitchy fearfulness had leached away with his blood. They walked down to him, twelve steps. Ewert knelt and examined the dead body as if hoping to find something, anything. He knew of course that he wouldn't. Lang was an experienced hitman who knew all about precautions like wearing gloves and he left absolutely nothing behind.

They were waiting for Ludwig Errfors. Ewert had phoned him immediately. That decision had been easy. With someone like Lang, you had to get your side of it right. Errfors was not one for making mistakes. He was simply the best.

A few minutes more, just enough time for Ewert to sit down on a step and think about the dead man. He wondered if Oldéus was the sort who had thought about dying. If he knew the speed with which his drug-taking hurried him on towards death? If he had been afraid? Or did he want to die? Bloody fool. It was easy to work out that with his lifestyle he'd end up like this, cluttering up an ugly stair-case, before he was thirty years old. Ewert sighed, snorted at the unresponsive corpse.

I'd like to know where I'll end up, he thought as he got up and went over to Hilding again. Will I be in the way too? Will someone snort at me? There's always some sod who snorts.

Ludwig Errfors was a tall, dark man, about fifty years old. He arrived wearing his civilian outfit, jeans and a jacket, just as he always did in his office at the forensic medicine headquarters in Solna.

He said hello and pointed at the body that until recently had been Hilding Oldéus.

'I'm afraid I'm in a hurry. Can we get started right away?'
Ewert made a small gesture.

'Ready when you are.'

Errfors knelt down to examine the body. He started to talk, with his face still at floor level.

'Who is this?' he asked.

'Dealer, small time, heroin addict. His name was Hilding Oldéus.'

'Why call me in?'

'We're after the butcher who did this. We've been chasing him for a while and need a proper examination of the corpse.'

Errfors moved his black bag closer. After pulling on a pair of surgical gloves, he waved his white hands irritably at Ewert to make him go away. At least up to the top step.

He felt for the pulse. Not there.

Next, the heartbeat. Nothing.

He shone a light into both eyes, recorded the rectal temperature, palpated the abdomen.

His routine examination did not take very long, ten or fifteen minutes. Opening the body up, the real work, came later and took longer.

Sven had escaped from the stairwell long ago and stood looking down the eternity of blue corridor that ran from the lift area to the ward doors. He remembered the last time he had seen Errfors at work. He had left the room in tears. It was just as tough for him now. He couldn't cope with death, not like this, not at all.

Errfors changed position, looking quickly from Ewert to Sven and back to Ewert again.

'He can't handle it,' he said in a low voice. 'Remember last time.'

Ewert called to his colleague.

'Hey, Sven.'

'Yes?'

'The witness statements. I want you to take them now.'

'We've only got Öhrström.'

'That's fine.'

'And we've already talked to her.'

'Talk to her again.'

Sven cursed his inability to handle death, but was grateful to Ewert for understanding how he felt. He got up, walked away from the stairs and towards the end of the corridor and opened the door to the ward that Hilding Oldéus had left in terror just hours ago.

Ludwig Errfors watched him go and then concentrated on the corpse lying at his feet; a human life turned into nothing much and soon reduced to a few notes on a form. He cleared his throat and started speaking into a Dictaphone.

'External examination of a dead male.'

He kept it brief, one set of observations at a time.

'Pupils dilated.'

Pause.

'Four fingers broken on left hand. The haematomas indicate that the fractures occurred prior to death.'

A couple of breaths.

'The left knee appears to be crushed. Oedema indicates that the injury was sustained prior to death.'

He was precise. Considered every word. Grens had asked for an unassailable report and he would get what he wanted.

'The abdomen is contused in several places and distended. Palpation and percussion indicate the presence of free fluid, possibly due to an intra-abdominal haemorrhage.

'Several injection punctures of varying age, some infected. Drug addiction is the likely cause.

'Time of death estimated to be approximately thirty and no more than forty minutes prior to inspection of body. This is supported by a witness statement.'

He carried on talking into the Dictaphone for a minute or two. The autopsy would take place later, when the body had been transferred to the forensic medicine building, but was not likely to change anything significant in his on-site report. He had done enough of those to know that.

*　　*　　*

Jochum took his hand from Slobodan's face. The cheeks were marked with red blotches which moved when he spoke.

'Did I hear you right, Jochum? Someone saw you?' Slobodan slipped his fingers over the hot spots on his face and sighed. 'Not so good. If there are witnesses, we'll have to talk to them.'

'Not witnesses. Just one witness, a doctor.'

The interminable rain made it difficult to see out. When the warmth of their bodies and their breathing and mutual aggression hit the car windows from the inside, the condensation eliminated what little vision they had had before. Slobodan waved at the windows and pointed to the fan.

Jochum nodded and handed the car key back.

'I can't go back in there,' he said. 'Not now. That doctor's still there. And the cops are probably there too, now.'

Slobodan waited in silence, watching the moisture slowly evaporate from the windscreen. Let the fucker stew for a bit. The power balance between them had shifted. Every time it tipped Slobodan's way, Jochum lost the same amount.

When half the window had cleared, he turned to Jochum.

'OK. I'll fix it.'

Jochum hated running up a debt of gratitude, but he had no choice.

'Lisa Öhrström. Thirty to thirty-five. Tallish, about one metre seventy-five, and slim, almost thin. Dark shoulder-length hair. Glasses, narrow with black frames, but she keeps them in the breast pocket of her white coat.'

They had exchanged a few words, so he knew how she spoke.

'Trace of dialect from somewhere up north. Light voice and a slight lisp.'

Jochum settled back, stretched out his legs and turned the fan off.

He watched in the rear-view mirror as Slobodan passed the automatic doors and disappeared into the entrance hall.

She was singing. As always when she was upset and worried, she sang her song.

Lydia Grajauskas
Lydia Grajauskas
Lydia Grajauskas

She sang it quietly, under her breath, because she couldn't risk being discovered.

She wondered how long it would take before the unconscious guard came back to life. It had been a hard blow, but he was a big man and might be able to take quite some force. Maybe he had raised the alarm already.

Lydia walked along the brightly lit corridor underneath the big hospital, her mind still full of how it had felt to press the gun to the guard's temple when he hesitated. She was back in the world of the nine-year-old, in the room where her father was kneeling while the military policeman kept hitting his head and shouting that death was too good for weapon smugglers.

She stopped and checked her notebook.

The Polish nurse had let her have the hospital information booklet she had asked for, and Lydia had studied the maps of the various floors very carefully. Lying in bed, watched by the guard, she had made shaky copies in her notebook and added notes in Lithuanian.

Yes, she was going the right way to the mortuary.

She walked faster, with the carrier bag in her right, functional hand. She walked as fast as she could, but her hip ached and made her limp. The sound of each firm step with her good leg seemed to echo along the corridor and she slowed down again, didn't want to be heard.

She knew exactly what to do next.

No Dimitri-Bastard-Pimp would ever again order her to undress and let a stranger look her over to decide which part of her naked body he had bought the right to touch.

A few people had passed her, but didn't seem to see her. She was aware of their eyes clocking her and felt they must know that she was in the wrong place, until she realised that she was invisible, because she looked like every other patient walking along a hospital corridor in her hospital clothes.

That was why she was unprepared.

She had relaxed and she mustn't.

When she saw who it was, it was too late.

Perhaps it was his way of walking that she noticed first. He was tall and took long strides. His arms had a long reach. Then he said something, quite loudly, to his companion, another man. She recognised his light, slightly nasal voice. She had heard it from close quarters.

He was one of them. One of the men who liked to hit her. Here, he wore a white coat. In a matter of moments they would be face to face; he kept walking straight ahead and so did she, and the length of corridor that separated them was brightly lit and had no doors.

She slowed down even more, her eyes down, her right hand on the gun inside the billowing hospital coat.

She almost touched him as they passed each other.

He smelt the way he had when he pushed into her.

One brief moment and he was gone.

He hadn't noticed her at all. The woman he had paid to penetrate every fortnight for a year usually wore a black dress and underwear of his choice. Her hair was loose, her lips red. He hadn't ever seen the real her, the woman he had just passed in the corridor. Her face was bruised and beaten; one of her arms was in plaster. She walked in white slippers with the hospital logo stamped on them. He didn't see her now either.

Afterwards she was surprised, more than anything else. Not frightened, hardly panicked, but surprised, verging on angry. He just walked around here, like everyone else, and nothing showed on the outside.

The last stretch of hospital corridor. Lydia stopped at the door she was about to open.

She had never been in a mortuary before. There was an image in her mind of what it would look like, but she knew it was made up from scenes in American films she had seen in Lithuania. It was all she had to go by, and what she had based her plans on. From her sketch in the notebook she had an idea of its size and how many rooms there were. Now she was about to go in and she had to be very calm, stay calm and cope with both the living and the dead.

She hoped there would be someone alive in there. Preferably more than one.

She opened the door. It resisted, as if she was pushing against a draught, but there were no windows, she knew that. She heard voices, but the sound was muffled and seemed to come from the room next door. She stood still. They were alive and in there. Now it was up to her. She had the gun and the explosives that Alena had managed to get for her. Lydia had already knocked the guard out and found her way here. The voices told her that she had been lucky, there were people there.

She took a deep breath.

She had to do what she had planned.

She would make sure that it would never happen again.

There were at least three voices, maybe more. She couldn't understand what they were saying, an odd word here and there perhaps, but it didn't help. Her Swedish was non-existent and it made her angry with herself now. She freed the gun from the tape and took it in her good hand. Slowly she walked towards the voices, through the empty room she had entered. It was long and narrow, a little like a hall in a flat, and unlit.

Then she saw them.

She stopped on the dark side of the doorway and watched. They were busy with each other, observing something which she couldn't see at first.

There were five of them and she realised that she had seen them all only a few hours ago.

They had stood around her bed. One of them was a little older than the rest; he wore large glasses and his hair was going grey. This was the doctor who had examined her after she had been admitted. This morning he had returned with his four medical students to show them her injuries, shown her body to them, pointed at the wounds on her back and talked a great deal, about things like the cattle-whip and how wide and long the gashes were and how well they might heal, or not. The four students had listened in silence, wondering how many body defects they would have to learn about in order to understand and be able to treat them.

The group was standing in the middle of the room, quite a bit away, but Lydia could make out more now. They were gathered round a trolley with a body on it, lit by the focused light from two large lamps in the ceiling. She guessed it must be a dead body, it was so pale and still. No breathing movements. The grey-haired man with the large glasses was pointing with the same kind of laser torch that he had used on her. The four medical students were as silent and grim-looking in front of the corpse as in front of a living human being who had been humiliated and wounded.

Lydia hung back in the anteroom. They hadn't seen her.

Then she took eight steps into the room before they discovered she was there. She stopped two or three metres away from them.

They saw her and yet did not see her.

They recognised the female patient with the lash wounds who had smiled so sadly from her bed that morning, but this woman, who looked quite similar, had a very different aura. She wanted something. Her eyes demanded their attention. She raised her gun and pointed it at them while she took a few more steps forward. The overhead light illuminated her face, which looked badly hurt, but showed no pain. This woman was intense and calm at the same time. The grey-haired doctor had been interrupted and in a deliberate manner began a new sentence about some part of the cadaver, but soon stopped again.

The woman had released the safety catch on the gun and raised it until the muzzle was pointing straight at his face. And then at the other faces, the gun moving from one pair of eyes to the next.

Each time she held it long enough for every one of them to feel that terrifying cramp in the stomach which she knew from when Dimitri-Bastard-Pimp had aimed at her temple.

No one spoke. They waited for her to say something.

Lydia pointed to the floor with the gun.

'On knee! On knee!'

They knelt, all five of them, in a ring round the trolley containing the remains of what had once been a living person. She tried to gauge how frightened they were, but no one met her eyes, not one of them. The only female student and one of the men had closed their eyes. The rest stared straight past her or through her. They didn't have the strength to do anything else, not even their teacher. Not even him.

She was nine years old again, back in that room with the military police, the gun pressed against her head, and her dad, his hands tied behind his back, was forced to kneel, then to lie face down on the floor. She remembered how he fell forward, the thud when his face hit the concrete, a heavy fall, and that he bled from both nostrils afterwards.

And now here she was, holding the gun.

Lydia took one last step forward.

She stumbled, almost lost her balance and realised that she had to be careful, not just because Dimitri had kicked her hard enough to make her limp, but because her sense of balance had been funny for almost two years. One of the punters had wanted to do something extra, slap her around a bit; he had promised to pay twice as much to hit her in the face and she had said yes. He hit her across her left ear and the pain had been unbearable. She lost some of the hearing on that side for ever and the mechanism inside the ear to do with balance was damaged. She didn't quite understand the connection, but whatever it was had taken more of a beating than it could stand.

She managed to steady herself in mid-step, stumbling but not falling, all the time keeping the gun trained on the five people crouching in front of her.

It was important to keep her distance, she knew. A couple of metres away, no more, no less. She made certain that they had both knees on the floor and then stuck her gun hand quickly inside her coat and pulled the carrier bag out from her panties and away from her stomach. Dropped it to the floor.

She used her foot to rummage in the bag, rolled out the ball of string and kicked it across to the trolley.

The gun swung to aim at the female student.

Lydia screamed at her.

'Lock! Lock!'

She watched the terrified woman, who tried to make herself as small as possible. They looked quite similar; both were blonde, with a tinge of red in their shoulder-length hair; they were almost the same height and more or less the same age. Not long ago the student had been standing and looking down at Lydia.

Lydia nearly smiled. Now it was the other way around, she thought. Now she is the one lying down. Now I am the one standing up, watching from above.

'Lock!'

The young woman stared vacantly ahead. She was aware of someone holding a gun to her head, and that someone was screaming. But she couldn't hear anything, she couldn't bear to listen and take it in. She couldn't think about words and what they meant. Not now. Not with a gun to her head.

'Last time! Lock!'

The older doctor understood. Cautiously, he turned his head to the student, made eye contact and spoke to her softly.

'She wants you to tie us up.'

The young woman looked at him, but didn't move.

'She wants you to tie us up with that string.'

His voice was calm. She seemed to listen and met his eyes before turning to look at Lydia with a scared expression.

'I don't think she'll shoot. Do you understand? If you tie us up she won't shoot.'

She nodded, slowly, slowly. Then she repeated the movement towards Lydia, to show that she had understood, and leaned forward to pick up the ball of string. Using the knife that had just made an incision into the abdomen of the cadaver, she cut a length of string, which she wound round her teacher's wrists.

'Hard! Very hard! You lock hard!'

Lydia took another step forward and waved with the gun. She watched until the string had been pulled tight enough to cut into the flesh.

'Lock!'

The young woman went on, moved round with the knife, tied everybody's wrists together and didn't stop pulling at the string until blood showed at every knot. When she had finished she turned to Lydia. She was breathing heavily and waited until they made eye contact.

Lydia pointed with the gun. The student was to turn round and kneel. Using her weak left hand, Lydia managed to tie the student's wrists as hard as she could.

The whole thing had taken six to seven minutes, a little longer than Lydia had planned. True, she hadn't expected five of them. One or two, yes, but not five.

Someone must have found the guard by now, realised that she was missing and probably alerted the police.

She didn't have much time.

She quickly searched the pockets of all five white coats, then the trouser pockets. Everything she found was piled up on the floor: key rings, wallets, loose change, ID cards, plastic gloves, half-empty packets of throat tablets. The doctor had a mobile phone. She tested it and noted that it was almost fully charged.

Five people kneeling in front of her, hands tied behind their backs, cowering before the gun in her hand.

One dead man, partly dissected, on a brightly lit trolley.

She had hostages.

Hostages mean that you can make demands.

She was crying.

It was a long time since he had made her cry. She hated him for it. Lisa Öhrström hated her brother.

The bloody call he had made from the metro station just two days ago, she could still hear his voice in her head, wheedling as usual when he was trying to make her give him money. She had refused, as she had been told to do at the courses for relatives.

Tears, a lump in her throat, her trembling body. She had picked him up so often from care homes and clinics. Every time he had promised it was the last time, he would never touch it again. He had caught her the way only he could do, looked into her eyes and, as time passed, unknowingly sucked her dry, sapped all her strength and wasted bloody years and years of her life.

Now he was lying there, slumped in a stairwell at her work.

This really was the last time, and just for a moment she felt almost relieved that he wouldn't bother her any more, until it dawned on her that this was the one feeling she would never learn to live with.

Sven Sundkvist, interview leader (IL): I know that to you
    Hilding Oldéus was not just another patient. However,
    I must ask you to answer my questions about him.
Lisa Öhrström (LÖ): I was just going to phone my sister.
IL: Believe me, I do understand that it is hard for you. But
    you were the only one here. The only eyewitness.
LÖ: I want to speak to my sister's kids. They adored their
    uncle. They only saw him when he was just out. He
    was clean then and nicely dressed. His face had some
    colour. They've never met the man who is lying on the
    stairs.
IL: I need to know how close you got to the other person.
    The visitor.
LÖ: I was going to phone just now. Aren't you listening?
    I'm trying to explain to you.
IL: How close?

    They were sitting on hard wooden chairs in the ward
sister's glass booth. It was located in the middle of the sixth-
floor corridor.
    Lisa couldn't stop crying and her dignity was slipping
away. She tried hard to hang on to it, but felt her grip on
life was weakening.
    He was her brother.
    She simply couldn't deal with this any more.
    The last few times he had come to her for help she had
refused, and all the tears in the world could not wash away
that guilt.
    Sven Sundkvist paused and watched her. Her white coat
looked rumpled; her eyes were half closed. He continued to
wait while she blew her nose and pulled her fingers through
her long hair. He had met her before. Not her, but people
like her. He often had to interview them, the women who
stood hovering in the background, supportive souls who
always felt guilty and exposed. He thought of them as guilt-

ridden and knew only too well that they could cause trouble. Their capacity for blaming themselves often complicated things, even for an experienced interrogator. They behaved as if they were the culprits and interpreted whatever you said as an accusation; actually, every one of them construed her life as one long accusation. Even when completely innocent, their anxieties obstructed investigations, which had to move on.

LÖ: Was it?
IL: Was it what?
LÖ: My fault?
IL: Look, it's only natural that you feel guilty. I understand. But I can't help you. It's something you have to deal with yourself.

Lisa looked at him, the policeman sitting in front of her with one leg crossed over the other and demanding something from her.

She disliked him.

He seemed nicer, gentler than the older man, but she disliked him all the same. The police had some kind of perennial aura of authority, and this wasn't a proper interrogation, more like a confrontation, the start of a quarrel she couldn't bear to take part in.

IL: The man who was here, he was probably the one who killed your brother. How close did you get to him?
LÖ: As close as you and I are now.
IL: In other words, close enough to get a good look at him?
LÖ: Close enough to feel his breath.

She turned, glancing at the glass wall. What an unpleasant place this was. Whoever passed by could see them there, curious eyes disturbing her sense of privacy. She found it hard to concentrate and said she was going to sit with her back to the window.

IL: Can you describe his build?
LÖ: He was frightening.
IL: Height?
LÖ: Much taller than me and I'm quite tall, one metre seventy-five. Maybe like your colleague. Another ten centimetres.

Lisa nodded towards the end of the corridor, where Ewert was standing at the top of the stairwell, next to the medical examiner, staring at the dead body on the floor. Sven automatically turned the same way and mentally measured Ewert.

IL: His face?
LÖ: Strong. Nose, chin, forehead.
IL: And hair?
LÖ: He didn't have any.

There was a knock at the door. Lisa Öhrström had been sitting with her back to it, so she hadn't noticed someone approaching and therefore got a fright. A uniformed policeman opened the door and came in. He handed over an envelope and then left.

IL: I've got some photos for you to look at. Pictures of different people.

She got up from her chair. No more. Not now. She didn't want to have anything to do with the brown envelope in the centre of the desktop.

IL: Please sit down.
LÖ: I'll have to get back to work.
IL: Lisa, look at me. It wasn't your fault.

Sven rose too, took a step forward and put his arm round the shoulders of the woman who wanted to return to her guilt and grief. He pushed her gently down on the chair, moved two case-note folders aside to make more free space on the desk and emptied out the contents of the brown envelope.

IL: Please, try to identify the visitor, the man whose breath you felt in your face.
LÖ: I suspect you know who he is.
IL: Please, concentrate on the photos.

She picked them over. One at a time, she had a good look, then put them to the side systematically, face down. After some thirty photos of men standing against a white wall, she suddenly had a sensation of something tightening in her chest. It was the same feeling as when she was little and scared of the dark. She had described it then as a jittery, dancing feeling, as if her fear was light and lifted her.

LÖ: That's him.
IL: Are you certain?
LÖ: Quite certain.
IL: For the record, the witness has identified the visitor as the man in photograph thirty-two.

Sven was silent for a while, uncertain of his reactions. He knew well that grief eats people from inside and that this woman was almost suffocating with sadness, but even so he had forced her to keep her feelings at arm's length and carry on nonetheless. He had known that she could break down at any moment and had ignored it, because it was his duty.

But now, now she pointed to the person they had wanted her to pick out.

He only hoped she was strong enough.

IL: You have identified a man who is generally thought to be very dangerous. From experience, we know that witnesses who identify him are always subjected to threats.

LÖ: What's the implication?

IL: That we are considering giving you personal protection.

That was something she did not want to hear. She wanted to undo the whole thing, to go back home, undress and go to bed, sleep until the alarm went, wake up, have breakfast, get dressed and go to work at Söder Hospital.

It wouldn't happen. Not ever again.

The past would never cease to be, no matter how much she wanted it to.

Sitting there on the hard chair, she tried to cry again, tried to expel a part of whatever it was that was eating her from inside. It didn't work. Crying, damn it, wasn't an option. Sometimes, it just isn't.

She was about to get up again and walk off somewhere else, just away, when the door to the ward sister's glass booth opened.

Pulled open by someone who didn't bother to knock, just stepped straight in.

She recognised the older policeman, who had held her hand for a little too long when they met. His face was flushed, his voice loud.

'Shit! Sven!'

Sven Sundkvist seldom got irritated with his boss, unlike the rest of them. Most of his colleagues disliked Ewert Grens, some even hated him. As for himself, he had decided simply to accept, the good and the bad, to put up or shut up. And so he put up.

With one exception.

'For the record. The person who has interrupted the interrogation of the witness Lisa Öhrström is Ewert Grens, DSI at the City Police, Stockholm.'

157

'Sven, I'm sorry. It just . . . it's bloody urgent.'

Sven leaned over to the tape recorder, switched it off, then gestured at Ewert. OK, talk away.

'That woman. You know the one we carried out of the flat in the Atlas district. She was unconscious.'

'Flogged?'

'Yes. She's disappeared.'

'Disappeared?'

Ewert nodded.

'She was admitted to one of the surgical wards and was here until very recently. I had a call from Control. She's not there any more. And she's armed with a handgun. Knocked out the guard assigned to look after her. She's probably still somewhere in the hospital, ready to shoot.'

'Why would she do that?'

'I only know what I've just told you.'

Lisa Öhrström put photograph number 32 back on the table. Then she looked first at one policeman and then the other, and pointed at the ceiling.

'Up there.'

'What?'

'Up there, next floor. The surgical wards.'

Ewert stared at the white ceiling and was on his way out of the room he had just barged into when Sven grabbed his arm.

'Stop. Wait. We just got a one hundred per cent clear, unhesitating identification of Jochum Lang.'

The large, clumsy man stopped, nodded at Lisa and smiled at his colleague.

'Now we'll see. Won't we, Anni?'

'What did you say?'

'Never mind.'

Sven stared uncomprehendingly at Ewert and then turned to Lisa, putting his hand lightly on the young doctor's shoulder.

'Ewert. Dr Öhrström needs to have protection.'

It was just after lunch on Wednesday 5 June.

Ewert Grens and Sven hurried up one of the hospital's many staircases, from the sixth to the seventh floor.

It had been a strange morning.

They had been restless for a few minutes, all five of them. Carefully moved a leg, slowly tilted a head against a shoulder. As if their bodies were aching, as if they didn't dare attract her attention, and for precisely that reason were unable to sit still.

Lydia sensed their fear and left them to it. She knew how hard it was even to breathe when you were sitting down, looking up at someone who had just claimed the right to your body. She remembered the *Stena Baltica* ferry and how the threat of death silenced your instinct to cry for help.

Suddenly one of them collapsed and fell forward on his face.

One of the young men, a medical student, had lost his balance and fallen out of the circle around the body.

Lydia quickly aimed the gun at him.

He lay bent over, face down, his knees still on the floor, his hands tied behind his back. His body shaking, being upright required too much effort. He was weeping with fear. He had never imagined anything like this before; life had just happened. He was young and everything was eternal; only now did he realise that it might end instantly, when he was only twenty-three years old. His body kept shaking. He wanted to live for much longer.

'On knee!'

Lydia went over and pressed the muzzle against the back of his neck.

'On knee!'

Slowly he straightened up, still trembling, tears running down his cheeks.

'Name?'

Silence. He just stared at her.

'Name!'

He found it hard to speak; the words stuck, didn't want to come.

'Johan.'

'Name!'

'Johan Larsen.'

She leaned over him and pressed the muzzle against his forehead. Like the men on the *Stena Baltica* had done. She kept it there while she addressed him.

'You, on knee! If again . . . boom!'

He sat up straight now. Held his breath. His body . . . he couldn't get it to stop trembling, not even when the urine started trickling down his leg, staining his trousers without him being aware of it.

Lydia looked them over, one by one. Still no one met her eyes, they didn't dare. She felt around inside the plastic bag with the supermarket logo, pulling out the explosive and the detonators. There was a small stainless-steel table next to the trolley and she divided up the pale brownish dough, kneaded it, still holding the gun in her good hand, until the mass had became soft and pliable enough to fix round the door she had only recently come in through and the other two doors in the room. She used half of it. She divided up the remaining half, putting a fifth of it on each of the people kneeling on the floor in front of her, around the trolley containing a dead, naked body. When she had finished, they carried death between their shoulders, a pale membrane of plastic explosive stuck at the back of their necks.

She had been in the mortuary for over twenty minutes now. It had taken her about ten minutes to get from the surgical ward on the seventh floor down to the basement.

She realised that her disappearance would have been discovered some time ago, that the police would have been alerted and be looking for her.

Lydia went over to the female student, the one who looked like her, with her reddish-blonde hair and thin body. The one who had tied the others up.

'Police!'

Lydia held the doctor's mobile phone up in front of the student's face. Then, after putting her hand on the explosive taped to the other woman's shoulder as a reminder, she cautiously loosened the ties.

'Police! Call police!'

The student hesitated, frightened that she might have misunderstood. She looked around anxiously and tried to make eye contact with the greying doctor.

He spoke to her, keeping his voice calm and steady, hiding his own fear. 'She wants you to call the police.'

The student had understood and nodded. The older man made his voice sound reassuring, he obviously had to force himself. 'Do it. Just do what she asks. Dial one, one, two.'

Her hand shook, she dropped the phone, picked it up again, dialled the wrong number, looked quickly at Lydia and said sorry. Then she got it right: one, one, two. Lydia heard the line connecting. She was satisfied and indicated to the student that she should lie down on her stomach. She took the handset from her, went over to the doctor and pressed the phone to his ear.

'Talk!'

He nodded, waited. His forehead was glistening with sweat.

The room was silent.

One minute.

Then a voice answered. The doctor spoke with his mouth close to the phone.

'Police.'

Silence, waiting. Lydia stood at his side, holding the phone. The rest of them had closed their eyes or were looking at the floor in front of them, lost, far away.

A new voice.

The doctor replied.

'My name is Gustaf Ejder. I am a senior registrar at the Söder Hospital. I am calling from the hospital mortuary, in the basement. I was here with four medical students when a young woman dressed as an inpatient came and took us all hostage. She is armed with a gun and is aiming at our heads. She has also put what I think is plastic explosives on our bodies.'

The student called Johan Larsen, the young man who had collapsed a little earlier, shaking uncontrollably, suddenly shouted at the phone.

'It is plastic explosive! I know! It's Semtex. Almost half a kilo. There will be a big fucking bang if she detonates it!'

Lydia's first reaction was to swing the gun towards the shouting man, but then she relaxed.

She had picked up the word *Semtex* and his voice had been so wild that the message would get across to whoever was listening at the other end.

She took out the pages she had torn from her notebook and, with the phone still pressed against the doctor's ear, lined up the pieces of paper on the floor in front of him with an almost empty sheet on top. It had just a couple of words written on it. Then she indicated that she wanted him to keep talking.

He did what she wanted.

'Are you still there?'

'Yes.'

'The woman wants me to read a name she has written

on a piece of paper. It seems to have been torn from a note-book. It says Bengt Nordwall. That's all.'

The voice asked him to repeat what he had just said.

'Bengt Nordwall. Nothing else. What she has written is pretty hard to read, but I am certain I've got it right. Her English when she speaks isn't that easy to understand either. My guess is that she comes from Russia. Or maybe one of the Baltic states.'

Lydia took the phone away from him and indicated that she wanted him to sit upright again.

She had heard him pronounce the name she had written down.

She had also heard him say Baltic.

She was satisfied.

Bengt Nordwall stared up at the sky. Grey, solid grey. The rain had followed his every step this summer. He sighed. This was supposed to be a time for winding down and relaxing, for gathering your strength for yet another winter. It would be one of those autumns again when, by mid-October already, people went into hiding in their offices, fed up with everything except their own company.

Silence everywhere, nothing to distract you from the sound of raindrops pattering on the cloth of the parasol.

Lena was sitting next to him, engrossed in a book. As usual. He wondered if she actually remembered the stories beyond the next day, let alone the next book, but reading was her way of unwinding. She would curl up in a chair, stuff a cushion behind her back and forget everything around her.

He was sitting in the same place as he had two days ago when Ewert had been next to him on the garden seat and it had rained just as hard. They had both been soaked to the skin, but their conversation was more important. They were so close, a closeness that can only develop with sufficient time.

He hadn't guessed then that he would meet up with Ewert

only the next day, outside that Baltic whore's flat. Bengt could still see her. The skin on her back, torn apart by the whip. He felt bad, worse than uncomfortable. Not her. Not another terrible beating again. Not now.

Their garden wasn't big, but he took pride in it. It was good for the kids, somewhere for them to run around. The last two years he had worked part-time, he was fifty-five and would never again experience young lives growing up around him. He had just this one chance and wanted to enjoy the children as much as possible. They were older now, of course, and could do most things on their own now, but he wanted to be there for them and joined in their playing from a distance. This summer even the kids had got fed up with playing outdoors. The sodden lawn was left alone, no footballs slammed into the roses and no one hid in the lilac bush while someone else counted to a hundred. Instead they sat holed up in their rooms, in front of their computer screens, caught up in an electronic world he knew absolutely nothing about.

Bengt looked at Lena again and smiled. She was so lovely. The long, blonde hair, her peaceful, intent face – a peace that he had never found. He remembered Vilnius. For a few years he had been the head of security at the Swedish embassy there and one day she had materialised at a departmental desk, a young and curious civil servant. He couldn't understand why she had chosen him, but that was exactly what she had done: she had picked him, and somehow he, who had already been discarded once, had been lifted back into the realms of the eligible people who married and settled down.

A washed-up policeman, twenty years her senior.

He was still terrified that she might wake up one morning, look him in the eye, realise that she had made a mistake and ask him to leave.

'Sweetie . . .'

She didn't hear. He leaned towards her and lightly kissed her cheek.

'Lena?'

'What?'

'Let's go in.'

She shook her head.

'Not yet. Soon. Just three more pages.'

Rain. He had been certain it couldn't be any worse, but now it got heavier and sounded like it would soon rip through the protective material above their heads. The lawn around them slowly surrendered to the water and became boggy marshland.

Bengt looked at his wife. She was holding the book up in front of her face with both hands, hiding behind a chapter with three more pages to go.

But the other woman was insistent.

Lena was in front of him, but it wasn't her he saw. Instead Bengt saw the other woman, her whipped back slashed, her skin ripped to shreds, congealing blood everywhere. He tried to push the sight out of his mind, but the image of the bloody whore wouldn't go. When he closed his eyes it just got clearer; he saw her carried out on a stretcher, unconscious. He opened his eyes again but she was still there, her stretcher being manoeuvred through the splintered door. He cowered behind the feeling of unease, which then tipped over into a fear he didn't want to feel.

'What's the matter?'

Lena had put the book down on the armrest and was looking at him.

He didn't reply at first. Then he shrugged. 'Nothing.'

'I can see something's up. Penny for your thoughts?'

Another light shrug of his shoulders, as carelessly as he could. 'Nothing, really. I'm fine.'

She knew him too well, knew that whatever it was, it was definitely not nothing.

'It's a long time since I've seen you like that. You seem scared.'

The fucking awful welts on one of them, and the other

one running round the flat screaming. Naked, beaten young bodies. Perhaps he ought to tell Lena. She had every right to know. The images haunted him. He had been utterly unprepared for it.

'Your phone's ringing.'

He looked at her, at her finger that was pointing at his jacket pocket, and he scrabbled to find the phone. The noise was stressing him out. Only four rings, then it would stop.

'Nordwall.'

He held the phone pressed to his ear. The call didn't take long, just a minute or so. He looked at his wife.

'Something's happened. They need an interpreter. I have to go.'

'Where?'

'Söder Hospital.'

He got up, kissed Lena's cheek again and then bent his head to get out from under the parasol. Out into the pouring rain.

Söder Hospital. The Lithuanian girl. A mortuary.

Fear sunk its claws into him again.

The guard in the green uniform was sitting on the only bed in the room, with a bandage wound round his head. He had bled a great deal and the white fabric was stained a pale red. The nurse standing next to him had a Polish name on her ID tag. She had brought him two brown tablets that Ewert assumed were painkillers.

The guard didn't have much to tell.

Lydia had been in the dayroom, quietly watching TV. The two lads from Ward 4 had been there too. The lunchtime news was on, some channel or other, he couldn't remember which. She wanted to go to the toilet, no harm in that. Why refuse her? She was so small and frail, with one arm in plaster and a bad hip that made her limp. He hadn't considered her dangerous, and besides, he couldn't follow her when she went to the toilet, could he?

Ewert smiled. Of course you bloody well should. Your job was to watch her: when she slept, when she went for a dump.

The guard's head hurt and he patted the bandage, touched the back of his neck. It had been a hard blow. She had flushed the toilet – he heard that, the water had rushed into the bowl twice. When she came out, she had signed to him that she wanted to go back to bed and that he should come with her. He didn't think there was anything strange about that. He had followed her back here, to Room 2, and closed the door behind him, as per usual.

And then suddenly she had a gun in her hand.

He didn't know how. All he knew was that she knew how to use it. He heard her cock the gun before holding it to his head. After a few moments, he realised that she was serious.

It was a bare, shabby room.

The guard had felt the back of his head gingerly, sighed and left. Ewert had stayed, sitting in the visitor's chair and looking around.

A metal bed. Next to it a bedside locker on castors. By the window a small table and a chair, the one he was sitting in. It was a spacious room, meant for four patients, but it had been cleared to let one badly abused woman recover alone.

He sat in silence. His thoughts bouncing off the cold, white walls.

He was waiting, mustering his strength. He needed it more than he had realised when the call on the way back from Arlanda Airport made them switch lanes and drive over the Väster Bridge towards the hospital. Then it had been all about a sad murdered junkie and the chance he had waited for, to tie a crime firmly to the man who had ruined his life together with Anni. Now the situation had spiralled into a hostage drama with enough Semtex to blow parts of this crowded building to smithereens.

Ewert Grens was a senior policeman and better than most at investigating murders. But big operations, that was different. It was a long time since he had stopped doing big operations, the mobilisation of cars and men while events were still taking place.

So he had just stood there, with a fresh eyewitness

statement against Lang in his possession, one floor below the room where another drama had unfurled: a prostitute had knocked her guard down and escaped.

And seven floors above the mortuary, where the same woman had taken five people hostage, and slapped some light-beige death between their shoulders.

He had a patrol car bring his police uniform from the cupboard at Kronoberg where it was kept.

Soon he would be appointed Gold Command, in charge of both operations.

Two human dramas had landed on his desk.

On his way into the hospital, Slobodan glanced quickly back at the car. He could see Jochum Lang's shaved, tanned skull and broad neck through the wet car window. Truth be told, he was fond of that fucking baldie, who had been like an older brother, someone you were maybe a bit scared of, but mostly admired. But it was about self-respect: at thirty-five a guy had to look after himself, get some respect even from those who didn't expect it. Too bad if some folk had different ideas. Besides, this time it was Jochum who was up shit creek; he shouldn't have let a witness see him when he was about to waste that screwball junkie.

Lisa Öhrström. Dialect from up north. Between thirty and thirty-five years old. One seventy-five, dark hair, narrow black-rimmed specs, usually kept in breast pocket.

Slobodan took the lift to the sixth floor, followed the empty corridor to the medical wards and stopped halfway along at a glass booth with a woman inside.

Her back was turned; he knocked lightly on the glass, and she turned round. Not her. At least twenty years too old.

'I'm looking for Doctor Öhrström.'

'She isn't here.'

Slobodan smiled. 'I can see that.'

She didn't respond to his smile.

'Doctor Öhrström is busy. Can I help you?'

This was the ward sister, or so her ID tag said. She seemed tense and her expression was worried.

'The police have been here. They have just finished talking to Doctor Öhrström. Is that what it's about?'

'Yes, in a way. Where did you say I could find her?'

'I didn't.'

'Where is she?'

'She's with her patients. And there's more waiting. It's been quite a busy day and we're running late.'

He stepped out into the corridor, pulled out a chair and settled down, a demonstration that he had no intention of going away.

'I'd like you to fetch her, please.'

He was sitting at a small table by the window in the room that had until recently accommodated an abused victim and was now a crime scene, using his mobile to issue commands. When the battery ran out he replaced it with a newly charged one and carried on.

Ewert had called for all available patrol cars to come to the Casualty unit at Söder Hospital, a place he had judged to be a suitable distance from any potential explosion. He wanted all traffic from the ring road stopped. The hospital access route was already blocked and the chief executive had agreed to evacuate the area where the mortuary was situated. Everyone must leave.

He stood up, glanced at Sven Sundkvist, who was just entering the room, and pointed at the door. Without a word they both went out into the corridor. The last few minutes had been intense.

'I want an explosives expert.'

'Right.'

'Can you sort that out?'

'Sure.'

They were at the lifts and Sven turned to the one that had just arrived. 'Going down? Or shall we use the stairs?'

Ewert waved a hand. 'Not yet.'

He produced an envelope and handed it to his colleague.

'I found this by her bed. The one thing in the entire room that didn't belong to the hospital.'

Sven took the envelope, looked quickly at it and gave it back, before walking into the nearest ward. He found what he was looking for on a shelf above the wash basin and returned, pulling on a pair of disposable surgical gloves.

'Right. Let me see it.'

He opened it. A notebook, blue covers. Nothing else. He glanced at Ewert, then started leafing through it. Some of the pages had been torn out, four were covered with tightly written script. A Slavic language of some sort, as far as he could see.

'Hers, presumably?'

'Presumably.'

'I don't understand a word of it.'

'I want it translated. Sven, can you take care of it?'

Ewert watched Sven restore the blue notebook to the envelope and then held out his hand, taking charge of it. He pointed towards the stairwell.

'We'll use the stairs.'

'Now?'

'We don't want to be stuck in a lift if something happens.'

They started to walk down the steep concrete stairs and passed the big red stain that until recently had been Hilding Oldéus. The green-uniformed lads had carried off the rest. Ewert shrugged as they passed.

'We'll have to deal with that later.'

After a few more steps, Sven stopped. He stood still for a second or two, turned and went back to the red stain.

'Ewert, hang on.'

He stared at the stain, his eyes following its edges. The blood had splashed high up on the wall.

'What drives us? Look, the remains of someone who was alive not so long ago. What drives people?'

'Sven, we haven't got time for this.'

'I don't understand. I know something about how human beings work, up to a point, but I don't understand it.'

Sven crouched down; his body swayed a little and he almost lost his balance. He stood up again.

'We know who Hilding Oldéus was. He had quite a lot going for him. He was bright, for instance, no question about it. But he hauled a burden of shame about on his back. Just like most of the rest of us fools. Shame, where does it come from?'

'We've got to get moving. Bloody quick.'

'You're not listening to me, Ewert. Shame eats you up from inside. Shame drives a lot of people. We shouldn't be chasing criminals, you know, we should go for the shame that make criminals commit crimes.'

'I don't have time, Sven. Come on.'

Sven didn't move. Ewert's irritation was only too obvious, but he ignored it.

'Hilding thought he knew who he was, at heart. And decided he would have nothing to do with that person, didn't want to know the real Hilding, not at any price, because he was ashamed of him. Why do you think that was?'

Ewert sighed. 'No idea.'

'He probably had no idea either. Heroin shut off that awareness. That much he did know. It shut the door on his shame.'

Sven looked down at Ewert. He hadn't been listening and was already heading down the stairs.

'Listen, we've got a prostitute who's pointing a gun at the people down there, so please excuse me, Sven. Let's talk about this some other time.'

One floor down. Sven caught up with him.

'Hey, Sven.'

'Yes.'

'A negotiator. I need someone who is good at hostage negotiations.'

'He's on his way.'

'What?'

'It was her only demand.'

Ewert stopped in mid-step. 'What the hell are you talking about?'

'I just heard when I phoned in your request for reinforcements. She got one of the hostages to speak for her, a senior doctor. He described the mortuary situation on her behalf, as it were. She doesn't speak Swedish and not much English either.'

'And?'

'When he was done with the preliminaries, she made him read out a name she'd written down for him on a piece of paper. Bengt Nordwall.'

'Bengt?'

'Yep.'

'Why?'

'Search me. Control took it to mean that she wanted him here. I would've come to the same conclusion.'

Ewert hadn't come across Bengt on police business for a long time. Then, yesterday, there he was outside that broken-down door. Now they were to meet again, only a day later. He preferred their private relationship, talking in the rain, breakfasts. His one friendship out of uniform.

They hurried through the ground floor, following a few hundred metres of corridor leading straight to Casualty. They gave cursory nods to the hospital staff they met, hoping to escape their questions. No time to stop and explain, not yet. Along to the front door and out on to the ramp where the ambulances usually pulled up several times daily, unloading heavy stretchers and injured people.

This was the point where all available patrol cars had been told to meet up. Not much time had passed since the alert went out, but already Sven counted fourteen cars parked in the large waiting area. Or fifteen, including the one coming through the large automatic gates with its blue light still rotating.

Ewert waited for another five minutes. Eighteen marked cars, pulled up side by side. He had unfolded a map of metropolitan Stockholm across the roof of the nearest one.

The men gathered behind him. No one said much. They were all waiting for him to speak. He was the boss here, Gold Command, a large, noisy DSI with thinning grey hair, a slight limp and a stiff neck after a tricky encounter with a wire noose. Said to be a peppery old bastard. They had all heard of him, but no one had worked with him or even seen him in action. He was known to skulk in his room, working on his investigations alone and listening to Siw Malmkvist. Not many people were allowed in, but then, hardly anyone fancied knocking on his door in the first place.

They waited patiently until he turned round and looked thoughtfully at them. Seconds went by before he started to speak.

'We have a female perpetrator. Yesterday she was carried unconscious from her pimp's flat. She was brought to this hospital and has been cared for here. So far, so good. So far, we've come across this kind of thing before.'

He looked around. They were listening intently. How young they are, he thought. Good-looking and strong, but what do they know? They probably hadn't come across this kind of thing before.

'But, for some reason, at lunchtime today, she recovers enough to do something we could never have foreseen. She gets hold of a handgun, God knows from where. She can hardly move but all the same she damn well manages to knock her guard out cold and walks off, gun in hand. Finds her way to the mortuary in the basement and steps inside, locking the door behind her. And then she takes the five people who were down there hostage. Then she sticks plastic explosive all over them and phones us.'

Ewert Grens spoke calmly, addressing colleagues he had never seen before and who had probably never seen him.

He knew what he had to do, what was expected of him.

He arranged for an even bigger evacuation. According to the information from the mortuary, she had about half a kilo of explosives and detonators, but she could have rigged some more or hidden it anywhere. She had passed through large parts of the hospital on her way down there and could have stuffed the shit into all sorts of nooks and crannies.

He extended the area to be cordoned off outside the hospital. Not only was the access road closed, but he also had tall wire-net barriers erected along the ring road, the whole way, where the commuter traffic was just now growing dense.

Through the proper channels, he also asked for assistance from the national police force, especially that the Flying Squad should be available and prepared for a possible raid within the hour. He had phoned one of the squad's senior men, John Edvardson, whom he had met several times and knew to be a clever man, as well as a Russian speaker. They talked through the situation. Even with Bengt there, Ewert felt it was important to have a second man on hand who could communicate in the language they would be negotiating in.

Sven was standing a couple of metres away watching his colleagues clustering at the ramp and taking orders from Ewert. They were there, completely alert. Truly present. Concentrating on the situation at hand and nothing else.

He wasn't. Deep down he didn't give a rat's ass about the prostitute from across the Baltic, pointing her gun at five medics who had had the bad luck to be in the mortuary at the wrong time, or that Jochum Lang had just been identified as Hilding Oldéus's killer, a few floors up.

Sven didn't mind his job. It wasn't that. He even liked it and still set out for work with a light heart in the morning. True, he had considered doing something else, something that didn't mean having to deal with the consequences of violence, something a little easier to live with. But he had always rejected the idea, tried to think of it as a game or a dream. He liked being a policeman, and had no real urge to start over in another job.

But right now, he wasn't there.

He wanted to go home. Today he belonged with Anita and Jonas. He had promised. This morning he had kissed their sleeping cheeks and whispered that he'd be home soon after lunch. They could enjoy being a family again then.

He backed away a little further. Partly hidden behind a waiting ambulance, he phoned home. Jonas answered, as always stating his full name, Hello, my name is Jonas Sundkvist. Sven explained that he wouldn't be coming home and felt awful, and Jonas started to cry because he had promised, and Sven felt even worse and then Jonas shouted that he hated him, because Mummy and Jonas had made everything nice, with a cake and candles. By now Sven couldn't take much more, so he just held the phone out in front of him and looked over at Ewert, who was nearing the end of his briefing, and at the massed colleagues, who were starting to disappear quickly in all directions. Sven took a few deep breaths and pulled himself together enough to mumble 'Please forgive me' into the electronic void that is created when someone hangs up.

It was June and high summer, so when a major hospital in central Stockholm was evacuated and the main traffic arteries were blocked and lined with tall wire fences, there were whoops of joy in the media. They could smell blood and chaos, some real news to satisfy a distrustful public, bored by silly-season trivia. The flashing blue lights of eighteen cars converging on the hospital had been noted and followed. Now the newshounds were mingling with the general public outside the two narrow Exit-Only passages, where uniformed police were opening and closing the barriers for hospital staff who were still coming out.

Ewert Grens had asked the police and hospital press officers to organise a press conference as far away as possible,
and then to give away as little as possible to the journalists. He wanted to have some peace in the room that had
been set aside as a centre of operations, and total calm in
the basement corridors near the mortuary. He recalled with
horror a hostage drama on the west coast a few years ago,
when the hostage-takers had been ensconced in a private
villa and kept the hostages covered with high-calibre
weapons. The perpetrators had been violent men, well known
to the police, and they had just entered negotiations and
were waiting for the next call when a journalist from one
of the national TV channels, who had managed to find out
who the negotiator was and get his mobile phone number,
called during a direct broadcast and tried to blag himself
an interview.

Ewert knew all this wouldn't help. He could send the
hacks miles away to utterly pointless press conferences, but
they still wouldn't leave anyone in peace.

An Eastern European prostitute who has been beaten up
and then takes hostages in the hospital where she's being
treated – it was a red-hot story.

They would hang on until the bitter end.

One of the three emergency surgery theatres near the Casualty
entrance had been designated centre of police operations.
Two of the theatres were in regular use, but were free at
the moment, and the third was on stand-by, fully equipped,
but rarely used. After much pushing and shoving, the once
sterile tables now served as temporary desks and the members
of the operational command group, never fewer than three
and never more than five, had already found themselves
special places to sit.

Ewert had to use threats, and then more threats, against
the telephone company to extract the number of the mobile
phone used to contact the police on the emergency number.

The number was ex-directory, but was registered to the man who had made the phone call, a senior registrar called Gustaf Ejder. Ewert printed the number in colour and put it up on the wall, next to the number of a stationary phone in the mortuary that was already hanging there.

His place was at what had been a surgical trolley, jammed in between two stainless-steel cabinets. He had been waiting and drinking coffee from paper cups for almost two hours, and he was getting impatient.

'She's winding us up.'

Nobody heard him. Maybe it helped to say it out loud.

'Maybe she knows exactly what she's doing. Knows that silence will stress us out. Or maybe she's packed it in, realises it's all going to pot and can't take any more.'

He drained the latest paper cup, scrunched it up and started to pace about the room, glancing now and then at Sven in the far corner, where he was seated at one end of another trolley. Sven had had a phone glued to his ear.

'Ewert, that was Ågestam on the line, just back from a meeting with Errfors about the autopsy. He said he'd like to do Hilding Oldéus as soon as possible. This afternoon, preferably. Then he became curious and wanted to know what we were up to. He had heard about the alert and the evacuation and must have a fair idea that this is something pretty big.'

Ewert stopped in the middle of the room and threw the crumpled paper cup hard against the wall.

'That little creep! He reckons this case smells big, prosecution-wise. Good for his career, so now he wants in on it. But when we ask him to hold Lang he's not so keen. Mafia hitmen who beat junkies to death, oh dear! Not such good material for interviews.'

Ewert didn't like Lars Ågestam.

Generally speaking, he had no time for the young public prosecutors, all prissy hairdos and shiny shoes, kids with no experience, only university degrees, but who could still tell him what was permissible evidence or sufficient grounds for a charge. He and Ågestam had locked horns and come to dislike each other about a year ago, when Ågestam had been appointed as head of investigation in a case involving sexual abuse of minors. Ågestam had performed to the cameras after each day in court, and had been repeatedly told to go to hell and stay there by Grens. Since then, the wannabe leading prosecutor had been obstructive on several occasions and they had continued to shout at each other. This time he swallowed his irritation. When he walked away from Lydia Grajauskas's empty hospital bed almost two hours ago, he had already realised that having to put up with Ågestam was a distinct possibility. The Grajauskas affair would be right up the young prosecutor's street, with the promise of plenty of publicity, and he would surely bow and scrape and brown-nose whoever he needed to, to be seconded to this case.

Ewert paced up and down under the intrusive overhead glare. The harsh strip lights were powerful enough to illuminate surgery, but were just annoying now. He waved crossly upwards. As if that would help.

Sven Sundkvist sat quietly in his corner of the room, resting his hands on the trolley desk and pretending not to notice Ewert's pacing and waving.

'Don't you see, Ewert, history is repeating itself. Grajauskas is driven by shame, just like Oldéus. Do you see what I mean? Shame is what motivates her actions.'

'Sven, not again. Not now.'

'Do you remember what we found in the bathroom cabinet at Völund Street? The vodka and Rohypnol? What do you think they were for? She needed to switch off too. She was ashamed, couldn't bear to face herself.'

Ewert deliberately turned his back on Sven and asked a question. 'How long has she been down there now?'

'You do actually understand, don't you? They humiliate

her over and over again. She hates what is happening to her, but has to carry on. In a way she allows it to happen, but wants nothing to do with it. She tries to live with her shame, but it's impossible, of course.'

Ewert didn't turn round, only slammed his fist into the wall and almost screamed out his question. 'I asked how long? Sven, you heard me. For how long has that woman been threatening to kill five people who she just happened to come across? Answer me!'

Sven took a couple of deep breaths, looked up and turned his head towards the man who was shouting at him. He sighed. Then he checked the clock next to the phone on his trolley.

'It is one hour and fifty-three minutes since Control received her call.'

'How long has she been down there?'

'Our guess is about two hours and twenty minutes. Her guard had a pretty good idea of what time it was when she knocked him down. The lunchtime news had just started when she went to the toilet. Say she spent a few minutes there. Add the few minutes it took to ask him to come along and then attack him. We've timed a slow walk to the mortuary and added it all up. I would say that she has been down there for two hours and twenty minutes, give or take.'

Ewert stared at his watch.

'Two hours and twenty minutes in a closed room, with hostages, but no demands. True, she asked for Bengt, so she can communicate in Russian. Since then nothing but long, bloody suffocating silence. She knows that we're getting tense. Let's turn the tables.'

When Ewert had realised that a command group was required for this operation, he had instantly decided that Sven must be at his side, as well as Edvardson from the national force. Next he contacted Homicide and asked for Hermansson, the young female locum with a broad Skåne dialect. He had seen before that she was careful and systematic and now she had proved to be tough as well. She hadn't batted an eyelid at the Oldéus interrogation when he tried to provoke her, thrusting his crotch and shouting insults, nor when she gave the little drug-crazed idiot a hard slap.

The four of them made up the core command group. He turned to Hermansson, whose desk space was at the other end of Sven's trolley.

'I want you to ring Vodafone. I've already told the suit in their marketing department that they have to comply with our every wish. Tell them to block that woman's bloody mobile. No outgoing calls. None. Next, phone the hospital switchboard and tell them to do the same to the land line they have down there in corpse city. That should do it.'

She nodded, understood. The prostitute, who spoke only Russian and was threatening people with a gun, would not be able to call the shots. They would manage the means of communication and she would have to accept their terms.

Ewert Grens went over to the kettle that someone had put on a stool, and filled it with some water from the jug on the floor beside it. Then he took a plastic cup from the pile and heaped in three teaspoons of instant coffee.

'So now *we* decide if there's going to be any talking. Now *we* are the ones stressing her out. *We* make *her* wait. Not the other way round.'

He didn't wait for an answer.

'And Bengt, where is he?'

Bengt had held on to her. His hands had grabbed her belt, and when he couldn't hold on any longer, she had been dragged away, out of the van while it was still moving.

Twenty-five years. Almost. He was close.

When this mortuary business was done.

There was a witness upstairs. Finally, the sentence Lang had deserved for so long. His punishment for Anni.

Sven pointed in the direction of the door.

'Nordwall is sitting out there, in the waiting room. Sharing a sofa with some of the last Casualty patients.'

Ewert looked, and waited before he spoke.

'I want him in here. In half an hour we'll have the Flying Squad boys in place outside the mortuary. That's when he'll make the first contact.'

The kettle hissed angrily. He turned it off, filled his cup with hot water and gave it a stir with the spoon before blowing on it and attempting to sip the scalding, dark-brown fluid. Then a phone rang, the one that had been put on a cupboard in the middle of the room and had only one designated function.

Hermansson had just had time to get through to the hospital switchboard to tell them about disabling the mortuary phone, but the police emergency call centre had recognised the number and transferred the call, just as they had been instructed.

Ewert checked the caller's number on the screen.

He stood still, letting it ring.

Fourteen signals. He counted them.

When they stopped, he was smiling.

Lydia Grajauskas looked at the clock above one of the doors. She had just tried to ring again. As before, the female student had dialled the number and then held the handset to the doctor's ear.

Fourteen rings. She had waited as the dull note rang out again and again. No reply. It bewildered her. Maybe the call hadn't got through, or maybe the police had simply ignored it.

She had made the hostages line up with their backs to a wall and was now sitting on a chair in front of them, about three metres away. It seemed a good distance; she had full control without getting too near. No one had said a word since the first phone call; they had all withdrawn into themselves and kept their eyes closed a lot of the time. They were afraid. You could always tell.

She looked around. The mortuary, she knew, consisted of several rooms.

There was the narrow room, like a hall, where she had stood for a while, steeling herself before taking the gun out of the plastic bag and marching into the big room where five white coats had been examining a corpse.

In the wall behind the five kneeling hostages a door

opened into an even larger room. A storeroom of some kind, with filing cabinets and trolleys and electronic equipment.

She had known all this before she came here. She had studied the information brochure that the Polish nurse had lent her, and then drawn the ground plan in her notebook and ripped the page out.

There was another room, behind her, and she knew about that too.

She hadn't been in there yet; she had had enough to do with the hostages, who must be made to respect her enough to obey her and had to be watched. But she knew what was behind the large grey metal door. It was the biggest of the rooms, the cold store where the used bodies were kept.

Suddenly one of the male students, the young medic who had wept earlier, started to gasp for breath faster and faster until he was hyperventilating.

She stayed where she was, lowered her gun and looked on as he fell forward again, with his hands tied behind his back. He was shaking badly where he lay, his face pressed against the floor.

'Help him!' The doctor who had spoken for her on the phone earlier sounded hoarse now. He shouted but he couldn't move. He stared at her, his cheeks and neck red with distress.

'Help him! Help!'

Lydia hesitated and observed the man shaking on the floor. Then she got up, raised the gun again and went over to him. Her eyes scanned the others to check they stayed put, backs against the wall, as they were meant to be.

Which was why she didn't notice.

Didn't notice that his hands were free.

He was lying there, shaking, face down, with his untied hands behind him.

She bent down, ready to press her plaster cast against the back of his neck, and that was when he threw himself at her and she fell over backwards. He kept hitting her head with one hand, while trying to pull the gun from her grip.

He was much stronger than her. He was like the rest of them. The men who had lain on top of her, hitting her, raping her, men she hated and would never allow to abuse her again.

That must have been what gave her strength.

At least that was what she thought later.

His hand was tugging at the gun, but she was able to hold on for long enough, until her finger squeezed the trigger and the shot echoed in the quiet room. The man who was humiliating her suddenly let go, fell over sideways. His body was heavy when he hit the floor, his face contorted with the pain that radiated from his leg.

The bullet had hit him just below the kneecap.

He wouldn't walk again for a long time.

A team of men from the Flying Squad were investigating positions in the basement when a faint voice called out from just outside the door to the mortuary suite. Even as they got closer, it was hard to make out any words, it was more like groans. When they saw him, he was lying on his side across the corridor, face down and with his head just outside the mortuary door. He was bleeding from his knees and his head. It was obvious that he was in need of immediate medical care due to blood loss.

They belonged to an elite group and moved slowly, step by measured step, taking every precaution as they had agreed earlier. The bleeding man might have been set up as bait, but they had to bite. Nothing happened when they reached him and lifted his damaged body on to a field stretcher.

Twelve minutes later they carried the casualty into the operations centre, where Ewert was waiting impatiently. He had been informed about an incident involving a man, a medical student called Johan Larsen, who had been one of the five hostages. The former patient had used a large-calibre weapon to shoot him through both kneecaps and then repeatedly used the butt of the gun to hit his face, especially his forehead. As soon as the stretcher arrived, Ewert went over to it, but was brusquely shoved out of the way by the A&E doctor who told him to hold it, the patient needed medical care.

He had so many questions.

He needed so many answers.

Lydia sat back down in the chair, watching the four remaining hostages. She felt tired. It had been a horrible few minutes.

As soon as she had shot him, she had understood that it wasn't enough. From the start she had demanded their respect, tried to impress on them that she was serious. It hadn't worked. When he was on top of her, pushing her down, just like all the other men, she had realised exactly what she had to do.

Push down, push down, again and again. She must keep her grip on power and they must be made to fear her.

She didn't want any more rebellions. They might succeed next time.

She had been on the floor, gun in hand and the student screaming with pain and holding his right knee. She had got up, checked the four lined up against the wall, then looked at the man who had attacked her. She showed them her weapon, pointed to it.

'Not again. If again. Boom.'

Then she had taken a few steps towards him until she was positioned straight above him, astride his body. She had shown the gun to the four over by the wall again and then another shot rang out, his left knee this time. He screamed wildly; she leaned down, looked at the others and then she said Boom, boom and shoved the muzzle into his mouth, holding it there until he was silent. She pulled it out, turned it around and used it to beat him about the face until he lost consciousness, hit him the way the others had always hit her.

Then she pulled the pad of plastic explosive off from between his shoulders and pointed at the woman and the older man. She loosened the rope around their wrists enough to make it possible for them to pull the unconscious man to the entrance, using sign language to make them understand. They were to put him outside in the empty corridor then return to be tied up.

She stayed quite still, aiming at them with her gun.

Soon the man she had shot would be found. They'd take him away and make him talk.

That was good.

What he had to tell them would surely convince them that she meant business and would never give in. For as long as this lasted she would have the respect she wanted.

She wanted to talk to them, the people outside.

No more waiting. It was time to let them know what she wanted.

She gestured with the gun. The woman was to use the mobile again. It would be her third phone call. First the call to announce that she had taken hostages, then the useless attempt.

The student dialled the number and put the phone to the older man's ear. He waited, then he cocked his head. 'Dead.'

She heard him, but wasn't sure she had understood and waved with her gun. 'Again!'

'Dead. No tone.'

He drew the edge of his hand across his throat, like they did in American movies when someone was going to die.

Lydia understood. With the gun still aimed at the hostages, she checked the phone on the wall behind them.

She lifted the receiver. Silence.

Two telephones, her only means of communication. They had cut them off.

She screamed something incomprehensible in Russian at the hostages, shouting and gesturing towards the storeroom. They understood and got up, their legs and backs aching after hours on the floor. They trooped next door, where they sat down again with their backs against another wall.

She felt sure they would obey her, but all the same, before closing the door on them, she pointed at the safety catch, waved the gun at them and said: 'If again. Boom.'

Then she closed the door and hurried past the corpse towards the metal door in the wall opposite.

She opened it and went alone into the large space which was the actual mortuary.

John Edvardson had been only thirty-four years old when he was offered the post as operational head for the national Flying Squad. He had trained as an interpreter, studied Russian and politics at university, and then gone to police college. After graduating, a few years of active police service had been enough to speed him past the queue of self-selected candidates for the Flying Squad post. It had caused a lot of grumbling in the ranks, as always when egos smart, but John had turned out to be the excellent choice his superiors had hoped for. He was wise and popular, a no-nonsense man who didn't feel the need to shout about it.

Ewert had met John several times. There was no friend-ship between them – Ewert wasn't interested in that – but he had learnt enough about the other man to understand what kind of person he was and how good he was at his job, a perfect partner to have at your side in the makeshift operations centre with its clutter of hospital kit.

John took hold of Ewert's arm and led him away from the young man with a bullet in each knee.

'You don't need to interview him now. Not yet. I asked one of my lads to talk to him while they carried him here.'

Ewert listened with his eyes fixed on the doctor who was examining the damaged knees.

'I need to know.'

'You won't get a lot out of him. Maybe later. Anyway, the casualty, Larsen, is positive that the stuff is Semtex. We don't know how he can be so sure. He clammed up at that point. His description fits well enough. It's a "pale brown dough" which she has distributed over the hostages and every door in the room. She also seems to have detonators. Larsen is convinced that she will use them if she needs to.'

'He should know.'

'You see what all this means, don't you?'

'I think so.'

'We can't act. A raid is impossible. If we go in, it's almost certainly goodbye to the hostages.'

Ewert turned to face John and slammed his hand hard on a wheeled stainless-steel table. The noise was terrific. The impact set the metal vibrating.

'I don't get it! Since when did lousy prostitutes carry arms and take hostages?'

'Larsen kept talking about her control. It was very frightening, he said. She was well prepared, had brought rope to tie them up and enough ammunition and explosives to keep us off her back.'

'Control, eh?'

'That's what he said. Control. And courage. He repeated it several times.'

'I don't give a damn about her control. John, I want you to position your men wherever you think is best. And I want police marksmen. If we have to, we'll shoot her.'

Edvardson was on his way out when Ewert called him back. The envelope with the blue notebook was on top of one of the unused trolleys. Ewert handed over a pair of surgical gloves and then slipped the notebook into John's gloved hands.

'This is Grajauskas's. Can you read it?'

John turned the pages slowly. He shook his head.

'No, I can't. Sorry. It's Lithuanian.'

'Sven! What's happening about that bloody interpreter?'

As Ewert Grens turned to the corner where Sven was sitting, the A&E doctor examining Johan Larsen's bullet wounds waved to attract his attention.

'DSI Grens!'

'Yes?'

Ewert was all set for a quick interrogation of Larsen, but the doctor raised his hand, making a stop sign.

'No. Not yet.'

'I need answers.'

'Hold it. He's in no condition to answer anything.'

'Couple of damned kneecaps! People are being held at gunpoint down there!'

'It's not his knees. Can't you see? Shock is setting in. If you don't respect it you might never get any answers.'

Larsen's face was white and absent. He was dribbling. Ewert's hand closed over the handkerchief in his pocket, the one he used to wipe her chin. He closed his eyes for a moment, then opened them to glance at Larsen's drooping, half-open mouth. He had been about to thump the steel table again, but held still with his arm outstretched.

'She takes hostages and tells us all about it. She fills the whole sodding place with explosives, but she makes no demands!'

He completed the movement of his arm, the steel surface reverberated and the sound bounced off the walls.

'Sven!'

'Yes?'

'Phone her. Phone her now! It's time for a chat.'

Lydia had never been inside a real mortuary before. She stopped and looked around as the grey metal door slammed behind her. The room was bigger than she had imagined, twice as big as the Klaipeda dance hall she and Vladi had gone to in their teens. It had pale yellow walls, with white tiling near the autopsy tables. The light was harsh and clinical. Cold boxes, stacked three rows high, running almost all the way along one wall. They had steel doors, the same size as small fridges, about fifty by seventy-five centimetres.

Fifteen per row. That made forty-five boxes with people inside. Chilled bodies, resting. She couldn't grasp it, didn't want to.

She thought of Vladi, as she sometimes did. She missed him. They had grown up together, gone to the same school, had liked walking hand-in-hand. They went for long walks together, making plans to leave Klaipeda. Sometimes, if they reached the edge of the town, they would turn round to look at it, the massed houses and tower blocks, and together dream for something else.

She thought of him as hers. He thought of her as his.

Lydia crossed the hard floor. Large grey tiles. She hadn't seen Vladi for three years and wondered where he was, what he was doing, if he ever thought about her.

She thought about her parents. Her dad in the Lukuskele prison. Mum in the Klaipeda flat. They had both done their best. There hadn't been much love, perhaps, but there hadn't been any hatred or violence. They each had their own things to deal with. She wondered if they too had had dreams once, if they had walked to the edge of the town and looked around, longing for something different.

It was good that her mum didn't know where she was now, a beaten-up whore in a mortuary who was using a gun to threaten people. It was good too that Vladi wouldn't know. She wondered if he would've understood, and thought he might. He would have realised that when someone has been kicked around for long enough, there comes a time when she has to kick back. That's just the way it was. You simply reached a certain point and there was nowhere else to go.

It took a few seconds before she registered that the

telephone was ringing. The one on the wall in the other room, near the trolley with the dead person. She guessed it had rung four times, maybe five.

She ran past the cold boxes, opened the grey metal door, picked up the receiver and waited. She was in pain; the chemical effect of the morphine was starting to wear off and she found it harder to move now. She realised it could only get worse.

A moment or two later, a voice spoke in Russian and she was unprepared for that. A man was speaking Russian with a Scandinavian accent and it didn't twig until he had introduced himself.

'Bengt Nordwall. I'm a policeman.'

She swallowed. She had not expected this. Hoped, yes, but hadn't dared to believe.

'You demanded that I came here.'

'Yes.'

'Your name is Lydia? Is that right? I will listen as long as you—'

She interrupted him at once, tapped the receiver with one finger and spoke loudly.

'Why did you cut the phones?'

'We have—'

She rapped the receiver again.

'You can call me, but I can't call you. I want to know why.'

He paused, and she realised that he was looking to the other policemen around him for support. No doubt they were nodding at each other, making gestures.

'I don't know what you mean. We haven't cut off any phones. We have evacuated large parts of the hospital because you have taken hostages. But we haven't blocked any lines.'

'Explain better.'

'Lydia, we've evacuated the hospital switchboard too. That's probably why you've got problems with your telephone.'

'Telephones! Not one, both of them. Do you think I'm stupid? Some stupid whore from Eastern Europe? I know how telephones work! And now you know I will hurt people if I need to! So don't give me that crap! You've got five minutes. I want the lines connected. Exactly five minutes for you and your mates to fix it. If you don't, I'll shoot one of the hostages. And this time it won't be in the legs.'

'Lydia, we—'

'Don't try to get in here, or I'll blow up the whole lot. The hostages and the hospital.'

He hesitated, looked at his colleagues again. Then he cleared his throat.

'If we fix the phones, Lydia, what do we get in return?'

'What do you get? You're spared finding a dead hostage. Four minutes and fifteen seconds to go now.'

Ewert Grens had listened in to the call and Edvardson had given a simultaneous interpretation. When it ended, he put his earphones down between Sven and Hermansson and drank what was left of his last cup of cold coffee.

'What do you think?'

He looked at each of them in turn. Sven, Hermansson, Edvardson and then Nordwall.

'Well? Is she bluffing?'

John Edvardson was dressed exactly like the men he had just positioned in the hospital. Black leather boots, camouflage-patterned uniform trousers with large square pockets on the thighs, grey waistcoat laden with spare magazines for the gun he had put down on one of the trolleys, and underneath it a flak jacket. The room they were in had already become overcrowded and hot. John was sweating, his forehead glistened and his shirt had large dark stains under the armpits.

'She has demonstrated that she's prepared to injure the hostages.'

'OK. But is she bluffing this time?'

'She doesn't have to. She has the advantage.'

'Why risk losing it?'

'She won't. If she shoots one she has still got three more to go.'

The two men's eyes met. Ewert shook his head.

'Why the hell take hostages in the mortuary? No windows. No other escape routes at all. Even if she shoots the whole lot, we will get her in the end. As soon as she tries to escape, or one of the marksmen gets her in his sight. She must realise that, must have known it from the outset. I don't get it.'

Hermansson was sitting in the middle of the room, but had so far been silent. Ewert had noticed that she had said very little since she arrived. Perhaps chattering wasn't her thing, or perhaps being the only woman made her reticent, as the men were all experienced and automatically took all the space they needed.

But now she stood up and looked straight at Ewert.

'There is another possibility.'

He liked her broad dialect, it inspired trust. He felt he had to take what she said seriously.

'Explain.'

She paused. She wasn't going to let this thought go: she was confident she was right. Still, there was that odd feeling of insecurity. She detested it but couldn't suppress it, not when they looked at her like that, like she was a little girl. She knew they didn't think of her like that, yet that was how she felt.

'Grajauskas is badly injured and must be in pain. She can't hold out for much longer. But I don't think she thinks like you. She has gone beyond the limit already and done things she probably thought herself incapable of. I think she's made up her mind. My feeling is that she has no intention of trying to come out of the mortuary.'

Ewert stood very still, a rare sight. He constantly had to fight his restlessness, his heavy body was always pacing about, and even when he sat down he moved his arms or his feet, stamping or gesticulating or twisting his torso from side to side. Never still.

But now he was. Hermansson had just said what he should have understood himself.

He sighed, started moving again, circled their temporary desk.

'Bengt.'

Bengt was standing in the doorway, holding on to it.

'Yes?'

'Bengt, I want you to phone her again.'

'At once?'

'I have the feeling we're in a bloody hurry.'

Bengt went off to the phone in the middle of the room, but didn't sit down at once. Precious seconds were slipping away and he had to fight down the awful sense of dread, the same feeling he had had in the garden when her torn back had haunted him.

He knew who she was.

He had known ever since he stood outside the flat at Völund Street.

The feeling of unease, of dread, was worse now.

Bengt glanced at the paper on the wall to check the number he was to use, then at Ewert, who was putting the earphone in place.

He dialled. Eight rings went through. Nothing.

He looked at the wall, at the paper displaying the enlarged number of the mobile phone.

He tried again. Eight, ten, twelve rings. No reply.

He shook his head and put the receiver down.

'She's turned them off. Both of them.'

Bengt's eyes followed Ewert, who kept walking in worried circles and whose face was bright red when he shouted.

'A fucking prostitute!'

He was about to shout more abuse when he saw the time. He checked his watch, then he looked at the clock. He lowered his voice.

'One and a half minutes to go.'

She knew the hostages would obey. They were sitting still. Just in case, she had a look. There they were in the store-room, the air thick with archive dust. They were sitting silently in a row with their backs pressed against the wall, their heads turned towards the noise of the opening door and they saw her. She showed them the gun, aiming it at them for long enough to remind them how death felt.

Her dad had fallen forward. His hands had been tied behind his back. She should have run up to him then. She hadn't dared to. There was a gun against her head; it hurt when the man who held it there increased the pressure against the thin skin over her temple.

She shut the door and checked the time. Their five minutes was up.

The receiver was off the phone on the wall, now she returned it to its cradle. She turned the mobile handset on, pressed the button with the green icon and dialled in the code the doctor had told her to use.

She waited only a few seconds.

They phoned, as she thought they would. The black tele-phone on the wall.

She let it ring a few times and then picked up.

'Your time is up.'

Bengt Nordwall's voice. 'Lydia, we need—'

Her hand hit the mouthpiece hard. 'Have you done what I asked?'

'We need more time. Just a little longer. To sort out the fault on the lines.'

Cold sweat was pouring off her. Every breath seemed to whip inside her body. It was hard to keep her thoughts together and fight the pain. She used the gun to hit the mouthpiece. Several blows this time, harder and harder. She said nothing.

Bengt Nordwall waited, heard her walk away and her footsteps growing fainter. She knew he would consult with the others, the men who were listening in, standing with their earphones on and trying to understand.

He gripped the receiver and called out, as loudly as he dared.

'Hello!'

He picked up an echo. His one word danced around the room.

'Hello!'

And then the sound he didn't want to hear. The noise of the gunshot drowned out everything.

She had fired in an enclosed space, and the force hitting the mouthpiece was violent.

It was hard to know. Maybe only a few seconds had passed. Maybe it was much longer.

'Now I've got three live hostages. And one dead. You have another five minutes. My phone lines are to be open for outgoing calls. If they don't work, I'll shoot another one.'

Her voice was steady.

'I advise you to remove the men who're in the corridor outside. I'm about to set off a few charges.'

Ewert had heard the shot. He had waited out her silence. When she spoke he had concentrated on the sound of her voice, to sense if she was calm or just pretending to be calm. That was all he could do; he didn't understand one word of their bloody Russian anyway.

John was leaning over to get close, mumbling the translation of what she was saying. Ewert took it in and swore.

He swung round in Sven's direction. 'Fix the goddam phones, Sven. She has to have her outgoing calls and as fast as hell.' Then back to Edvardson. They agreed that his men should retreat a good bit away from the mortuary entrance. 'No bugger is going to stand outside and get killed!'

Ewert paused for a second, breathing heavily, then put his hand on Sven's shoulder and looked him in the eyes.

'Sven, get a flak jacket and put it on.'

Sven almost twitched, Ewert's hand on his shoulder; he realised he had never touched him before.

'I want you to go down there. Down into the basement. I need to know what's happening. Your immediate impressions. Eyes I can trust.'

Sven settled down at a point where one corridor split in two, about fifty metres from the main door to the mortuary suite. He sheltered behind the wall of the second corridor together with three men from the Flying Squad. After less than two minutes he heard the door they were guarding open and went down on his stomach, pushed himself forwards and looked in the mirror that had been positioned further down the passage.

The corridor was dark, but was lit indirectly by the strong light from behind the opened door. A man was moving about the faint circle of light, just an outline of his dark body, leaning over and pulling at something.

It took a little while before Sven realised what it was.

The man was pulling at an arm. He was dragging a body.

Sven pulled out night-vision binoculars from a bag next to a police officer, considered the risk of showing himself, crawled to the corner of the corridor and directed the binoculars at the man.

It was difficult to make out his features. But he saw him suddenly let go of the arm, disappear through the door and slam it shut.

Sven crept forward, taking deep breaths, pressing the radio to his mouth.

'Grens. Over.'

It crackled. They always did.

'Grens here. Over.'

'I saw a man, just now. Dragging a lifeless body from the mortuary. He's gone back in, left the body in the corridor. I saw the wires. We can't go to it. It's fused!'

Ewert was just about to reply when his voice was drowned by a strange noise. The sound of a human body exploding.

The radio went silent.

Or perhaps it hadn't, and Sven's cry had been there all the time.

'She did it! Ewert! She's blown up the person who was lying there.'

His voice was weak.

'Did you hear me? Ewert! Shit, that all that's left. Only shit!'

Lisa Öhrström was frightened. She had lived with a pain in her stomach for a long time, now a burning, screeching pain that forced her to stop mid-step to check if she could still breathe normally. She had seen the man who had presumably thrown the punches and let the wheelchair roll down the stairs, and knew that the images would haunt her for as long as she could endure living with them.

She hadn't eaten anything, had tried a sandwich, then an apple, but it wasn't any good. She couldn't swallow, wasn't producing any saliva.

She couldn't quite take it in.

That he was dead now.

What she couldn't work out was whether it was a relief to know exactly where he was, what he was *not* doing, that he wasn't hurting himself or others – or was it grief? Or simply that she was preparing herself for having to tell Ylva and Mum?

She spent more time thinking about how to make Jonathan and Sanna understand than anything else. They were Ylva's children, but she loved them like her own. They were her substitute children, the children she'd never had herself.

Your Uncle Hilding is dead.

Your Uncle Hilding was killed when he fell down a staircase.

Lisa went back to the kitchen, needing the coffee she had made this morning. One of the policemen, who had been ordered to stay behind in the ward, had given in to her pleading and, in the end, told her more than he should. She had learnt more about the visitor with the shaved skull who had killed her brother, the man she had recognised in police identification photograph thirty-two. His name was Lang; he was a professional hitman, someone who was paid to threaten and use violence. He had been charged with crimes of violence quite a few times, and in many more cases had been suspected and arrested but gone free because the witnesses had changed their minds about testifying. That was how these people worked, using threats to instil fear, because frightened people don't talk.

Jochum stayed in the car outside the hospital entrance, but didn't bother to look round after Slobodan. The guy was no doubt running around trying to be boss, getting a hard-on because it was him who was tidying up after Jochum this time.

I shouldn't have been seen, he said to himself, but that's what happens, sooner or later you take your eye off the ball, and risk your position. The little guys are after you in a flash, they forget quickly and need to be reminded.

He turned the ignition key to check the time. The figures lit up. Twenty minutes. More than enough. Slobodan should've had time to tell her a thing or two.

Lisa was leaning against the kitchen sink. The coffee was stronger than it should be but she drank some all the same. It felt good to be able to swallow. She wasn't even halfway through her list of patients. A long day ahead, as if the morning hadn't been enough.

She was just about to put the cup down when the ward sister came in, flushed and agitated.

'Dr Öhrström! Shouldn't you go home?'

'Not alone. I couldn't bear it, Ann-Marie. I'll stay here.'

The sister shook her head slowly. She still looked flushed.

'A patient has been murdered and you saw it. Shouldn't you get in touch with the staff counsellor? At the very least?'

'Patients often die.'

'It was your brother.'

'Ann-Marie, my brother died a long time ago.'

The ward sister looked at Lisa and gently touched her cheek.

'There's someone here to see you.'

Lisa caught the other woman's eye, as she drained the remains of the coffee.

'Who?'

'I don't know. But I don't like the look of him.'

'A patient?'

'No.'

Ann-Marie sat down at the table with its red-and-white-checked tablecloth.

'And what does he want?'

'No idea. But he wouldn't go away. Needed to talk to you, he said.'

As Lisa pulled a chair up to the table, she felt the floor under her feet move and heard the cups in the cupboards rattle.

It felt like the whole place was shaking.

She knew that parts of the hospital had been evacuated, but did not know why. The kitchen was shuddering and she had the distinct impression that a bomb had gone off. Not that she had ever experienced a bomb blast, but that was her only thought in the after-shock of the explosion.

Jochum Lang turned the key again, checked the time, started the windscreen wipers so he could see out while he waited. What a day. The rain was set to carry on until after dark.

Then it happened.

He heard it clearly, a dull thud from somewhere inside the hospital. He turned around, tried to peer through the wet glass of the automatic doors. Explosives. He had no doubt. It was that kind of noise.

He prepared himself for more, but that was it. Just the one bang and then silence.

The room was too brightly lit. The bloody overhead light had irritated Ewert ever since he came into the Casualty operating theatre and started to move things that were in the way. He had just heard the noise of a human body exploding, followed by Sven's desperate shouts over the radio.

Bloody lights, he thought. Can't stand it for a moment longer. How can anyone live with all this light? He sat down, then stood up again and almost ran across the room, past the trolley where Edvardson and Hermansson were standing, threw himself at the switch and turned off the light.

A quiet moment. No exploding bodies. No prostitutes taking charge of other people's lives. A quiet moment. The light, his irritation, the dark, the light switch were all tangible things he could understand. And he needed to understand if he was to fathom what had happened. Just a quiet moment.

It was still light enough for them to see each other. Ewert started pacing again; he needed his circling and forgot the darkened lamps. Concentrated on his breathing, felt the blood return to his face. He stopped when he reached the corner where Bengt was sitting with the earphones still on, and put his hand on his friend's shoulder.

'Call her.'

The shaking stopped as abruptly as it had started. Lisa Öhrström was still at the table. She leaned forward and put her hand on top of the ward sister's.

'Ann-Marie.'

'Yes?'

'Where is he?'

'Outside your office. He frightens me. I can't think why, but what with Mr Oldéus being murdered and the police snooping about all morning . . . I don't know, it's too much.'

Lisa was silently looking at the red-and-white-checked pattern on the tablecloth when there was a knock on the door. She turned. A man, dark hair and moustache, slightly overweight. She caught a glimpse of Ann-Marie nodding. It was him.

'Sorry to trouble you.'

His voice was soft, his tone friendly.

'Was it you who wanted to see me?'

'That's right.'

'What is it about?'

'A private matter. Is there somewhere we could talk?'

Lisa's stomach churned. One part of her wanted to scream and run away, the other was suddenly furious. Her attacks of fear had nothing to do with her own life and everything to do with Hilding and his damned addiction. Her whole life had been dictated by his attempts to escape and he controlled her still; even after his death, he was draining her strength.

She shook her head, didn't reply straight away. Her stomach was burning, fear tugging at her mind.

'I'd prefer to stay here.'

Ewert wanted him to call her. Bengt reached out for the receiver; he would have preferred to wait a little longer, a few more moments of peace. He had disliked that shuddering movement under his feet.

His mouth felt so dry, he swallowed, but that wasn't enough. Nothing could rid him of the fear that crawled all over him, the persistent unease. He kept wondering if he should speak up, admit that he knew who she was.

Not yet.

It wasn't necessary yet.

He had better do as Ewert asked. When he leaned forward to dial the number of the mortuary, the phone rang.

He turned, caught Ewert's eye and saw that he was putting in his earpiece. Two rings and then Bengt replied.

'Yes?'

'Nordwall?'

'Yes.'

'You heard that, didn't you?'

'Of course.'

'And you all know what it means?'

'Yes, we do.'

'Shame that it took another dead hostage to make you understand.'

'What do you want?'

'Let me make two points clear. One, I don't negotiate. Two, you can't get in here without blowing the whole place up.'

'We have understood that too.'

'The hostages are fused and so is the mortuary.'

'Lydia, if you keep calm I'm sure we can come to an agreement. But we have to know why you're doing all this.'

'I will tell you.'

'When?'

'Later.'

'What do you want now?'

'*You*. I want you down here.'

Now he knew why she had taken hostages. Somehow, he had known all along. The sense of vague dread now turned into something else, a feeling he had never experienced before. The anguished fear of death.

He closed his eyes and spoke. 'What do you mean?'

'It's hard to keep watching the hostages at the same time as I'm running about playing games with telephones. I want you here. You and I will speak Russian together. You can make the phone calls when it's time to contact your colleagues.'

Bengt's breaths came in bursts. Ewert was listening in but didn't understand. John had left the room to update his boss.

Bengt explained briefly what she had demanded. Ewert shook his head vigorously.

No, no. Not that.

Not ever.

The two police officers patrolling the Söder Hospital precinct noticed the car at once, as soon as they approached the main entrance. It was brand new, expensive and illegally parked, with two wheels up on the narrow pavement. It was hard to see inside because of the pouring rain, but there seemed to be a man sitting in the passenger seat. The driver's seat was empty. They went to either side of the car and tapped lightly on the front windows.

'You can't park here.'

The man was heavily built and bald. His tan looked unreal. He wound the window down, smiled, but didn't answer.

'This whole area is cordoned off. No cars are allowed.'

The guy just sat there smiling.

The officer on his side lost patience and glanced quickly at his colleague to see if he was ready to go for it.

'Your identity card, sir.'

The man in the passenger seat didn't move, as if he hadn't heard or hadn't made up his mind to obey.

'We need proof of your identity. Now, if you don't mind.'

The man sighed exaggeratedly. 'Sure.'

His wallet was in his back pocket. The police officer took the ID card and leaned against the car door while he radioed.

'Check this. Hans Jochum Lang. ID number 570725-0350.'

A minute or so, then they could all hear the answer.

'Hans Jochum Lang. ID number 570725-0350. On the wanted list since this morning.'

Jochum laughed as they manhandled him out of the car.

When they had him belly-down on the wet tarmac, he asked them who their witness might be. He laughed even louder as they searched and cuffed him, then shoved him into the back seat of the patrol car they had called and drove off.

Bengt watched Ewert as he shook his head vigorously. The negative was obvious.

Lighter, that was how he felt. Stronger.

Ewert had decided. He had said no.

Bengt spoke into the receiver again. 'I'm sorry, but that's not possible. Won't happen.'

'No?'

'If I was to come down to the mortuary . . . it's against our policy in hostage negotiations.'

'Killing people is against policy, but I've done it all the same. And I'll kill another one if you don't come down here.'

'There must be alternatives. Let's talk about it.'

'The police get the hostages, the ones that are alive, only when *you* come down here. Three hostages against one. So far.'

He was convinced now. He knew where they were going now.

'Nope. Sorry.'

'I want you. You speak Russian. You've got thirty minutes. Then I'll kill another hostage.'

The tearing, haunting anguish. He was so very afraid.

'Lydia, I—'

'Twenty-nine minutes and fifty seconds.'

Ewert pulled out his earpiece, walked across to the switch and turned on the overhead light.

They looked at the clock on the wall. It was eleven minutes past three.

The man who was standing in the doorway to the medical ward kitchen addressed the ward sister.

'You'd better go.'

Ann-Marie got up, looked at Lisa, who nodded. A nod in return and then the sister left, her eyes fixed on the floor, hurrying out through the door into the empty corridor.

Slobodan watched her as she vanished and then turned to Lisa with a smile. She was about to smile too when he moved quickly close to the table.

'Let me explain.'

He paused.

'All you need to know is, you haven't seen a frigging thing. You haven't got a clue who visited Hilding Oldéus today.'

She closed her eyes. Not more of this. Not now.

A stomach spasm. She vomited into her lap and on the tablecloth. Bloody Hilding. She kept her eyes closed, didn't want to see, not again, not any more. Hilding, Hilding. Fuck him.

'Hey.'

Her eyes were still shut. Her body was still racked by pain, more spasms; she wanted to throw up again.

'Lisa. Look at me!'

Slowly she opened her eyes.

'All you have to do is keep your mouth shut. Simple, isn't it? One word, and you're dead.'

Ewert Grens had expected to feel something more when he got the message that Jochum Lang had been arrested. He had waited for so long and this time had a reliable pair of eyes that had seen Lang in action, someone who could testify to the murder all the way to a life sentence.

But he felt nothing.

It was as if he were anaesthetised. Thinking about Grajauskas, who was holed up in that basement hellhole, playing games with hostages' lives, stole all his energy. Later, when Grajauskas had been dealt with, then he could take the good news on board.

But he did leave the room so he could find a place where he could phone that prosecutor prat in peace. Ågestam had to know that they had a witness this time, a hospital doctor who had seen Lang come along to beat up Hilding Oldéus. They also had a motive. A recent report from two regional detective constables indicated that Lang was acting on behalf of his Yugoslav bosses, who had taken a strong aversion to Oldéus's trick of cutting their speed with washing powder.

Ewert promised himself that under no circumstances would he end the call before Ågestam had understood and had agreed to charge Lang on the grounds of a reasonable suspicion of murder and then ordered a complete body search, mainly for traces of the victim's DNA and possibly some blood. The beating must have caused a fair amount of splashing.

Lisa couldn't hold back any more. Her stomach was in pieces and she leaned over the table and threw up again. She sensed that the man who was threatening her had come closer.

'Lisa, Lisa. You're not well, are you? As I had to wait to speak to you, first downstairs, what with the cops crawling all over the place, and then again outside your office, I made a few phone calls to pass the time. Get that, Lisa? A few quick calls to the right people, that's all it takes, and then you're king of the castle, eh? Know everything you need to know.'

His face came closer still.

'You can't answer. Maybe you should listen instead. Your name is Lisa Öhrström. You are thirty-five years old and have been a doctor for seven. You have worked in this place for the last two years.'

Lisa sat very still. If she didn't move, didn't speak, it might be over soon.

'You are unmarried. No children. Still, never mind, you have these photos pinned to your noticeboard.'

He showed her the photographs. In one of them it was

summer and a six-year-old boy was lying on a wooden jetty next to his older sister. The sun was shining and they both looked a little too red. The other picture was of a Christmas tree and the same children, surrounded by wrapping paper and ribbon, their faces winter-pale but full of anticipation.

Lisa closed her eyes again.

She saw Sanna, she saw Jonathan. They were all she had. She was so proud of them both, felt like another mother to them. There were times when they stayed at her place more than at home with Ylva. They would soon be grown up. In this horrible world. She prayed that they would never have to deal with someone close to them being an addict. Prayed that neither of them would ever be haunted by the sick behaviour patterns driven by addiction. Prayed that they would never have to feel the terrible fear that gripped her now.

She kept her eyes closed and would keep them closed until all this was over.

What you don't see doesn't exist.

'Ewert?'

'Yes?'

'What's going on?'

'I don't know.'

Ewert had no idea. He still couldn't feel anything. She had given them half an hour. Why not twenty minutes? What about that? Or ten? Why not just one minute? What did it matter, when they had no choice?

'Ewert?'

'Yes?'

Bengt Nordwall was holding on tightly to the edge of the trolley. He found it difficult to speak, even to stand up straight. Why ask? Why am I pushing this? he thought. I'm saying things I don't want to say, which means that I'll have to do things I don't want to do. I don't need this. Some bloody awful terror is tearing me apart. I don't want to think about it. Not the commotion in the stairwell, not her lashed back. Not the *Stena Baltica*. None of that.

'Ewert, you know that I have to. We have no choice.'

Ewert knew it was true.

He knew it wasn't true.

The minutes were ticking away. Find a solution, only there isn't one.

He wanted to leave the room, but had to stay.

He had completed the Lang negotiations with Ågestam and looked around for Edvardson, who was still sitting in another room, keeping his boss up to speed with the situation. He tried to contact Sven, who was down in the basement corridors, waiting for the mortuary door to open again.

He needed them there. Hermansson was a good police officer, but he didn't know her in the same way he knew the other two. As for Bengt, well, it was all about him, so he was the last person he ought to discuss the situation with.

'She wants you with her. She will free the others in exchange for you.'

Ewert went over to his colleague, his old friend. He waited.

'Are you listening? I don't understand. Do you?'

Bengt still had the earphones on. He had put the receiver down a while ago, but their conversation was still going round in his head: he heard what she said and he heard what he said and the dialogue got nowhere, the same sentences, over and over again.

He had understood. He would never admit it.

'I don't understand either. But if you want me to, I'll go in.'

Ewert went over to the phone that was their link to the mortuary. He listened to the monotonous tone in the receiver, shouted at it, incoherent phrases about whores and wired-up bodies on the floor and detonators and clocks ticking away time to think.

The colour in his face didn't fade even when he had put the receiver down and circled the trolley a couple of times.

'It would be a breach of duty to order you to go down there. You know that.'

'Yes, I know.'

'And so?'

Nordwall hesitated. I can't, he thought. I can't, I can't, I can't.

'It's your decision, Ewert.'

Ewert carried on pacing, completing one circle after another.

'Hermansson?'

He looked at her.

'Yes?'

'What do you think?'

She looked at her watch. Three minutes to go.

'You can't use the Flying Squad. Half the hospital has been evacuated because we know she has explosives, which she has in fact already used once and threatens to use again. You can't persuade her to do what you want, you've tried that, but she's determined. There's no time to look for other ways to get in there.'

The time, again. She continued:

'She picked a closed room, a perfect one. For as long as she is in there with her gun aimed at the hostages, we simply get nowhere. What do the rules say? Sure, it would be seriously unprofessional to send someone down there on her terms. Is there any alternative? Not really. We have sent police officers in before, in exchange for hostages. There are three people down there who may live for a little longer.'

Just over two minutes to go. Ewert started on another circle. He had listened to what Hermansson had said and realised that he should have asked her opinion much earlier on. Later, when he had time, he would make a point of telling her so. He threw a quick glance at Bengt, who was still sitting there with the earphones on; Bengt, who had two small children and a lovely wife and a garden outside his house . . .

The radio went live.

Sven's voice.

'A gunshot. From in there. No question about it. Just one shot.'

Bengt heard this, but couldn't take any more. He took the earphones off. The tearing feeling in his chest wouldn't let up, intensified.

Ewert got hold of the earphones and shouted into the mike.

'Christ almighty! What's up? We've got two minutes to go. At least!'

Sven seemed to move about. The radio crackled.

'Ewert.'

'Speak.'

'The mortuary door is open. One of the hostages is in the corridor. He or she is pulling at the arm of a body on the floor, dragging it out, same as before. It's hard to make out the details from where I am, but I'm pretty sure the body is . . . lifeless.'

Bengt Nordwall was waiting in one of the dark basement corridors, the one furthest from the lift that led straight to the mortuary door. He was freezing. It was the middle of summer but the floor was cold against his bare feet, the air-conditioning too chilly for naked skin. He had undressed: plain underpants, a small microphone, and an earpiece mounted to his ear.

He had no illusions about what was awaiting him in the mortuary. He knew who she was, that it was a matter of life and death. For him. For the others. He was responsible for the fact that several people's lives were in danger.

He turned round, as he had twice already, to check that the three armed policemen were right behind him.

'Ewert. Over.'

He kept his voice low, trying to maintain contact for as long as possible.

'Receiving, over.'

There was nothing to hold on to.

He wasn't sure that he would be able to stand upright for much longer.

He thought of Lena, somewhere in their shared home,

curled up with a book in her hand. He missed her. He wanted to sit beside her.

'Just one thing, Ewert.'

'Yes?'

'Lena. I want you to tell her. If anything happens.'

He waited. No reply. He cleared his throat.

'OK. I'm ready.'

'Good.'

'Ewert, I'll go in there whenever you say.'

'Now.'

'Now. Is that right?'

'Yes. Walk to the door and stop there. Hands above your head.'

'Right. I'm walking.'

'Bengt?'

'Yes?'

'Good luck.'

He walked noiselessly, bare feet on the concrete floor. So cold. The place was so cold. Standing in front of the mortuary door he was freezing. The Flying Squad guys were some ten or fifteen metres behind him. He waited, though not for long; he counted the seconds and less than half a minute had passed when a middle-aged man with grey hair came out. The man, who wore a white coat with a name tag saying Dr G. Ejder, stepped past Bengt without looking at him. A string of plastic explosive lay between his shoulders. Ejder held up a mirror, angling it so that whoever was standing just inside the door, breathing audibly but out of sight, could see that the new arrival was alone and undressed.

'Ejder?'

Bengt whispered, but the doctor's eyes didn't focus on him. Ejder lowered his hand, waved a little with the mirror. They were to go inside.

Bengt didn't move at once. Just one more moment.

Eyes closed.

Breathe in through the nose and out through the mouth. He shut out the fear. From now on his task was to observe. He was responsible for all their lives.

Ejder wanted to go in and seemed impatient. They stepped over the body on the floor. As they left the corridor Bengt pressed his shaking finger gently to the electronic gear in his ear, making sure it was still there.

He was freezing. He was sweating.

'Ewert.'

'Receiving, over.'

'The hostage in the corridor is dead. No visible blood, so I can't make out where she shot him. But the smell is odd, strong. Harsh.'

He saw her the moment he stepped inside. It was her. He recognised her. The *Stena Baltica*. The other day he hadn't really been able to see her face, only the lashed back and the stretcher blanket covering most of her. Now he was certain.

He tried to smile, but it felt like cramp in his lips.

She was standing near the middle of the room, holding a gun to the head of a young man in a white coat.

She was small, frail, her face swollen and scratched, one of her arms in plaster. She supported her weight heavily on one leg; the other must be painful, a damaged hip or knee.

She pointed at him. Spoke. 'Bengt Nordwall.'

Her voice sounded as calm and collected as ever.

'Turn around, Bengt Nordwall. Hands up all the time.'

He turned, observing the explosives covering every door frame.

One turn, then he faced her again. She nodded.

'Good. Tell these people they can leave. Go through the door one by one.'

Ewert sat down on the floor of his temporary operations office and listened to the voices from the mortuary. John Edvardson was back at his side to translate the Russian.

Hermansson had also got hold of a pair of earphones and sat at her trolley making notes of the absurd exchanges, attempting to alleviate the stress by giving her hands something to do.

Bengt was in there. He had done what Grajauskas had asked and told the hostages they could leave. Now he was the only one left.

Suddenly he spoke again in Swedish, his voice strained but managing to stay calm. Ewert recognised the tone well, knew how close he was to cracking up.

'Ewert, it is all one fucking big con. She hasn't shot anyone. All the hostages are still here. All four of them are alive. They've just walked out. She has got about three hundred grams of Semtex round the doors, but she can't detonate it.'

Her voice now, sounding agitated. 'Speak Russian!'

Ewert heard what Bengt had said. Heard it, but didn't understand. He looked at the others and saw his own bafflement reflected in their faces. There must have been more people in there from the start, more than five. One of them had been kneecapped, one blown to bits and one more had been dragged outside the door a few minutes ago. But there were still four people who left, walked out of there alive.

There was Bengt's voice again, still speaking Swedish. He seemed to be standing still, facing her.

'All she's got is a handgun. A nine-millimetre Pistolet Makarova. Russian army officer's sidearm. The explosive. She can't detonate it without a generator or a battery. I can see a battery, but it isn't connected to any cables.'

'Speak Russian! Or you'll die!'

Ewert sat there, listening to John's translation.

She told Bengt to stay still in front of her. No talking.

She spat on the floor in front of him, then demanded that he take off his underpants.

When he hesitated, she took aim at his head and threatened him until he obeyed.

Grens got up quickly. She had tricked them somehow and Bengt was defenceless. He looked at John, who nodded.

He radioed the men, issued instructions for an immediate break-in and gave permission for the marksmen to use live rounds.

'You are naked.'

'That's how you wanted it.'

'How does that feel? What is it like to be here, in a mortuary, standing naked in front of a woman with a gun?'

'I have done what you asked me to do.'

'You feel humiliated, don't you?'

'Yes.'

'All alone?'

'Yes.'

'Afraid?'

'Yes.'

'Kneel.'

'Why?'

'On your knees. Hands behind your head.'

'Haven't you done enough?'

'On your knees.'

'Like this?'

'There, you can do it.'

'Now what?'

'Do you know who I am?'

'No.'

'Don't you remember me?'

'What do you mean?'

'What I say. Do you remember me, Bengt Nordwall?'

'No.'

'You don't?'

'No.'

'Klaipeda, Lithuania. The twenty-sixth of June, two thousand and two.'

'I have no idea what you're talking about.'

'The *Stena Baltica*. The twenty-sixth of June, two thousand and two. At twenty-five minutes past eight in the evening.'

Ewert had seen Lydia Grajauskas only once, just over twenty-four hours ago. She was unconscious inside the flat with the broken-down door; he had just pushed past the shit they called Dimitri-Bastard-Pimp and was walking quickly through the hall towards Lydia's naked body. One of her arms was broken, her face was swollen and bruised and her back was a mass of bleeding gashes, more wounds than he could count. He had come across girls like her before, different names, but the same old story. Young women who opened their legs and were beaten up, then cared for until they healed, so they could open their legs and be beaten again. They would go off the radar as suddenly as they had turned up, moved on to a new flat somewhere else and a new set of customers, do the rounds a couple of times before they disappeared for good and were replaced by new women. There were always new ones to be bought from people who traded in people, three thousand euros for young girls, who also coped better with the beatings.

He had seen her carried out on a stretcher.

He could understand her hate; it wasn't hard to understand that constant humiliation would force you in the end to choose between giving up and going under, or trying to humiliate someone else as a payback.

But how she found the strength to keep her broken body upright, to occupy a mortuary and threaten people in her faint voice, that was utterly beyond him. And why was she targeting doctors and policemen? What was she actually after? He didn't understand, not even at the point when he interrupted John's translation and shouted out loud.

'The *Stena Baltica*? That's a bloody boat! This is something personal! Bengt, over! Fuck's sake, Bengt. Stop it! Squad, move in! All clear. Repeat, move in!'

*　　*　　*

Afterwards all their accounts differed slightly, mostly in the time dimension, but then it's often a fact that time is the most difficult thing to pin down when someone stops breathing. In general, their observations with regard to the events were consistent, what happened and when. After all, they had stood side by side in the Casualty operating theatre, listening to the same radio and heard the sounds of two shots in quick succession, then one more shot shortly after, followed by the crash when the Flying Squad battered down the door to the mortuary suite and went in.

NOW
PART TWO

Every death has its consequences.

Ewert Grens knew that. He had worked with the police for thirty years; most of them had been spent investigating murders, which meant that his work often started with death. That was what he did, worked with death and its consequences.

And the way the dead continued to live on afterwards was always so different.

Some just disappeared quietly, no one asked for them, no one missed them, it was as if they never existed.

Others seemed to be more alive in death than in life, with all the commotion, all the investigation, the endless words from friends and strangers that had never been spoken out loud before, but were now repeated over and over again until they became true.

You breathe and then a moment later you don't breathe any more.

But the consequences, the consequences of your death, depend entirely on what caused you to stop breathing. When the sound of the three shots rang out in his earphones, Ewert knew instantly that something terrible had happened. The sound invaded his mind, his very being.

So he should have been able to understand his grief, the grief he did not allow himself to feel, but that would continue to gnaw at him until he too ceased to exist. He should perhaps have also sensed the loneliness that would follow, that it would be even worse than he had feared.

But not the rest.

Despite having listened to the strange and violent death, Ewert Grens could never have anticipated that he would think back on the days that followed, and the consequences of this death, as the most hellish time of his life.

He did not cry. It is hard to say why – he himself has no explanation – but he could not cry. He doesn't cry now. Afterwards, he didn't cry when he entered the mortuary through the splintered door – when he saw two people on the floor with holes through their heads, the blood that had not yet dried.

Bengt was lying on his back. He had been shot twice.

Once through his left eye. Once in his genitals, which were covered by his blood-soaked hands. She had aimed between his legs first and he had instinctively put his hands there.

He was naked, pale bare skin against the grey floor tiles. Lydia Grajauskas lay next to him with her plastered arm twisted oddly under her. She had shot herself in the temple and must have hit the floor hard, almost bouncing, to end up lying face down.

Ewert moved cautiously along the new marker lines dividing up the room. He had to get an overview, had to be efficient, that was what he always did, to escape his feelings, work work work to shut out everything else. He didn't need any drugs to block off his emotions, he just got on with the work in hand, head down and no let-up until the worst had passed.

He gently prodded the bare white thigh with his foot.

You bloody fool.

How can you lie there without looking at me?

Sven Sundkvist was standing at a distance. He saw Ewert prod Bengt Nordwall's body with his foot and then silently bend over the dead man, a body surrounded by a white outline. He went and stood just behind his boss.

'Ewert.'

'Yes.'

'I can take over now.'

'I'm in charge of this operation.'

'I know. But I can take over down here. Just for a while. I'll manage the site examination. You don't need to be here, not now.'

'Sven, I'm working.'

'I know it must be—'

'Sven, how did a prostitute manage to take us to the cleaners like this?'

'Ewert, please. Just go.'

'Can you tell me that? If not, move over. You must have things to do too.'

You bloody, bloody idiot.

Say something.

You're not saying anything.

Just lying there on the floor. Not saying a word. And not a stitch on.

Get up!

Ewert recognised the four forensic technicians who were down on their hands and knees, crawling all over the mortuary suite looking for the sort of things forensics look for. Two of them were his own age, and for years they had met just like this, at crime scenes where life had slipped into death. They would stay in touch for as long as the investigation continued, then nothing for a few months, until there was another suspicious death. Then they would meet up again and chat. He touched Bengt's thigh for a second time and then walked over to the nearest of the technicians, who was hunched over a supermarket carrier bag, examining it for fingerprints.

'Nils?'

'Ewert, I'm very sorry. I mean that Bengt—'

'Please, not now. I'm working. That bag, is it hers?'

'Seems to be. Quite a few bullet magazines left. Some explosive and a few detonators. A couple of pages torn from a notebook. And a video.'

'How many people have handled it?'

'Two. Small hands. Two rights, two lefts. I'm pretty sure they were both made by women.'

'Two women?'

'One set is probably hers.'

The technician, whose name was Nils Krantz, nodded in the direction of Lydia Grajauskas's still body. Ewert glanced at her and then pointed at the video.

'Let me have that when you've finished with it.'

'Sure. Give us a couple of minutes more.'

Ammunition. Explosives. A video. Ewert's eyes were fixed on her lacerated back.

'What were you after? What did you really want?'

Suddenly someone was calling out, a man's voice out in the corridor.

'Ewert!'

'Yes! I'm here.'

'Come and see this.'

Ewert hadn't realised that he would get there so quickly, but was glad that he had come as asked.

'Look.'

Ludwig Errfors stood in the middle of fragments of what had once been a human body, the body Grajauskas had made them carry out and blow up in order to make her message absolutely clear to everyone.

'Ewert. Look at this. A dead body.'

'I don't have time for games.'

'Please. Have a closer look.'

'What the hell's your problem? I heard the blast. I know he or she is as dead as you get.'

'This is a dead person and was a dead person at the time of the blast, and has been a dead person for about a week.'

Ewert reached out and touched the arm that Errfors was holding. It was colder than he had expected. Earlier he had felt, somehow, cheated, without understanding why. Now he knew.

'Look around. No blood. Just a peculiar smell in the air. Can you smell it, Ewert?'

'Sure.'

'Describe it.'

'Bitter. A little like bitter almonds. Bengt said he picked up an astringent smell just before he went in.'

'It's formaldehyde.'

'Formaldehyde?'

'She blew up one corpse and she shot another. Not the hostages. The first time, yes, she shot the student who attacked her. But he was the only person she shot.'

Errfors took one more look at the arm that had been lifeless for at least a week, shook his head and put it back where it had been. Ewert left him examining the remains in the corridor, moving from one body part to the next.

No blood anywhere. And that smell.

She had used the dead bodies and left the hostages alone. She had only wanted to get Bengt there. That was all.

That was all she had really wanted.

He went back inside, to Bengt's naked body, to the woman in her oversized hospital clothes.

You're not saying anything.

Bengt.

Talk to me, for Christ's sake!

He almost stepped in the blood from the wound on her temple when he went closer to them.

So it was him you wanted all along.

Bloody whore!

I don't get it.

He didn't hear Nils coming up behind him, nor that he

231

asked him to take the sealed plastic bag with the video in it. Nils tapped Ewert on the back, repeated what he had just said and held out the sealed plastic bag.

'The video, Ewert. The video is all yours now.'

Ewert turned.

'Right. OK. Good, Nils. Any prints?'

'Same as on the bag and the rest. Two different people, probably women. Grajauskas and someone else.'

'And it was with the ammunition?'

'Yep. In that carrier bag.'

Nils made to go. Ewert called after him.

'Do you need it back?'

'Yes. Chain of custody. You know.'

Ewert watched Nils as he pulled on white fabric gloves and went off to investigate a door to some kind of equipment store. She had smeared pale brown dough around the frame.

'Ewert?'

Sven Sundkvist was sitting on a stool by the wall-mounted telephone from which she had rung – the one they blocked for outgoing calls, and then unblocked. Ewert closed his eyes and tried to visualise her, gun pointing at the hostages, talking into the phone, threatening, but demanding nothing. A frail creature with one arm in plaster, who had forced them to evacuate one of the largest hospitals in the country and had practically every policeman and journalist in the city on the run. For a few hours that little whore had kept as many men busy as she had ever fucked.

'Ewert.'

'What is it?'

'The widow. Remember.'

Ewert heard Bengt's voice, the conversation they just had, when his old friend, his link with the past, was still alive. He had stood there in his underpants in that bloody corridor and asked Ewert to speak to Lena, *if anything happens I want you to tell Lena.* As if he had known or had a premonition of what awaited him behind the mortuary door.

232

'What's that, Sven?'

Sven shrugged.

'Just that you know her. You should go over there.'

He hadn't noticed before, but now he registered that the pale body looked almost calm: hands resting close together on his belly, his legs straight, feet turned slightly outwards and no trace of the distress he must have felt when the gun was pressed to his forehead.

I have to tell Lena.

Talk to me!

I have to do it.

I am still alive.

Dead!

You're not alive.

You are dead!

Grens knew that he had kept them waiting for too long. Lang had to have a full body search. Every minute that ticked by reduced their chance of finding crucial remains of blood or DNA from Hilding Oldéus.

He had insisted on being present because he wanted to be in complete control until the man he hated was locked away. Ewert commandeered a patrol car, with blue light flashing. When he arrived at Berg Street, the building looked empty. He thanked the driver and took the lift to the cells. The surgery was at the end of the corridor and Ewert hurried past the rows of thick metal doors leading on to tiny cells; his limping footsteps echoed in the ugly, bleak place, where even the light seemed tired.

He had been to the surgery before to attend informal interrogations and meetings. It was properly equipped with a few impressive-looking pieces of electronic machinery, an examination bench pushed up against a wall, steel instruments lined up on a mobile table and a couple of electronic instruments; Grens had no idea what they were used for.

He scanned the room slowly.

All these people. He counted them. Ten.

Lang stood in the middle of the floor, his body lit by a powerful lamp. He was naked and handcuffed. Bulging muscles, shaved skull, oddly staring eyes. He looked up when Ewert entered the room.

'You as well.'

'What's that, Lang?'

'You want to see my dick too?'

Ewert just smiled. Trying to provoke me, are you? Can't hear you. Not this time. My best friend just died.

He exchanged silent nods with the others. Four uniformed men, three guards and two technicians. All familiar faces.

He took note of the stuff on the bench, a pile of paper bags, one for each item of Lang's clothing. One of the technicians, wearing transparent rubber gloves, was just putting a black sock in the last bag. His colleague was holding what looked like a tube-shaped lamp.

The forensic technician looked up. No more waiting about, Grens was here at last.

He turned on the lamp and directed it at Lang. Its blue light started a slow sweep from face to feet, but soon stopped at a possible spot of blood on the skin. The other technician picked up a sample on a cotton swab for later analysis. Carefully they went over the naked man's big body, one part after another, looking for evidence that could make or break the case against him.

'Hey, Grens. What do you think?'

Lang stuck his tongue out and thrust his pelvis backwards and forwards.

'What d'you reckon? Every bloody time. Same thing. You all come over for a look.'

More action, faster now. Lang moaned and stuck his tongue out at the two nearest officers.

'I mean, look at them. Not real policemen, are they? Grens, admit it. More like fucking Village People – be proud, boys. Be gay. Sing with me now, *It's fun to stay at the YMCA*.'

Lang took a step forward, legs apart, still thrusting with his crotch. One of the two young policemen was thoroughly fed up by now. His breath came more quickly and he moved closer to Lang.

'You there. Step back.'

Ewert stared angrily at the officer and didn't look away until the man was back in his original position.

Then he turned to Lang.

'You're going down. For life this time. The sentence you should have had twenty-five years ago. We've got a witness.'

'Life? For GBH? You're kidding.'

One last pelvic thrust, another 'Be proud, be gay' and a smacking kiss.

'Look, Grens. Fucking identity parades get you nowhere. You know that.'

'And threatening behaviour.'

'I've been cleared of that as well. Six times.'

'Perverting the course of justice. That's what we call it.'

Jochum Lang stood still again. The technicians glanced at Ewert, who nodded. Carry on. The bluish light started and stopped. Cotton swabs delicately mopping up DNA fragments in one of Lang's armpits.

Ewert had seen what he came for. The lab report would be ready in another day or two.

He sighed.

What a bloody awful day.

He knew what he had to do next. He had to go, go to her, to Lena, bringing death to her home. For her, Bengt was still alive.

'Hey, Grens.'

He turned. Jochum Lang was still standing there, stark naked in the middle of the room, while a technician prodded under his toenails.

'Yes?'

Lang's mouth pursed for a kiss.

'So-o sad, Grens, about your old mate. I heard about the

shoot-out in the mortuary. He isn't with us any more, is he? Out cold on the floor? What a shame. You two got on so well. Just like you used to with that uniformed chick of yours. Life is tough, don't you think? Eh, Grens?'

More smacking noises, little kisses in the air.

Ewert Grens stood very still, controlled his breathing, then turned on his heel and left.

It took them less than twenty-five minutes to reach Eriksberg, the suburb where Ewert had been only two days earlier. They were silent for the whole journey. Sven was sitting beside him, driving. He had phoned Anita and Jonas first to say he'd be even later than he had thought, so maybe they should have the birthday cake tomorrow instead. Ludwig Errfors was sitting in the back, as Ewert had asked him to bring tranquillisers and to be there, just in case. People react so differently when death knocks on their door.

Mentally, Ewert had still not left the police surgery. Lang had stood there naked and scornful, his mocking movements and all the rest taking him one step closer to a life sentence than before. Lang didn't realise that if he continued behaving like all the other bloody thugs, that as long as he remained silent, and played the predictable interrogation game – denying everything or saying nothing whatsoever, lying – as long as he didn't admit that he had at least roughed up Oldéus, he would be up for a murder as well. The bastard didn't know that there was a witness who dared to speak up, threats or no threats. Ewert Grens was struck by how ironic it was that, right now, when they had finally found someone who was courageous enough to stand witness against Lang in connection with his violent crimes, he was on his way to tell Bengt's wife about the death of her husband; another meaningless killing in the same building where Lang had been careless enough to be seen by the wrong person.

Anything. He would give anything not to be on his way to this person, who still didn't know.

Ewert wasn't really that close to her.

He had sat in their garden and their sitting room, talked and drunk coffee in their company once a week since they moved in, ever since Lena married his best friend. She had always been warm and friendly and he had responded in his way, as best he could, but they had never become close. It could be the age difference, or that they were simply too unlike one another. But they had both cared for Bengt, and shared love was perhaps enough.

When they pulled up outside Ewert sat in the car for a while and looked at the front of the house. Lights on in the kitchen and the hall, but the upstairs rooms were dark. She was probably downstairs then, waiting for her husband. Ewert knew that they usually had a late supper.

I can't bear this.

Lena is in there and she knows nothing.

He is alive and well as far as she's concerned.

As long as she doesn't know, he's still alive. He dies only when I tell her.

He knocked on the door. There were young children in the house and they might be asleep; with any luck they would be. When did children go to sleep? He waited on the gravel path, with Sven and Ludwig close behind him. She was slow in answering. He knocked again, a little harder, more persistently, heard her quick footsteps, saw her take a look through the kitchen window before coming to unlock the front door. He had been a messenger of death many times before, but never to someone he actually cared about.

I shouldn't have to stand here.

If you were alive, I wouldn't be standing here at your door, with your death in my hands.

He didn't have to say anything. He just stood there and held her in his arms, on the steps, with the door wide open. He had no idea for how long. Until she stopped crying.

Then they all went to the kitchen and she made some

coffee while he told her everything he thought she might want to know. She didn't say a word, nothing at all, until the first cup of coffee, when she asked him to repeat everything in detail. Who the woman was, how Bengt's execution had been set up, what he had looked like and what the woman had really wanted.

Ewert did as she asked, describing the events blow by blow until she couldn't take any more. He knew it was the only thing he could do, talk to her, tell her again and again, until she finally started to understand.

Lena wept for a long time, now and then looking up at him, Sven and Errfors.

Later she edged close to him, grabbed his arm and asked him how he thought she should tell the children. Ewert, what do you want me to tell the children?

Ewert's cheek was burning.

They were back in the car, going along the almost empty E4 towards the city centre. The street lamps would come on soon.

She had hit him hard.

He hadn't expected it. They were just about to leave, out in the long hall, when she rushed over to him, shouting, *You can't say things like that* and slapped him. He was baffled at first, but had had time to think that she had the right to hit out before she raised her arm again, screaming, *You can't say things like that*. He stopped. What else could he do? He couldn't do any of the usual things he did when people threatened to hit him. When her voice rose to a shriek, Sven grabbed her arm and led her firmly to the kitchen.

He looked at Sven now, sitting beside him. He was driving back to town a little too slowly in the middle lane, lost in thought.

Ewert rubbed his cheek. It felt numb; her hand had hit the bone.

He didn't blame her.

He was the bringer of death.

It was past ten o'clock, but a light summer's night, quite beautiful now that the incessant rain had actually stopped. Sven had dropped him off at the police headquarters. They had been just as silent on the way back, as they had on the way there. Lena's despair had lingered, more powerful than words.

Ewert Grens went into his office. His desk was laden with yellow and green Post-it notes, informing him about journalists who had tried to contact him and would call again. He binned all the messages. He would arrange more press conferences as far away from here as possible and get the PR pros to field the questions he didn't want to hear. Sitting at his desk, he spun on his chair a couple of times, stopped and listened to the silence, spun round again, stopped. He couldn't really think, tried to go through the events of the last hours in his mind. Bengt's death and Grajauskas's death. The unharmed hostages. Bengt, unseeing, on the floor. Lena holding his arm and wanting him to tell her every detail, one at a time. It was hopeless. He couldn't do it. They weren't his thoughts, so he sat there, spinning around and around, without pursuing anything.

One and a half hours alone, spinning on his chair without a single thought.

The cleaner, a smiling young man who spoke decent Swedish, knocked and Ewert let him in. His presence broke the monotony. For a few minutes there was someone who emptied the waste-paper basket and pushed a mop around. Better than the thoughts he could not think.

Anni, help me.

Sometimes he missed having people, sometimes loneliness was just ugly.

He dialled the number he knew by heart. It was late, but he knew she would be awake. When life is one long half-sleep, maybe rest matters less.

One of the young care assistants answered. He knew who she was. She had worked extra in the evenings for a few years now, to top up her student loan, to make life a little easier.

'Good evening. Ewert Grens speaking.'

'Hello, Mr Grens.'

'I'd like to talk to her.'

A pause. She was probably looking at the clock in reception.

'It's a little late.'

'I know. Sorry to trouble you, but this is important.'

He heard the young care assistant get up and walk down the corridor. A few minutes later her voice came back.

'She's awake. I told her that you're waiting to talk to her on the phone and asked someone to help her with the receiver. Connecting you now.'

He heard Anni breathe, between the gurgling and mumbling she usually made on the phone. He hoped someone was around to wipe away the dribbles.

'Hello, Anni. It's me.'

Her shrill laughter. His body grew warm, almost relaxed.

'You have to help me. I don't understand what's going on.'

He spoke to her for nearly quarter of an hour. She panted and laughed now and then, mostly staying silent. He missed her the moment the call ended.

Getting up from the chair his body felt heavy, but not tired. He walked along the corridor to the far too large meeting room. The door was never locked.

He fumbled about in the dark, looking for the switch on the wall and found it higher up than he remembered. It was for not only the lamps, but also the TV and the video and the whirring overhead projector. He had never got a grip on how these bloody things worked and swore a great deal before he managed to find a channel that worked with the video.

Wearing plastic gloves, he extracted the cassette from the bag he had been given at the mortuary, which he had kept hidden in the inner pocket of his jacket.

The first images were drowning in bright bluish light. Two women were sitting on a sofa in a kitchen with sunlight pouring in through a window behind them. Obviously whoever was holding the camera wasn't sure how to balance brightness and focus properly.

The women were easy to recognise all the same.

Lydia Grajauskas and Alena Sljusareva. They were in the flat with the electronic locks, where he had seen them for the first time.

> *They wait in silence, while the cameraman moves the lens up and down, then turns the microphone on and off, presumably to test it. They look nervous, the way people do when they are not used to staring at the single eye that preserves whatever it looks at for posterity.*
>
> *Lydia Grajauskas speaks first.*
>
> " *Это мой повод. Моя история такая.* "
>
> *Two sentences. She turns to Alena, who translates.*
>
> 'This is my reason. This is my story.'
>
> *Grajauskas looks at her friend and says two more sentences.*
>
> " *Надеюсь что когда ты слышишь это того о ком идет речь уже нет. Что он чувствовал мой стыд.* "
>
> *She nods with a serious expression and waits, for Alena, who turns to the camera again and translates.*
>
> 'When you hear this, I hope that the man I am going to talk about is dead. I hope that he has felt my shame.'
>
> *They speak slowly, careful to enunciate every word in both Russian and Swedish.*

Ewert Grens sat in front of the TV for twenty minutes.

What he saw and heard did not exist. Lydia was transformed once more from perpetrator to victim, from whore to abused woman.

He got up and slammed his fist on the table as he usually did, hit it several times, hard enough to hurt. He shouted and hit. Sometimes there was nothing else you could do.

I was there a few hours ago.

It was me who had to talk to Lena!

Who do you think is going to tell her about this?

She doesn't deserve this.

Do you hear me?

She must never know this.

He must have shouted out loud; he thought it was only in his mind, was certain of it. But his throat felt rough, which it wouldn't if he had been silent.

Ewert looked at the empty, flickering screen and rewound the tape.

`'When you hear this, I hope that the man I am going to talk about is dead. I hope that he has felt my shame.'`

He listened to their introduction again and then rewound it again.

He could see them on the mortuary floor. She was face down, her arm twisted underneath her body. Bengt naked, his genitals ripped by the bullet, the hole through his eye.

If only you had admitted you knew her when she asked.

Bengt. Fucking hell!

She asked you!

Maybe if you'd said yes . . .

Maybe if you'd told her that you knew who she was.

Then you might still be alive.

That might have been enough.

That you acknowledged her, understood.

He hesitated, but only for a few seconds. Then he pressed

the red button with REC on it in white letters. He was going to wipe what he had just seen. From now on it no longer existed.

Nothing happened.

He pressed the same button again, twice, but the tape didn't move. He checked the cassette and saw that the safety tab on the back was broken. It was their story and they had done everything they could to make sure that no one stole it from them, recorded over it. Ewert looked around. He knew what he had to do.

He got up, stuffed the tape into his pocket and left the room.

It was after midnight by the time Lena Nordwall stood at the sink with the four mugs that still smelt of coffee. She rinsed them in hot water, in cold, in hot and in cold again. It took her half an hour before she felt able to let go. She dried them one by one, needed them to be absolutely dry, using a clean towel to make sure. Then she lined them up on the kitchen table. They gleamed in the lamplight.

Lena picked the mugs up, one by one, and threw them against the wall.

She was still standing by the sink when one of the children came downstairs, a little boy in his pyjamas. He pointed at the shards of china and said to his mother that mugs make an awful noise when they break.

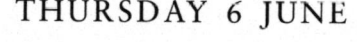

THURSDAY 6 JUNE

Ewert's back ached.

The office sofa was really far too small; he had to get it changed. His sleep had been troubled. Bengt's lie, Grajauskas and the other girl on the video, Anni's hand that he couldn't get hold of, the tears that had drained him. His clothes were wrinkled and his breath was stale. He had tried to work when the hours dragged, but he couldn't concentrate on the investigation of the Oldéus and Lang case. Grajauskas and her friend had commandeered his thoughts. They had looked pale and spent when they talked about his best friend and the shame they hoped he would feel. He had tried to get back to sleep, twisting and turning until the light forced him to get up.

He absently touched the plastic parcel in his pocket. He had tried to wipe the tape and had failed. He had made up his mind and wasn't going to change it. It had to go.

The police house was still totally empty. He bought a dry cheese sandwich and a carton of juice from the machines in the corridor, breakfasted and then went to the locker rooms and had a long shower.

I must see her again soon.

Last time I brought death.

This time must I bring shame?

The water was hammering on his skull and shoulders. That damned mortuary was being washed down the drain and the tension began to slip. He used somebody's forgotten towel, dressed and got another coffee from the machine. Black, as usual. Slowly he woke up.

'Good morning, sir.'

He heard her voice from one of the rooms in passing. She was sitting on a chair in the middle of the floor and surrounded by papers, on the sofa, the desk, the top of the bookshelf, and the floor.

'Hermansson. You're in early.'

She was so young. Young and ambitious. That usually wore off.

'I'm reading the witness statements from the hospital. They're really interesting. I wanted to have time to go through them properly.'

'Found anything I should know about?'

'I think so. Well, I haven't got them all yet. The statements from Grajauskas's guard and the boys who were watching TV in the dayroom are being printed now.'

'And?'

'For one thing, the link between Grajauskas and Sljusareva looks strong.'

Perhaps it was her nice dialect, or her calm manner, whatever it was, he listened to her now, just as he had listened to her yesterday in the temporary operations centre, though it was too late. He should tell her. That she was good, that he trusted her and that didn't happen often.

'Tell me more.'

'Can you give me a couple of hours? I'll have a clearer picture then.'

'Right. See me after lunch.'

He was about to go. He ought to tell her.

'Hermansson.'

'Yes?'

She looked at him and he had to go on.

'You did a good job yesterday. Your analysis . . . well, what you said. I'd like to work with you again.'

She smiled. He hadn't expected that.

'Praise! From Ewert Grens. That's very special.'

He stood there, feeling something new. Abandoned perhaps, or exposed. He almost regretted having complimented her and switched tack; anything really, as long as it was different.

'You know the store where electronic stuff is kept?'

'Sorry?'

'I need a couple of things from in there, but I've never been. Do you know where it is?'

Hermansson got up. She was laughing. Ewert didn't understand why. She looked at him and laughed, making him feel uncomfortable.

'Sir? Just between us?'

'Yes?'

'Tell me, have you ever praised a woman officer before?'

She was still laughing when she pointed out into the corridor.

'And the store is right there, next to the coffee machine.'

She settled down on the chair again and started rooting around among the papers on the floor. Ewert looked at her and then walked away. She had laughed at him. He didn't understand why.

Lisa Öhrström had kept her eyes closed for a long time.

She had heard the dark man who threatened her get up and leave; she had remained seated, not daring to move until Ann-Marie left her glass booth in the corridor and came to see how she was. The older woman had taken Lisa in her arms and talked soothingly, sat with her. At one point they had started playing the childish game of slapping one hand on top of the other.

Afterwards she had gone home. She had tried to see her

patients, but was too frightened and drained. She had never felt such fear.

It had been a long night.

She had reasoned with herself, trying to banish the ache inside. Her heart was racing and she took deep, slow breaths to settle down, but instead was alarmed by the way she gasped for air. No peace of mind, she didn't dare go to sleep, scared that she would never wake up, didn't want to, couldn't sleep, couldn't close her eyes, not any more.

Jonathan and Sanna. She couldn't keep them away.

All night long they had insisted on being let in.

She had tried to banish them by taking slow breaths, calm. She loved them like she had never dared to love anyone else, except perhaps Hilding, way back, before he had made her stop feeling. The children were different, they were part of her.

That man knew that the children existed. He had found her photos.

The damned pain in her chest.

The children were her weakness and her protection at the same time, little human beings she could not bear to lose and who strangely also made her able to control the panic that almost overwhelmed her.

The detective who had questioned her after Hilding's body had been found, and who had made her identify that man Lang, DI Sven Sundkvist, had phoned early in the morning when she was still in bed, apologised, explained that they were working hard on the case and asked her to come to the station as soon as she could.

She was waiting in a dark room somewhere inside the main City Police building. She wasn't alone. Sundkvist was there too and a lawyer, who presumably represented the accused, had just come through the door.

DI Sundkvist told her to take her time. There was no hurry and it was important that she did everything in the correct way.

She went and stood at the window. He assured her that it was a one-way view only. Only those on the police side could see through it. The men on the other side just saw their own images in the mirrored surface.

There were ten of them, all about the same height, roughly the same age, and all had shaved heads. Each man had a label hung round his neck, a large white board with a black number on it.

They stood shoulder to shoulder, staring straight at her. At least that's how it felt – as if they were waiting and watching to see what she would do.

She looked at them without seeing.

A few seconds for each one, scanning them from their feet to the top of their head. She avoided their eyes.

'No.'

She shook her head.

'None of them.'

Sven Sundkvist took a step closer. 'Are you quite certain?'

'Yes, I am. He wasn't one of these men.'

Sundkvist nodded at the window.

'They're going to walk in a circle now, one at a time. I want you to watch carefully.'

The man furthest to the left, number 1, took a few steps forward and walked slowly round the relatively spacious room. Her eyes followed him. She saw him this time, his slightly rolling gait, a self-assured way of moving. It was him.

That was Lang all right.

Bugger, bugger Hilding.

She saw him return to the line. It was number 2's turn. The men ceased to look alike as she watched one after the other do the circuit of the room. They had all looked the same before when they were standing still, and now she saw their differences.

DI Sundkvist had been standing next to her, silently observing the parade. He turned to her when number 10 was back in his place.

'So you've seen them again now: their faces, how they moved, their posture and so on. I need to know if you recognise any one of them.'

Lisa didn't look at him. She couldn't.

'No.'

'Nobody?'

'Nobody.'

Sven took a step closer and tried to meet her evasive eyes.

'Are you quite certain? Positive that none of these men was the one you observed before he killed Hilding Oldéus, your *brother*?'

He looked at the woman in front of him. Her reaction surprised him. The death of her brother did not seem to sadden her. Instead it seemed to make her angry, or something akin to that.

'You're thinking about sisterly love, aren't you? I did love him once, the Hilding I grew up with. But not the one who died yesterday. That was Hilding the heroin addict. I hated him and hated the person he forced me to become.'

She swallowed. Everything she felt inside, the rage and hatred and fear and panic. She tried to swallow it all.

'Anyway, I repeat, I don't recognise any of the men in there.'

'You haven't seen any of them before?'

'No, I haven't.'

'You are absolutely certain?'

The lawyer, who had come into the room last, spoke up for the first time. He was a man in his forties, dressed formally in suit and tie. His voice was edgy, almost upset.

'That is surely enough, Inspector. The witness has stated quite clearly that she doesn't recognise anyone, still you keep pressurising her.'

'Not at all. There is a discrepancy between Dr Öhrström's response today and her previous witness statement.'

'You're using undue pressure.'

The lawyer came closer to Sven.

'And now I must insist that you let Mr Lang go. At once. You can't hold him.'

Sven took the lawyer's arm and led him towards the door.

'I'm going to have to ask you to leave. I know the rules, don't worry, but we still have some things to discuss.'

Once the lawyer had been ushered out of the room, Sven checked that the door was properly closed. Lisa had turned towards the viewing window, staring at it, into the empty room behind.

'I don't understand.'

Sven went over to the window and stood between her and the empty room.

'I don't understand. Do you remember our interview yesterday?'

Lisa's neck blushed, her eyes pleaded.

'Yes.'

'Then you also recall what you said?'

'Yes.'

'You identified the man on photograph thirty-two. I told you that his name was Jochum Lang. You said, several times, that you were certain that he was the man who had injured and killed Hilding Oldéus. I know it and you know it, which is why I fail to understand why, when you see him directly in front of you today, you come nowhere near even a tentative identification.'

She didn't answer, just shook her head and looked fixedly at the floor.

'Have you been threatened?'

He waited for her reply. It didn't come.

'That's how he usually operates. He silences people with threats. It allows him to carry on maltreating people at will.'

Sven was still trying to meet her eyes, still waiting.

Finally she looked up. She wanted to avoid this, but she stood her ground.

'I'm sorry, Inspector. I really am sorry. Please understand – I have a niece and a nephew. I love them dearly.'

She cleared her throat.

'You do understand, don't you?'

The morning traffic had died down and it had been easy to cross the city centre. The motorway was clear and the journey took about half an hour this time. Suddenly he was there, for the second time in less than twelve hours.

Lena was happy to see him.

She came outside, stood on the steps waiting and then gave him a hug. Ewert was not used to physical contact and his first instinct was to back away, but he didn't. They needed it, both of them.

She went in to get a jacket as the air was chilly, even though the rain had stopped. It was that kind of summer, no real warmth.

For almost twenty minutes they walked together in silence, deep in thought, following the path across the fields towards the Norsborg reservoirs. Then she asked again who that woman was. The girl who had shot Bengt, the one who had lain beside him on the floor.

Ewert asked her if it was important and she nodded. She wanted to know, but couldn't bear to explain. He stood still, telling her about the first time he had seen Lydia Grajauskas, inside a flat with an electronic lock, where she had been beaten senseless, with great red, swollen welts all over her back.

She listened, walked on a little, then asked another question.

'What did she look like?'

'How do you mean? When she was dead?'

'No, before that. I want a picture of who she was. She has taken the rest of our life together, Ewert. I know that you, of all people, can understand that. I watched the news for as long as I could bear. Then as soon as I woke up this morning I looked through both the morning papers, but there are no pictures of her. Maybe there aren't any anywhere.

Or maybe what she looked like doesn't matter to anyone else. Maybe what people need is to know what she did, how she ended up.'

The rest of our life together.

Ewert had thought exactly that, said it too.

A wind had started to blow. He buttoned his jacket while they walked. I've got them here, he thought. In my inside pocket – the photographs we got from the Lithuanian police.

Lena, I have that bloody video too. The one that will soon disappear. There's so much that you must never know.

'I have a photo.'

'A photo?'

'Yes.'

He unbuttoned enough to get the envelope out and handed over a black-and-white photograph of a girl.

The girl was smiling. Her long blonde hair was pulled back and held with a ribbon tied into a bow.

'That's her. Lydia Grajauskas. She was twenty. From Klaipeda. The picture was taken about three years ago. She disappeared soon afterwards.'

Lena stood very still, fingering the photo, touching the face as if seeking something she could recognise.

'She's pretty.'

Lena wanted to say more, he could sense it, but she only looked at the picture of the girl who had killed the most important person in her life.

She said nothing.

Sven had got home late last night.

Anita had been waiting for him in the kitchen when he arrived a little before midnight, just as she said she would. He held her tight and then went to fetch a silver candelabra they were both very fond of. He lit the white candles and they looked at each other. They drank wine and ate half the birthday cake by candlelight, celebrating the start of his forty-second year.

Later he went upstairs to see Jonas, kissed him on the forehead and instantly regretted it when the boy woke and seemed confused, mumbling something inaudible. Sven stayed by his bedside, gently caressing his cheek, until Jonas fell asleep again. He found Anita in the bathroom and told her how lovely she was. He held her hand hard when they went to bed. She was naked, and afterwards they went to sleep in each other's arms.

He had woken early.

Their little house was very quiet when he left.

He realised he was being a bit keen – they had a photo identification after all – but as soon as he got to his office he had contacted Lisa Öhrström and asked her to come in for an identity parade that morning. He was aware that it would be seen as unprofessional to put a witness through two identifications, but the pressure was on and he wanted to make sure. They needed all they could get to persuade the prosecutor, Ågestam, that he must not let Lang go free, not this time.

Which was why he was furious when he left Dr Öhrström by the one-way window that separated her from the ten men who were lined up with numbers on their chests. He tried not to show it, because he knew in his heart of hearts that she was not to blame. If anything, she was a victim too, terrified by the death threats. But he didn't manage to control himself. He became sarcastic and condescending.

He hurried out, made his way to the Kronoberg interview room.

Lang would not be released.

Roadworks somewhere between Skärholmen and Fruängen made Ewert bang the dashboard and shout out loud. He was in a hurry to get back, would pass by Kronoberg and the City Police Building to run a quick errand, then walk over to the St Erik's Street restaurant where he had just arranged to meet Sven for lunch.

He knew he wasn't any good. He had stood with his arm around Lena and tried to say the kind of things he felt he ought to say, all the while feeling useless. He wasn't any good at hugging or comforting people; he never had been. While the wind blew across the fields, Lena had stood with the photo of the Lithuanian girl clutched in her hand, until he gently made her give it back.

Why had he gone to see her? All he had done was intrude into her grief. Was it because he missed Bengt? Because there was nobody else for her just now? Or because he himself had nobody?

The cars crawled ahead, three lanes merged into one. The minutes dripped off his forehead. He would be late. He had no choice.

He had to get to the office electronics store before lunch. Sven would have to wait.

The interview room was as bleak as ever.

When Sven got there he was out of breath, his anger had propelled him through the building at an unnecessary speed. Lang was sitting at the table. He was smoking and didn't even look up.

Sven Sundkvist, interview leader (IL): You visited Hilding Oldéus, who was in one of the medical wards at the Söder Hospital, immediately before he died from the injuries inflicted on him.

Jochum Lang (JL): That's what you say.

IL: We have a witness.

JL: Really, Sundkvist? That's good news. You could bring them here and set up an identity parade.

IL: The witness showed you to the ward where Oldéus was.

JL: You know what I mean, don't you? Like, they come along and look at me and nine other blokes through a one-way window. Fucking brilliant. You do it, Sundkvist.

Sven was raging inside. The man opposite him was trying to make him lose control and was close to succeeding. Must keep calm, must ask my questions and no matter what he says, just keep asking until I get what I want.

He saw that Jochum Lang was smiling. His lawyer would already have informed him that the parade had been a washout. Lawyers were quick off the mark with that kind of thing. Never mind, no way was this ruthless thug going to leave, not yet.

He was going to answer the questions again and sooner or later he would say more than he wanted to, enough to satisfy Ågestam that he should keep the suspect locked up and carry on with his preliminary investigation.

IL: We picked you up in a BMW that was parked illegally at the hospital entrance.

JL: Busy man, aren't you? No idea you did parking fines as well.

IL: Why were you sitting in the passenger seat of a car left inside the cordoned-off area?

JL: I can sit wherever I fucking like.

IL: We won't let you go this time.

JL: Sundkvist, get off my back. You'd better return me to the fucking cells! Or else I might do something that I *could be* charged for.

It was ten minutes past twelve when Ewert parked outside the police building. Sven was probably waiting impatiently in the restaurant by now.

He hurried inside, down the corridor leading to his room, and stopped near the coffee machine. Not for a coffee, though; he went into the storeroom, which was next to it, just where Hermansson had said.

Brown cardboard boxes containing blank videocassettes were stacked on shelves at the back of the stale-smelling little room. He took one out, tore off the plastic cover and checked that it looked exactly like all other videotapes. Then he went to his office, picked up Grajauskas's carrier bag and placed the new video in it.

Lena's shame? Or hers?

Lena was alive. She was dead.

Grajauskas's true story did not exist any more. Well, it did, deep down in the water off Slagsta beach, where he had stopped on the way back from Eriksberg. The burden of shame is so much heavier when you're alive.

Ewert yawned and swung the carrier bag with the new videotape in it a couple of times. Then he put it back in the box with the rest of her belongings.

Ewert found a table in one of the furthest, darkest corners, where he was unlikely to be seen by someone who had just stepped inside for a look. What a dump, he thought, this small restaurant on the busy corner of St Erik's Street and Fleming Street, quite a walk from Kronoberg. Too bad. He had no choice. Reporters had been chasing him all over the Kungsholmen area and knew where he usually went for lunch. He had been on his way there when he spotted a few hacks already buzzing about outside.

He wouldn't give them any answers. He'd give them nothing. The police press officers could work for their wages, they could explain as little as possible at one of those press conferences where everybody shouted at the same time.

He had turned on his heels, phoned Sven who was already sitting in there waiting, and walked to a place he knew a few blocks away where he had sheltered before when someone's death had caused excited headlines and words. Here he would be left in peace to consume the foul food.

He picked up a newspaper someone had left behind, opening to a six-page news feature about the hostage drama at Söder Hospital.

'I had just been served, you know.' Sven patted him on

the shoulder. 'That's sixty-five kronors' worth down the drain.'

He sat down, looked around and shook his head.

'And for what? Great place you've chosen.'

'At least nobody hangs around asking questions here.'

'I can see why.'

They ordered beef stew, Skåne style. Served with pickled beetroot.

'How is she?'

'Lena?'

'Yes.'

'She's grieving.'

'She needs you to be with her.'

Ewert sighed, shifted about restlessly on his chair and put the paper down.

'Sven, I have no idea what you're supposed to do or say. I'm no good at things like that. Take this morning. Lena wanted to see what Grajauskas looked like and I showed her the photo.'

'If that's what she wanted.'

'I'm not sure. It didn't feel right. Her reaction was odd, as if she didn't . . . almost as if she recognized Grajauskas. She looked at the picture, touched it and tried to say something, but didn't.'

'She is still in shock.'

'She doesn't need to know what her husband's dead killer looked like. I felt like I was rubbing it in her face.'

A few pieces of meat, swimming in gravy. They ate because they had to.

'Ewert.'

'What?'

'This morning was a complete disaster.'

Ewert chased a slice of beetroot across his plate, but gave up when it sank in a pool of brown gravy-powder sludge.

'Do I want to know this?'

'Not really.'

'Tell me, all the same.'

Sven relived the morning.

He had sensed Lisa Öhrström's fear and unwillingness from the moment they met, he said, and went on to describe the line-up, her first negative and his request that she should observe the men moving. All the time, he was aware that she neither dared nor wanted to engage with what she was shown. Then her give-away plea that she loved her nephew and niece, his own anger when he realised that she had been intimidated and her refusal to substantiate her earlier statement. Finally her shame, and the lawyer who insisted that Lang should be released.

Sven knew what would happen next.

Putting down his knife and fork, Ewert went bright red in the face, his eyes narrowed, a blood vessel began to pulsate at his temple. He was just about to thump the table when Sven grabbed his arm.

'Ewert. Not here. We don't want to attract attention.'

Grens's breathing was ragged and sheer rage made his voice fall into a low register.

'What the hell are you saying, Sven?'

He got up and walked round the table, kicking each one of its legs.

'Ewert, I'm just as mad as you are. But pack it in now, we're not in the office.'

He remained standing.

'Intimidation! Lang threatened the doctor! Threatened the kids!'

Sven hesitated before he continued. The strange morning replayed in his mind. He took a small audio recorder from his jacket pocket and put it on the table between their half-eaten platefuls.

'I questioned Lang afterwards. Listen to this.'

Two voices.

One wanting to talk. The other determined to end the conversation.

Ewert listened with concentrated attention, his every muscle tensing when Jochum Lang spoke. When it was all over and Sven switched the tape recorder off, Ewert came to life.

'Play that again. Only the last bit.'

Sounds, a chair scraping on the floor, someone breathing. Then Lang's voice.

'Sundkvist, get off my back. You'd better return me to the fucking cells! Or else I might do something that I could be charged for.'

This time Ewert howled, and every one of the few remaining customers turned to stare at the big man in the far corner standing by a table waving his fist in the air.

'Ewert! For Christ's sake! Sit down.'

'That's it! There's no way I'll let Lang decide any more. He'll stay put in the cells and I don't give a rat's ass about the consequences.'

He was still standing. He pointed at Sven. 'Her telephone number. Lisa Öhrström's.'

'Why?'

'Do you have it or don't you? Give me her number! We're going to do some real police work, you and I, right here in the restaurant.'

The waitress, a girl rather than a woman, approached their table timidly and appealed to Sven, ignoring Ewert. It took great effort for her to tell them to please be quieter, show some respect for the other guests or she would have to call the police. Sven apologised and promised it wouldn't happen again. They were just about to leave, could they have the bill?

'Here.' He handed Ewert his opened pocket diary. Dr Öhrström's phone number was neatly written down. Ewert smiled. All the case contact names were ordered alphabetically. That was how he operated, this young colleague of his.

He got out his mobile phone and dialled her number.

He caught her somewhere on the ward. She had gone in to work immediately after the identity parade.

'Dr Öhrström? DSI Ewert Grens speaking. In an hour I'll fax you some photographs. I want you to have a good look at them.'

She paused, as if she was trying to work out what he had said.

'Please explain. What is this about?'

'Robbery, grievous bodily harm and murder.'

'I still don't understand.'

'What's your fax number?'

Another pause. She wanted nothing to do with whatever it was. 'Why do I have to see these pictures of yours?'

'You'll understand when you see them in an hour's time. I'll ring you back.'

Ewert waited impatiently while Sven finished his half of lager and fumbled for the money he said he knew he had somewhere. Ewert waved this away. No problem, he'd pay for both of them. He handed over a larger tip than the food had deserved.

They were just about to step out from the smell of stew into the snarled-up traffic on St Erik's Street when Ewert spied two journalists of the kind he definitely wanted to avoid. He pushed Sven back into the restaurant, kept the door ajar and waited until they passed and disappeared down the street.

Back in his room, Ewert picked up a couple of black-and-white photographs and went off to find the fax machine.

'Sir?'

There she was. She had laughed at him earlier on that morning.

'Hermansson. You promised me a report after lunch. It's after lunch now.'

He wondered if he sounded brusque. He hadn't meant to.

'It's done.'

'And?'

'I've gone through all the statements now. Quite a few interesting points have turned up.'

Ewert was holding the photos and she gestured to him, Fax them, of course, I'll wait, but he put them down and asked her to elaborate.

'Take the hospital guard's account. He mentions a woman who walked past and went into the toilet at the end of the corridor just before Grajauskas went in. From his description, I'm sure it was her friend Alena Sljusareva.'

He listened to her and remembered this morning, when he had praised her and then felt awkward, weak and exposed. He hadn't quite understood why, still didn't. He wasn't normally laughed at by young women.

'The next statement I read was given by the two lads who were sitting next to Grajauskas, watching the lunchtime news. One of them remembers the same woman going by and his description is identical to that of the guard. A perfect description of Alena Sljusareva again. I'm positive.'

Hermansson had brought a folder full of papers, a twenty-four-hour-old investigation into a murder and a suicide in a hospital mortuary. She handed it to him.

'It was her, Grens. Sljusareva supplied Grajauskas with the firearm and explosives, I'm sure. In other words, she is an accessory to aggravated kidnap and murder. We'll find her soon. She has got nowhere to go.'

Ewert took the folder and cleared his throat. The young detective was already walking away.

'Look, Hermansson.'

She stopped.

'By the way. You're the second policewoman I've praised. And I ought to do it again, it seems.'

She shook her head.

'Thanks. But that's enough for now.'

She started to walk away again, when he asked her to wait. One more question.

'What you said this morning. Am I to take it that you think I have a problem with female officers?'

'Yes. That's what I meant.'

Not a moment's hesitation. She was as calm and matter-of-fact as ever, and he felt just as exposed.

He took the point, though, and remembered Anni.

He cleared his throat again and got himself a coffee from the machine. He needed the simplicity of it, black and hot in a plastic cup. It calmed him down and he pressed for a refill. He knew why he had a problem with female officers. With women in general. Twenty-five years. That was how long it was since he had held a woman in his arms. He could hardly remember what it felt like, but knew he missed it, what he couldn't remember.

One more.

He drank the last coffee slowly. Mustn't allow himself more than three, so better savour the peaceful feeling it gave him. He sipped and swallowed and sipped and swallowed until he realised that he was still holding the photographs.

He glanced at them, certain that they'd do the trick.

Lisa Öhrström replied after five rings.

'One hour exactly. You're very punctual.'

'Please go to your fax.'

He heard her walk down the corridor, visualised the layout of the ward and knew where she was standing.

'All right?'

'Coming through.'

'What do you think?'

'I don't understand what it is you want.'

'Describe what you see.'

He waited.

She sighed. He waited until she was ready to speak.

'What do you want me to say?'

'You're the doctor. Look at the pictures. What do you see?'

Lisa Öhrström was silent. He could hear her breathing, but she said nothing.

'Come on. What do you see?'

'It's a hand, a left hand, with three fractured fingers.'

'The thumb. Is that right?'

'That's right.'

'Five thousand kronor.'

'I'm sorry? I don't understand.'

'Index finger is one thousand, little finger is one thousand.'

'You've lost me.'

'Jochum Lang's rates and his trademark. The photo was taken by a technician during an investigation into a case of GBH, which was later dropped. This guy, with a pretty useless hand, owed seven thousand kronor. One of Lang's victims. That's how he operates, the man you are protecting. And he'll carry on doing this kind of thing for as long as people like you protect him.'

He said nothing more, just waited for a while before putting the receiver down. She would sit there with the three broken fingers in front of her until he got in touch again. A door opened along the corridor and Ewert turned to look. Sven was hurrying towards him with swift footsteps.

'Ewert, they phoned just now.'

Ewert sat down on top of the fax. His leg ached the way it sometimes did and he didn't register the machine's thin plastic cover creaking under his weight. Sven did, but couldn't be bothered to say anything. He looked at his boss.

'From the ferry port. A Russian interpreter is on the way.'

'And?'

'She was about to board the boat to Lithuania.'

Ewert waved his arms about impatiently.

'What's this about?'

'Alena Sljusareva. They've arrested her, just minutes ago.'

They had talked about it so many times.

He had sat with Bengt in interview rooms and pubs, in Bengt's garden or sitting room, and time and again they had ended up talking about the truth and agreed that when all is said and done, it's bloody simple, there's the truth and the rest is lies. And truth is the only thing that people can bear to live with in the long run. Everything else is bullshit.

Lies feed on each other, one lie leads to another and then to another, until you're so hopelessly caught up in the tangle that you no longer recognise the truth, even when that is all you have.

Their friendship had been built on this respect for the truth, their shared belief that you should always dare to say what you think, even when it saps your strength or undermines your position. Now and then, when one of them realised that the other was being evasive, maybe keeping quiet out of kindness, they would have a row, shout at each other, slam the door to the corridor shut and only open it again when everything had come out – the truth.

Ewert shuddered. What a bloody lie! How had he believed that he and Bengt shared the truth and nothing but the truth?

He sat hunched over his desk, his thoughts circling a video that he had carried around for the best part of a day and night, only to let it sink to the bottom of Lake Mälaren.

And now I'm lying.

Lying for Lena's sake.

The plain truth.

I'm lying in order to protect your lie.

Ewert Grens pulled over a cardboard box that was sitting on the edge of his desk. He leaned forward, opened the lid and peered inside. The contents belonged to Alena Sljusareva. She had been arrested a few hours earlier by two policemen, who had also impounded all she carried with her.

Ewert turned the box upside down. Her life scattered over his desk. Nothing much to it, only the essentials for someone on the run. He picked over her possessions, one by one.

A money clip with a few thousand kronor, her pay for opening her legs twelve times a day for three years.

A diary. He broke the lock and leafed through it. Cyrillic letters making up lots of words he didn't understand.

A pair of sunglasses. Cheap plastic, the kind you buy when you have to.

A mobile phone. The model was quite up to date, more functions than anyone could ever cope with.

A single ticket for the ferry from Stockholm to Klaipeda for today, 6 June. He checked his watch. The ticket had ceased to be valid.

He started putting her life back in the box, read the chain-of-custody list, signed it and put it in with the rest.

Ewert knew more than he wanted to. Now he had to interrogate her. And she would repeat exactly the things he didn't want to hear. So he would listen and forget, tell her to pack her bag and go home.

For Lena's sake. Not for you. But for her.

He rose, followed the corridors to the lift that would take him to the custody cells. The duty officer was expecting him and led the way to the cell where Alena had spent the last hour and a half. The officer used the small square hole in the door to check on the prisoner. She was sitting on the narrow bunk, doubled up, her head resting on her knees. Her long dark hair almost reached the floor.

The guard unlocked and opened the door and Ewert stepped into the tired little room. She looked up. Her eyes . . . she had been crying. He nodded a greeting.

'I am Detective Superintendent Grens. I believe you speak Swedish?'

'I do, a bit.'

'Good. I am going to ask you some questions now. We are going to sit here, in the cell, with the tape recorder between us. Do you understand?'

'Why?'

Alena Sljusareva tried to make herself smaller. She did that sometimes when someone had been too rough, when her genitals hurt, when she hoped no one would look at her.

Ewert Grens, interview leader (IL): Do you remember seeing me before?

Alena Sljusareva (AS): In the flat. You're the policeman who hit a stick on his stomach. Dimitri-Bastard-Pimp. He fell down.

IL: You saw me doing that, but you ran away all the same?

AS: I saw Bengt Nordwall too. I panicked. I just wanted to run away.

He was sitting on a hard bunk in a police cell, next to a young woman from a Baltic state; his back ached from sleeping for a few hours on the office sofa and his leg ached as usual. His breathing was laboured, he was tired and he didn't want to be there any longer. He didn't want to destroy the one thing he had left, his pride, his identity. He hated the lie that he had to live with, that forced him to carry on lying.

AS: I know now. Lydia is dead.

IL: Yes, she is.

AS: I know now.

IL: Before she died, she shot an innocent policeman dead. Then she killed herself, one shot through the head, using the same gun. A nine-millimetre Pistolet Makarova. I would very much like to know how she got hold of that gun.

AS: She is dead. She is really dead! I know now.

She had kept hoping, as one docs. If I don't know whatever it is, it hasn't happened.

Alena crossed herself and burst into tears. She wept bitterly, the way you weep only when you finally understand that a person, whom you will miss, no longer exists.

Silently Ewert waited for her to stop, watching the tape unwind. Then he repeated his question.

IL: A nine-millimetre Pistolet Makarova.

AS: [inaudible]

IL: And plastic explosives.

AS: It was me.

IL: Me?

AS: I went to get it.

IL: Where from?

AS: The same place.

IL: Where is that?

AS: Völund Street. The basement.

Grens slammed his fist into the tape recorder, almost hitting her. How the hell had this broken, scared girl on the run managed to slip past the guard outside the building, raid the basement and carry off enough explosives to blow up a substantial part of a large hospital?

He frightened her, this man who hit out, just like the rest. She made herself smaller still.

He apologised and promised not to do it again.

IL: You knew what she was going to use it for.
AS: No.
IL: You handed over a loaded gun, without asking why?
AS: I knew nothing. And I asked nothing.
IL: She didn't explain?
AS: She knew that if she did I would have insisted on being there.

Ewert switched off the recorder and removed the tape. The lie. Questions and answers which would never be transcribed. This cassette must vanish, just like the film of their shared story had vanished.

He looked at her, she looked away: didn't want anything more to do with him.

'You're going home.'

'Home? Now?'

'Now.'

Alena Sljusareva got up quickly, stuck her feet in the regulation prison slip-ons, pulled her fingers through her hair and tugged at her blouse.

They had promised each other that they would go home together. That would never happen now.

Lydia was dead.

She was on her own now.

Ewert called a taxi. The fewer police involved, the better. He escorted her to the Berg Street door. An older man with his younger woman, or perhaps a father with his grown-up daughter. Few passers-by would have guessed at a detective superintendent from Homicide sending a prostitute back home.

Alena sat in the back as the taxi manoeuvred through the city afternoon traffic, from Norr Mälarstrand to Stureplan, down Valhalla Way to join Lidingö Way, the route to the harbour. She would never come back here, never; she would never leave Lithuania again. She knew that; she had completed her journey.

Ewert paid the taxi driver and accompanied Alena into the ferry terminal. The next departure for Klaipeda was in two hours' time. He bought her a ticket and she held it tightly, determined not to let go until she arrived in her home town.

It was so hard to imagine it, the place she had left as a girl of seventeen. She hadn't hesitated for long when the two men had offered her a good, well-paid job only a boat trip away. All she was leaving behind was poverty, and little hope of change. Besides, she'd be back in a few months. She hadn't discussed it with anyone, not even Janoz. She couldn't remember why.

She had been a different person then. Just three years ago, but it was another life, another time. Now she had lived more than her peers.

Had he tried to find her? Wondered where she was? She saw Janoz, had kept an image of him in her mind that they had never managed to take away. They had penetrated her and they had spat at her, but they had never been able to get at what she had refused to let go of. Was he still there? Was he alive? What would he look like now?

Ewert told her to come along to the cafeteria at the far end of the terminal and bought her a coffee and a sandwich. She thanked him and ate. He bought two newspapers as well. They settled down to read until it was time to go on board.

The day was not over yet.

Lena Nordwall was sitting at the kitchen table and staring at something or other. When you stared, it had to be at something.

How long would it take? Two days? Three? One week? One year? Never?

She didn't need to understand. She didn't need to. Not yet. Did she?

Someone was sitting behind her. She sensed it now.

Someone in the hall, at the bottom of the stairs. She turned; her daughter was looking at her, in silence.

'How long have you been there?'

'Don't know.'

'Why aren't you outside playing?'

''Cause it's raining.'

Their daughter was five years old. *Her* daughter was five years old. *Her* daughter. No matter how hard she searched, she wouldn't find another adult in this house now. She was the only one, alone. The responsibility was hers. The future.

'Mummy, how long will it be?'

'How long will what be?'

'How long will Daddy be dead for?'

Her daughter's name was Elin. Lena hadn't noticed that she still had her wet, muddy wellie boots on. The little girl got up and walked to the kitchen table, leaving a trail of wet soil. Lena didn't see it.

'When will he come back home?'

Elin sat down on the chair next to her mother. Lena noted this, but nothing else, nor did she really hear that Elin kept asking questions.

'Won't he come home, ever?'

Her daughter reached out a hand and stroked her cheek; she could only just reach.

'Where is he?'

'Your daddy is asleep.'

'When will he wake up?'

'He won't wake up.'

'Why not?'

Her daughter sat there throwing questions at her. Each one made a physical impact; she was being bombarded with these things that crawled over her before boring into her skin, into her body. She stood up. No more attacking words. Enough. She shouted at the child, who was trying to understand.

'Stop it! Stop asking questions!'

'Why has he become dead?'

'I can't . . . it's too much, can't you see that? I can't bear it!'

She almost struck the child. The impulse was there – it came in an instant, as the questions crashed against her head. Up went her arm. She could have slapped her, but she didn't. She never had. She burst into tears, sat down again and hugged her daughter close. *Her* daughter.

Sven had laughed out loud as he walked back alone from the sad little restaurant to Kronoberg. It wasn't the food, even though that was laughable, those small, fatty pieces of meat in slimy powder gravy. He had laughed at Ewert. He thought of his colleague marching round the table, kicking its legs and then stopping to curse the tape recorder and Lang's threatening voice, until the waitress tiptoed over to ask him to calm down or she'd have to call the police.

Sven had burst out laughing without thinking and two women walking towards him looked concerned. One of them mumbled something about alcohol and not being in control. He took a deep breath and tried to calm down. Ewert Grens was a lot of things, but at least he was never boring.

Ewert was going to question Sljusareva, good. Sven Sundkvist felt sure that she had information that would help them understand more about the case. He decided to abandon the Lang case for the moment, concentrate on the hostage-taking instead, and walked faster, hurrying back to his office. The mortuary business made him feel deeply disturbed, and not just because it was all about death.

There was something else, something incomprehensible. Grajauskas had been so driven and brutal. Medics held hostage with a gun to their heads, corpses blown apart, her demand for Nordwall, only to shoot him and then herself. All that without letting them know what it was she really wanted.

Back at his desk he ran through the events again, scrutinising 5 June minute by minute, noting the exact time for each new development. He started at 12.15, when Lydia Grajauskas had been sitting on a sofa in the surgical ward watching the news, and ended at 16.10, when several people agreed that they had heard the sound of two gunshots in their earpieces. The two shots had been followed by one more. Then a great crash, when the Flying Squad men forced the door.

He read the statements made by the hostages. The older man, Dr Ejder, and the four students seemed to have the same impression of Grajauskas. They described her as calm and careful to make sure she stayed in control at all times. Also, she had not hurt anyone, except Larsen who had attacked her. Their descriptions gave a good picture, but not what he needed most. Why had she acted like this?

He went through the chain-of-custody list and the technical summary of the state of the mortuary at around 16.17, but no new angles came to mind. All very predictable, nothing he hadn't expected.

Except that.

He read the two lines several times.

A videotape had been found in her carrier bag. The cassette had no sleeve, but had been labelled in Cyrillic script.

They swapped newspapers. He bought them another cup of coffee and a portion of apple pie and custard each. She ate the pie with the same hearty appetite as the sandwich.

Ewert observed the woman opposite him.

She was pretty. Not that it mattered, but she was lovely to look at.

She should have stayed at home. What a bloody waste. So young, so much ahead of her, and then . . . what? To be exploited every day by randy family men looking for a change from mowing the lawn. From their ageing wives and demanding kids.

Such a terrible waste. He shook his head and waited until she had finished chewing and put her spoon down.

He had brought it in his briefcase, and now he put it on the table.

'Have you seen this before?'

A blue notebook. She shrugged. 'No, I haven't.'

He opened it to the first page and pushed it across the table so she could see it.

'Do you understand what it says here?'

Alena read a few lines and then looked up at him. 'Where did you find this?'

'Next to her bed in the hospital. The only thing that was hers. Seemed to be, anyway. Is it hers?'

'It's Lydia's handwriting.'

He explained that because it was in Lithuanian, no one had been able to translate the text during the hostage crisis, when she was still alive.

While Bengt was alive, he thought. While his lie didn't yet exist.

Alena leafed through the book, then read the five pages of text and translated it for him. Everything.

Everything that had happened barely twenty-four hours earlier.

In detail.

Grajauskas had planned and written down precisely what she later put into action. She had worked out how the weapons would be delivered, together with a ball of string and the video, and left in a toilet waste bin. That she would hit the guard over the head, walk to the mortuary, take hostages, blow up corpses. And demand the services of an interpreter called Bengt Nordwall.

Ewert listened. Now and then he swallowed. It was all there, in black and white. If only I had known. If only I had had this stuff translated. I would never have sent him down there. He would have been alive now.

You would have lived!

If only you hadn't gone down there, you would be alive. You must have known!

277

Why didn't you say?

You could have spoken to me. Or to her.

If only you had admitted that you knew who she was. At least you could have given her that.

Then you would still be alive.

She never wanted to shoot you.

She wanted confirmation that what had happened in those flats wasn't her fault. That she had never chosen to wait around, ready to undress for all those men.

Alena Sljusareva asked if she could keep the notebook. Ewert shook his head, grabbed the blue cover and put it away in his briefcase. He waited until twenty minutes before the departure time, then accompanied her to the exit. Alena had her ticket in her hand, showed it to a uniformed woman in the booth, then turned to him and thanked him. Ewert wished her a good trip.

He left her in the queue of passengers and went over to a corner of the terminal building from where he had an overview of people arriving off the ferry, as well as those waiting to go on board. Leaning against a pillar, he tried to think about the other ongoing investigation, about Lang in his cell and Öhrström studying the faxed pictures. She would soon get some more. But his mind drifted, he was too preoccupied with the two women from Klaipeda. Absently he observed the strangers milling about, something he had always enjoyed doing. The arrivals walked with the sea still in their bodies. They all had somewhere to go, the ones with red cheeks and large duty-free bags full of spirits who had drunk, danced and flirted the night away before falling asleep alone in their cabins below deck. Others dressed in their best clothes had been saving for years for a week's holiday in Sweden, on the other side of the Baltic. And there were a few who wore rumpled clothes and had no luggage at all, having left in a hurry just to get away. He studied them all – it was all he could bear to do right now – and forgot about time for a while.

Alena Sljusareva would be on her way soon.

Ewert was just about to walk away when he saw what was probably the last group of passengers coming off the ferry.

He recognised him immediately.

After all, it was less than two days since he had seen this man at Arlanda being given a dressing down by a plump little Lithuanian diplomat, and then manhandled through security flanked by two big lads there to see him off on the one-hour flight to Vilnius.

Dimitri-Bastard-Pimp.

He was wearing the same suit that he had been wearing when he was escorted up the steps to the plane, the shiny suit he had had on when he stood blocking the broken-down doorway on the fifth floor, having flogged Lydia Grajauskas unconscious two days earlier.

And he wasn't alone. Once through passport control, he waited for two young women, or rather girls, sixteen or seventeen years old. He held out his hand and they both gave him something they had ready for him. Ewert didn't need to see any more to know what it was.

Their passports.

In debt already.

A woman wearing a tracksuit with the hood pulled down over her head hurried forwards to meet the little group, keeping her back turned. Ewert watched her as she greeted the three arrivals and, as he believed was customary in the Baltic states, kissed them all, light little kisses on the cheek. Then she pointed towards the nearest exit and they followed her. None of them had much luggage.

Ewert felt sick.

Lydia Grajauskas had just shot herself in the temple. Alena Sljusareva had fled and was now only a short voyage from home. Both had been ruthlessly exploited for three years in flats with electronic locks. They had been threatened, abused and had to pretend they were turned on as they were going to pieces inside. And it only took twenty-four hours, twenty-four hours, before they had been replaced. A day and a night was all it took to find two young women who had no idea of what lay ahead, who would be trained to smile when they were spat at, so that those who traded money for sex could still count on one hundred and fifty thousand kronor per girl every month.

In a couple of minutes, the ferry would pull away from the quay. He stayed where he was. They disappeared in the crowd, the hooded Baltic woman, Dimitri-Bastard-Pimp and the girls, barely old enough to have breasts, teenagers who had just given away their passports.

There was nothing he could do, not now. Lydia and Alena had dared to question and fight back, but that was unusual. At least, it was the first time Ewert had heard about it. The two new girls were children, frail and scared. They would never dare to testify at this point, and that motherfucking pimp would deny everything.

Consequently, no crime existed yet.

Maybe it didn't, but he was sure that he or a colleague would come across them. There was no telling where or when, but sooner or later they too would go straight to hell.

As soon as Sven had seen the entry in the technical account – one videotape in a plastic bag with two sets of fingerprints, identified as Lydia Grajauskas's and Alena Sljusareva's – he put everything else to one side. First he looked for it in the forensic science department, where it should be.

It wasn't there.

He asked the language experts, who might have taken an interest in the Cyrillic writing, and the night duty crew.

It wasn't there either.

He also drew a blank in the impounded property store, which was the last of the likely places. Not there.

His stomach was contracting again. A sense of unease

that grew and intensified, turning into irritation, and then into anger, which wasn't like him, and he hated it.

He located the technician who had been first on the scene, good old Nils Krantz, who had been around for as long as Sven could remember, and well before that. Krantz was at work, a domestic violence case in a flat in Regering Street, but he took time off to speak to Sven on the phone. He described where they had found the video, what they had found with it, basically confirming what Sven already knew from the documentation.

'Good, thanks. And what was on the tape?'

'What do you mean?'

'I mean, what was on the tape?'

'I don't know.'

'You don't know?'

'That's not my job. It's up to you lot.'

'That's why I'm investigating it.'

Sven hung on while Krantz talked to someone in the room for maybe half a minute.

'Anything else you want to know?'

'One more thing. Where is it now? The tape, I mean.'

Krantz gave an exasperated laugh. 'Don't you lads ever speak to each other?'

'What do you mean?'

'Ask Grens.'

'Ewert?'

'He wanted the tape. I handed it over to him after we had done the prints. You know, down in the mortuary.'

Sven took a deep breath. Pain in his stomach, irritation. And definitely anger.

He got up from his desk, went to Ewert's office four doors down, and knocked.

He knew that Ewert was interviewing Alena Sljusareva. He tried the door. It wasn't locked.

He went in and scanned the room. It was an odd feeling. He was there to pick up a scene-of-crime item, but in that instant was an intruder, entering unbidden and without permission. He couldn't remember ever having been in Ewert's office alone. Had anybody? He only had to look for a few seconds. He saw the video on the shelf behind Ewert's desk, beside the old cassette player that filled the room with Siw Malmkvist. The label on the back was in Cyrillic script, which he couldn't read.

After putting on plastic gloves, he weighed the videotape in his hand, fingered it pointlessly. She had planned every move in detail, never hesitated, had a motive for every step she had taken towards her death. Sven flipped the video over, felt its smooth surface. This tape was not there by chance. There was a reason for it. She had wanted to show them something.

He left, closing the door carefully, and went along to the meeting room. He loaded the tape. He was sitting in the same chair where Ewert had been sitting the night before.

But watching something different. Jonas, his son, used to call such an image the War of the Ants. A tape with a loud rushing noise and no picture, just a white flicker against a grey background.

This was a tape that shouldn't exist. It was unregistered, had no entry in the official lists, held no filmed images.

That feeling in his stomach that had been unease earlier had now turned to anger, a sudden rage that made him sick.

Ewert, what the hell are you up to?

Alena was safely on board. The ferry had left the port and was negotiating the Stockholm archipelago on her way to the open sea. Her route crossed the Baltic Sea and ended in Klaipeda. Soon Alena would be home and would never look back.

Ewert Grens waited for a taxi that never came. He swore and called back to find out why. The operator apologised, but she had no record of a taxi request for Grens from the ferry terminal to Berg Street. Should she register a request now? Ewert swore again, launched into a litany that included organisations and bureaucrats and clowns, demanded to know the operator's name and altogether managed to be more offensive than he cared to remember afterwards.

Then finally a cab turned up and he got in.

He suddenly caught a glimpse of the house on the other side of the bay.

Blood was pouring from her head.

I leaned against the side of the van, holding her, and it never stopped pouring from her ears, her nose, her mouth.

He missed her; he longed for her. The feeling was stronger now than it had been for years, and he didn't want to wait until next Monday morning. He should tell the driver to go across Lidingö Bridge, past the Milles Museum and stop in the car park outside the nursing home. Ewert would run inside and stay with her. Just be there, together.

But she wasn't there, not the woman he missed and longed for. She hadn't existed for twenty-five years.

Lang, you took her from me.

The afternoon traffic was growing heavy and the taxi slowed to a halt more than once. It took half an hour to get to Kronoberg, and by the time he had paid and got out of the car, he had cooled down.

The air felt milder now. The effect of all that rain seemed to be wearing off and summer was making another attempt. The wind had died down and he felt the sun warming him. Weather: he had never got his head round it.

Back in his office he started his music machine and Siw's voice came through the tinny mono speaker. Together they sang: 'Lyckans ost', (1968), original English version 'Hello Mary Lou'.

Ewert opened the folder on the investigation into the Jochum Lang case. He knew the photos would be there.

He studied them, one at a time. Their subject was a dead person on a floor and the quality was not great. The photographs were grainy and so poorly lit the outlines had become almost blurred. Krantz and his boys were good technicians, no question, but none of them could handle a camera. He sighed, picked three halfway decent ones and put them in an envelope.

Two telephone calls to round off the morning.

First he rang a stressed Lisa Öhrström, who answered from somewhere in the hospital. He told her briskly that he and DI Sundkvist would come to see her soon in order to show her some more pictures. She protested, saying that she had quite enough to do without spending her time on more photos of broken body parts. Ewert replied that he looked forward to seeing her and hung up.

His next call was to Ågestam, who was in his office at the State Prosecution Service. Ewert told the prosecutor that he had someone who was prepared to witness against Jochum Lang in connection with the Oldéus incident, a hospital doctor called Lisa Öhrström, who had unhesitatingly identified Lang as the perpetrator. Ågestam was unprepared for this and asked for further information, but Ewert interrupted him with a reassurance that there would be more to come, conclusive evidence clinching both the current cases by tomorrow morning, when they were due to meet.

She was still singing her heart out, was old Siw. He tuned in and sang along, moving about the room with a bounce in his step. 'Mamma är lik sin mamma', (1968), original English version 'Sadie the Cleaning Lady'.

Not many passers-by noticed the car that had stopped in front of the door to number 3 Völund Street. It was a modest car, driven decorously. The driver was a middle-aged man, who climbed out and opened the rear door for two girls, teenagers of about sixteen or seventeen. They were both pretty and seemed curious about their surroundings.

Could be a father with his daughters.

The girls looked up at the building with its rows of identical windows, as if they hadn't seen it before. Presumably they didn't live there, so maybe they were visiting somebody.

The driver locked the car and walked ahead to open the door. Just as he pulled at the door handle, he turned and said something which made one of the girls give a little scream and burst into tears. The other one, who seemed the stronger, put an arm round her, patted her cheek and tried to make her come with them.

In the lobby, the man kept talking and the anxious girl kept crying.

Any native observer would have found their language strange-sounding and incomprehensible, which meant that even if the older man had said something to the effect that they owed him now and that was why he was going to break them in and screw them until they bled, nobody would have understood it.

Sven left the meeting room with the empty videotape in his hand. He stopped for a coffee, added plenty of milk because he needed nourishment but had to be careful. Now that he had become angry, his stomach was in constant protest.

That video was a blank. He was convinced Grajauskas hadn't intended it, she had planned everything so meticulously and had stage-managed every aspect of her last hours. He knew that her tape had a purpose.

He phoned Krantz again from his office. The technician, still in the Regering Street flat, answered at once, preoccupied and cross.

'What's up with the damn tape now?'

'All I want to know is – was it new?'

'New?'

'Had it been used?'

'Yes, it had been used.'

'And how do we know that?'

'I can't speak for you lot, but I know because when I checked there was dust inside. Another thing I know is that the safety tab had been broken off. Which is what you do if you want to make sure the recorded stuff won't be wiped.'

Sven inspected the video under the desk lamp. It was so new it shone, not one grain of dust in sight. The safety tab was intact. He spoke again.

'Krantz, I'm coming to see you.'

'Later, I don't have time now.'

'I want you to look at this videotape again. Krantz, it's important. Something's not right.'

Lars Ågestam didn't know whether to laugh or cry. Grens had announced that he was going to provide conclusive data about the deaths of both Lydia Grajauskas and Bengt Nordwall – as well as Hilding Oldéus – and about Alena Sljusareva and Jochum Lang; about two simultaneous catastrophes linked by time and place. Almost a year had passed since he last worked with Ewert Grens. That too had been a strange business, a trial of a father who had shot his daughter's killer. At the time, Ågestam had been the youngest prosecutor in the state service, keen to land a major case and was then almost crushed when the big one landed in his lap. He had been picked to be in charge of the interrogation, which formally meant that he outranked DSI Grens, a man he had heard much about and admired from a distance and whom he now would work with and against.

They were meant to work together, but their collaboration had been a disaster.

Grens seemed to have decided from the outset that mutuality simply wasn't on his agenda and, collaboration or not, he couldn't be bothered even to be civil.

Now Ågestam had a choice, and he decided to laugh, which was the easier option. Fate would have it that he was to work with Grens again, on not one, but two investigations in connection with the events at Söder Hospital. And the argument was – this was when he laughed rather than cried – that they had worked together the last time Grens had a big case; the powers-that-be had kept an eye on it and noticed that the teamwork gave good results.

Teamwork? My ass.

Ågestam's thin body shook as he laughed. He pulled off his jacket, sat back with his shiny black shoes on the desk, tugged at his nicely cut blond hair and laughed until tears came to his eyes at the thought of Grens, the teammate from hell.

The sky above Regering Street should have been summer blue. Sven stared at it and it stared back, grey and dull and mean-looking. Soon it would rain again. He had been standing there for a while. He knew that he should get back to the office, but was uncertain whether he could take any more. Back in the office he would have to continue the work he had started, work that was pushing him to the breaking point.

Nils Krantz, stressed and irritable at being interrupted in the middle of a crime scene examination, had glanced at the videotape for a few seconds, no more, then he handed it back, saying that this was not the tape he had found and analysed in the mortuary. Sven knew that already, but hadn't been able to stop hoping that he was wrong, as one does when all is not as it should be.

Still, now he knew for certain. Or, rather, he knew nothing whatsoever.

The Ewert Grens he knew and looked up to wouldn't dream of interfering with evidence.

The Ewert Grens he knew was an awkward bastard, but a straight and honest bastard.

What he had done now was different, something else altogether.

The dull sky was still glaring down at him when his mobile rang. Ewert. Sven sighed, uncertain if he could deal with him now. No, he couldn't. Not yet.

He listened to the voice message instead. They were going

to drive over to Söder Hospital and show Lisa Öhrström a few more of Ewert's photographs. Sven was to wait where he was; Ewert would pick him up soon.

It was difficult to look at Ewert, and Sven avoided all eye contact with his boss. He would do it later, he knew that, when the time was right, but not now. He settled gratefully in the passenger seat, where he could keep his gaze fixed on the anonymous car a few metres ahead in the slow-moving rush-hour mess on Skepp Bridge and up the slope up towards Slussen and Södermalm.

He wondered about the woman they were going to see. He was still feeling upset about the failure of the identity parade. Öhrström's reneging on her previous statement had turned the whole thing into a fiasco. Members of her family had been threatened and he understood how terrified she was, but there had been something else as well, something more than fear. She was also riddled with shame, the shame he had tried to explain to Ewert earlier. This had become obvious during their first interview, when she had told him that she grieved over the loss of her little brother but was disgusted with Hilding for being an addict and angry with him for indirectly being the cause of his own death.

She hadn't been able to prevent it and that was what made her feel ashamed and gave her another reason, in addition to the threats, for not recognising Lang behind that one-way window. Sven felt sure that she was one of those people who agonised about being inadequate, always tried to help, but never felt they had done enough. Hilding was probably the reason she had chosen to study medicine; she was family and therefore believed that she had to save and help and save and help.

And now he was dead, despite all her help.

She might never be rid of her shame now. She would have to live with it for ever.

When they walked into the ward, she was sitting in the

ward sister's glazed cubicle. Her face was pale; the look in her eyes was weary. Grief and fear and hatred can each corrode your strength; together they consume your whole life. She didn't greet them when they stepped inside the glass box, only looked at them and radiated something close to loathing.

Ewert ignored her manner – or possibly didn't notice it – he just reminded her briefly of their previous conversation. She didn't seem to care. It wasn't easy to read whether her indifference was pretence, or whether she simply couldn't bear to listen to what he was saying.

Ewert asked her to turn around. He had brought more photos.

It took some time before she stopped studying something on the wall, before she looked at the black-and-white photograph on the table in front of her.

'What do you see here?'

'I still have no idea what you're trying to prove with this game.'

'I'm just curious. What do you see?'

She stared at Grens for a while, then she turned her head.

She glanced at the photo, noting that it was printed on unusual, slightly rough paper.

'I see a fractured elbow. Left arm.'

'Thirty thousand kronor.'

'I'm sorry?'

'Remember the pictures I faxed to you? I'm sure you do. Three broken fingers; that is, one thumb at five thousand and two fingers at a thousand each. I told you that Lang operates with fixed charges, and also that he usually signs off a job by breaking a few fingers. Then I said that the poor sod had owed seven thousand kronor. That wasn't quite true. In fact he had been in debt to the tune of thirty-seven thousand. It meant the elbow had to go as well. Losing an arm is worth thirty thousand, you see.'

Sven was sitting a little to one side, behind Ewert. He felt bad, ashamed. Ewert, you're trampling all over her, he thought. I know what you want and I agree we need her as a witness, but not this, you're going too far.

'I have another picture. What would you say this is?'

The photograph showed a naked man on a stretcher. The whole body was in the frame and the picture had been taken from the side, in poor light as before, but it was easy to see what it was all about.

'You seem to have nothing to say. Let me help. This is a dead man. The arm you have been looking at is part of his body. Look! There are the fingers. You see, I told another fib. This guy didn't just owe thirty-seven thousand kronor, his debt amounted to one hundred and thirty-seven thousand. Lang charges one hundred thousand for a killing. This man's bad debt has been cleared. He has paid. One hundred and thirty-seven thousand in all.'

Lisa Öhrström clenched her jaw. She didn't speak, didn't move, pressed her lips tightly together to stop herself from screaming. Sven watched her, then looked at Ewert. You're getting there. You're close. But, Ewert, your tactics are out of order. You are hurting her and will soon do it again. I'll put up with it, despite feeling ashamed, ashamed of you, ashamed because of what you're doing, though I have to accept that you're the most skilful operator I've ever met in the force. You need her to testify and you will make her do it. But what about the other investigation? I should be helping you here, should be happy that you'll soon have her where you want her, but, Ewert, Ewert, how are you dealing with the Grajauskas case? What underhand tricks are you playing? I've just been to see Krantz, which is why I can't concentrate on what is going on here, can't even bear to look you in the eye. Which is also why I'd like to lie down on this table and shout until you listen. Krantz told me what I already knew. There's another videotape, another video, Ewert!

Ewert sat back and waited for Öhrström to cave in. Let her take her time.

'Come to think of it, I've got another set of pictures for you here.'

Lisa whispered. Her voice was too weak. 'You make your point very clearly.'

'Good. Excellent. You'll find the new set even more interesting.'

'I don't want to see them. And . . . there's something I don't understand. If what you tell me is true, if this is what Lang does and the sums you mentioned are his fixed charges, as you say, why hasn't he been locked away long ago?'

'Why? You should know. You have been threatened, haven't you? You know all you need to know about how Lang operates.'

That man who had come to the ward kitchen and had got hold of her photos of Sanna and Jonathan. She felt it again, the ache in her chest, the trembling that wouldn't stop.

Ewert put another envelope on the table, opened it and pulled out the first photograph. A different hand. Five fractures this time. You didn't need to be a qualified doctor to see that all the fingers had been crushed.

She was silent. He didn't taunt her, only placed another picture next to the hand. A cracked kneecap, very clear too.

'It's a little like a jigsaw, isn't it? A knee here, a hand there. It's fair to assume they belong together. They do, but this time the motive had nothing to do with money. This time it was respect.'

Ewert held both pictures in front of her face.

'This time the message was that you must never spike Yugoslav amphetamine with prison-issue washing powder.'

Still holding the two images in front of her face, Ewert took a third one from the envelope and held it even closer.

It had been taken by someone standing in a staircase, a few steps up, positioning the camera at head-height and pointing the lens at a recently dead man. An overturned wheelchair lay next to him. The blood that had flowed from the man's head had formed a pool around him.

She realised what the picture was and quickly turned her head away. She was crying.

'And that is what this guy had done. He had messed around with a big dealer's product. His name, by the way, was Hilding Oldéus.'

Sven had made up his mind during the car journey back from the hospital. He would keep a low profile for now and say nothing; he would not leave the police building until he had located the videotape.

Back at his desk, he picked up the pile of transcribed interrogations from the floor and started to leaf through them. He knew he had seen it somewhere.

He would read all of them again. Slowly. It was in there and he mustn't miss it.

It didn't take long, just about a quarter of an hour.

He had started with the statement made by the female medical student. The interview session had been brief, presumably she was weak and in shock. It would be a while before she had digested it all. Next he read the older man's statement. The interview with Dr Ejder had taken longer and been more like a conversation. Ejder had controlled his fear by using his logic. As long as he was rational, he could avoid getting over-emotional. Sven had come across the need to suppress fear many times before and noted different ways of keeping panic at bay. Ejder's self-control and intellectual approach also made him an exceptional witness. He was one of those people who spoke in images detailed enough to make the listener feel that they had been there. In this case, sitting at Ejder's side, tied up and powerless, on the mortuary floor.

Somewhere in the middle of this statement Sven found what he had been looking for. The doctor had been questioned about the plastic carrier bag where Lydia had kept her weapons. Suddenly, he described a videotape.

Sven followed the lines with his finger, reading one word at a time.

Ejder had seen the black tape when Lydia Grajauskas had pushed the sides of the bag down to take out the Semtex. It was at an early stage, when Ejder thought he should try to talk to her, win her confidence. At least it might help to calm the others. He had asked about the video, and after first refusing to answer, she had then decided to explain in her limited English.

She had said that the video was truth. He had asked her which truth, but she simply repeated the word. *Truth. Truth. Truth.* She had been silent while she concentrated on shaping the plastic dough, then she turned to him again.

Two tapes.

In box station train.

Twenty-one.

She had demonstrated the number by showing him first two fingers, then one.

Twenty-one.

Gustaf Ejder insisted that he recalled every single word, in the right order. She had said very little, with such effort, that it was easy to remember.

The truth. Two tapes. In box station train. Twenty-one. Sven read the passage once more. In a railway station. In box 21.

He was convinced now. There was another video in storage locker number twenty-one, almost certainly at the Central Station.

That tape would also have the safety tab removed and the video would contain images, not just a flickering greyness.

He put the pile of documents back on the floor and got up. He would be there soon.

The way he had forced those images on her, in her face.

Lisa was beyond hating anyone. Maybe she never had, and maybe she had never loved either; she had just filed hate and love away as two words for the same emotion, assuming that if she couldn't feel one, she couldn't feel the other either. But that had changed: she actually hated this policeman. The past twenty-four hours had been so strange; her grief for Hilding that wasn't really grief and, after that vague threat, her fear for the children that wasn't really fear. It was as if, at the age of thirty-five, all her feelings had been put under a spotlight; she had to force them all back in, throw away the key, hide behind her shame and not get to know herself. She had had no idea what they looked like, these unknown emotions, so strong and naked and impossible to escape.

And in the middle of it all that limping policeman had turned up and rubbed her face in it.

She had seen immediately that the last picture was of Hilding lying dead on the stairs and had got up from her chair, grabbed the photograph, torn it up and thrown the pieces against the glass wall.

She knew where she was going now, running down the corridor towards the main exit. She had a few more hours to do on her shift. For the first time in her life she couldn't care less. She ran out on to the tarmac outside, and turned in the direction of Tanto Park, across the railway tracks and through the park, not even aware of the unleashed dogs that pursued her fleeing body, propelled by panic. She carried on running, past the Zinkensdamm housing estate, stopping only when she had crossed Horn Street and could stand in the shade of the huge Högalid Church.

She wasn't tired, didn't register the sweat that trickled down over her forehead and cheeks. She stood for a while to get her breath back before walking down the slope to the house where she stayed as often as she did in her own flat.

The door to the flat on the fifth floor of number 3 Völund Street had been replaced. The large hole in the panel was no more. There was nothing to show that just a few days earlier the police had broken in to stop an incident of gross physical violence, a naked woman lashed across the back thirty-five times.

The two girls, still in their teens, stood behind the man who could have been their father while he unlocked the door. When they went into the flat, they saw the electronic locks on the door, but didn't know what they were. The man closed the door and showed the girls their passports. Then he explained again that the passports had cost him. Therefore they owed him money and would have to work to pay it off. The first customers were due two hours from now.

The girl who had started to cry downstairs was still crying; she tried to protest, until the man, who until only a few days earlier had been called Dimitri-Bastard-Pimp by two other young women, pressed the muzzle of a gun to her temple. For a brief moment she thought he would shoot.

He told them to undress. He was going to try them out. From now on it was important that they knew what men liked.

Lisa was feeling hot after running all the way from the hospital. She had only stopped when she could see Ylva's house in Högalid Street.

She hadn't been thinking straight earlier. She was capable of love, of course she was, not for a man, but for her nephew and niece; she loved them more than she loved herself. She had put off coming here. Normally she'd pop in to see them every day, but she had lacked the strength to walk into the house and tell them that their uncle had died, that he had crashed down a stairwell the day before.

They adored their Uncle Hilding. To them he wasn't a hopeless junkie. They had only met the other Hilding, straight out of prison, round-cheeked and easy-going, full of a calm that had always vanished a few days later, when the world around him began to look dangerous, reminding him of the shadows he couldn't cope with and couldn't confront. They had never seen that awful junkie. They had never seen the change. He was only there for them for a few days at a time, and then when he changed into something else, he disappeared.

She had to tell them, though. They must not be informed by having black-and-white police photographs pushed into their faces.

Lisa held Ylva's hand in hers. They had hugged each other before going to sit side by side on the sofa. Both were feeling the same way: not quite grief, more a kind of relief that they knew where he was and where he wasn't. The sisters weren't certain that they should feel that way, but now that they were together, it seemed easier to accept these impermissible feelings.

Jonathan and Sanna sat in the two armchairs opposite the sofa. They had sensed that this wasn't one of Auntie Lisa's usual visits. Not that she had said anything yet, but as soon as she opened the front door they had started to prepare themselves for what she would say. The way she had pressed down the door handle, said hello, and walked to the small sitting room all made it obvious that this was not just an ordinary visit.

She didn't know how to begin. There was no need to worry.

'What's the matter?'

Sanna was twelve, and still in the zone between little girl and young teenager. She looked at the two grown women she trusted implicitly and repeated her question.

'What is it? I know something's wrong.'

Lisa leaned towards the children, reaching out to put one hand on Sanna's knee and the other on Jonathan's. Such a little boy, her fingertips met easily around his leg.

'You're right. Something is wrong. It's to do with your uncle.'

'Hilding has died.'

Sanna spoke unhesitatingly, as if she had been waiting to say this.

Lisa's hands tightened their hold. 'He died yesterday. In the hospital, on my ward.'

Jonathan, only six years of life inside his small body, watched as his mum and Auntie Lisa cried. He hadn't grasped this, not yet.

'Uncle Hilding wasn't an old person, was he? Was he so old that he had to die?'

'Don't be so silly. You don't understand a thing. He killed himself with drugs because he was a junkie.'

Sanna glared at her little brother, making him the target of the bad thoughts she didn't want to have any more.

Lisa's hand moved to stroke Sanna's cheek. 'Don't think about him like that.'

'But he was.'

'Don't say these things. What happened was an accident. He died because he lost control of his wheelchair and it fell down the stairs.'

'I don't care what you say. I know he was a junkie. And I know that's why he's dead. You can pretend what you like, because I know anyway.'

Jonathan listened but didn't want to know. He got up from his armchair, crying now. His uncle wasn't dead, he couldn't be.

He shouted at his sister. 'It's your fault!'

He ran from the room and all the way downstairs and across the concrete flags on the courtyard, screaming all the way.

'It's your fault! You're stupid! It's your fault, if you say that!'

The afternoon was fading into evening. Lars Ågestam was surprised to see Ewert Grens open his office door without knocking. His looks, his massive body, thinning grey hair, the straight leg that made him limp, none of that had changed.

'I thought you weren't coming until tomorrow.'

'I'm here now. And I've brought you some information.'

'Information about . . . ?'

'The murders. That is, the investigations into the incidents at Söder Hospital, both of them.'

He didn't wait for Ågestam to offer him a seat, he simply grabbed the nearest chair and carelessly dumped a pile of papers on the floor. Then he sat down opposite the young prosecutor, whom he had mentally consigned to his large category of 'stuck-up prats'.

'First, Alena Sljusareva. The other woman from Lithuania. She is on her way home now. I have questioned her and she has got nothing to offer us. Didn't know who Bengt Nordwall was, didn't know where or how Grajauskas had got hold of arms and explosives. She had never heard of any kidnapping plans. I helped her to catch the ferry to Klaipeda and so forth. She needs her home and we don't need her.'

'You sent her home?'

'Any objections?'

'You should have informed me first. We should have discussed the entire matter, and if we both agreed that sending her home was reasonable, the final decision would still have been mine.'

Ewert Grens stared at the young man with distaste. He felt the urge to shout, but refrained. He had just created a lie and presented it to the prosecutor. For once he chose to hide his anger.

'Anything else?'

'You have sent home a person who could be guilty of a serious gun crime, as well as being an accessory to the potential destruction of property and aggravated taking of hostages.' Lars Ågestam shrugged.

'But if this woman is on board a ferry . . . that's it. End of story.'

Grens fought his contempt for the young man on the other side of the desk. He couldn't explain it properly; he always despised people who used their university education as a reference for life, who hadn't actually lived, only pretended to experience.

'Right. Next, about Jochum Lang.'

'Yes?'

'Time to lock him up for good.'

Ågestam pointed at the papers which Ewert Grens had dumped on the floor.

'Grens, that pile is interview transcripts, one after the other. No result. He's stonewalling. I can't hold him for much longer.'

'You can.'

'I can't.'

'You can and you can even inform him that he is a suspect for the murder of Hilding Oldéus. We have a positive identification.'

'Do you indeed? Who?'

Lars Ågestam was slightly built, wore small round glasses and his short hair combed forward in a half-fringe, and, although he had just celebrated his thirtieth birthday, looked more like a little boy than ever as he leaned back in the large leather chair and listened.

'A doctor in the ward where Oldéus was a patient. Woman called Lisa Öhrström. She is Oldéus's sister.'

Ågestam didn't reply at first. He pushed his chair back and got up.

'According to a report from your colleague, DI Sundkvist, an identity parade did not have the expected outcome. Not so good. Lang's lawyer won't leave me alone, of course. He demands that his client be released instantly, as no one has identified him.'

'Listen to me. You *will* get your identification. I'll bring it in tomorrow.'

The prosecutor sat down again, dragging his chair closer to the desk, and then raised his arms in the air, as people do in films when someone points a gun at them.

'Grens, I give in. Explain what you're up to, please.'

'You will get your identification tomorrow. No further explanation required.'

Ågestam pondered over what he had just been told.

He was in charge of two separate investigations into three deaths that had taken place in the space of a few hours in the same building, and in both cases Ewert Grens was the man who reported directly to him. Somehow the stories Grens had just told didn't ring true. Too simple.

Sljusareva had been sent home already, Lang had been identified – he should be satisfied that the superintendent running both shows insisted that everything was well in hand.

But Ågestam was not reassured. Something wasn't right, something just wasn't right.

'The media are pestering me, you know.'

'Sod them.'

'I'm being asked about Grajauskas's motive. Why would a young female prostitute want to kill a policeman and then herself? In a closed room, for Christ's sake, a mortuary? I don't know. I need answers.'

'We haven't got the answers. The case is under investigation.'

'In that case we're back to square one. I simply don't understand you, Grens. If the motive is still unknown, why let Sljusareva go? A woman who is possibly the only person who might know something.'

Ewert Grens's anger welled up, his permanent rage at these interfering prats. He was just about to raise his voice, but his burden, Bengt's damned lie, stopped him, making him again into someone he was not, someone who looked before he jumped. He had to be cautious, just for once. Instead his voice dropped, almost to a hiss.

'Look Ågestam, don't treat me like you're interrogating me.'

'I've been reading the transcripts of the communications you had with the mortuary before the shooting started.'

Ågestam pretended not to hear the threat in his voice,

didn't look at the large policeman as he searched for the right sheets of paper in the bundle on his desk. He knew where they were, somewhere in the middle. He found what he had been after. He followed a few lines with his finger and read out loud.

'Grens, this is you speaking, or shouting, actually. And I quote: "*This is something personal! Bengt, over! Fuck's sake, Bengt. Stop it! Squad, move in! All clear. Repeat, move in!*"'

Ågestam looked up and spread his thin, suit-sleeved arms in a gesture.

'End of quote.'

The telephone on the desk between them suddenly started to ring. Both men counted the signals, seven in all, before it stopped to make space for their exchange.

'Quote away. You weren't there, were you? Sure enough, that's how I felt at the time. That some personal issue was at stake. I still think that, but I don't know what it was.'

Lars Ågestam looked Grens in the eye for a while before turning to the window and scanning the view of the restless city. You couldn't get your head round it all, it was too much.

He hesitated.

The intrusive sense that something was not right had made him formulate what could be taken as an accusation against this powerful man, and he didn't want to say it out loud. But he should, he must.

He turned to face Grens again.

'What you're telling me is . . . nothing. I don't know what it is, I can't put my finger on it, Ewert – I think that's the first time I've called you that, Ewert – but what are you doing? I am aware that you're investigating the murder of your best friend and understand that it must be hard for you, maybe too hard. I can't help wondering if it is a good idea. Your grief . . . you're grieving, I'm sure, it must hurt.'

Ågestam took a deep breath and jumped in.

'What I'm trying to say is . . . do you want to be replaced?'

Ewert Grens rose quickly.

'You sit here behind your desk with your precious documents, you ambitious little penpusher, but you'd better get this. I was investigating crimes, flesh-and-blood crimes, before your daddy got into your mummy's knickers. And I've not stopped.'

Grens half turned, pointing at the door.

'Now I'm going off to do exactly that: investigate crimes, that is. Back down there, with the hard men and the whores. Unless there was something else you wanted?'

Lars Ågestam shook his head and watched as the other man left.

Then he sighed. Detective Superintendent Grens seldom failed. It was well known. He simply didn't make silly mistakes. That was fact, regardless of what you thought about his social skills or ability to communicate.

He trusted Ewert Grens.

He decided to carry on trusting him.

The evening had patiently dislodged those who spent hours of their lives commuting between their suburban homes and city-centre jobs. Stockholm Central Station was quiet now, preparing for the following morning when the commuters would be back, scurrying from one platform to the next.

Sven Sundkvist sat on a seat in the main hall, pointlessly staring at the electronic Departures and Arrivals board. Half an hour earlier he had gone in search of the downstairs storage boxes. He knew of them, of course, lock-ups intended as a service for visitors, but mostly used by the homeless and criminals in need of somewhere to stash belongings, drugs, stolen goods, weapons.

He had located box 21 and then stood in front of it considering what he should do. Would it not be best if he were to forget about having checked the hostages' statements? No one else would read through them again.

Then he could go home to Anita and Jonas.

Nobody would give it another thought.

Home sweet home. No more of this shit.

As he hovered, he felt the rage come back, the pains in his stomach; it was more than just a feeling now. He remembered the talk with Krantz earlier and how certain the elderly technician had been. He had recorded the find of a used videotape with a broken safety tab.

Now, it was nowhere.

You're risking thirty-three years of service in the force. I don't understand you.

That's why I'm here, standing in front of a locker door in Stockholm Central Station. I have no idea what I will find, what it was Lydia Grajauskas wanted to tell us, only that it will be something I'd rather not know.

It had taken him the best part of a quarter of an hour to persuade the woman inside the cramped left-luggage office that he really was a detective inspector with Homicide and needed her help to examine the contents of one of the boxes.

She had kept shaking her head until he got fed up with arguing and raised his voice to emphasise that it was within his rights to order her to open the locker. When he had added a reminder that it was her duty as a citizen to assist the police, she had reluctantly contacted the station security officer, who held spare keys to the boxes.

When Sven Sundkvist saw the green uniform in the main station entrance, he went to meet the man. He identified himself and they walked together to the lock-ups.

In the heavy bunch of keys, number 21 was indistinguishable.

The door opened easily and the security officer stepped aside to let Sven Sundkvist come closer. Sven peered inside the narrow dark space, divided by two shelves.

There wasn't much to see.

Two dresses in a plastic bag. A photo album with black-and-white studio photographs of relatives wearing their nicest clothes and nervous smiles. A cigar box full of Swedish paper money in one- or five-hundred kronor notes. He counted quickly. Forty thousand kronor.

The estate of Lydia Grajauskas.

He held on to the metal door. It struck him that her life had been stored in this box, what little past she still had, as well as her stake in the future, her hope, her escape, her sense of existing somewhere other than in that flat, in a real place.

Sven Sundkvist put the things he had found into his brief-case.

Then he reached up to the top shelf and took down a video with a label on the back in Cyrillic script.

She had run after him, across the courtyard, through the hallway and out on to Högalid Street. He stopped there, barefoot and tearful. She loved him and hugged him close and carried him home in her arms, saying his name over and over again. He was Jonathan, her nephew, and what she felt for him must surely be what you feel for your own child.

Lisa Öhrström stroked his hair; she had to go soon. It was late and dark, as dark as it could be a few weeks before midsummer; darkness was gently edging into what had been daylight until now. She kissed his cheek. Sanna had already gone to bed. Ylva was there and she met her sister's eyes before closing the door behind her.

There were so few of them left. Their father was gone, and now Hilding. She had seen it coming, of course, and now there it was, the enveloping loneliness.

She decided to walk. She had been there before and knew the way, across Väster Bridge, along Norr Mälarstrand, then through side streets to the City Police building. It would take half an hour or so, not long on a summer's night. She knew that he usually worked late, he had said so, and he was that sort, one of those who didn't have anything else. He would sit hunched over the investigation that had to be completed, just as the week before there had been an investigation to complete and next week would bring another one to serve as a reason for not leaving the office.

She phoned to tell him that she was coming. He replied quickly, sounded as if he was expecting her, possibly even certain that she would come.

He met her at the main entrance and led the way along a dark, stale-smelling corridor, his uneven steps slapping and resounding against the walls. Christ, how grim it was. How strange that anyone should choose to work in surroundings like these. She looked at him from behind, broad and overweight, a bald patch on the back of his head, his limping, slightly bent body. How odd that he should seem strong, but he did; at least in this shabby place he radiated the kind of strength that gives a sense of security, the result of having made a choice. Which was what he had done, he had actually chosen to work in this place.

Ewert Grens ushered her into his office and offered her a seat in his visitor's chair. She looked around and thought it a bleak room. The only things with a personality setting them apart from the dull, mass-produced office furniture were an ancient monster of a ghetto-blaster and a sofa, ugly and sagging, which she felt sure he often slept on.

'Coffee?'

He didn't really mean it, but knew that he should ask.

'No thank you. I'm not here to drink coffee.'

'I guessed not. Anyway.'

He raised a plastic cup half full of what looked like black coffee from a machine and drank the lot.

'What can I do for you?'

'You don't seem surprised. To see me.'

'I'm not surprised. But I am pleased.'

Lisa Öhrström realised that what had come over her, what was tugging at her mind, was tiredness. She had been so tense. Now she relaxed as much as she dared to and the recent past weighed heavily on her.

'I don't want to see any more of your photographs. I don't want any more images of people I don't know and never want to know thrust in my face. I've had enough. I'll testify. I will identify Lang as the man who came to see my brother yesterday.'

Lisa Öhrström put her elbows on the desk, leaning forward with her chin on her clasped hands. So very tired. Home soon.

'But there's one thing I want you to know. It wasn't only the threats that made me hold back. Quite a long time ago I decided that I would never again allow Hilding and his addiction to influence how I lived. This last year, I haven't been there for him any more, but it didn't make any difference. I still couldn't escape him. Now that he's dead, he still drains me of strength, perhaps more than ever. So I might as well testify.'

Ewert Grens tried to keep the smile from his face. This was it, obviously.

Anni, this is it.

Closure.

'Nobody is blaming you.'

'I don't need your pity.'

'Your choice, but that's how it is. Nobody blames you because you didn't know what to do.'

Grens went over to root among his audiotapes, found what he wanted and put it into the player. Siw Malmkvist. She was sure it would be.

'One thing more. Who threatened you?'

Siw Malmkvist. She had just taken the hardest decision in her life and he was listening to Siw Malmkvist.

'That's not important. I will stand witness. But on one condition.'

Lisa Öhrström stayed where she was, chin resting on her hands. She was leaning forward, getting closer to him.

'My nephew and niece. I want them to have protection.'

'They already have protection.'

'I don't understand.'

'They have been under protection ever since the identity parade. I know, for instance, that you went to see them today. One of the kids ran outside without his shoes on. And they will continue to be protected, of course.'

Fatigue paralysed her. She yawned without even trying to hide it.

'I must get home now.'

'I'll get someone to drive you. In a plain car.'

'Please, to Högalid Street. To Jonathan and Sanna. They'll be asleep.'

'I suggest that we step up the level of protection and put someone inside the flat as well. Do you agree?'

Evening had really come.

Darkness. Silence, as if the whole big building were empty.

She looked at the policeman and his tape recorder; he was humming along, knew the jolly tune and the meaningless text by heart.

He sang under his breath and she felt sorry for him.

FRIDAY 7 JUNE

He had never liked the dark.

Winter darkness that lasted for an eternity had been part of his childhood in Kiruna, well to the north of the Arctic Circle, and police college in Stockholm had meant a series of night shifts, but he couldn't resign himself to the dark, couldn't get used to it. To him, the dark would never be beautiful.

He was standing in the sitting room, looking out through the window at the dense forest. The June night lay as deep under the trees as summer darkness ever can be. Sven Sundkvist had got home a little after ten o'clock with the video in his briefcase. First he had gone to see the sleeping Jonas, kissed the boy's forehead and stood for a while listening to his quiet breathing. Anita had been in the kitchen doing a crossword. He managed to squeeze in next to her on the chair, and after an hour or so, only three squares in three different corners were empty. Typical, just a few letters short of posting the completed crossword to the local paper in the hope of winning one of three Premium Bonds.

Afterwards they made love. She had undressed him first and then herself; she wanted him to sit on the kitchen chair and she settled in his lap, their naked bodies so close, needing each other.

He had waited until she had gone to sleep. It was after midnight when he got out of bed and pulled on a T-shirt and tracksuit bottoms. He carried his briefcase into the sitting room.

He thought it better to be alone when he watched the video.

Alone with the overwhelming feeling of unease.

What Anita and Jonas didn't know couldn't hurt them.

The dark outside. Staring into it he could just make out some of the trees.

He checked his watch. Ten past one. He had spent an hour looking at nothing in particular. He couldn't put it off any more.

She had told Ejder about two videotapes.

She had made a copy. Just in case. Someone might wipe one of the tapes, or record on top of her film, or simply try to lose the whole thing and replace it with an empty cassette.

Sven Sundkvist could not be sure that what he was watching was identical to the recording on the other tape.

He assumed that it was.

> *They look nervous, the way people do when they are not used to staring at the single eye that preserves what it looks at for posterity.*
>
> *Grajauskas speaks first.*
>
> *"Это мой повод. Моя история такая."*
>
> *Two sentences. She turns to Sljusareva, who translates.*
>
> *'This is my reason. This is my story.'*
>
> *Grajauskas speaks again, two sentences, with her eyes fixed on her friend.*
>
> *"Надеюсь что когда ты слышишь это того о ком идет речь уже нет. Что он чувствовал мой стыд."*
>
> *Her face has a serious expression. She nods and again Sjusareva turns to the camera and translates.*

'When you hear this, I hope that the man I am going to talk about is dead. I hope that he has felt my shame.'

They speak very distinctly, careful to enunciate every word in both Russian and Swedish.

He leaned forward and stopped the tape.

He didn't want to go on.

What he felt was no longer unease or dread, rather an overwhelming anger of a kind he only rarely had to confront. No more doubt. He had hoped, as everyone always does. But now he knew, he knew that Ewert had manipulated the tape and had a motive for doing it.

Sven Sundkvist got up, went into the kitchen and put on the coffee machine, a strong brew to help him think. It would be a long night.

The crossword was still lying on the kitchen table. He moved it to make room for a sheet from Jonas's drawing pad, picked up one of the boy's marker pens, a purple one, and drew lines, haphazard at first, on the white surface.

A man.

An older man. Massive torso, not much hair, piercing eyes.

Ewert.

He smiled at himself when he realised. He had in fact drawn Ewert in purple marker ink.

He knew why, of course. A long night was staring him in the face.

He had known Ewert for nearly ten years. To begin with he had been ordered about and shouted at – they all had – but at some point he had suddenly become aware of something like friendship with his difficult boss and had become one of the few who were addressed normally, men whom Ewert invited into his office and confided in, as much as he ever did. Later Sven had come to know Ewert Grens well enough to realise how little he understood him. He had never been to Ewert's flat, and you couldn't really know people whose homes you'd never seen. On the other hand, Ewert had been here, for supper or just for a cup of coffee, and had sat at this very table flanked by Anita and Jonas.

Sven had invited Ewert to his home, a place where he could be himself. Ewert had never reciprocated.

He looked at the drawing and started to fill in the purple man's jacket and shoes with more purple. He knew nothing about the private person. He knew the policeman, DSI Grens, who was first in the office every morning, long before everyone else, played Siw Malmkvist songs with the volume turned up, worked all day and all night, often stayed overnight in his office to carry on with an unfinished investigation when dawn broke. He was the best policeman Sven had ever encountered, incapable of making simple errors and always prepared to pursue every case to its conclusion, regardless of consequences. To him, the investigation alone mattered, to the exclusion of everything else.

But now he didn't know any longer.

He drank the rest of the coffee in his cup and refilled it. He needed more.

Another marker pen, a screaming shade of green this time. He used it for making notes in the space next to the purple man.

Ejder sees the video in LG's carrier bag.

Krantz finds it at the scene, notes that it has been used. He records two sets of probably female fingerprints. One set is LG's.

Krantz hands it to EG in the mortuary. EG takes charge of it, but does not record anywhere, i.e., not with the duty staff or the forensic boys.

SS finds a video in EG's office. The tape is blank.

In the interview, Ejder states that LG told him that a copy of the video is deposited in a Central Station storage locker.

SS gets access to the locker, brings the tape home. SS

creeps around the house at night, watches the video and can confirm that it is not blank.

He stopped making notes. He could have added, *SS is too soft to carry on watching it*, but instead he just sat and looked at the ink version of Ewert. What have you done? I know that you deleted evidence, and I know why. He scrunched up the paper and threw it across the table towards the sink. Then he tried to solve the crossword, testing one letter after another in the three empty squares, but gave up after a quarter of an hour.

He wandered back to the sitting room.

The videotape demanded attention.

He could have not collected it. Or not brought it home. Now he has no choice. He has to watch it.

> *Lydia Grajauskas again. The camera slips out of focus, a few seconds pass and then the cameraman signals to carry on.*
>
> "Когда Бенгт Нордвалл встретил меня в Клайпейде сказал он что это была хорошая высокооплачивая работа."
>
> *She looks at her friend, waiting for her to translate. Sljusareva strokes Lydia's cheek before she turns to the camera.*
>
> 'When I met Bengt Nordwall in Klaipeda, he said it was good job and very well paid.'

Sven Sundkvist stopped the tape and fled into the kitchen again. He peered into the fridge, drank some milk straight from the carton and closed the door quietly. Mustn't wake Anita.

He had not put it into words, but this was exactly what he had feared.

A different truth.

When the truth changes, lies emerge. A lie can only be dealt with when it is known to be a lie.

He went back into the sitting room and settled on the sofa.

He had just started to be part of Bengt Nordwall's big lie.

He was convinced that Ewert had watched this very film and realised the same as he had. Ewert had watched and then wiped it, to protect his friend. Now Sven faced the same dilemma. Bengt Nordwall's lie had become Ewert's. If he himself did nothing, he too would have to live with it. He could do the same as Ewert: look away to protect a friend's reputation.

He started the video again and fast-forwarded it to find out how long the film was. Twenty minutes. He checked the time. Half past two. If he started from the beginning and watched the whole of Lydia Grajauskas's story, he would be finished before three. Then he could tiptoe into the bedroom, leave a note on the pillow explaining that he had a night job, get dressed and take the car into town. The drive took only twenty minutes.

It was nearly four o'clock when he opened his office door. Morning had already arrived, bringing light from somewhere out at sea, from the east, light that had followed him along the deserted stretch of motorway between Gustavsberg and central Stockholm.

He got himself more coffee, not so much to stay awake – his mind was alive with ideas, and sleep was simply not an option – but because he hoped the coffee would help him to sharpen up and get a grip before the buzzing in his head took over and crystallised into its own conclusions, the way thoughts do at night.

He cleared his desk by piling papers and photographs and folders on the floor. When he sat down at the bare desktop, the wooden surface seemed new to him. He had probably never seen it like this, not for years anyway; he had worked here for five or six years.

He took a ball of paper from his pocket. It was the drawing of Ewert, rescued from the kitchen sink. He flattened it out in the middle of the desk. Now he knew that the purple man had gone beyond the point of no return and tampered with evidence, in order to protect his own interests, to protect a lie that wasn't his.

Absently retracing the outline of the man he had drawn, Sven Sundkvist felt an impotent rage. He had no idea what to do with this knowledge.

Lars Ågestam did what he usually did when he couldn't sleep. He dressed in his suit and black shoes, put only the minimum in his briefcase and left his house to walk into work with the dawn – three hours through Stockholm's western suburbs.

It had been an odd conversation, hard to follow too. As a rule he didn't have problems understanding but this time Ewert Grens, a man he both admired and pitied, had insisted that on the one hand the police had no notion of Lydia Grajauskas's motive for knocking out her guard, taking five hostages and killing a policeman before shooting herself, but that, on the other hand, her best friend Alena Sljusareva knew nothing that had any bearing on the case and could therefore be left to her own devices back home in Lithuania.

Sleep had been impossible.

At the time, he had decided to trust Grens after all.

Now, in the light of the rising sun, he walked with purpose. He had already phoned Söder Hospital to say he wanted to visit the mortuary once more.

He didn't knock. Nothing odd about that, Ewert Grens never knocked.

Sven started and looked at the door.

'Ewert?'

'Bloody hell, you're early, Sven. What's up?'

Sven blushed, aware of how obvious it was. He stared down at his desktop, embarrassed and exposed. There he was, staring at his purple version of Ewert.

'I don't know. It seemed a good idea.'

'For Christ's sake, it's just gone five in the morning. Normally there isn't another soul around at this time.'

Grens made a move to step into the room. Sven Sundkvist

glanced nervously at his drawing and covered it with his hand.

'Come on, son. What's on your mind?'

Sven was not much good at lying, especially not to people he liked.

'Nothing special. There's just such a lot to do at the moment.'

He was suffocating. Must be as red as a beetroot.

'Ewert, you know how it is. Söder Hospital, all that. The media are on our backs. And you'd rather give all that a miss. But we need some kind of basic story for the press office.'

No more of this, I can't handle it, he thought, looking down at the desktop.

Ewert Grens took a step forward, stood still for a moment, then backed out, talking as he went.

'Good. I'm sure you know what you're doing, Sven. And I'm pleased you're dealing with the hacks.'

Söder Hospital was a huge lump of a building, usually ugly, but now in the early sunlight it was almost beautiful, coated in a pale red glow that cast its reflection on gleaming windows and roofs. It was nearly six o'clock when Lars Ågestam walked through the main hall, which was barely awake.

He took the lift down to the basement, the same route Grajauskas had taken two days ago, a badly injured woman with a plastic bag hidden under her hospital clothes, whom no one would beat up again.

The last part of the corridor was cordoned off with blue and white police tape, from roughly the point where Sven had been lying in wait, some thirty metres away from the door, but close enough to see that it was no longer there. Ågestam bent down under the tape, avoided the bits of broken wall, and made for the hole where the door had been. It was sealed with a criss-cross of tape that he ripped off.

A hallway, then the room where they had been found on the floor. Their outlines in white chalk were close. Her body so near his. Their blood mingling. He had died with her. She had died with him. Ågestam felt certain it had been deliberate, this final resting place of theirs, side by side.

It was silent down there. He looked around the room. Death terrified him; he didn't even wear a watch any more as it just measured time. And yet here he was in a mortuary, alone, trying to understand what had happened.

The tape recorder. He placed it in the middle of the floor.

He wanted to listen to them talking.

He wanted to be part of it, afterwards, as he always did.

'Ewert.'

'Receiving.'

'The hostage in the corridor is dead. No visible blood, so I can't make out where she shot him. But the smell is odd, strong. Harsh.'

Bengt Nordwall's voice. Steady, at least it sounded steady. Lars Ågestam had never met him and never heard his voice before.

He was trying to get to know a dead man.

'Ewert, it is all one fucking big con. She hasn't shot anyone. All the hostages are still here. All four of them are alive. They've just walked out. She has got about three hundred grams of Semtex round the doors, but she can't detonate it.'

He noticed the man's fear. Nordwall continued to observe and describe what he was seeing, but the tone of his voice had changed, as if he had understood something which the listeners upstairs had not and which Ågestam, a late listener, was trying to grasp now.

'You are naked.'

'That's how you wanted it.'

'How does that feel? What is it like to be here, in a mortuary, standing naked in front of a woman with a gun?'

'I have done what you asked me to do.'

'You feel humiliated, don't you?'

320

'Yes.'

'All alone?'

'Yes.'

'Afraid?'

'Yes.'

'Kneel.'

Not even two days had passed. The recorded voices were alive still, even the Russian interpreter's version. Every word was distinct. They were speaking in a closed room. She had made up her mind, Lars Ågestam was certain of that. She had decided from the start what would happen. She was to die there. He was to die there.

She would humiliate him and afterwards they would both cease to breathe.

For all eternity they would lie together on a mortuary floor.

Ågestam didn't move from where Nordwall had stood, wondering if he had known that he had only a few seconds left, a fraction of a moment, and then nothing.

Ewert Grens couldn't concentrate.

He hadn't slept at all and told himself that he should've kipped down on the office sofa. There was too much on his mind that needed attention, stuff that had to be mulled over and over, interminably. Sleeping at home was not an option.

He had promised to have lunch with Lena, who wanted to carry on talking about Bengt. He said no at first, he didn't want to. He missed his old friend, of course he did, but he was also aware that the man he missed was someone other than the Bengt Nordwall he had learnt more about recently.

If only I had known then what I know now.

Did you think about her? Did you ever? And when you came home, did the two of you make love? I mean, after-wards?

I'm doing this for Lena.

You are not alive.

When she had asked him again later, he agreed to have lunch with her.

Lena ate nothing, only played with the food on her plate and drank mineral water, two whole bottles. She had been weeping, mostly for the children, she said, it is so hard for them and they don't understand, and if I don't understand either, Ewert, how can I explain to them?

Afterwards he was glad that he had been with her. She needed him, needed to say the same things so many times that they gradually sank in and she could begin to understand.

He didn't have the courage to grieve properly.

It felt right to watch somebody else doing it.

Lars Ågestam listened to the tape over and over again. He had stood in the middle of the room listening, and then sat with his back to the wall just like the hostages. He had lain down one last time where Bengt Nordwall had been, protected his genitals with his hands, and stared at the ceiling. He was aware of the white chalk outline, drawn around a body larger than his own. He listened to the whole exchange between Bengt Nordwall and Ewert, and was now convinced that Nordwall, who had ended his life just where he himself was lying now, had known exactly who Lydia Grajauskas was, and that they somehow belonged together, which was what Grens had sensed or maybe even knew and why for some reason he was prepared to throw away a whole life in the police force in order to protect the truth.

By the time he was ready to leave, Ågestam had spent two full hours in the mortuary. Suddenly he was panicking about death, had to get away, needed to eat breakfast in a large café packed with people who were noisy and hungry and alive.

'I had this area cordoned off.'

Lars hadn't heard him come in: Nils Krantz, a technician from Forensics. They had met, but didn't know each other.

'I'm sorry, I had to get in. I was looking for some answers.'

'You're trampling all over the crime scene.'

'I am the prosecutor in charge of the investigation.'

'I know, but to be frank I don't give a damn who you are. You stick to the marker lines like everyone else. I'm responsible for any evidence here that's worth having a look at.'

Ågestam sighed loudly, suggesting that he wouldn't waste time arguing about trivia. He turned away, picked up his tape recorder and his notebook, put them in his bag. Time for breakfast.

'You're in a hurry.'

'You gave me the impression I was to get off site as quickly as possible.'

Nils Krantz shrugged, started studying the remains of explosive round the door frame to the store and suddenly spoke in a loud voice.

'Thought you might be interested to hear that the test results are in.'

'What test results?'

'From the other investigation, the one involving Lang. We did a body scan.'

'Yes?'

'Nothing.'

'What do you mean, nothing?'

'We went over every square inch. No trace of Oldéus anywhere on his body.'

Lars Ågestam had been on his way out, but stopped when Krantz raised his voice. Now he felt empty, couldn't muster the energy to move.

'There you go.'

He stood still, looking glumly at Krantz, who carried on prodding the area round the door frame with his gloved hands. Finally he managed to pull himself together enough to pick up his briefcase and start off towards what had once been the door. He was just about to step through the hole in the wall when Krantz called after him again.

'Wait.'

'What is it now?'

'Lang's clothes, we did them too, of course. And the shoes. There it was. Traces of blood and DNA – Oldéus's blood and DNA.'

After lunch, Ewert Grens had left Lena alone in the restaurant. She told him that she wanted to sit for a bit longer, ordered a third bottle of mineral water and hugged him. He had started walking towards Homicide when he changed his mind and took the slightly longer route via the police cells.

He couldn't resist it.

It wouldn't be enough to have a reliable doctor identifying him from photographs, even if she insisted with one hundred per cent certainty that he was the killer. If that same killer managed to threaten and frighten the witness once more, neatly timed for the identity parade, so that no identification was made after all, then the law said that he could go free to kill again.

This time was different. This time it would be enough.

Grens took the lift and got out on the second floor, where he told the guard he wanted a word with Jochum Lang, that he wanted to fetch him himself and take him to the interrogation room.

The guard led the way past silent, closed doors, stopped in front of number eight. Ewert nodded to the guard who then pulled back the little flap to let Ewert peer inside.

He was lying on his back on the bunk, his eyes closed. He was sleeping. There was nothing much else he could do, locked up for twenty-three out of every twenty-four hours, confined to a few lousy square metres without newspapers or radio or TV.

Grens shouted through the opening.

'Hey, Lang! Time to wake up!'

No response, not a twitch. He had heard all right.

'Now. Time for a chat. Just you and me.'

Lang moved a little, lifted his head when Grens shouted, then turned on his side with his back towards the door.

Irritated, Grens slammed the flap shut.

He nodded to the guard, who unlocked the door. Grens stepped inside the cell, saying that he wanted to be alone with the prisoner. The officer hesitated. Jochum Lang was classified as dangerous. He decided to stay put. Grens explained, as patiently as he could, that he would take full responsibility for the prisoner for the duration, and that if there was a cock-up, it would be his fault and his alone.

The officer shrugged, and closed the door behind him.

Grens took a step closer to the bunk.

'Lang, don't mess with me. Get up.'

'Piss off.'

One last step and he was close enough to touch the body lying there. Instead he grabbed the edge of the bunk and shook it until Lang got up.

They stood facing each other. Staring hard. Staring.

'Interview time, Lang. Get moving.'

'Fuck off.'

'We've found matches with his blood group and DNA. We have a witness. You'll be put away, Lang. For murder.'

Ten or twenty centimetres between their faces.

'Grens, you're a stupid twat. I have no idea what the fuck you're talking about. Perhaps you should take it easy, be a bit more careful. You know that policemen have hurt themselves falling out of cars before.'

Ewert Grens smiled, showing plenty of stained teeth.

'You can threaten me as much as you like. Whatever. There's nothing I can lose now that isn't worth putting you away for good. You'll be wanking behind bars until you're sixty.'

It was hard to tell which of them hated the other more.

Each man looked into his enemy's eyes, searching for something that should be there. When he spoke, Lang's voice was low, warm puffs of air in Grens's face.

'I'm not taking part in any more of your interrogations. Period. Just so you know, you old shit. If you or any other pig turns up to drag me off to just one more chat show, I'll hurt the poor fucker badly. Take my word for it. Fuck off now. And shut the door behind you.'

Sven Sundkvist had phoned home and tried to explain why he had disappeared in the middle of the night without a word, just leaving a note. Anita had been upset; she didn't like the fact that he hadn't spoken to her, especially as they had promised never to take off suddenly like that without saying why. They ended up having a row, and when Sven tried to make it better, it just made things worse.

He had been on his way home, feeling cross at the world, speeding a bit now that the queues had thinned out. He had just passed the stupid oversized boats moored at the Viking Line terminal, when Lars Ågestam rang and started to speak quietly.

He wanted Sven to come to the prosecutor's office for a meeting after hours. Just the two of them.

Sven Sundkvist had stopped the car, phoned Anita again and made everything worse still. Now he was back in town again, alone, not sure what to do with all the spare time. It was in fact only an hour or two, but just then an eternity.

It was one of those mild, warm June evenings. He walked slowly from Kronoberg, circling the streets, not taking in the music from far away and the smells from the restaurant terraces and pavement tables. Life was all around him and he should have been smiling, should even have joined in for a while, but he didn't, hardly even noticed.

He was beginning to feel tired after a long night and what seemed like an even longer day.

He couldn't bring himself to think about the video and about the awful truth he carried with him.

Is that what did Ågestam wanted to go over?

Did he want to have a go at shaking Sven's loyalty?

He was too tired for that kind of thing. No such decisions, not yet.

They met at the Kung Bridge entrance a few minutes after eight o'clock. Ågestam was waiting. He looked the same as ever: fringe, suit, shiny shoes. He shook hands and opened the door with his ID card. They didn't say much in the lift. Time enough for that later.

They got out on the eighth floor and Ågestam ushered Sven into his office, where he caught a glimpse of the view of the city through the window, the summer night overpowering the day.

He found a chair and sat down. Ågestam went off for a moment to get them both a cup of coffee. He also brought a plate of biscuits, which he put down next to a couple of massive investigation reports.

'Sugar?'

'Just milk, please.'

Ågestam was doing what he could to lower the palpable tension, to tone down any hint of drama, but his efforts weren't all that successful. Both of them of course knew that their meeting had nothing to do with sharing a nice coffee break. It was too late for a start; everyone else had gone home by now, allowing them to talk together in confidence, without being overheard.

'I didn't sleep well last night.' Ågestam stretched, raised his arms above his head, as if to demonstrate how tired he was.

Nor did I, Sven thought. I didn't sleep at all, what with that damned video and worrying about Ewert. Is that what you want to talk about? I still don't know what to think.

'I kept thinking about your friend, your colleague, Ewert Grens.'

Not now. Not yet.

'I had to discuss this with you, Sven. I believe there's a problem.'

Ågestam cleared his throat, shifted in his chair, but didn't get up.

'You know that Ewert and I are not the best of friends.'

'There's quite a few people who feel the same.'

'Yes, I know. However, I thought it was necessary to point out that this has nothing to do with my personal feelings for him. I'm worried about Ewert Grens in his professional capacity. Especially as he is in charge of the police work in an investigation that I am ultimately responsible for.'

He shifted position again. This time he got up, glanced at Sven and started pacing the room, clearly upset.

'Take yesterday. I had a very strange meeting with Grens. He was just back from the Baltic ferry terminal. He had put Alena Sljusareva on board a ferry back to Lithuania. Without checking with me first.'

He stopped and waited for a reaction. He didn't get one.

'Early this morning I went back to the hospital mortuary, in an attempt to understand. During the day I've interviewed some of your colleagues. One of them, Detective Sergeant Hermansson, a very sensible officer who was new to me, quoted statements by two independent witnesses confirming that a woman went into the toilet at the end of the corridor before Lydia Grajauskas went in, just before she started running around with a gun and taking hostages. Both witnesses describe a woman who could be Sljusareva. It's easy then to suppose that it was Sljusareva who provided Grajauskas with weaponry. So why then was Grens in such a hurry to send her back home?'

Sven Sundkvist did not answer.

The video. He had feared this meeting would be about the lost evidence, removed by a serving policeman in order to protect a colleague. The video that he now knew about. The video that would soon force him to choose between speaking the truth and lying.

'Sven, I must ask you this. Is there anything you know that I ought to know?'

Sven still did not answer. He had no idea what he should say.

Lars Ågestam repeated his question.

'Is there something?'

He had to answer.

'No. I have no idea what you're talking about.'

Ågestam began pacing the room again, breathing rapidly, nervously. He had barely begun.

'One of the best officers in the force, so I should relax, shouldn't I? Sit back and wait for the results of his investigative work, right?'

A couple of deep breaths before he carried on.

'But I can't relax because something is not right. Don't you see? Which is why I lie awake at night. Which is why I feel compelled to go to work absurdly early and lie inside the chalk lines around the position of a dead body on a mortuary floor.'

He turned round and stopped in front of Sven, looked at him. Sven tried to meet the other man's eyes, but stayed silent. He knew that no matter how much he said, it would never be enough.

'Sven, I phoned Vilnius.'

Ågestam didn't move away.

'I asked our Lithuanian colleagues to locate Sljusareva. They found her in Klaipeda, back at her parental home.'

He perched on the edge of his desk and held up a bundle of papers, the documentation on the case he was talking about.

'There is no transcript of the interview with Sljusareva that Grens claims to have carried out. He decided unilaterally that she should leave this country. What he says is all we know.'

His voice cracked, knowing well that he was about to say something he should never say, not to a policeman, not about a colleague in the force.

'Ewert Grens is telling a story and it doesn't hold water.'

He paused.

'I have no idea why. I think Grens is tampering with the evidence in this investigation.'

Ågestam pressed Play on the tape recorder on his desk and the two men listened to the end of an exchange they had both heard before.

'*Stena Baltica*? That's a bloody boat! This is something personal! Bengt, over! Fuck's sake, Bengt. Stop it! Squad, move in! All clear. Repeat, move in!'

No decision about choosing loyalty or truth. Not a word. Not yet.

'Sven!'

'Yes?'

'I want you to go to Klaipeda. You are not to mention this to anyone, nor that you are going to interrogate Alena Sljusareva. You will report the results of the interrogation directly to me. I want to know what she really has to say.'

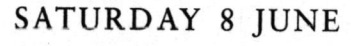

SATURDAY 8 JUNE

A strong smell hung in the air at Palanga Airport. The moment he passed the gate on his way to the luggage carousels, the smell of perfumed disinfectant hit his nose. The floor was still wet from washing and the smell told him that he was abroad, in a foreign place where they used chemicals and scents long since banned in Sweden. One hour and twenty minutes, he thought, one bleeding hour and they even clean the floors differently.

This was his second visit to Lithuania. He couldn't remember much from his first trip, not even which airport they had flown into. It had been a big thing for him, a new recruit to the force, to be asked to escort a high-profile criminal on a journey outside Swedish borders. Now that prison was probably all that was left of his memory. It had felt like travelling back in time, with barking dogs, damp corridors, stale air that weighed on his lungs, tuberculosis warnings posted everywhere and pale, silent prisoners with shaved heads sitting in their small, overcrowded cells. A strange experience, one he had never really spoken about, not even with Anita.

He left the terminal building and summoned one of the waiting yellow cabs. Klaipeda was twenty-six kilometres south of Palanga. He was going to see Alena Sljusareva and hear things he didn't want to know.

He had phoned home from Arlanda to say good morning to Jonas and promised him a present, something secret, a surprise. Sweets, no doubt, bought in a hurry in the airport shop. He didn't have much time in Lithuana; he was due back in Stockholm early the next morning, and he knew that what he had to do here would take up every waking hour.

The driver took his time on the road from Palanga to Klaipeda. Sven Sundkvist considered telling him to speed up, but refrained. Settling into his seat, he told himself that the few minutes gained wouldn't make up for the time it would take him to explain to the driver what he wanted.

It looked pretty, the landscape lit by the sun. He knew that it was a poor country, with eight out of ten of its people living precariously close to the poverty line, but he felt that there was a kind of dignity in what he saw this time, something likeable. Nothing to remind him of that prison. The news reports at home showed clichés every time, so like everyone else he believed what he was shown, because it looked like what he had been fed before: all these grey people living in permanently grey weather. This was different. It was summer in a place full of real people, real lives, real colours.

He told the driver to take him straight to the hotel. He was too early to check in, but Hotel Aribò was far from full and he was given a room at once.

He wanted a little rest and tried the bed, the narrowest he had ever seen. Only a few minutes while he tried to visualise the woman he was about to meet, to remember what she looked and sounded like.

The scene in the flat had been chaotic. Alena Sljusareva had been upset, screaming about her friend who was lying unconscious on the floor, and about the man in a shiny suit, whom she called Dimitri-Bastard-Pimp, who was standing nearby next to a hole in the apartment door. Sven Sundkvist didn't have a chance to take a proper look at her and of course had had no idea that later the same week he would watch her in a video and meet her in a strange city on the other side of the Baltic.

Alena Sljusareva had been standing in the room next door, just as naked as her unconscious friend.

She was dark, darker than most of the Baltic prostitutes who had ended up as items in the documents on his desk.

While they took care of the injured woman and confronted the pimp, who was making a fuss about his Lithuanian passport and diplomatic status, she had disappeared. That is, until she was arrested at the Baltic ferry terminal, about to board a boat that was ready to depart.

Ewert had interrogated her and, a few hours later, decided that she could go home to Lithuania after all.

Sven Sundkvist got up and had a shower. He put on lighter clothes; he hadn't realised it would be so warm. The grey cliché must have stuck in his mind. He opened his briefcase, looked thoughtfully at the small tape recorder and then closed the case again. He would interrogate her, but the old-fashioned way, taking notes. He didn't know why, maybe he was afraid of what she would tell him, afraid of her voice explaining what he didn't want to record.

He walked through the centre of the town, the buildings beautiful but breathing from another time, the people he met, traces of Lydia Grajauskas in their faces, over and over again.

She had instructed him to walk to the lakeside and take the small ferry across Lake Curonia to Smilty Island. The heat that had struck him first in Palanga, then in Klaipeda, was now more intense. The sun scorched the back of his neck during the short boat trip and he realised he should have brought some sunscreen. He would turn brick red before the evening.

Once he stepped off the ferry he was to turn right and

walk along the beach to an old fort housing an aquarium, a big one, the posters told him, with one hundred species of Baltic fish and a dolphinarium. She had explained that she wanted to be among people, and at lunchtime this place was full of schoolchildren and other visitors who came along to watch the fish. The two of them could stroll about among the tanks and talk for as long as they liked without anyone taking notice.

He stopped at the main entrance, where she had told him to wait for her, and checked the time. He was early, with almost twenty minutes to spare. It wasn't easy to estimate how long it would take from the centre to this aquarium-cum-museum of Baltic fish on the island of Smilty.

He picked a seat with a good view of the aquarium entrance. The sun played over his skin, and he leaned back and narrowed his eyes to watch the comings and goings, searching among the strangers for somebody like himself, as he always did. Somewhere, in this flow of people he would never know, was someone who was him, or at least like him; a man his age, with a woman he loved at his side and, walking a little ahead of them both, their beloved child. A man, who wanted to be at home but who spent most of his time elsewhere, and who might be a policeman or something else that required a strong sense of duty and long evenings at work. Someone in this crowd who lacked Ewert's aggressiveness, Lang's stubborn self-belief, Grajauskas's capacity to resist, stay upright and take her revenge on those who had humiliated her. Perhaps the man who was Sven would be a little dull, ordinary, lacking in all the qualities you needed to be anything other than predictable.

He did see himself. Several versions. Had he been born here, he might have been any one of them. He studied them and smiled when he spotted a man in a short-sleeved shirt and light slacks on his way into the aquarium.

Then she tapped his shoulder.

He hadn't seen her arrive, nor heard her call him, so

preoccupied had he been with his little game. She stood in front of him, hidden behind sunglasses, wearing a thin sweater and jeans that were a little too big. She fitted his image of her quite well. Not tall, lovely face and long dark hair. Traded for three years, humiliated countless times a day. It didn't show, not on the outside. She looked like women do in their twenties, life just starting. Inside, he knew, she was old inside. That's where she kept her scars. It was that woman who would never be whole again.

'Sundkvist?'

He nodded and stood up.

'Yes. I am DI Sundkvist.'

They had no trouble speaking to each other. His English was a little rusty, hers had been polished during three years abroad and she seemed to prefer it to Swedish.

'You recognise me?'

'I saw you in the flat.'

'It was very chaotic.'

'I would know you were Swedish anyway, even if I'd never met you. I've got to know what Swedish men look like.'

She made a gesture towards the entrance and they walked side by side. He paid for their tickets, and once in, tried to sense when would be the right time to start questioning her. She helped him.

'I'm not sure what you want to know. I will tell you everything. I would like to begin now, please. I trust you. I saw you at work in the flat. But I would like to get this over with. I want to go home. Forget. Do you understand?'

She looked pleadingly at him. Behind her, a wall of glass, and fish slipping through the water. He tried to appear calm, calmer than he was, now that he was going to hear the answers he had been anticipating.

'I'm afraid I can't tell you how long this will take. It depends. But of course I understand. I'll do my best to keep it as brief as possible.'

337

He couldn't really see the point of aquariums. Or zoos, for that matter. Caged creatures didn't appeal to him and he found it easy to block it all out of his mind: the strolling groups of people, the fish they were meant to be looking at. He would concentrate. On Alena Sljusareva, on her and her answers to his questions.

On her story, the story he had been dreading.

The tale of events he wished hadn't taken place.

It wasn't a normal interview, but whatever it was went on for almost three hours. She spoke about her flight from the flat and her time spent alone in the city, how her body rejoiced at being free, how she was scared that she would be found, anxious about Lydia. The worry about her unconscious beaten friend never let up. They had sworn never to leave each other until they were both free together, but just then, the instant when Alena had decided to run away, she had been convinced that she would be of more use to Lydia well away from that fifth-floor flat.

He interrupted her whenever she seemed to hesitate, and she would clarify, never try to change the story, at least not as far as he could make out.

They walked slowly among the people watching fish. She told him about going to the harbour and Lydia calling from her hospital bed to ask for the weapons and the other things that she would later put to use in the mortuary.

Her voice was a near-whisper when she begged him to believe that she had had no idea of what her friend had been planning to do.

He stopped, looked into her eyes and explained that the purpose of his inquiry was not to establish whether she had been an accessory to kidnapping and murder.

She asked what his reason was, in that case.

'Nothing. And everything. Leave it like that.'

A cluster of simple chairs and tables. He bought them each a cup of coffee and they sat down among the parents and children and the big fish on the blue plastic table-cloths.

She told him about the locker in Central Station, how she had broken in to the cellar and the carrier bag, which she was to deposit in the hospital toilet.

He decided to check the truth of what she was telling him.

'What was the number?'

'Number?'

'The box at the station.'

'Twenty-one.'

'What was in it?'

'Mostly my things. Lydia wanted only money for extras.'

'Extras?'

'Hitting. Spitting. Filming. Use your imagination.'

Sven Sundkvist swallowed, sensing her discomfort.

'And Lydia? What did she keep in your box?'

'Her money. And her two videotapes.'

'What tapes were they?'

'The truth. That's what she named them. *My Truth.*'

'Which was . . . ?'

'She told it like it was. How we came to Sweden. Who was buying and selling us as products. And what the policeman she shot had done to make her hate him. I helped her translate.'

'Nordwall?'

'Bengt Nordwall.'

Sven Sundkvist did not tell her that he had opened their box 21 and watched the tape, listening to them both. He did not mention that one of the tapes had gone missing because one policeman was protecting another and had decided to lose it, nor did he explain how ashamed he felt at his own inability to decide whether their humiliations were more or less important than his loyalty towards a colleague and a friend, and whether he ever would make official what only he knew now: there was another tape, a copy of the truth.

'I saw him.'

'Who?'

'Bengt Nordwall. I saw him in the flat.'

'You saw him?'

'He saw me too. I know he recognised me. And I know he recognised Lydia.'

After that he found it difficult to listen to her.

She carried on talking and he asked her his questions, but his mind was elsewhere.

He was furious. As furious as he had ever been. He wanted to scream.

He didn't, of course. He was after all one of the ordinary blokes, a little dull. He suppressed the scream, sensing the pressure inside his chest.

Instead he carried on pretending to be calm, unafraid of what she had to tell him. He mustn't frighten her. He understood how brave she was, how the memories gnawed at her.

He cried out.

Cried out, then apologised to her. He had a pain, he explained. It wasn't her, he had a pain here, in his chest.

By the time they had boarded the ferry back to the centre of town, he knew in detail what had happened during her hours of freedom, from her escape down the stairs at Völund Street to her arrest at the harbour. Fury was churning inside him, from chest to belly and back, but he felt their talk had not yet ended. He wanted to know more, about how it all worked: about those three years, the slave trade, how it was possible for a woman's body to be sold so that someone else could top up his bank account or buy himself a new car.

He asked if she would have dinner with him.

She smiled.

'I don't think I can cope with any more now. Home. I want to go home. I haven't been at home for three years.'

'The Swedish police will not trouble you again in this matter. You have my word on that.'

'I don't understand. What more do you want to know?'

'I spoke to the Lithuanian ambassador to Sweden just a couple of days ago. He had gone to the airport to see off the man you call Dimitri-Bastard-Pimp, and spoke to us afterwards about the extent of the world you've just escaped from. He was despairing. I want to learn more about it. Tell me.'

'I'm so tired. Too tired.'

'Just one evening? Just talking. Then never again.'

He blushed suddenly when he saw himself demanding her attention like the Swedish men she had learnt to hate.

'Please forgive me. I didn't intend this as some kind of come-on. You mustn't take it that way. I truly want to know more. And I'm a married man and a father.'

'They always are.'

He marched back to the hotel quickly. Another shower to wash away the heat and another change of clothes, the second in the eight hours since his arrival.

She had asked two older women coming to board the ferry about a good place for a meal and they had suggested a Chinese restaurant called Taravos Aniko, saying that the portions were nice and big, and if you were lucky enough to get one of the right tables you could watch the food being prepared.

She was already there when he arrived, wearing the same jeans and sweater. She smiled, he smiled. They ordered bottles of mineral water and a set menu that someone else had worked out, starter, main course, dessert for two, all suitably put together and priced.

She searched for words and he waited quietly. He didn't want to push her.

Then she started speaking, beginning somewhere in the middle, with a remembered impression, and afterwards unravelling their story. She took him on a journey to a world that he thought he knew something about and made him realise he knew nothing. She cried and whispered for a while, but she couldn't stop talking and he didn't interrupt. This was the first time she had described to someone else what her adult life so far had been; it was the first time she had listened to herself. He listened too and was increasingly amazed at her strength and her integrity. Despite everything, she had stayed whole.

He waited until she had finished or maybe couldn't bear to say any more. Until she fell silent, her unseeing eyes empty. Now it was over, she was done and would never again tell her story on demand.

Sven reached down for his briefcase and put it on the table.

'I've brought a few things which don't belong to me.'

He took out a small brown box and two neatly folded dresses.

'I believe these things are Lydia's.'

She stared at the box, at the dresses. She knew where they had been. There was still a question in her eyes when she met Sven's. He nodded, confirming that she was right.

'Your locker is empty now. Let to someone else. I wanted to give you these. I suppose the dresses are hers. And the box too. It contains forty thousand Swedish kronor, in smallish notes.'

Alena didn't move, said nothing. 'Do what you like. Keep the money. Or give it to her family, if there is anyone left.'

She leaned forward and caressed the smooth, black material of one of the dresses.

All that was left.

'I went to her home yesterday. I wanted to see her mother. Lydia often talked about her.' She lowered her eyes. 'She is dead. She died two months ago.'

Sven waited. Then he gently pushed Lydia's belongings towards Alena.

'I would like to know more about Lydia. Who she was. All I have seen is a badly beaten human being who stood up again and took hostages.'

Alena shook her head. 'It's enough now.'

'I think some part of me understands why she acted as she did.'

'No more, not today. Not ever.'

They stayed for a while longer, without talking much. The waiter finally asked them to please leave, the restaurant was closing. They got up and were just about to go when the front door opened and a man in his early twenties came in. Sven gave him a quick once-over. He was tall, blond and suntanned, easy-going, not confrontational. Alena walked over to him, kissed his cheek and put her arm through his.

'Janoz. I left him. He was still here. I am so grateful for that.'

She kissed his cheek again and pulled him closer as she told Sven how Janoz had tried to find her for seven long months, spending time and money until he had to give up.

And she laughed. For the first time that evening, she laughed. Sven smiled and congratulated them both. For a moment, at least, not everything seemed hopeless.

'What about Lydia? Was there someone waiting for her?'

'There was someone called Vladi.'

'And now?'

'He got what he wanted from her.'

She said no more and he didn't ask. They went out in the street. Before going their different ways Sven Sundkvist repeated his promise that she would never again have to speak to the Swedish police about this case.

A few steps only and then she turned round.

'One more thing.'

'Of course.'

'Today, in the aquarium. The interview. Why was that necessary?'

'The case is still open. The police have to gather all the evidence.'

'Yes, I see. I have no problem with that. But you, the police, you already knew.'

'What do you mean?'

'What you asked, it was the same as the other policeman.'

'The other policeman?'

'He was there in the flat too. Older than you.'

'His name is Grens.'

'That's the one.'

'The same questions?'

'Everything I told you this afternoon in the aquarium I have already said to him. The same questions, the same answers.'

'Everything?'

'Everything.'

'You told him about Lydia calling you from the ward and the mortuary? About how you went to look for the things she wanted? About the video from the locker? About the gun and the explosives? About how you left it in the hospital toilet?'

'All of it.'

It was two o'clock in the morning by the time Sven was ready for the narrow hotel bed. He hadn't got anything for Jonas. He decided to sleep for a few hours and then go to St John's Lutheran church and light a candle for Lydia Grajauskas and her mother, who had been buried there. Then take a taxi to the airport. There was a duty-free shop there, where he could get sweets, the jelly ones and the shiny gold chocolate bars.

He lay in the dark. The window was open on a silent Klaipeda.

He knew his time was running out.

He must decide. The truth was there and now he had to decide what to do with it.

SUNDAY 9 JUNE

He had test-fucked the two new girls and they hadn't been up to much.

True, they were practically virgins, apart from that incident in the ferry cabin, and weren't actually too bad; they seemed to be getting the hang of it. It was their third day in the Völund Street flat and it wouldn't be long now before they too serviced twelve a day, like that mad bitch Grajauskas and her dirty little friend had. Or had done, until they lost their cool and went berserk.

The new girls needed to get their act together, though. Not hot and eager enough, he reckoned. Customers paying good money had a right to feel they were attractive and drove girls crazy, and that they were part of a couple, just for a while. Otherwise they might as well wank in the toilet.

He had knocked the new girls around a bit, just to keep them in order. Just a few more days and he'd have put a stop to their snivelling. It got on his nerves, all their bloody whining.

He had to admit it, Grajauskas and Sljusareva were pros. They got on with it, took their kit off and acted randy as hell. But it was a relief not to have their sneering grins in your face all the time. And he was tired of being called Dimitri-Bastard-Pimp every time he showed them who was boss.

The first one would be here soon. It was just after eight in the morning.

Mostly they came straight from home, having left the wife who was starting to get fat, just wanting to experience something, an extra stop going to work.

He would watch the girls today. Exam time. Find out if their fucking was up to standard or if they needed some more tuition.

He'd start with the one in Grajauskas's room. She looked a bit like her and he had put her there deliberately; it was easier on the old customers. She was tarting herself up, as she should, and putting on the bra and panties her client wanted her to wear. So far, so good.

A knock on the door. She looked at herself in the mirror. The locks were disabled now that he was keeping an eye, so she could open the door and greet the man outside with a smile. The client wore a grey suit of some kind of shiny material, pale blue shirt and black tie.

She kept smiling, used her smile even when he spat or, more like, let the gob just fall to the floor in front of her feet in their high-heeled black shoes.

He pointed.

His finger was straight, pointing downwards.

She bent down, still smiling as she had been told. Then down on her hands and knees, almost folding double as her nose touched the floor. Her tongue came out to take the spit into her mouth and she swallowed.

Then she stood up straight, her eyes shut.

The client slapped her with his open hand. She smiled and smiled at him, just as he had taught her.

Dimitri liked what he saw, gave the thumbs-up to the man in the grey suit, got thumbs-up in return.

She had passed.

He would book her up now.

Lydia Grajauskas didn't exist any more, not even here.

He always felt a pang of fear when a plane touched down and the ground came into clear view, the snap when the wheels were released and the thump when they made contact. And it never got easier; rather his fear seemed to increase the more he travelled. In little planes like this one, only thirty-five seats and so cramped that you couldn't stand up straight, take-off and landing were especially scary. He kept worrying until the bouncing changed into a smooth forward movement.

Sven Sundkvist breathed out again and went to find his car. If the traffic was reasonably light it took only half an hour to drive from Arlanda to central Stockholm.

Anywhere, just anywhere not to think about Ewert.

He was sixteen for a while and with Anita who he had just met and held naked for the first time and he was with Jochum Lang who stood at the top of a staircase in Söder Hospital and beat the life out of Hilding Oldéus and with Lydia Grajauskas lying on the floor in the mortuary next to the man she had hated and with one-year-old Jonas in Phnom Penh saying Dad just two weeks later and with Alena Sljusareva sitting in a Chinese restaurant in Klaipeda in her big red sweater telling him the story of a three-year-long humiliation and with . . .

With anyone at all, in order to avoid thinking about Ewert.

Roadworks outside Sollentuna meant that the cars were confined to one lane and there was a long queue. He inched forward in low gear, sped up a bit, slowed again, came to a halt. Everyone else was doing the same, sitting and waiting for the time to pass, staring blankly ahead. They probably had their own Ewerts to think about.

He gave an involuntary shudder, as you often do when you're tense.

Then he decided to take the long way round by keeping south, via Eriksberg, where she lived. Lena Nordwall.

He needed more time to think.

The wooden bench was hard. In his time, he had sat on it for hours on end, enduring pointless court cases against refusenik villains. They were alone in the back row and the tired room was silent. Ewert Grens quite liked the old high-security court in the Town Hall, despite the hard seats and the chattering lawyers, because coming here was a kind of settlement, confirmation that his investigation had led to something concrete and the case could be closed.

He looked at his watch. Five minutes to go. Then the guards would open the doors, escort Lang into the room and tell him where to sit during the remand proceedings, the lead-in to a long prison sentence.

Grens turned to Hermansson, who was sitting next to him.

'Feels good, doesn't it?'

He had asked her to come along. Sven had disappeared without a trace, refusing to answer the phone; Bengt had been found dead on a floor, and he couldn't offer Lena any comfort. He had wanted to be here with someone and that someone turned out to be Hermansson. He had to admit it, he really liked her. Her barbed comments about him and policewomen, or all women, should have infuriated him, but she had sounded so down-to-earth and calm, maybe because she was right. He would ask her to consider staying with the City force when her locum came to an end; he'd like to work with her again and perhaps talk to her more. She was so young that he didn't want to come across as a dirty old man, because what he felt had nothing to do with the beauty of a younger woman, it was more a kind of surprise that there were still people around whom he wanted to get to know better.

'Yes, it does. It feels good. I know what we've achieved,

what with Lang and the hospital hostages and everything. Makes my time to Stockholm worthwhile.'

A courtroom is a bare, dull place without judges, magistrates, prosecutors, lawyers, accused and accuser and, of course, a curious public. The drama of a crime needs to be articulated, in terms of interference and vulnerability, a process in which every word adds to the act of recognising and then measuring the offence.

Without all that, no heart.

Grens looked around at the dark wooden panelling, the large filthy windows facing Scheele Street, the far-too-beautiful chandelier, inhaled the smell of an old legal tome.

'It's strange, Hermansson. Dealing with professional criminals like Lang is my job, I've done it all my life, but I still don't understand any more now than I did when I started. Take the way they act up under interrogation or in court. Well, clam up. Whatever we say or ask, they ignore it. *Don't know. Never heard of it.* They deny everything. I can see some point in their strategy, of course. For a start, it leaves it up to us to prove that they've done whatever we say they've done.'

Ewert Grens raised his arm, pointing at the wall opposite, at a door made of the same heavy, dark wood as the panelling.

'In a few minutes Lang will come in through that door. And he'll play the same lousy old game. He'll say nothing, deny, mumble *I don't know*, and that is, Hermansson, that is exactly why he'll lose this time. This time that game will be the biggest mistake in his life. You see, I think he's innocent. Of murder, that is.'

She looked surprised, and he was just about to explain when the door opened and four guards came in, followed by a uniformed and armed constable on either side of Jochum Lang, who was handcuffed and dressed in prison-issue clothing, blue and baggy. He looked up, Ewert Grens smiled and waved.

Then he turned to speak to Hermansson, lowering his voice.

'You see, I have read the technical report and what Errfors has to say in the autopsy report. Oldéus wasn't murdered. Lang broke five of his fingers and crushed one kneecap, as he was instructed. But no one had ordered and paid for death. I think Oldéus lost it and the wheelchair careered down the stairs and into the wall.'

Ewert pointed ostentatiously at Lang.

'Watch him. There he sits, the stupid bastard. Today he'll get himself ten years in the jug for keeping his mouth shut. He'll receive a sentence for murder when he could have talked himself into two and a half years for GBH.'

Grens waved again, in the direction of his hate. Lang stared, as forcefully as the day before when they had confronted each other in his cell, before turning away. Behind him, behind his shaved skull, people were filing into the room.

Ågestam came in last. He and Grens nodded at each other.

Briefly, the policeman's thoughts touched on their last meeting and he wondered what the prosecutor had made of it and of the lies he had dished out.

He dismissed the thought – he had to – and leaned towards Hermansson, whispering: 'I know that's what happened. It wasn't murder. But believe you me, I'm not going to say a word. Lang is going down. Boy, is he going down!'

Dimitri was pleased. Both girls were young, nice smooth skin, fucked like rabbits. He had bought them on credit and decided from the outset that if they were no good he wouldn't pay.

But they worked. He'd pay up.

The cop wasn't around any more, of course, but the woman he worked with had done a good job without him. She had delivered two new whores, as agreed. She was waiting for him now. Time for his second payment, one third of the total cost: three thousand euros for each girl.

He opened the door to Eden. A naked woman on the stage, her tits against an inflated doll, making provocative thrusts and groans, whining a bit. Everyone at the tables, all men without exception, had their hands down their trousers.

She was sitting in her usual place, in a far corner near the fire exit.

He went over to her table and they nodded at each other.

She always wore the same tracksuit. Always, with the hood pulled down around her face.

She wanted him to call her Ilona, and he did, even though it annoyed him. It wasn't her name, he knew that.

They didn't talk much, never did. A few polite phrases in Russian, that was all.

He gave her the envelope. She didn't bother to check the money, just put it away in her bag. Agreed to meet next month.

One more month, one more payment and then the girls would be his. His property, both of them.

Ewert Grens got up and waved at Hermansson that she was to follow him. They left just as the remand procedure was concluded. He hurried down the three flights of stairs to the basement and along the corridor to the underground car park. Hermansson asked where they were going, and he replied that she would soon see.

This haste had made him gasp for breath, but he didn't stop until he was almost suffocated by the stuffy under-ground dust. He looked around, saw what he wanted and then walked towards a metal door which led to the lifts that went all the way up to the cells.

He planted himself in front of the door, knowing that Jochum Lang would be brought here on the way back to his cell.

He only needed to wait for a minute or so before the four guards, two policemen and Lang came into view, heading towards the metal door.

Ewert Grens went to meet them and asked the officers to wait a few metres away while he had a word with Lang. The officer in charge of the prisoner wasn't best pleased, but agreed. Grens normally got what he wanted in the end anyway.

They glared at each other, as they always did. Grens waited for Lang to react, but he just stood there, hand-cuffed, his large frame swaying as if he couldn't decide whether to hit Ewert or not.

'You stupid bastard.' They were standing so close, Grens need do no more than whisper for Lang to hear. 'You kept your mouth shut, as you always do. But you were remanded and you'll be sentenced later. I know you didn't kill Oldéus. But what are people to believe? As long as you behave like a villain, refusing to say anything, only to deny everything, I'll tell you what they'll do. They will make you pay. It will cost you six or seven years, on top of what you might have got regardless. Enjoy!'

Ewert Grens turned and called the guards back.

'That's all, Lang.'

Jochum Lang didn't say a word, didn't move, didn't even turn to look at Grens when he was moved on by the guards.

Not until the guards had opened the door and he was on his way through and Grens shouted for him to turn round. Then Lang turned and spat on the ground as the superintendent shouted at the top of his voice, reminding Lang about the body scan session, the way he had taunted him about his dead colleague and made kissing noises. Grens screamed, *Do you remember?* And the kisses were returned, flying through the air. Grens stood with pursed lips and made loud smacking sounds as Lang was led back to the lift and the cells.

Sven Sundkvist parked in a street of terraced houses, crowded with kids playing hockey in between two home-made goals that blocked the traffic. They had noticed the car, but didn't bother about it at first. He had to wait until two nine-year-olds finally moved the cages, sighing loudly about the old fart who was messing things up.

He knew now. Knew that Lydia had already decided to kill Bengt and then herself. She had wanted to tell the truth, give voice to her shame. Ewert had denied her that.

What gave him the right to do that?

Lena Nordwall was sitting in the garden. Her eyes closed, she listened to the radio, a commercial station of the kind that interrupts the music with jingles about its name and frequency.

He hadn't seen her since the evening they came to tell her about Bengt's death.

Ewert wanted to protect a friend's wife and children.

But by doing so, he denied a dead woman the right to speak out.

'Hello.'

It was a warm day and he was sweating, but she had greeted the sun in trousers and a denim jacket over a long-sleeved sweater. She hadn't heard him arrive, and when he went closer, she jumped.

'Oh. You startled me.'

'I apologise.'

She made a gesture inviting him to sit down. He moved the chair, now sitting facing her, the sun burning his back.

They looked at each other. He had phoned and asked if he could come. It was up to him to start talking.

He found it hard. He didn't really know her. They had of course met on birthdays and so on, but always in the company of Bengt and Ewert. She was one of those women who made him fumble for words, feeling inadequate and too old. He didn't know why. She was beautiful, true, but beauty didn't usually affect him. It was her poise that made him insecure, like some people do.

'I'm sorry to disturb you.'

'Well, you're here now.'

He looked around. The only other time he had been in this garden was some five, six years earlier, on Ewert's fiftieth birthday, when Bengt and Lena had had a dinner for their friend. It was the only celebration Ewert had ever permitted. Sven and Anita had sat on either side of him at the table. Jonas had been a toddler then and had run around on the grass with the Nordwall children. There were no other guests. Ewert had been unusually quiet all evening; Sven had thought he was happy, just uncomfortable about being celebrated.

She kept rubbing the sleeves of her jacket.

'I'm so cold.'

'Now?'

'I've felt frozen ever since you were here last, four days ago.'

He sighed.

'Please forgive me. I should have understood.'

'I have to dress warmly even on a day like this, almost ninety degrees in the shade. Can you understand that?'

'Yes. Yes. I think I can.'

'I don't want to be cold.'

She stood up suddenly.

'Would you like a cup of coffee?'

'No, you mustn't trouble yourself.'

'No trouble. Do you want one?'

'Yes please.'

She went in through the open French windows and he listened to the kitchen noises and the shouting of the hockey players. Maybe someone had scored a goal, or another boring old bloke was interfering with their game.

She served the coffee in tall glasses, topped up with foaming hot milk, the way they served it in the cafés he never had time to go to.

He drank a mouthful, then put the glass down.

'How well do you know Ewert?'

She studied him with that special look in her eyes, which

made him feel awkward. 'Is that why you're here? To discuss Ewert?'

'Yes.'

'What is this? Some kind of interrogation?'

'No, not at all.'

'What is it then?'

'I'm not sure.'

'Not sure?'

'No.'

She rubbed her sleeves again in that chilly gesture.

'I don't understand.'

'I wish I could be more helpful, but I can't. Please see it as me thinking aloud. As far from police work as you can get.'

She sipped from her glass, finishing her coffee before she spoke.

'What can I say? He was my husband's oldest friend.'

'I know. And you, how well do you know him?'

'He isn't an easy man to know.'

She wanted Sven to go, didn't like him. He was aware of her dislike.

'Tell me something. Please try.'

'Does Ewert know about this?'

'No, he doesn't.'

'Why not?'

'If he did, I wouldn't need your answers.'

It was hot, his back was soaking. It would have been better to sit somewhere else, but he felt he shouldn't fuss, the situation was tense enough.

'Has Ewert spoken to you about what happened? In the mortuary? About what happened to Bengt?'

She wasn't listening any longer. Sven could tell. She was pointing at him, holding her hand up for so long that he felt uncomfortable.

'He was sitting there.'

'Who?'

'Bengt. When you lot called him in. To the mortuary.'

He should not have come. He should have left her in peace with her grief. The trouble was that he was desperate to hear about another side of Ewert, the positive side, and surely Lena would be able to help him. He repeated his question.

'What has Ewert said to you about that day? About what happened to Bengt?'

'I asked my questions. He didn't tell me anything I couldn't have read in the papers.'

'No? Nothing else?'

'I don't care for this conversation.'

'For instance, you haven't asked him why the prostitute chose to shoot Bengt?'

She was quiet for a long time.

He had put off asking the question, his real reason for being here. Now it was done.

'What are you implying?'

'I just wanted to know what Ewert might have said to explain why it was Bengt she killed.'

'Do you know why?'

'I asked you.'

Her eyes were fixed on him.

'No.'

'And you never wondered?'

Suddenly she burst into tears. She looked so small, curled up in the chair, shaking with grief.

'Of course I've wondered. And asked. But he won't say, he's said nothing that makes sense. It was chance, that is all he says. It could've been anyone. It was Bengt.'

Someone was standing behind him. Sven Sundkvist turned. A little girl of five or six, younger than Jonas, was dressed in white shorts and a pink T-shirt. She had come from the house, now stopped in front of her mother, observing how she was upset.

'Mummy, what's wrong?'

Lena Nordwall leaned forwards and gave her a hug.

'Nothing, sweetheart.'

'You're crying. Is it that man? Is he being horrid to you?'

'No, no, he isn't horrid at all. We're just talking.'

The little pink-and-white body swung round. Sven met her wide-open eyes.

'You see, Mummy is very sad. My daddy is dead.'

He swallowed, trying to look kind and serious at the same time.

'I knew your daddy.'

Sven Sundkvist looked at the woman who had been left a widow with two young children for four days now. He could sense her deep pain and realised why Ewert thought the last thing she needed was the truth and had chosen to protect her.

Ewert Grens couldn't wait until the next day. He longed to be with her.

Sunday traffic meant that it was easy to cross the city and the Värta motorway was almost empty. He put on a tape and was singing along with Siw as he crossed Lidingö Bridge. The rain started up again, but he didn't notice.

He pulled into the usually empty car park and realised that it was full. He was baffled, thought for a moment that maybe he had taken a wrong turn, until he remembered that today was a Sunday, the most popular day for visiting the sick.

The receptionist looked surprised. Mr Grens didn't normally come on Sundays. He smiled at her surprise.

She called out after him.

'Mr Grens. She isn't there.'

He didn't catch it.

'She isn't in her room.'

He stopped. In the time it took for her to draw breath before continuing, he felt all that he had felt back then. He died. Again.

'She's with the others on the terrace for Sunday afternoon coffee. We try to get everyone outside in the summer. Even when it rains, the parasols are big enough.'

He didn't hear what she was saying. Her lips were moving, but he didn't hear.

'Go out and see her. She'll be pleased.'

'Why isn't she in her room?'

'I beg your pardon?'

'Why isn't she in her room?'

He felt dizzy. A chair. He took off his jacket and sat down.

'Are you all right?'

The young woman knelt in front of him. He saw her now.

'On the terrace?'

'Yes, that's right.'

Most of the decking outside was protected from the rain by four large parasols, emblazoned with an ice-cream manufacturer's logo. Ewert recognised some of the staff and all of those who were sitting about in wheelchairs or with Zimmer frames parked next to their chairs.

She was sitting in the middle of the group, with a cup of coffee beside her, a half-eaten cinnamon pastry in her hand. He heard her childish laugh above the patter of rain on the umbrellas and the sporadic singing. He waited until the group of singers had finished their tune and then joined the crowd on the terrace. His jacket was already wet.

'Hello.' He greeted one of the white-coated women, who had a familiar face.

She smiled pleasantly.

'Mr Grens, how nice to see you. And on a Sunday too!'

She spoke to Anni, who stared blankly at them. 'Anni, look! You've got a visitor.'

Ewert went to her. As usual he put his hand on her cheek. He turned to the care assistant.

'Do you mind if I take her inside? I've got something to tell her. Good news.'

'Of course. We've been here for quite a while. Anyway, Anni, you don't want all of us around when you have a gentleman visitor.'

She released the brake on Anni's wheelchair and he took over.

Anni was wearing a different dress today, a red one. He had bought it for her a long time ago. It was still raining, but only lightly, and she barely got wet as they dashed from the parasols to the side of the building. He steered the wheelchair in through the door and down the long corridor to her room.

They sat as they always did. She in the middle of the room. He, on a chair at her side.

He caressed her cheek again, kissed her forehead and took her hand in his. For a moment he thought she squeezed his hand in return.

'Anni.'

He tried to make sure that she was looking at him before continuing.

'It's over now.'

It was one o'clock and Dimitri had promised her an hour's rest. She had been working non-stop since the morning, since the first customer came and spat on the floor and she had to lick it up with a smile.

She was crying.

That man. Then seven others. Four more later. Twelve a day. The last one was coming just after half past six.

One hour's rest. She lay on the bed in the room she thought of as hers.

It was in a pleasant flat, on the fifth floor in a nice block.

A couple of the men had called her Lydia. She had told them that that wasn't her name, but they insisted that for them, that was what she was called. She knew now that Lydia was the woman who had been there before her and a lot of the men had been Lydia's customers. She had inherited them from her.

Dimitri didn't beat her so much these days.

He had said she was learning the ropes, she had to make more noises, that was what was missing, she had to groan when they pushed inside her, and whimper a little, with pleasure, of course. The customers liked noises; it made them feel they weren't paying her to do it.

She only cried when she was alone. He hit her more if he saw her cry.

One hour. She had closed the door and would cry in peace for an hour. Then she had to smarten up and smile in the mirror and cup her hand over her genitals, as the two o'clock man wanted.

Ewert Grens had been back in his office for only an hour or so, but already he felt restless. He couldn't concentrate on anything. He went to the toilet, got a coffee from the machine and asked reception to fix a pizza delivery for him, but that was that. Now, all that was left to him was his office.

It was almost as if he were waiting.

He listened to Siw Malmkvist's warm voice and held her close, dancing with her in the tight space between his desk and the sofa.

He had no idea where Sven was and Ågestam hadn't been in touch.

He turned up the volume. Soon it would be evening once more and he could hardly figure out how. His room was warm after a day of summer sunshine and he sweated as he moved to the rhythms of the Sixties.

Bengt, I miss you.

You pulled a fast one on us.

You see that, don't you?

Lena knows nothing.

Not a thing.

362

You, who had her.
You, who had the children.
You, who had something!

He switched off the tape recorder and put the tape back in its box.

He looked around. No, not this place, not tonight.

He left, walked along the empty corridors and stepped outside into the fresh air, to the car left unlocked as usual. Settling in the seat, he decided to go for a drive. He hadn't done that for a long time.

It was half past six and she had spread her legs for the twelfth and last time today.

He had been quite quick and he hadn't wanted to hit her or anything, and no spitting. He had only penetrated her anally, but barely, and told her to whisper that it turned her on, so it hadn't hurt much at all.

She showered for a long time, even though she had washed several times already. It was the best time for crying, when the water was pouring over her.

Dimitri had told her that she was to be fully dressed and smiling by seven o'clock, sitting on her bed. The woman who called herself Ilona, the one who had met them when they came off the ferry, was coming to see them, to check that they were all right. Dimitri explained that the woman still owned a third share of them, so her approval was important. For another month, anyway.

The woman arrived punctually. The kitchen clock: thirty seconds to seven. She was wearing her tracksuit with the hood up, just as before. She didn't take it down as she passed the electronic locks and came into the flat.

Dimitri said hello, asked if she wanted a drink. She shook her head. She was in a hurry, just wanted to give the girls a quick once-over. After all, she did still have a stake in them.

When the woman popped her head round the door, the

girl looked as happy as she could, just as Dimitri had instructed her. The woman asked how many men she had seen today and she replied twelve. That pleased her and she said that was good going for such a young Baltic pussy.

She lay down on the bed and cried again. She knew that Dimitri didn't allow it and that he would soon come in and hit her, but she couldn't help it.

She thought of the men who had forced themselves on her, the woman with the hood and that Dimitri had said that they had to pack their bags again as they were moving to another flat in Copenhagen, and all she wanted to do was die.

Ewert Grens had been driving aimlessly for almost two hours. He had started in the centre of the city, navigating the most heavily congested streets with their traffic lights and jaywalkers and imbeciles who punished their car horns. Later, he crossed to Södermalm via Slussen, made his way along Horn Street and Göt Street; the south side, which was supposed to be so damn bohemian, but to him this looked like any sad provincial dump.

Back to the northern side again and past the soulless facades in posh Östermalm, a loop round the TV building at Gärdet and then a run on Värta Road to the harbour, where large ships were arriving packed with Baltic whores. He yawned. Valhalla Road next, endless roundabouts as far as Roslag Junction.

All these people. All these people on their way somewhere.

Ewert Grens envied them. He had no idea where he going.

He was tired. Just a few minutes more.

He drove through the city centre to St Erik's Square in the slowing evening traffic. After drifting on along the smaller streets for a while, he turned left, past the Bonnier building and into Atlas Street. Downhill, left again. He parked in front of the door, suddenly surprised at the thought that less than a week had passed since he had come here for the first time.

He turned the engine off. How silent it was, as silent as a big city can be when the working day is over. All those windows, all those fancy curtains and potted plants. Places where people lived.

He sat in the car and time passed. Maybe a minute. Or ten. Or sixty.

Her back had been torn and inflamed. She had lain naked and unconscious on the floor. Alena Sljusareva had been screaming in the next room, hurling abuse at the man she called Dimitri-Bastard-Pimp.

Bengt had been on the landing. He had been waiting there for almost an hour. Grens recalled the scene perfectly, where Bengt had stood.

You must have known even then.

Ewert Grens stayed where he was for a little longer. Not time to leave yet. Another minute, several minutes, whatever it took for him to calm down. He had to go to the place he still called home, although he often had no wish to be there.

Another couple of minutes.

Suddenly the heavy door opened.

Four people came out. He looked at them, recognised them.

Only a couple of days ago, he had taken Alena Sljusareva to the port to ensure that she boarded a ferry that would take her over the Baltic Sea, back to Lithuania and Klaipeda.

They had got off the ferry when it docked on Swedish soil. The man was wearing the same suit he had previously, another time in Völund Street. Dimitri-Bastard-Pimp. As soon as he had cleared passport control, he turned round and waited for two young women – girls, in fact, of sixteen or seventeen. He held out his hand and demanded to have their passports, their debt. A woman in a tracksuit, with the hood pulled up over her head, had come forward to meet them and kissed them lightly on each cheek, the way people from the Baltic states do.

Now, they filed out of the door in front of him: Dimitri first, followed by his two new girls with bags in hand, and the hooded woman.

Grens watched them walk away.

Then he phoned the Ministry of Foreign Affairs, was put through to the person he wanted and asked a few questions about Dimitri Simait.

God knows he had enough on his plate, but never mind. He wanted to know if that fucking pimp still had the right to claim diplomatic immunity and asked to find out who his female contact was.

A little additional information and then he'd have both of them in the bag.

When this was all over. When Lang was inside. When Bengt had been buried.

When he was certain that Lena was able to go on, without the lie.

The day had passed without him noticing.

He had woken up in a narrow hotel bed, in Klaipeda, then driven from Arlanda to Lena Nordwall, where she sat freezing in the hot sun, then on to his Kronoberg office and from there to the Prosecution Service building, where Ågestam had been waiting, nearly at the end of his patience.

Sven Sundkvist wanted to go home.

He was tired, but the day that was almost done had not quite finished with him yet. Instead it seemed its longest hours were waiting for him.

Lena Nordwall had run after him as he walked away from their futile talk in the garden, towards the hockey kids and his car. She had been short of breath when she grabbed his arm and asked if he knew about Anni. Sven had never heard the name before. He had known Ewert for ten years, had worked closely with him and come to regard him as a friend, but he had never heard the name before. Lena Nordwall told him about a time when Ewert had been in charge of a patrol van, a story about Anni and Bengt and Ewert and an arrest which had ended in tragedy.

He tried to stand still, but wasn't able to stop trembling. There was so much in life he didn't understand.

He had no idea where Ewert lived. He had never, not once visited him. Somewhere in the centre of Stockholm, that was all he knew.

He laughed a little, but his face wasn't smiling.

Strange, how one-sided their friendship had been.

He kept inviting and Ewert allowed himself to be invited. Sven believed in sharing, thoughts, emotions, strength, while Ewert hid behind his right to privacy.

He got Ewert's home address from the police staff records. He lived on the fourth floor of quite a handsome block of flats in the middle of the city, on a busy stretch of Svea Road. Sven had been waiting outside for nearly two hours. He had tried to distract himself by scanning the rows of windows. Not that he got much out of it. From a distance they all looked identical, as if the same person inhabited all the flats.

Ewert arrived just after eight o'clock, his big body rolling on his stiff leg. He opened the door without looking round, and disappeared into the building. Sven Sundkvist waited for another ten minutes, feeling nervous and lonelier than he could ever remember.

He took a deep breath before pressing the intercom button. No reply. A longer ring this time.

The loudspeaker crackled as a heavy hand picked up the receiver on the fourth floor.

'Yes?' An irritated voice.

'Ewert?'

'Who is it?'

'It's me, Sven.'

The silence was audible.

'Hello, Ewert? It's me, Sven Sundkvist.'

'What are you doing here?'

'I'd like to come up.'

'Come up here?'

'Yes.'

'Now?'

'Now.'

368

'Why?'

'We need to talk.'

'We can talk tomorrow. Come to my office.'

'It would be too late. We have to talk this evening. Open up, Ewert.'

Silence again. Sven stared at the still live intercom. A long time passed or, at least, it felt like that. Then the lock clicked and Ewert's voice spoke, low and indistinct.

'Fourth floor. Grens on the door.'

The pain in his stomach was bad now, as bad as when he'd watched that video. He had carried this pain for long enough. Time to hand it over, as it were.

He didn't need to ring the bell. The door was open. He peered into the long hall.

'Hello?'

'Come in.'

He couldn't see anyone, but Ewert's voice was calling from a room further in. He stopped on the doormat.

'Second door to your left.'

Sven Sundkvist wasn't quite sure what exactly he had expected, but whatever, it wasn't this.

It was the biggest flat he had ever seen.

He looked around as he walked slowly down a hall which never ended. Six rooms so far, possibly seven. High ceilings, elegant tiled stoves everywhere, plush rugs on perfect parquet floors.

Above all, it was empty.

He tiptoed, hardly breathed, feeling like an intruder even though nobody was about. He had never before been any-where that felt so deserted. It was so large and clean and unimaginably lonely.

Ewert waited in something that might be called the library, one of the smaller rooms with bookshelves along two walls, from floor to ceiling. He was sitting on a worn black leather armchair in the light of a standard lamp.

Sven hardly noticed the rest of the room, because a few things caught his attention. On the wall by the door was a small embroidered wall hanging with MERRY CHRISTMAS in yellow letters on a red background. Next to it two black-and-white photographs, one of a man and the other of a woman, both in their twenties, both in police uniform.

A huge, never-ending place. But it was obvious. The two photos and the embroidered cloth were at its very heart.

Ewert looked at him, sighed, gestured to him to come in. He kicked a stool that he had been resting his feet on in the direction of his guest. Sven sat down.

Ewert had been reading when he rang the bell and interrupted. Sven tried to see what the book was, to find a way of starting the conversation, but it was lying to one side and he couldn't see the title. So instead he got up and pointed at the door.

'Ewert, what is this?'

'What do you mean?'

'Have you always lived like this?'

'Yes.'

'I've never seen anything like it.'

'I spend less and less time here.'

'Our little terraced house would fit into your hall.'

Ewert nodded at him, wanted him to sit down. He closed his book, leaned forwards, red in the face. He was getting impatient with this meaningless chitchat.

'Sven, it's Sunday night, I believe.'

Sven did not answer.

'After eight o'clock. Isn't that so?'

It wasn't really a question.

'I have a bloody right to be left alone. Don't I?'

Silence.

'Why this invasion of my privacy? Can you tell me that?'

Sven tried to stay calm. He had encountered this anger before, but never the fear. He was certain of that. Ewert had never shown that before. But here, sitting in his own leather armchair, his aggression was masking his fear.

He looked at his older colleague.

'The truth, Ewert – you know how hard it is to face.'

Sven ignored Ewert's obvious wish that he should stay put. He stood up and wandered over to the window, stopped to look down at the cars in the street as they hurried from one red light to the next, and then went to lean against a bookshelf.

'Ewert, I spend more time with you, just about every day of my life, than with anyone else, more than with my wife and my son. I haven't come to see you because it seemed like a nice idea. I'm here because I have no choice.'

Ewert Grens was leaning back, looking up at him.

'What a lie, Ewert. What a fucking big lie!'

The man in the armchair didn't move, only stared.

'You have lied and I want to know why.'

Ewert snorted.

'Seems I'm being visited by the inquisition.'

'I want you to reply to my questions, yes. Snort away. Call me names, by all means. I'm used to it.'

He went back to the window. There were fewer cars and they drove more slowly. He longed to get out there, once this was over.

'Officially, I've been on sick leave for two days.'

'You seem fine to me. Well enough to play the interrogator anyway.'

'I wasn't ill. I was in Lithuania. In Klaipeda. Ågestam asked me to go.'

Sven Sundkvist had anticipated an outburst, of course. He knew that Ewert would stand up and shout.

'That little prat! You went to Lithuania on his orders? Behind my back!'

Sven waited until he had finished. 'All right. Sit down again, Ewert.'

'Fuck off!'

'Sit down.'

Ewert looked briefly at Sven and sat down, putting his feet on the stool.

'I met Alena Sljusareva in an aquarium, a Klaipeda tourist trap. I got the answers we needed, step by step, the whole story. How she delivered the gun and explosives to Grajauskas. Very instructive.'

He waited. No reaction from Ewert.

'I know that the two women communicated by mobile phone, several times. Before and during the hostage drama.'

He watched the silent man in the armchair.

Say something!

React!

Don't just stare at me!

'Before Sljusareva and I parted company outside a Chinese restaurant at the end of the evening, something odd happened. She wanted to know why I had asked all those questions, as she had already answered them. In an interview with another Swedish policeman.'

He said nothing.

'Has the cat got your tongue?'

Nothing.

'Say something!'

Ewert Grens burst out laughing. He laughed until tears came to his eyes.

'What do you want me to say? What's the point? You're fucking babes in the wood, you two! Haven't got a clue!'

He laughed even louder, wiping his eyes with his shirt-sleeve.

'As for Ågestam, it goes without saying. But you, Sven! Christ, little boy lost!'

He stared at his uninvited guest, who had invaded his house and taken away his right to be alone.

He was still chuckling, though, and shaking his head.

'The perpetrator, Grajauskas, is dead. The plaintiff, Nordwall, is dead. Who cares about the whys and wherefores?

Who? Eh, Sven? Not the taxpayers who pay our wages, that's for sure.'

Sven Sundkvist stayed by the window. He felt like shouting to drown all this out, but kept quiet. He knew what it was about, after all, this fear masquerading as anger.

'Is that how you see it, Ewert?'

'It's how you should see it too.'

'I never will. You see, we talked for a long time, Alena Sljusareva and I. We went for a meal together. And when I asked, she told me about the three years she and Grajauskas spent in flats all over Scandinavia, being bought and sold as sex slaves. Made to perform twelve times a day. I thought that I was well informed, but she told me things about imprisonment and humiliation that I will never truly under-stand: about Rohypnol to endure it and vodka to deaden their senses, just to be able to live, to cope with the shame, in order to never let it get close.'

Ewert got up and walked towards the door, waving at Sven to come with him.

Sven delayed a little, looking at the photos of the two young people. Full of hope. The man's eyes fascinated him especially, so alive and eager, different eyes which he hadn't seen before. They didn't fit in with this flat.

They had dreams, were full of life.

There was only emptiness here, as if life had ground to a halt.

He tore himself away from the eyes and the room, walked past two more rooms and into a third. It was a kitchen of the kind Anita dreamt about, large enough to cook in comfort and have space left for people to sit down together.

'Hungry?'

'No thanks.'

'Coffee?'

'No.'

'I'm having a cup. Sure?'

The electric coil glowed bright neon red. Ewert filled a saucepan with water.

'I don't want your bloody coffee, Ewert.'

'Sven, get off your high horse.'

Sven Sundkvist searched inside himself for the strength to carry on. He had to keep going with this.

'Alena also told me about how they came here. About the journey here on the ferry. Who arranged it and came with them. Ewert, I know that you know who it was.'

The water boiled. Ewert made a mug of instant coffee. Turned the cooker off.

'What are you suggesting?'

'Am I not right?'

Grens took his mug and went to sit down at the kitchen table. It was round and there were six chairs to go with it. Ewert's face was still flushed. Sven wondered if he was still angry or if it was fear.

'Are you listening to me, Ewert? Of course they couldn't shut out what was happening to them. Rohypnol and vodka weren't enough. So they tried other ways of dealing with it. Lydia Grajauskas didn't have a body. She couldn't feel it when they penetrated her and abused her, it wasn't her body.'

Ewert Grens scrutinised his mug of coffee, drank some, said nothing.

'And Alena Sljusareva, she did the opposite. She was aware of her body, and how they exploited it. But she didn't register any faces. They didn't have any.'

Sven took a step forwards and pulled the mug away from Ewert, forcing him to look up.

'But you knew that, didn't you? Because they said it all in that video of theirs.'

Grens said nothing, only looked at his mug in Sven's hand.

'You see, I knew something wasn't right. I went through the reports to chase up the videotape she had brought to the mortuary. The scene-of-crime photos showed it lying on the floor and I got on to Nils Krantz, who confirmed that he had given it to you.'

Ewert Grens reached out for his mug, and finished his coffee. Once more he asked if Sven wanted one and once more Sven said no. They stayed in the kitchen, facing each other across a large island unit set out with cooking kit and a full set of kitchen knives.

'Where is your TV?'

'TV? Why?'

Sven went into the hall to fetch his case.

'Where did you say it was?'

'In there.'

Ewert pointed at the room across from the kitchen. Sven crossed the hall and asked Ewert to follow.

'We're going to watch a video.'

'I haven't got a VCR.'

'Thought not, which is why I've brought a portable one.'

He unpacked it and connected it to Ewert's TV.

'Right. Now we're going to watch this together.'

They settled in opposite corners of the sofa. Sven had the remote control. He used it to start the video he had just loaded.

Blackish image, lots of white flicker. The War of the Ants.

Sven turned to Ewert.

'This one appears to be empty.'

No answer.

'And it's probably supposed to be, because it isn't the tape you were given by Krantz. Is it?'

The tape was crackling, an irritating noise, letting his thoughts turn over and over in his head.

'I know it isn't, because Krantz confirmed that the tape found in the mortuary was used, rather dusty and with two sets of female fingerprints. None of which fits this cassette. There will be prints all right, but only yours and mine.'

Ewert turned away. He couldn't bear to look at the man whose boss he was.

'Ewert, I'm curious. What was on the original tape?'

He flicked the remote at the TV, shutting off the invasive noise.

'OK, let me put it another way. What was on the original tape that made it worth risking thirty-three years of service in the force?'

Sven bent down to get something out of his case.

Another videotape. He took out the first one and loaded the second.

> *Two women. They are out of focus. The cameraman moves the camera about and twists the lens. The women look nervous as they wait for the signal to start.*
>
> *One of them, a blonde with frightened eyes, speaks slowly in Russian, two sentences at a time. Then she turns to the dark woman, who translates into Swedish.*
>
> *Their faces are serious and their voices strained. They haven't done anything like this before.*
>
> *They speak for more than twenty minutes.*
> *That's how long it takes, their story of the past three years.*

Sven stubbornly stared straight ahead, waiting for Ewert's reaction.

There was none, not until the women had reached the end of their account.

Then he burst into tears.

He covered his face with his hands and wept, letting thirty years of grief flow out of him as he had never dared before in case he drained away and disappeared.

Sven couldn't bear to watch. Please, not this. He cringed with embarrassment at first, and then anger surged through his body. He got up, stopped the tape and put it on the table in front of them.

'You see, you only replaced one of the copies.'

Sven prodded it lightly and began pushing it towards Ewert.

'I reread the statements made by the hostages. Ejder mentioned that Grajauskas talked about two tapes. And a locker at the Central Station.'

Ewert took a deep breath, looked at Sven, but couldn't talk, still crying.

'I found it there.'

Sven pushed the tape past a vase with flowers until it was in front of Ewert. His anger, it had to be released.

'How dare you take away that right? They had every fucking right in the world to tell their story. And what was your reason? To keep the truth about your best friend from getting out!'

Ewert looked at the video in front of him, picked it up, but still said nothing.

'Not only that. You actually committed a criminal offence. You withheld and later destroyed evidence. You kept a self-confessed criminal out of court by sending her home, because you were scared of what she had to say. How much further were you prepared to go? How much is this lie worth to you, Ewert?'

Grens fingered the hard plastic case.

'This?'

'Yes.'

'Do you think I did it for my own sake?'

'Yes, I do.'

'What?'

'For your own sake.'

'So it wasn't enough that she lost her husband? Why should she have to face this as well? The bastard had lied to her!' He threw the cassette back on the table. 'Her empty life is more than enough! Lena doesn't need this crap! She doesn't ever need to know!'

Sven Sundkvist couldn't take any more.

He had confronted his friend, seen him weep and now knew about the grief that had filled most of his adult life.

He just had to get away. This day had been too much, he didn't want another minute of today.

'Alena Sljusareva.'

He turned towards Grens.

'You see, she spoke about her shame. The shame she had tried to wash down the drain, twelve times daily. But this . . .'

Sven slapped the TV screen, hit out against what they had just watched.

'This was because you couldn't face it, Ewert. You can't cope with the guilt you feel when you remember what you've done to other people, and the shame you feel when you think of what you've done to yourself. You can live with guilt. But shame is unendurable.'

Ewert sat there, his eyes fixed on the person, who kept talking.

'You felt guilty because it was your decision to send Bengt into the mortuary, to his death. That's understandable. There's always an explanation for guilt.'

Sven's voice grew louder, as often happens when you don't want to show how close you are to a breakdown.

'Shame, now, that's different. Much harder to understand! You were ashamed because Bengt had managed to trick you so completely. And you felt ashamed that you would have to tell Lena who Bengt actually was.'

Sven became louder still.

'Ewert, you weren't trying to protect Lena. You were protecting yourself. From *your own shame.*'

It was strangely cold outside.

June is meant to be midsummer and warm.

He waited at the crossing outside the building where Ewert Grens lived. The lights turned red eventually.

Now he had finally shed the burden of the lies he had been carrying.

The story of two young people, erased to protect a man from the truth.

Bengt Nordwall was a swine, the kind that even Sven Sundkvist could hate. Until the end, he had behaved exactly like the swine he was, unable to change even when facing a gun, naked, in that tiled place of death. He had refused to acknowledge the shame she felt, even then. And Ewert had carried on refusing, reducing her shame to a mere flicker, a War of the Ants.

The green man showed, and he crossed the road and started walking northwards. He needed to get away, deep into the summer night. At the Wenner-Gren Centre he turned towards Haga Park.

Lydia Grajauskas was dead. Bengt Nordwall was dead.

Ewert had put it succinctly. A case with no perpetrator and no plaintiff.

He had always liked Haga Park, so near the city centre and yet so silent. A man was shouting despairingly for his dog, a black Alsatian. A couple were lying on the grass, holding each other tight. No one else was in sight. The green space was as empty as all city places are during the few summer weeks when life happens elsewhere.

No one was going to speak for the dead, not now and not ever. He was breathing heavily. What if he testified against the best policeman he knew? What good would that do? Would it matter? Should he demand answers from those who were still alive? What was better, Ewert Grens working with the City Police, or Ewert Grens lost in that silent home of his?

The water's edge. He had reached the lakeside and saw the evening sun reflected in it, as it always was.

Sven Sundkvist was still carrying his case. A small VCR, some papers, two videotapes. He opened it and picked up the tape he had taken from box 21 at Central Station. The label with Cyrillic script was still there. He let the cassette fall to the ground and stamped on it until the plastic casing was in pieces. Then he ripped the tape out, metre after metre of curling ribbon, as if for a birthday present.

The Brunnsviken water was almost perfectly still, a rare kind of absolute calm.

He took a few steps closer, twisted the twirling ribbon round the remains of the cassette, lifted his arm and threw it as far as he could.

He felt both heavy and light. There might have been tears in his eyes, maybe he felt some of Lydia Grajauskas's sadness. As he observed the scene from afar, he realised that he had done exactly what he had just condemned.

He had stolen from her the right to be heard.

Ågestam would never know what Sljusareva had really said.

He felt ashamed.

THREE YEARS EARLIER

The flat is small, just two rooms and a kitchen.

There are five of them. Mum and Grandma. Her older brother and little sister. And herself, of course. She has never really thought about it before. It has always been like that.

She is seventeen years old now.

Her name is Lydia Grajauskas.

She longs to be somewhere else.

She wants a room of her own and a life of her own. This place, this life is so cramped. She is a woman now, or almost. Soon she will be a woman, grown up and needing space.

She misses him.

She often thinks of him. Dad, who was always there for her and always understood her.

She has asked, many times, but nothing can make her understand why he had to die.

She misses their walks together most of all. He would take her hand in his as they walked, lost in plans about the day they would leave Klaipeda.

They used to walk to the edge of town, just as she and Vladi do now. Then they would turn round to look back at the town, really take in what it looked like. Dad often sang for her, songs he had learnt as a child, which she had never heard anyone else sing. Their heads would be filled with longing. That was what they did; they longed together.

This flat. Too small, too crowded! Always someone underfoot. Always someone.

She remembers last night, the two men who came to the café. She had never seen them before. They shook hands with Vladi and they seemed nice.

Her Vladi, who has been her friend for ever, who had been next to her on the sofa when the military police burst in, shouting *Zatknis!* and pinning Dad to the floor.

The two men smiled at her and chatted while they ordered coffees and sandwiches. They spoke Russian, but one of them, the older man, didn't look Russian, more like people from Sweden or Denmark.

They had stayed for quite a long time. She refilled their cups twice. Then Vladi had left and she talked to them for a bit. They wanted to know what she was called and how long she had worked in the café and how much she earned. They seemed interested, nice and polite, not slimy at all. They didn't try anything on, didn't flirt, nothing like that. She sat down at their table later. She wasn't allowed to, but the place was almost empty right then and there was nothing much to do.

They talked about a lot of things. She enjoyed the talk, she really did. It was weird, she thought, to be with men who were so pleasant and easy. She laughed a lot and that was new too. There wasn't much laughter at home.

They came back.

Late today, just as she was getting ready to close, they both came back.

She knows now that their names are Dimitri and Bengt. Dimitri comes from Vilnius and Bengt is from Sweden. Bengt is a policeman, in Klaipeda to work on an investigation.

They seem to know each other well. They met many years ago. Although she isn't sure, she guesses that Dimitri must be part of the Lithuanian police force.

They were just as nice to her and asked again about her job. They seemed shocked when she told them what she earns waitressing at the café. Bengt told her what she could earn in Sweden for doing just the same thing. It is almost twenty times as much. Every month. It seems incredible, but they insisted. Twenty times as much!

She told them about her dreams. Told them about the small, cramped flat that is her home, about her walks with Vladi, about wanting to leave Klaipeda, which somehow doesn't offer her enough any more.

They ordered more sandwiches and invited her to sit down at their table.

They talked and laughed, which was lovely. Laughter clears the air.

They come back for the third day running.

She almost expects them now and before they order she has laid their table for coffee and sandwiches.

Yesterday they offered to help her, said that they could fix the paperwork, work permits and that kind of thing, if she was keen to work in Sweden. Just imagine, getting twenty times what she could earn here.

She laughed and told them it was crazy, she couldn't.

Today she brings the subject up herself, asks them what has to be done.

She needs a passport, but one which says she is older than she is. They can arrange it. It will cost a fair bit, of course, but they're happy to lend her the money until she gets paid in Sweden.

They have actually done this for other Lithuanian girls. When she asks who they are, they give her some names, but Lydia doesn't recognise them.

They tell her that they have a female contact in Sweden who makes the girls feel really welcome.

She says the coffee is on her and they sit about for quite a while.

She mustn't make up her mind until she's quite, quite

sure, they tell her. It's important that she thinks about it. If she really wants to stop just dreaming about other places and break free, she has to let them know soon. The next ferry, which they're travelling on themselves, leaves two days from now, and they assure her they can fix the passport in time.

It's warm when she gets to the harbour. The pouring rain has stopped, the sun is shining and there is hardly any wind. Vladi holds her hand and says he's happy for her. Her things are packed in one suitcase, mostly clothes and as many toiletries as she dared to take. A handful of photographs, her diary.

She hasn't told anyone. Mum wouldn't understand. She doesn't long to get away.

But she will phone as soon as she gets there. From her new workplace. She will tell them how much she is earning and how much money she will send home every month. Then Mum will realise what it's all about. Her new, different life.

They agreed to meet at the entrance to the ferry terminal.

She spots them easily. Dimitri, the dark-haired one, is wearing a grey suit. Bengt has got almost blond hair and is a little shorter than Dimitri. His eyes are so kind. He gives Vladi an envelope. Vladi looks very pleased, but doesn't meet her eyes afterwards, just gives her a hug and hurries away. A young woman, about her own age, comes and joins them. She has dark hair and looks pretty and friendly.

They say hello and introduce themselves. Her name is

Alena. She too has brought just one suitcase and also has a false passport.

The ferry is so impressive. Lydia has never been on board such a large ship. Quite a few of the other passengers are Swedish, some are Lithuanian and some she can't place. She smiles as she steps on board and leaves her past behind.

She and Alena share a cabin.

They get on really well. Alena is easy to make friends with; she's the sort who seems to invite you in, curious and eager to listen. She laughs a lot and it's easy to laugh with her. Lydia has a special feeling all over, now that she's on her way.

Soon it will be time to go for a meal.

First, they have to go up to meet Bengt and Dimitri in their cabin, which is just upstairs. Then they will go to the dining room, all four of them together.

They knock on the door to the cabin.

They wait. Just a little while.

Bengt opens the door with a smile, and gestures with his hand to invite them in. They exchange glances and feel a little shy. Stepping inside the men's cabin doesn't feel quite right.

Then everything falls apart.

One single breath.

That's all it takes.

The two men raise their hands and slap them hard in the face.

They keep hitting until the girls collapse.

They tear at their best frocks, rip the fabric to pieces and push balls of cloth into the girls' mouths.

They force open their legs and push deep inside them.

Lydia will never forget the sound of his panting in her face.

That night she doesn't sleep. She lies in her bed clutching a pillow.

They shouted at her. They hit her. They held the cold metal of a gun's muzzle to her head and told her that she could choose now to shut up or die.

She cannot grasp what has happened.

All she wants is to go home.

Alena is lying in the lower bunk. She doesn't cry quite so much. She says nothing, makes hardly any noise at all.

Lydia looks at her case. It's on the floor, next to the basin. The case she packed without telling anyone. She left home less than twenty-four hours ago.

She hears the noise of the waves hitting the ship's metal sides. She hears it through the window, which can be opened, but is too small to climb out through.

The journey ends in the morning.

She is still in bed.

She hasn't dared to move.

She tries to ignore them when they bang on the cabin door and shout that it's time to leave, they have to go ashore.

Dimitri walks just ahead of her, Bengt is behind her. They walk towards the exit and through passport control.

She wants to scream.

She doesn't dare.

She remembers the blows to her face and the pain when they penetrated her. She begged them to stop, but they didn't.

It's a large place, much larger than the terminal in Klaipeda. People meet and hug each other, delighted to be together again.

She feels nothing.

Only shame.

She doesn't know why.

She hands her passport to the uniformed official. *Shut up*. He leafs through it, looks at her, nods her through. *Or die*. She walks away. Alena is next.

Outside the gate, Dimitri turns to Lydia and tells her that he will take the passport. She owes him for it and he wants his money back, so now she has to work.

She doesn't really hear what he says.

The large hall empties slowly as the people around her leave. They wait at a newsagent's kiosk, a small distance from passport control.

Then she comes, the woman they are waiting for, who works with Dimitri and Bengt.

She is wearing a grey tracksuit. The top has a hood and she wears it pulled down over her face. She is quite young. The woman smiles at Dimitri, gives him a peck on the cheek, then smiles at Bengt and kisses him on the lips, as if they belong together. She turns to Lydia and Alena, still smiling, and says something they don't understand, presumably in Swedish.

'Well, hello there. So you are our two new little Baltic pussies.'

She kisses their cheeks, first Lydia, then Alena. She smiles and they try to smile back at her.

They don't notice when Bengt Nordwall leans close to the woman and whispers to her, his hand gently pushing back the edge of the hood.

'Lena, I've missed you so.'

But they hear what she says next, still turned towards them and smiling. She has switched to Russian.

'Welcome to Sweden. I hope you'll enjoy your stay.'

A NOTE ABOUT THE AUTHORS

Anders Roslund is the founder and former head of *Kulturnyheterna* (Culture News) on Sveriges Television, and for many years worked as the head of news at Aktuellt (Channel 1) and as a prize-winning investigative reporter at Rapport (Channel 2), the Swedish equivalents of CNN and the BBC.

Börge Hellström is an ex-criminal who helps to rehabilitate young offenders and drug addicts. He is also one of the founders of KRIS (Criminals' Return into Society) – a non-profit association that assists released prisoners during their first period of freedom.